They Speak of Night

Jo Jackson

First published 2023
© Jo Jackson 2023
ISBN 978-0-9956094-3-3

A CIP catalogue record for this book is available from the British Library

Published in Great Britain by Apedale Press

Cover image by Siby Unsplash.com

Printed and bound in Great Britain by Biddles Books Ltd

For Andy with love

Jo Jackson was born in Birmingham and went on to become a nurse, midwife and family psychotherapist. She has three grown up children and lives in Shropshire with her husband.

By the same author

Too loud a Silence

Beyond The Margin

It Can't Get Darker Than Midnight - novella

They Speak of Night

1

I slapped the station sign so hard my fingers stung. The cold metallic ring drowned the noise of roosting starlings. It was easier to take it out on that than to blame myself. Totteridge & Whetstone, the name had held such promise when I first heard it. I slumped onto a bench, the steps to the bridge too grey and forbidding to tackle. An orange plastic bag tumbled between the train rails and snagged on a bolt before breaking free and plastering itself against the wall.

I'd said yes. For the first time I'd said yes. So why was I sitting on an empty platform with twilight bleeding from bunching clouds when I should be in a bar laughing with my work colleagues, sipping wine, and swapping plans for the weekend?

Tying her long hair into a topknot, Jade had shouted across the office, 'Come on, Lily. We're going.' She'd turned to the others and told them to carry on, that we'd catch them up. Jade with her bright clothes and a smile that charmed the users of the care home organisation.

'I've got a thumping headache. Do you mind if I leave it tonight?' I heard my own pathetic excuse.

'Lily, just come. Come this once. Stop being …'

I hadn't waited to hear what I was being. 'Sorry.' I'd fled through the swing doors and onto the street into anonymity. I'd seen Jade shrug and hated myself for hurling friendship back in her face.

My invented headache was becoming real. Another overground train rattled into the station. A woman lifted a pushchair onto the platform and tucked a pink blanket around the sleeping child. She manoeuvred past a group of school kids who shared pieces of chewing gum and dropped the wrappings on the ground. A man gripping his laptop case sidestepped slower passengers and kicked my foot. He never noticed, and confirmation of my invisibility slowed the thumping of my heart. I waited until they'd all gone, let another train, and another, pass through, the carriages hurtling away to become silver streaks in the distance. Next week after work I *would* go out with them. I'd laugh, share funny moments from the week. Be normal. I made the promise that would get me through the weekend. I picked up my bag and climbed the steps, heading home, though that word meant nothing any more.

Letting myself in I closed the door and sucked in the silence. The flat was no more than a bedsit above a takeaway, but it was close to the station and just two stops from work. It had its own entrance over a concrete yard at the back. Scratch marks around the keyhole told a story of a stream of tenants. Junk mail spewed from a pile on the bottom stair – I should make the effort to throw it all away. Books from the charity shop waited on another step to be returned. I picked one up. Had I read it? I couldn't remember and I didn't care. Six paces took me across my room and past the kitchenette with its cream Formica worktops. I pulled back the curtains, left closed in the rush of the morning; a faint mustiness fanned into the room to compete with mountain-breeze air freshener. Leaning my head on the glass, I watched Friday-night traffic as it edged along the High Road, brake lights blinking like Christmas tree bulbs. There was already a queue outside the fish and chip shop and further along, couples were peering at the menu of the Indian restaurant before linking arms and going in.

I tossed a satin-striped cushion from the floor onto the sofa. One of a pair, the purchase a measure of my excitement when I'd bagged my first job and found this place. Fuchsia-pink and grey, they covered up where the velveteen chairs had worn thin. On the sideboard a spray of silk apple blossom in a black vase echoed the colours. I'd put Mum's photograph under them, knowing it's where she'd like to be. Tonight, I couldn't whisper 'Hi' as I usually did.

The needle-sharp water of the shower nudged me to a warmer place. It tamed my black hair into straggly ringlets from which water droplets ran down my back. I donned a favourite jumper; too big and stretched out of shape but as comforting as a hug. I reached for my leggings from the shelf at the top of the wardrobe.

There it was. The box. Pushed to the back. I halted, still balanced on tiptoe. It had lain there since the day I moved in, shoved out of sight. Slowly I edged it forward and lifted it down. Made of cardboard and the size of a shoebox, but light. Set on the floor it looked out of place, patterned with gaudy gold and black diamond shapes covered in glitter. Like something from an Ali Baba pantomime. So exactly you, Mum, that I hadn't been able to open it, too gay and bright for my mood at the time, my curiosity stultified.

I rapped on the lid, hearing only a hollow sound.

'Why, Mum? Why? Whatever were you thinking.' The thin woman in red wellies and a sun hat smiled at me from the photo frame.

I don't know who my father is. My mum didn't know either. She'd never made a secret of the fact and neither of us cared. It was just the two of us and always had been. The trunk filled with dressing-up materials provided endless opportunities for guesswork. Sometimes he was from Africa and an astrakhan hat on my head gave me tight black curls, or he was an Oxford student and I paraded around the room with a striped college scarf around my neck, my hair parted down the middle. It was a familiar game and always ended the same way in fits of giggles.

'I think maybe my eyes slant just a bit.' I squinted into the mirror with its frame of painted flowers, a charity shop find or from a house sale, like everything else we possessed.

'What do you think, Mum?' Her head appeared beside mine, same green-grey eyes that changed colour with the light, her purple-streaked hair scrunched into a bobble. Thirteen and I was nearly as tall as her.

'Hey, you might be right.' From behind, her fingers pulled my eyes sideways. 'Wait, let's see.' She scrabbled in her make-up bag and with an eyebrow pencil drew a thin line extending each of my eyes. 'That's it.' From atop the metal trunk that acted as a coffee table she grabbed the satin runner, wrapped it around my shoulders and rummaging inside she found a silk scarf to drape around her own. 'Not quite there yet. Don't move.' She raced upstairs returning with a pink powder puff with which she dabbed talcum powder all over our faces, finishing off with bright red lipstick. 'We're geisha girls and your father was a Japanese businessman, head of the biggest bank in Japan.' We minced across the floor and knelt beside the trunk, our hands demurely crossed and our eyes cast down. We poured imaginary tea into imaginary cups and passed them around the assembled dignitaries before collapsing in a heap on the rug, helpless with laughter. Not surprising that I chose English with Drama as my uni course.

Gold glitter flaked onto my lap as my fingers grazed the box. I placed it beside Mum's picture, sure that her smile widened at seeing it there. 'Lily, you can do it, go anywhere, be anything you want to. Conquer the world.' Just remembering her words doused in laughter sent me fleeing to my bed. The duvet over my head formed a dark cave with walls I could touch.

Where had she gone, the girl called Lily? Was she vomited down the toilet pan after that drunken June night, or did she die with the ring of the doorbell the next day?

2

The promise I'd made to myself hung over me all week like a predatory spider. It sat beside me when I travelled to work, it perched on my computer screen, it nestled between the pages of the book I was reading and became my last thought at night and woke me in the morning. Sometimes I could laugh at it, make it inconsequential, something I could achieve. At other times it would grow, turn shades of black and grey, its outline, blurred and barbed.

Friday came. Jade linked her arm through mine locking me to her side. We walked down the road to the wine bar where smokers milled on the pavement occupying stainless-steel tables ringed with beer stains. Her fingers made indents into my goose-pimpled skin as she coaxed me in. The smell of alcohol had me gagging. My eyes strafed the bar, my senses honed sharp as a blade. I saw the guy in the centre of a loud group, his jacket off, his tie loosened, holding forth with theatrical gestures, waving the pint that fuelled his performance. The party guy, charming, suave … the sort who would …

'Get a grip,' the voice in my head shouted. 'There's no way *he's* going to be here.' I tugged at my earring wanting to cover my ears and eyes, to close my nostrils.

'Hi, we saved you a seat.' Ben's familiar voice called across the throng. Our crowd was pressed against the back wall. 'White wine for both of you or is it a lager night?' Jade pushed me into the empty cushioned settle. She still clutched my thumb sensing I might run at any moment. I made a fist around hers to reassure her and say thanks.

'Yes please, make it prosecco, get a bottle. I'll buy the next round.' Jade answered for both of us, and I nodded to Ben, caught his eye, and practised a smile. His quick blink and a pat on the shoulder released the breath I hadn't realised I was holding.

I swirled the cold, sparkling prosecco around in the glass, the bubbles rising to the surface and escaping. At first mouthful the clean tang teased my tongue and wakened taste buds. Jade let go of my hand but contact with her thigh was my umbilical cord. An image of my yoga teacher in her pink leggings danced before my eyes. "Take deep breaths and exhale slowly," My heart, the moth trapped in a lampshade, stilled.

There were five of us, all head-office staff. The bright young things Ben called us. He was the oldest at thirty and head of recruitment. I was his assistant. Jade in PR, Amir in accounts.

Isaac was the joker, a skill he deployed in marketing. His sharp-nosed face, sallow skin, black-rimmed glasses, and black hair that flopped over his forehead had us all glancing at each other and raising eyebrows on his first day in the office. The man-bag he carried made us grimace. It swung like a satchel across his chest bumping against his hip. Not a discreet black leather but yellow, as bright as a canary. His first words to us as he looped it over his head and set it on his desk like an exotic bird, 'It's unisex. No one's going to accuse me of being a bad Jewish mother and not seeing her son off into the world well equipped.' He gave a downward flick of his wrist. 'It'll get you noticed,' he mimicked with such exaggerated assurance that we all laughed, and tension burst like a squeezed spot. 'Don't laugh, you'll never know how much it cost my mother to say that.' From that moment we loved his mother and him, and everything he was. We have never found out what else he carries in the bag other than his pasta salad, but whenever there's a crisis or we're feeling fed up he unzips it and peers very deliberately inside before coming up with another outrageous story. We never see him without it.

A girl shouted a greeting over the heads and pushed her way across to us. 'God deliver me from tourists,' she said.

Ben gathered her up and kissed her on the cheek. She wagged her finger around our circle. 'If any of you ask me a single stupid question tonight. I'll … I'll tip your drink over your head.' She flopped onto a stool.

'Well, if you take your badge from around your neck, perhaps we'll not be reminded you're a tour guide,' Ben said, easing it over her neck.

'Oh, Christ, I forgot. No wonder that creep by the door was peering at my chest. Hi, I'm Maisie. You must be Lily. Ben's told me all about you.'

Ben held up both hands. 'All good things, honest, guv.'

Isaac poured Maisie a glass of prosecco and topped up the rest of the glasses. 'Come on, Lily. You'll have to drink faster than that to keep up with these two. Not much of a drinker then?'

'I haven't had a drink for eighteen months.' It was out before I could stop it. I laughed to lessen the impact of my admission. 'And this one is beginning to go to my head.'

'Jeez. Imagine, no alcohol for eighteen months. Why?' Isaac sagged where he stood, his tongue lolling from his mouth. I think Jade must have kicked him or something because he jerked and hopped on one foot.

'That should be me.' Amir lifted his beer. 'As you can see, Lily, I am a thoroughly bad Muslim. Just don't tell my father. He still thinks he has a pious son worthy of the family name.'

As the banter was batted back and forth, I stopped biting the inside of my lip and wondered what it would be like to have a father to live up to.

A father. My father. Gripping the glass, my hand quivered halfway between the table and my lips. The noise and chatter floated to the ceiling, clarity a bubble in my head. Why hadn't it occurred to me before now? The box. That's what's in the box. A name, a photograph, a town, perhaps an address. A secret, Mum's to keep. Something that had never mattered before was suddenly squeezing my ribcage like a tourniquet.

'You all right, Lily?' Jade's question seemed to come from far away.

'Yes, I'm fine. It's been great, thanks for letting me tag along. I think I'll be off though – things to do. Next Friday? The same?'

Amir gave me a thumbs-up and Ben shuffled along the seat to let me out. 'Well done.' he whispered as I squeezed past. I blew a kiss to Jade.

'You faced the foe and conquered adversity. A Jewish proverb, or if it's not it should be.'

'Leave it, Isaac.' Amir cuffed him over the head. I felt them watching me as I eased my way to the exit. I turned and they waved, making me wonder how much I'd been the topic of their conversation previously. I waved back, flooded with warmth.

*

A crescent moon shone through the trees as I got off the train. With no one to see, I high-fived the station sign as I went past. 'A small achievement, but it felt like a giant one,' I whooped in the direction of the disappearing train and took the stairs two at a time.

In the dark of the flat, the box threw off sparkles of light reflecting the glow from the streetlamps. 'Don't let the feeling slip away,' I whispered to the shadows. I lit three fat cream candles, and the smell of vanilla surrounded me.

'Maybe it's the prosecco or maybe it's the effect of friends, but tonight, Mum, your box doesn't seem so daunting, so impossible to open. When did you intend me to have it? What's inside? What were you thinking when you put it together? I wish I could ask you. No tears, not tonight, I promise.'

I rummaged in the drawer for my notebook. Inside the front cover was the note I'd found on top of the box, secured by a snow scene paperweight. Mum's flowery scrawl. It didn't offer any clues, but I traced the letters with my finger and then touched her smile.

For Lily

XX

Sitting cross-legged on the floor, with both hands I eased off the deep lid.

3

The lid pulled off with a sucking sound, like a warning. I opened my eyes, not realizing how tightly I'd screwed them shut in the moment. Shiny copper colour filled the space. Another box, its sides glittered gold like the first one. My fingernail scraped at the roughness of the surface like a file on metal. I perched them one on top of the other. A smile I couldn't hold back became a giggle.

'Trust you, Mum. You made everything fun. Why should I have expected even something as important as this to be dressed in any other way? Who do you want me to be? Am I a pirate opening a captured chest aboard a pitching ship? A bank robber breaking into a vault, a child at Christmas suffused with delight at her kitschy, colourful present?'

A candle spluttered, laughing with me as wax spilt over. Shadow shapes capered over the walls and furniture, an audience to the great reveal. I shook the new box, it answered with a dull thud. Off came the copper top, another box, and then another, and another. Five alternately matching boxes formed a shiny, garish pyramid. I jiggled the smallest, the size of my hand. It wasn't empty but made a different sound. Photographs perhaps, an envelope, a letter, I tried to guess. Wriggling worms slinked from the pit of my stomach, dried my mouth and extinguished my excitement. I tipped the box and let the contents slide onto the floor.

Three packets of seeds: marigolds; marjoram; chard.

Bright images, orange, purple, rainbowed. The shadows stopped dancing. Tears pooled and overflowed as I recalled her voice.

'Times were mad back then, Lily. I was drunk on freedom. Young people protested on the streets about everything, experimented, lived and loved, believing they would be young forever. Consequences, responsibility, maturity, words with no relevance, applicable only to the boring and the old.'

'But I was your consequence, Mum. Did I spoil it all.?'

'Yes, you were my consequence and the best present anyone could have given me. Saved me from God knows what. From the minute I knew I was pregnant, you became all I wanted. I wasn't going to share you even if I'd known who to share you with. Was I selfish? Probably. Would I change anything? No, no, no.' Mum had looped her arm through mine and twirled me across the stones to the water's edge.

'It's January, Mum!'

'Let's paddle.'

She'd already pulled off her boots and socks. The water was freezing, it turned pink toes blue, the undertow piling shingle into dunes behind our heels.

'Yes, you were bloody selfish.' I shouted at the packets of stupid seeds and threw them across the carpet. 'What bloody use are these to me?' I slapped her photo face down so I couldn't see her smiling at her joke. Amir, it was his fault too for talking about his father in the way he had, giving me the crazy idea of what might be in the box. I tore at the scarf around my neck searching for air to breathe. I clasped a cushion and sobbed.

Nobody can cry forever, but I wanted to. My sobs became gulps, torn from a suppurating wound.

'Sorry if you're hurting.' A whisper blew the curtains making them tremble. I jerked upright with a retort. There was no one to hear it. She wasn't there. Just a gaping space where memories wisped like sea fret.

My mum had precious little, but what she had was love and a sense of fun. We lived in a cream-rendered council house, with a square of garden at the back and a matching patch at the front. Neighbours let the salt-laden winds and apathy defeat them, but every inch of our garden was covered in edible flowers and vegetables, mixed together in riotous chaos so that a cabbage nestled amongst the marigolds, and nasturtiums climbed as high as beans. 'My potager,' Mum called it. Often, I would catch her talking quietly amongst the plants. 'Who are you talking to, Mum?'

'To the birds and the bees and the butterflies of course. Listen, pause a minute, hear them answering.'

My playground had been the seashore. If I crossed the road in front of the house and over a stretch of grass that tumbled with flowering weeds in the summer, I was onto banks of shingle washed by the grey waves of the estuary. Across the water, the low hills of Scotland appeared and disappeared in the cloud that swept in from the Irish sea. In winter, on my way home from school, darts of rain would bend me double and sandpaper winds tear at my skin. On other days I would lie on the stones, listening to the rhythm of the waves with white clouds running races across the sky and gulls fluting in arcs over the water. My mum used to say I was a feral child, but I wasn't. Her lack of rules meant I made up my own which took away the need to rebel. Freedom fed my imagination. I drifted with the tides, beachcombed for coloured glass smoothed by time, and lay warm amongst dunes of marram grass.

The council had tried to smarten up the seafront; they'd laid a tarmac path above the shoreline and made a short circular walk around the town. Still the tourists flocked inland to The Lakes, but few ventured to the coast. Only locals sat on the beach in jackets, eating sandwiches behind a windbreak. The flat bleak seascape was a difficult place to like, unless it was home, the place I lived all my life until I was eighteen.

All my friends loved my mum, they called her Hettie. She said Henrietta was too much of a mouthful and didn't describe her. 'You become your name,' she would tell us though none of us knew what she meant.

They bemoaned the fact their parents were boring, had ordinary jobs, like working in factories, or were cleaners or care workers. 'Yours buys and sells things on eBay. How cool is that?'

'And we have a shed in the garden stuffed with other people's crap to prove that sometimes she's successful and a lot of the time she's not.'

But I was proud of her. On parents' evening, she stood out from the rest with her Doc Marten boots worn under flouncy chiffon, bright and striped like Joseph's coat of many colours. Over the top, she would wear a patchwork waistcoat and no matter how much she tried to tame her hair, wisps of it would escape and curl around her laughing, freckled face. She allowed sleepovers and never came to tell us whispering, giggling girls that it was time to go to sleep. She'd waken us in the morning with orange juice and yoghurt and we'd all sit wrapped in duvets mulling over the secrets we'd shared the night before.

On a few occasions, the two of us would pick nettles from the field and make them into soup or pesto, or when everyone else was hunkered indoors out of winter's grip we'd build a fire on the beach and tucked under a blanket we'd toast sausages and marshmallows over the flames.

In class I was serious and didn't mess around like some. Science and maths bored me but give me English, Drama and History and I was there. I was the Wife of Bath from *The Canterbury Tales*, or the luckless Ann Boleyn. I walked in their shoes and played out their lives in my head when I went to bed. The main parts in school productions were always mine. The audience would clap and whoop and I would seek out Mum, the bright butterfly in a sea of faces.

I called it anger, the weight that ousted sleep, but it wasn't. I tried disappointment but why should I be disappointed over something that had never been important? Grief was the word I wouldn't utter; surrender was not an option. Her avowal quivered in the room, 'Never regret, Lily. Hey, life's too short.' It was.

Each hour of that night was marked by the click of the clock. Clouds kept the sky black. First, it was a single note I heard. Mum had woken me once to listen. 'A robin, Lily. He's calling for a mate.' Back then I'd wanted to go back to sleep. 'Wait.' She'd snuggled in beside me and together the birds sang in the dawn just for us. Like now when they sang for me. I pulled up the bedroom blind. Faint daubs of salmon-pink nibbled at the night, backlighting the ugly, high-rise office buildings In the distance, the steeple of the dwarfed church was a black shard in the diminishing gloom.

The flat was suddenly too small, darkness clung in the corners. I scrambled into leggings and a top, grabbed a coat and bag, and burst into the cool air, still fresh in the breaking day. Round the corner, down the hill, past the station. Speed walking, pushing myself to go faster, my breath exhaled in short puffs through pouted lips. Up the hill, round the back of the pub and I was in fields. I'd been here before. An oasis found by accident when the city was suffocating me. My pace faltered. Draped over a gate I inhaled the smell of warm cowpats and mud where the herd, now peacefully grazing, had churned up the ground. A brown-eyed beast, its udder full, stopped chewing to appraise me before moving closer to the others, bony haunches rippling under its caked hide. Green fields, new leaves on the trees moist with dew, the miniature flowers of blackthorn like snowflakes in the hedgerows.

The sea. I need to see the sea, to taste it, smell it, and hear the waves breaking. The thought came like a full-on slap in the face. There was no sensible me to argue with the idea, just a hideous gut wrench that pitched me from the farmland back to suburbia, onto the Tube to the mayhem of London Bridge Station and aboard an early train to Brighton. I collapsed into a window seat of an almost empty carriage where the smell of antiperspirant and perfume lingered, remnants of the usual bored, crammed, weekday commuters. I closed my eyes to the blur of houses and flyovers rushing by and let the hum of the rails soothe me into sleep.

I woke to a man shaking my arm. 'Unless you want to go back to London you'd best get off here.' He grinned, gathered up his belongings and was gone. Passengers milled around and I struggled to remember where I was, to recall how I came to be here. Pain like the nick of a razor pricked the back of my eyes to remind me.

I'd never been to Brighton, but instinctively I turned towards the sea. The town was waking up, lights were going on in shops and a pile of newspapers tied with string sat outside the newsagents. A beady-eyed gull hopped aside on the pavement and then resumed its foraging under a rubbish bin. Across the promenade and there it was. Not my sea, but miles of restless grey water fading almost to white where it met the sky. I flung my arms out wide, and still it stretched beyond my fingertips. The smack of brine tasted better than caviar.

The stones, round and smooth, lumped beneath my feet, a scatter of beige, white and blue. I negotiated the gently shelving beach to sit with my back against a rowing boat pulled up beyond the waterline, a thick rope snaked to its mooring point.

The day's new sun, flecking gold leaf onto the waves, was bright even when I closed my eyes. I began to breathe again.

I'm staring at the sea. I tapped out the WhatsApp message to Louisa. I'd met her on our first day at Lancaster university. She'd knocked when she heard Mum leave and plonked herself on the foot of my bed. 'I'm in the next room. We're not supposed to cry, are we? Too grown up: lives before us and all that but if you don't tell neither will I.' She wiped her eyes with a tissue and passed it to me making us both laugh. Best friends ever since. She'd been with me. She understood.

My phone vibrated in my hand making me jump. Louisa's name was on the screen.

'Lily, God, where are you?' Her words were clogged with sleep. 'Are you all right?'

'I'm in Brighton, sitting on the beach staring at the water. I wanted …'

'Lily, tell me you're not going to do anything silly.' I could hear she was scrambling out of bed, talking, and walking. I heard a door close. 'Lily, say something. Is anyone with you?' Her voice was scratchy, urgent.

'Lou, it's so beautiful, I wanted to share it with you, that's all.'

'Christ, it's too early and it's Saturday. Why are you sitting on a bloody beach?'

'I needed to see the sea. I took a train to Brighton.' It sounded pathetic. 'Sorry, I never thought about the time.'

'Well, it's peeing down here in Manchester. Enjoy it while it lasts. You gave me a fright, messaging me like that. Are you going for a swim or something 'cos I'm going back to bed?'

'It's April, Lou! The water would be freezing. Go back to bed, I'm sorry.'

'Are you sure you're all right?' The question was laced with concern.

'I'm fine. I'll ring you later.'

'Sometimes Manchester feels too far away.'

'Yes, but I know you're only a train ride away. Speak soon.' I blanked the screen and the shush of waves was the loudest sound.

Away in the distance, a man walked along the tideline, his

dog running circles around him. No one else in sight. Swim? Crazy or what? I whipped off my outer clothes, and my shoes, felt the bruising stones as I ran and plunged into the water, the salt stinging my lips, and coating my skin. Murky green swirled above me, circles of light, strong strokes, limbs striving, lungs screaming. Water streamed off my hair and face as I surfaced, and the breeze drew goosebumps. Up the beach, patted dry and clothes on, I jumped up and down making wide sun circles with my arms. Deep breaths, slow breaths. Alive.

'A latte, scrambled egg on toast please and ... a muffin. Why not?' I grinned at the lady who was wiping the worksurfaces. A teasing aroma of coffee and bacon seeped from behind the counter. I rubbed a circle in the condensation on the window by my seat and sucked at a sugar lump from the bowl like a naughty child.

'You look like you need a warm drink.' The woman brought the tall glass over and I wrapped my hands around it. 'Your hair's all wet. Don't tell me you've been swimming in the sea.'

'I have and it's freezing. More of a plunge than swimming. I used to live in Cumbria, by the sea, and I've swum even in winter. Excruciating at the time, but afterwards it feels worth it.'

'You're mad, wouldn't catch me in there even in summer. I'll get your breakfast.' She came back with my steaming plate of scrambled eggs and a towel. 'Here, use this to dry your hair. My daughter is about your age, and I bet she's still in bed. On holiday, are you?'

The reason why I was here clouded in. 'No, just here for a day. It seemed like a good idea. I was pissed off.' It came out like a hiss. 'Sorry.'

'Don't be. I hear much worse than that in here sometimes. If it's a man, don't let him get to you. Another will come along and probably better too.'

'It's my mum.'

'Ah, we mums often get it wrong. My teenagers, their favourite expression is, "what do *you* know?" If I told them they might be shocked.' She winked and pulled a face leaving to serve a jogger who had just come in, music emitting faintly from his dangling earpiece. The bell over the door jangled as I left. She called across the tables. 'Make the peace. You'll feel better.' I waved and gave her a thumbs-up.

I wandered through the famous gardens where daffodils and crocuses embroidered the grass; imagined a Victorian lady walking there with her suitor, her hand resting lightly on his arm, a chaperone following discreetly at a distance. The Lanes were filling up with tourists, the owner of an antique shop polished a display of copper kettles in his window. An outside clock over a craft store told me it was past eleven. Louisa would be up by now.

I rang.

'Hi, Lou's phone.'

Lou? Only I got to call her that. From everyone else, she insisted on Louisa.

'Is she there?' I tripped on the words.

'She's in the bath. Hang on a minute, I'll take her the phone. Who is it?'

A smell of whisky and vomit came from nowhere and made me gag. For God's sake, I reasoned. She lives in Manchester; a scouse accent is not unusual.

'It's Lily.'

A prick of hesitation.

4

'Who was that?' It was a bark, not a question.

'He borrowed the sofa last night – out too late to get home.'

I heard water topping up the bath. 'Who is he, Lou? What's his name? A new man?'

'Lily, he's just … someone. Are you okay anyway?'

A thrum in my head said to leave it there. 'Yes, that's why I rang, to tell you I'm fine, and to apologise for earlier. I won't interrupt your day.'

'You're not. Hey, why don't we arrange a mad weekend, it's been a while.'

'That would be great, it's too easy to let work get in the way. I could do with a northern fix.' I tried to sound light so she would hear my smile. 'When?'

A pulse beat. 'Why don't I come to London, a proper girlie weekend in the capital? Find some good clubs or bars to hang out in?'

'Lou,' I rushed on not wanting her to hang up. 'Do you remember the box we found that day, in Mum's house, all glittery and bright, the one with the note, "for Lily", on a piece of paper, underneath a snowdome?' She clearly didn't remember but I needed to tell her. 'I finally opened it last night. Do you know what was in it?'

'What? Knowing your mum, it would be something unusual.'

'Five boxes stacked inside each other like a Russian doll. And in the fifth there were three packets of seed.'

Lou's laugh rang out. 'Yeah, that sounds like Hettie.'

'But what did she mean by it? Is it some sort of riddle I'm supposed to figure out the answer to? In my head, I'd built it up, thought it was going to be something big. I even got the idea it might be the name of my father or a letter or photograph. I felt fucking let down. I couldn't sleep. Three packets of seed! I haven't got a garden, just a concrete yard littered with crates most of the time. I haven't even got a window box. All night it has been driving me mad trying to work it out.'

I heard Lou's sigh. 'Lily, a series of boxes that's all. So what? Your mum probably thought you would like them. Maybe she forgot there was anything inside them. No big deal – they're just boxes. She … she didn't know you were going to live in a flat. Maybe you're making too much of this? Forget it. Throw them away or just have them as a keepsake.'

'You're probably right.' I forced out the words. 'Look, I must go. Speak soon.' I squeezed the phone like I could break it. Shoppers stepped around me with curious stares. Eventually I made myself walk towards the station.

Only a box, only a box. Lou's words were the rhythm of the train over the rails. By the time I reached the High Road near to home, I felt drenched in the stale smell of travelling. She was right, it was only a box. Lou, who never let me down. She had been with me when I needed her the most. A day I would never forget.

'Bloody hell what's happened to you?' Lou squatted, her face level with mine, the toilet pan between us. Her question smelt of wine, spirits and sweet smoke.

'Leave me alone, go to bed.' I wiped scraps of vomit off my chin with my sleeve.

'It must have been a bloody good party. You're half undressed!'

'A shower, to wash …' What was it I wanted to wash?

'No chance. Let's get you onto the sofa.' She was taking charge like I wanted her to. She hauled me up. Stomach-turning somersaults and pain carved a ravine between my legs as I clutched bruised ribs.

She lifted my top when I moaned. I dreaded what she saw. 'God, Lily, who did this?' With a thumb and finger, she picked up my bloodied pants from the bathroom tiles and threw them in the sink. The room was a whirling stream of light, and I held onto her sweater to stop myself from falling.

'Who, who did this? Who were you with? You need to talk to the police. Now. I'll call them.'

'No.' I spewed the word like sick. 'I was drunk, I am drunk. He was drunk. I don't know who he was. Off our heads. I can't remember, can't remember anything. Let me lie down, let me sleep.'

'Lily, Lily, wake up.' Lou's fragmented voice pummelled in my ears. Warm sunlight speared my eyes as I tried to open them. 'What time is it? God, my head. Leave me be.'

'Lily, you need to wake up. The police are here. They need to speak to you.' Her words scared me.

I pushed back the cover retching at the smell of myself and swung my bare legs to the floor. Two officers loomed in silhouette in front of the lounge window.

'No, Lou. No.' I think I yelled because my head thumped in reply. 'What have you gone and done? It's okay, really. She's wasting your time. I was drunk and ...'

'Lily.' Lou sat beside me, crying, her arm, a brace around my shoulders. She scraped back a strand of hair that had stuck to my cheek 'It's not about ... It's your mum.' Her sob punched me, her face ashen.

'I'm sorry young lady. Lily, isn't it? There's been an accident.' The officer shifted to block out the sun. 'Your mother suffered a severe head injury. The paramedics tried everything at the scene, but she died on the way to the hospital. I'm sorry.' A young policewoman knelt in front of me, put her hand on my knee and tucked in the duvet to cover my naked skin.

No, they were wrong. Words jumbled in my throat. I had to make them see. 'She doesn't have a car. It's not my mum. it's someone else's.'

'It wasn't a car accident. She fell off a ladder.'

'A ladder? Why was she up a ladder?' I begged for the detail that would prove it wasn't her, everything a puzzle, half the pieces missing.

The woman squinted up at her colleague. 'The neighbour said ... she was rescuing a pigeon trapped in netting over a downpipe.'

It *was* her. And I was a stinking wreck.

For a moment the memory was so vivid it stopped me from walking. I shook my head to dispel the pictures. Across the road, an old man wearing a kurta picked daffodils from his allotment. I'd seen him before; he was often there when I jogged early in the morning. He straightened slowly, arching his neck. I half waved when he looked across, but I don't think he saw me as he gave no response.

Back in the flat I lifted the cushions from the floor, made the bed and put on some coffee. Curled on the sofa with my eyes shut, I could see again the ripples of the waves as they broke into white foam on the shore, taste the brine and feel the eddy of the water above my head. 'Only a box, maybe you're making too much of this.' Practical Lou, down-to-earth Lou. She'd turned my twenty-four-hour roller-coaster trip into a simple ride on a fairground roundabout. But that man, the one who'd answered her phone? I tossed a niggling thought away to stop it from becoming ugly. I smiled; I can do this. I am going to label this a good weekend.

I collected up the scattered packets of seeds, scrabbled under the sideboard to where one had fled, and dropped them into the waste paper basket. The boxes I neatly stacked inside each other once more and put them back on the shelf in the wardrobe. 'Putting my life back in order,' I told Mum as I righted her photograph and polished the glass with my sleeve. Behind her, lime green flowers tumbled over the path, interspersed with pink. Her eyes fixed on mine. 'Okay, okay, you're right, better idea, I should have thought of it.' I retrieved the packets of seeds from the bin. 'I'll give them to Isaac for his mother. She can enjoy them.' Mum was laughing with me again.

5

Damn, I forgot to give those seeds to Isaac for his mum. Walking past the allotments after work and seeing the old Indian man there reminded me. He was sitting on a bench in front of his shed, smoke just visible from a cigarette. The sight of him, small and hunched, resting against the rickety structure with its boards of different colours, drew me across the road to a metal gate. I unlooped the chain that held it shut and followed a gravel path which took me past the first allotment. Manure was heaped in a wheelbarrow and flies buzzed around. Dead foliage from last year's plants was punctured by dandelions and emerging weeds.

'Hello,' I spoke softly, not wanting to surprise him. He squinted up at me with watery eyes. He was much older than I'd thought, deep furrows were etched into his face; his skin hung in folds like crumpled cloth.

'You've caught me. I allow myself one cigarette a day. I used to smoke many more but now … they tell me it's not good for me.' He tapped the bench beside him as if he'd been waiting for me. I sat down feeling prim in my office clothes. He didn't seem curious at my sudden appearance and I felt no compunction to rush into an explanation. He puffed quietly at his cigarette, then ground the stub with his foot. We stared across the acres of green and newly turned ground. Some of the enclosures had greenhouses, almost all had sheds of varying size and stability. A woman in a bright, multi-coloured wrap thrust a spade into the earth pausing occasionally to right the turban-like headgear she wore. He must have been watching her too because he said, 'Her name is Abeke. Her laugh is like a mountain waterfall. She's our light in the winter, our hope in the spring. When Abeke laughs we all do.'

'Is she from Africa?'

'Yes, from Nigeria. It is like the United Nations here. We come from all corners of the world.'

'And that's the thing I love most about living in London.'

He chuckled, 'Growing things is the language we share.'

'Growing things. That's the reason I'm here.' I couldn't work out why, but I didn't want this moment to end. I wanted to stop here with this quiet, gentle man until the pale sun disappeared. 'Sitting here, it's so lovely. All the noise and the traffic, and the busyness of the day is forgotten.'

'Nature weaves its own magic, don't you think? In India, where I came from, nature can be harsh, but she is also beautiful.'

I rummaged in my bag and found the three packets of seeds.

'My mum died, and she left me a box – these were inside. I have nowhere to grow them. Would you like them?'

He took them from me and brought them close to his eyes to see them better. He turned the packets over and shuffled them like a deck of cards. Abeke called goodnight and waved as she left by the far path. Now there were only the two of us.

'A herb, a vegetable and a flower. Your mother was full of sunshine.'

'Yes, she was. Why do you say that?'

'Because of these.' He stroked the packets of seeds. 'They worship the sun, and the warmth. Marigolds and marjoram are nectar to the bees.'

'She loved bees too, and moths and butterflies, all wildlife.'

'I think I would have liked your mother.' He shook his head. 'I won't plant them; she has left this gift of sunshine to you.'

He passed the packets back to me. I wanted him to change his mind. I wanted him to have them. He stroked his chin with its grey beard, and I saw that two of his fingers were only stumps, missing above the second joint.

'But I will show you how to plant them and you can have some space on my allotment. See, over there. It is too big for me to manage though I don't want to admit it.' A sparrow hopped in front of us and the man threw it some food from a bag in his pocket. 'One of my friends,' he said. 'In exchange, they eat the bugs.' He laughed and patted my knee. 'My name is Asadi. Perhaps you are a gift to me.' His voice tinkled with merriment. 'What is your name?'

'Lily.'

'Ah, fresh life and rebirth. Your mother must have loved her flowers to give you a precious name like that.'

'Is that what it means, fresh life and rebirth?'

'The sweet and innocent beauty of the lily flower.'

'I think you are a poet. You say such beautiful things.'

'All we Indians are poets. We are brought up on poetry. Why don't you come back another time and we'll plant your seeds?'

'I will, I'll come at the weekend. If that's all right.' I was already looking forward to it. 'Thank you. Talking to you has been the nicest thing that's happened to me in ages.'

He nodded, 'Your mother was also a wise woman.'

I wasn't sure what he meant but I liked him for saying it. 'It feels like you knew her.'

'I will get to know her through you. Now it is time for us to go before I stumble in the dusk.'

Over the last few days, I'd let my thoughts drift to the things Asadi had said. Now I needed to concentrate. I straightened my jacket and scanned the room of candidates awaiting their allotted interview slot. Three women and two men all hoping to be appointed as carers. One young man stood staring out the window lifting himself up and down on his toes, glancing at his watch then thrusting his hand into his pocket. An older woman sat reading a magazine while another, who made me think of Abeke from the allotments, busied herself handing out coffee in disposable cups from the machine. I wanted to tell them not to worry; unless they really messed up, they would all get a job. We continually needed carers, and low wages and hard work meant there was a frequent turnover.

I remembered when I was the one sitting and waiting in this very room. It felt like an age ago. I'd applied for the job of Recruitment Assistant but was too numb to care if I didn't get it. When Mum died the university were kind, said all the right things, offered support through my finals and gave me the opportunity to defer. What they didn't realise was I couldn't even make a decision about what to wear each day never mind about what my future should look like. It had been less than two months before my exams. Everything I had learnt over the past three years had fled into some impenetrable vault. Every creative, expansive idea in my head had withered and the thought of performing had me crouching in the toilet cubicle shivering like a cold child.

Lou barely left my side. She'd been with me when I went back home and into the house for the first time, past the ladder now laid on its side against the wall. She helped me to arrange the funeral, to choose a coffin, pine with brass, white or simple basket weave. I dithered, the woman in the funeral directors asked in a hushed tone perfected over years, 'What do you think your mother would like?' I wanted to scream. She wouldn't like any of them. She didn't intend to die. But I didn't, I focused instead on the arrangement of flowers that sat in an alcove on a velvet cloth.

The crematorium was full of faces from my childhood, neighbours, shopkeepers and school friends. A distant cousin said, 'There is so much love in the room. I had no idea Henrietta was so popular.' Even though I wanted to hit this person whom I didn't remember and would never see again, the sentiment stuck with me. My mum was loved.

Lou and I, but mostly Lou, packed up Mum's house, returning all the charity shop items to where they came from. I didn't want anything except a few things that I remembered Mum liked, like a ring she wore and a favourite mug and of course the box with my name on it. Sometimes now I recall other things, like the trunk with its content of fun, and wish I'd kept them, but it's too late.

I left university, put my few possessions from the student house into a suitcase, hugged Lou so hard she squealed in protest and took a train to London.

I'd seen the job advertised on LinkedIn: Assistant Recruitment Officer. London seemed about as far away as I could get. I applied. They listened without comment to my garbled story as to why I hadn't finished my degree, didn't push as to why the Creative Arts no longer interested me and said a simple 'sorry' when I told them about Mum. I would never have given me the job but for some reason they did.

'… don't you think?' The candidate who had been looking out the window was standing next to me. 'The panorama, it's dramatic, looking across to London.'

'Yes. It's beautiful. There's a lot of green, it softens the cityscape. I'm sorry, I was miles away.'

'I could see that. You looked sad.'

His eyes were pale, in his sallow face, like the blue had been washed from them. I smiled to reassure him. I was here to put the candidates at their ease not the other way around. 'Have you come far today?' I asked him.

'From Barnet, not far. But originally, from Poland. A village in the north ... within sight of the sea.'

'You miss it?'

'Of course. It is home. But there are not so many opportunities there. One day perhaps I will go back. Forgive me for saying but I think you too are missing something.'

I nodded. 'Well, good luck with the interview.'

'Thank you. My name is Aleksy.'

They were all given a job. I saw them as they left the building, each one looking relieved the interview was over. A lip being chewed, or cheeks puffed out. I smiled when Aleksy punched the air unaware of being observed.

'Well done. Your observations are impressive. Your summary of each candidate is spot on. Astute and empathetic at the same time.' Ben poured coffee for us both, tilted back his chair and stretched long legs onto his desk. 'Tiring day, but worth it. Are you joining the gang tonight? Round off a productive week.'

I nodded, 'Yes, for a bit. It ... it was all right.'

'Lily, you know I'm always here if you need to talk. We wouldn't want to lose you.' Ben was picking at a quick on his nail. 'Last week, in the bar you looked, well, terrified. I can't think of any other way to describe it. None of my business I know but ...'

'Thanks, Ben. I'll remember.' I gathered up the plastic cups and threw them in the bin.

He shrugged on a jacket. 'Right then. Let's go or we'll miss the first round. Must be Isaac's turn. He's been threatening to introduce us to his boyfriend. Don't want to miss that.'

A breeze tugged as we walked down the street crowded with people leaving their offices, heads down making for the Tube or stopping off at restaurants or cafés. Couples sat at tables on the pavement eating from bowls of steaming noodles or lifting cheese-draped pizzas to their mouths.

'A teacher and a mechanical engineer.' Ben shook his head. 'I wonder how long they'll stay with us.'

'Pardon.'

'Sorry, I was thinking of the interviewees. That woman from Uganda and the Polish guy. Remember, that's what they were in their own countries. You must have to be pretty desperate to apply for a carer's job. Imagine all those years of training gone to waste.'

'I guess you play the ball where it's landed.'

'Yeah, I suppose so. And where has your ball landed this weekend, Lily? Any more madcap plans to go for dips in the sea?'

I'd told them of my trip to Brighton but not the reason behind it. 'Actually, I'm going to plant seeds on an allotment, at the invitation of a very old man from India.' I couldn't help but grin at Ben's expression. 'I'm really looking forward to it.'

'God, I don't see you as a gardener, Lily. What other secrets are you hiding?' He pushed open the door of the wine bar. I sloughed off his words and followed him in.

6

I had woken this morning to fine drizzle and watched raindrops stir and stretch on the window. Uncertainty lodged in my chest like undigested food. Did the old man really mean for me to come? Would he be there in the rain? Why would he bother with me when I obviously knew nothing about plants?

'I've bought new wellies. Do you like them?' I felt slightly foolish standing in front of Asadi in my green boots decorated with sunflowers. In the shop they had seemed fun. Asadi laughed, the hairs of his beard quivering under his lip. 'They are quite the jolliest pair I have ever seen. Look at my old ones, plain black and muddy. I think yours might soon be dirty too. First, let us sit and you can tell me what you have been doing since I last saw you.' He reached under the bench and brought out a flask from which he poured thick beige-coloured liquid into small cups.

'Thank you. Tea?' I said, tasting sweetness and spice.

'Chai. Ginger chai to keep us warm. All friendships begin by drinking chai together.'

'You asked about my week; it's been nothing special. I haven't anything interesting to say. We held interviews for people wanting to be carers.' I found myself describing the lady who reminded me of Abeke and who had been a teacher in Uganda and the man from Poland who had been an engineer. 'It must be so hard starting over again in a new country, where there's different food, new places, a strange culture. I think I'd be too scared, too afraid of being rebuffed.'

'You make it work if you want it to, but yes, it is hard.' Asadi's long exhale cut short my ramblings.

'Oh, I'm sorry. What am I going on about? Of course, you know what it's like. You came over from India.'

'A long, long time ago.' He ran a blue-veined hand over the back of his neck then rubbed the stumps of his fingers. 'It was in 1947 when the world was a different place.' He pulled up the zip on his frayed gilet. 'Perhaps one day if you are not bored with an old man I will tell you. See, you did have lots to say after all. Come, did you remember to bring your seeds? I have these for you. A present.' He handed me a pair of new red gardening gloves. 'And I have cleaned my spade, in honour of the occasion. Perhaps you can carry it and I will bring the bucket.' His chuckle folded over me like soft silk. 'I think your mum is watching us.' He pointed at splashes of sunlight littering the ground.

With the thought that she might be, I brushed a sleeve across my eyes as I followed him to the far end of his allotment.

'Before you sow, you must dig to get rid of the weeds. A task that is hard for me but with young muscles, it will not be so hard I think.'

'How do I know which are weeds?'

His laugh cascaded to his boots. 'All of these are weeds. Over the winter, despite the cold, they grow, and their seeds are always the first to sprout. I will start at the other end and perhaps we will meet in the middle.' He ambled away with a lopsided gait, and I watched as he resolutely began to push a fork into the earth. How old must he be? If he'd come here as a baby, he could be sixty-five, but he was much, much older than that, I was sure. Generous, fascinating and full of knowledge, I couldn't ever imagine being bored by him.

I looked at the sprawling web of greenery at my feet and pulled a face. Mum had always tended the garden. She would sing as she worked and I liked to sit on the top step and listen; her happiness made me happy. She'd come in with dirty hands and smudges of soil on her face and I'd make tea and we'd share a piece of cake if there was any in the house.

I thrust the spade into the soil and turned over a clod, shook the weeds free and tossed them into the bucket. All around people seemed to be doing similar tasks. Two small children played tag, squealing with fun. A man, who I guessed was their father, erected a wigwam of canes. Occasionally he would shout to them but mostly they ran around absorbed in some invented game. Abeke waved a greeting and gave me a thumbs-up as I took a moment to straighten and take off my jacket before I became too hot and sweaty. Still bent over his patch of soil, Asadi had cleared an area only a fraction of the size I had.

After a while he came over to me and nodded. 'You have

done well.'

'I'm not sure about that.' His warm praise made me beam.

'Your blood, it runs with gardening genes, I think. Shall we plant the marigold seeds next to the path? You can scatter them around so they will become a profusion of oranges and yellows. The chard I suggest we sow in a neat row or two behind.'

He leant on the spade. Under his direction, I forged a shallow furrow and sprinkled in the seeds, covering them with soil. 'It's hard to believe they'll soon be something we can eat. I feel quite proud.' I surveyed the newly tended stretch of ground.

'I think it is time to stop for some lunch. Already you have a new friend; look at the robin pecking for worms. Time now to meet more friends.'

When I looked in the direction of his nod, I saw Abeke spreading a bright cloth, as vivid as her headgear, over a pile of pallets next to Asadi's bench. I squinted at him, he winked and took my arm to steady himself.

The younger man I had noticed earlier appeared from inside the shed carrying a pizza.

'Hi, Lily, I'm Adam.' He held out his free hand and waited while I peeled off my gloves. 'My two hungry kids will be right over when they smell food. I love that you look so surprised. I can see Asadi didn't warn you. This is a tradition; whenever someone new arrives in our corner of the allotments, we say hello by sharing food together. Nothing special but fun.'

'That's so lovely. I should have brought something.'

'Not this time. This is our welcome.'

Already there were crisps laid out alongside samosas and a colourful pasta salad with peas, tomatoes and peppers.

'These can't be from your allotments.'

'Some perhaps, like the peas and the peppers, if they've been frozen, but no, it's too early in the season for fresh produce but you wait – in the summer we have a banquet, all freshly picked. I sound like I know what I'm talking about. I don't, I'm a bit of a novice. The venture was Rosie's, my partner.' He turned from me, looking across to his space.

'Come on, honey. Help yourself. I'm Abeke. You have been working hard this morning, now you need some calories. Build you up. See, like me.' She patted a round stomach that heaved under her dress as she chortled. Her skin was the colour of a new conker, polished and shiny and every crease in her face spelt laughter. She gathered me up and propelled me towards the feast.

'Gulnar.' She shouted across to a figure still crouched on the ground. 'Lunch.' The woman lifted her head. She wore a black hijab and a coat over jeans. 'She is always the last. She is always working.' Abeke handed me a paper plate.

'Noah and Sam, come and say hello.' Adam ushered the boys over and they obediently said hello. 'We've got a swing,' the younger one said. 'You can play on it if you want to. It's over there.' He pointed with a grubby finger.

'Well, thank you. Maybe I just will one day.'

'You are very honoured.' Adam grinned, his eyebrows raised in exclamation. 'You two, go and wipe your hands and don't eat all the pizza.'

Everyone was chattering, different accents blending. Gulnar arrived with a basket of pakora, still warm and covered with a white cloth. She insisted I take two. Never had anything tasted so good. 'From my mother's recipe,' she said. 'In Pakistan they are a staple food.'

I moved to where Asadi sat on his bench. 'You've not much to eat. Can I fetch you something?'

'Enough for an old man. It seems appetite gets frail along with everything else.'

'Everyone is so kind, Asadi, especially you. I don't know what to say. I feel so … so wanted. Does that sound silly?'

'Not silly at all. We all yearn to be wanted.' His scored face folded into pleats. 'Here, I have three pots for you to take home. I will give you some compost and you must sow the marjoram in them. Put them somewhere warm, love and cherish them, and in a month or so we can plant them out.'

A sudden aching to be loved flooded over me like water bursting from a fractured pipe. I tilted my face to stem the tears that threatened. Rays from the sun touched my skin.

'Out of the wind the sun is inviting and it's only April.' I spoke to cover my confusion.

'I think there has been too little sunshine for you recently.' He said it so quietly I wasn't sure if I'd imagined it. When I turned to him, his eyes were closed but he patted my knee as he had done that first time we'd met. 'I'm glad you came.'

7

'Birthday time again.' Jade bounced into the office, in a sleek black leather skirt, black tights and long boots, her blonde hair vivid against a scarlet jumper. 'The Peach Tree for drinks at nine then back to my place to party, party, party. All of you – be there. My brother's bringing his rugby mates.'

'Yeah.' Isaac punched his arm into the air. 'Your parties are legendary. Rugby players, what's not to like?' He minced across the room in an exaggerated fashion and kissed her on both cheeks. 'Count me in.'

Amir piped up. 'And bring your boyfriend, Isaac. We're dying to meet him. You can leave your bag at home.' Everyone laughed.

'Bag or boyfriend, no contest, bag every time.' Isaac clapped Amir on the back. 'And what about you, Amir, will you bring someone? I bet you have a stunningly beautiful girl lurking in the shadows.'

Jade opened her arms wide. 'Bring whomever you like as long as you take away my misery at being twenty-five. Twenty-five, imagine? I may soon have to start acting maturely.'

I listened, wishing I could crawl under the desk and become invisible. Any moment the attention would swerve to me. Already a flush of heat was creeping up my neck, whipping my heart into a frenzied response. I stared hard at my computer screen to avoid their glances, then hit print to give me an excuse to hide in the print room. Breathe. Keep breathing. My hands were clammy, and the room began to spin. I fled to the toilet and sat down on the loo with my head between my hands.

'You're not coming, are you?' Jade pushed open the door and stood with a hand on the jamb. 'Why the hell not? What's wrong with you?'

I snapped back, 'I don't like parties.'

'If you were fifty, boring and old I would accept that. But you're not and whatever's eating you up will make you that way.'

'It's none of your business.' I could see she was fuming as I brushed past her. I ran down the stairs, through the foyer to the street, relieved to be free of the building and to feel the chill of the fresh air. Propping myself against the wall my fingernails scratched at the coarse brick imagining torn skin oozing blood. Nausea puddled below my ribs. A deep breath in, pause and let it out slowly. I focussed on a bus attempting to edge its way into the traffic but trapped by cars squeezing past. That's me – trying to rejoin the mainstream but always driven back. Finally, the bus driver forced his way out and a blue 4x4 squealed to a juddering halt; the noise of its horn drowned the obscenities mouthed by the woman inside.

'Lily … I'm sorry. I'm worried for you, that's all.' Jade wore her coat and held out my jacket at arm's length. 'Let's go for a walk. We don't need to talk or anything. They know we'll be gone for a bit.'

We walked down the street away from the shops, occasionally brushing arms as if to remind ourselves of each other's presence. True to her word she kept her silence and I loved her for that.

Memories, like splintered ice, rained images and sounds; breath laced with beer and spirits, spiky white-blond hair shaved short at the sides, a Scouse accent, stairs with a red carpet, stumbling half-way up clinging to a banister like it was the funniest thing in the world. The frantic beat of a song pulsing in tune with my gasps. His hands, a tearing zip, a crumpled bed, tongues, skin moist and hot. Naked, stretched-out limbs. Slaps, my head reeling sideways, pummelled ribs. Me pushing, pushing at his chest, scratched skin, pain, an eruption of climactic agony, torn-out hair in my closed fist. Words shouted. Words I don't remember. A rush of vomit. *Live Like We're Dying* stuck on the turntable of my mind. Later, much later, me, spent, dribble frothing on my chin, lying on the floor, knees drawn up, shivering in the chill of first light. Him, sprawled on the bed with legs spread wide. Waking, staggering out, the bang of a door and a 'sorry' rebounding off the walls settling in the farthest, darkest folds of my brain. And all the time music playing.

'Lily.' Jade threaded her arm through mine, nudging me back to the present.

We had reached a small green area where a path wove between hummocks of grass. Crocuses lay broken amongst the scattered clumps and a grey squirrel foraging on the ground paused, then scurried up a tree to safety.

'When I was at university I went to a party. There was always a party that someone knew of.' My chest tightened, squeezed my breath.

'And?' Jade's whisper came from far away.

'It was coming up to finals. I worked hard. I wanted a good degree. There were also new friends, music, dancing, talking, deep conversations long into the night, drinking, drugs if you wanted them. Freedom.' I faltered, telling felt like ripping open a sealed envelope.

Jade grimaced, then broke into a grin, 'I never made it to university, but I went to some wild student parties. Ugh, those hangovers!'

'You're too right.' A child's ball bounced across the path in front of us making us stop, giving us time to remember. 'It was exciting, real. You think it will last.'

I sat down on a bench; Jade close beside me as if trying to keep me warm. 'Spurs Forever' was carved into the arm of the seat. I fingered the jaggedly scored wood.

'You wouldn't recognise the person I was then.' I scanned her face wondering if she believed me. A small puff of warm sweet breath told me she was listening. 'Noisy, fun, popular ... and clever. Down for a first. My tutor thought energy, not blood, coursed through my veins.' I leant forward, arms crossed, elbows on my knees, trying to recall what that had felt like.

'There was a guy, doing a PhD, I fancied him like mad. We got together, a bit heavy, a bit quick. You know what I mean.'

'Guys, hey.' Jade's smirk was almost a smile.

'I was besotted. All evening I'd redo the make-up in case he came, forgive him when he didn't turn up or turned up late. He'd always 'lost' his phone or forgotten it so he couldn't call me. That's obsession – stupid or what? I sound pathetic, don't I?'

'We've all been there.'

'I guess. Well, I was on the bus this Thursday night when he got on. We talked and talked, his hand creeping up my thigh. He almost missed his stop, had to gather his things in a rush and run. He shouted over his shoulder, "Joel's place on Saturday. Big party." He blew a kiss and I waved as the top of his head disappeared down the stairs. A woman sitting opposite with a young child on her knee laughed. "That sounds like an invitation you can't turn down."'

'What's the expression? A dog with two tails, that was me.'

'I hate him already. You went to the party. He didn't show?'

'Oh, yes, he was there – with another girl. Just another notch on his bedpost, one of many, was how others laughed it off when I asked who she was. Seems everyone knew but me. I felt sick, twisted into knots. They smooched all night. He completely ignored me. I was of less significance than an ant. Have you ever felt naked in your clothes? Stripped, transparent, every organ exposed like on an X-ray. I got drunk. Whatever was offered I took it: lager, wine, spirits, weed, a cocktail of self-destruction. All to prove I didn't care. I danced harder and sang louder than anyone else. I clung round the necks of people I didn't know, and still humiliation blazed. To cut a long story short, I went upstairs with another guy, someone as drunk as me. The next thing I remember is waking up in the early morning bruised and bleeding.'

'He raped you?'

'Yes. No. That's it, did he, or did I want it as much as him? I don't know. Do I even deserve to know?'

'Christ, Lily that's horrible.' Jade wound her hair into a scrunchy on top of her head like she didn't want it to be contaminated. 'Did you report it?'

'No. Something else happened – the next day. My ….' I shook my head, the guilt too raw to touch. 'I couldn't even remember his name - if I ever knew it. We'd both been smashed. Sometimes, Jade, he's there, I see him in crazy moments, flashbacks that can be triggered by anything, the smell of alcohol, a beat of music, drunk people out of control. Pale hair, blue eyes, open, staring into me, through me. Eyebrows so fair they're hardly there. It's like he's watching. Everything that happened after … I blame myself for. If I'd not gone to that bloody party …' I stood up. 'We should go back. Thank you — for listening, for being here.' I held Jade briefly, rubbing free the light smell of her perfume.

She looked at her watch. 'Hell, I have a meeting at twelve. I've got to be there.' She wrapped her arms around me. 'There's more, isn't there? When you want to …'

'I know. Thanks.' Relief at telling made me feel dizzy, light enough to fly. 'Now come on.' I pulled her along the path out of the square, along the street, weaving between passers-by who tutted, stared, or moved aside for us. Two young women running together, Jade's hair escaping from its confines and spilling across her face. We arrived at the office with minutes to spare, laughing at each other, bringing in a smell of fresh air with a hint of car fumes.

'Lipstick, my notes and I'm ready.' Jade called across the room as she rushed out, leaving me standing there getting my breath back. The others were looking. Whatever conversation my hasty exit had provoked it was clear us returning in this way was not what they had anticipated.

'Sorry, folks. Stupid female hysterics. Hormones, ugh.'

Amir stepped from behind his desk and enveloped me in his arms. 'This is from all of us.'

Acceptance and friendship wrapped in a hug.

Isaac was fishing in his bag. 'Did I tell you the one about the rabbi who …?'

8

I spent a long time choosing a pair of silver hoop earrings to give to Jade for her birthday. It was ages since I'd given that much thought to someone else, and I squirmed at my own selfishness. The party had not been mentioned again but Jade had been so brilliant I didn't want it to be something she couldn't talk about in front of me.

'This is to say Happy Birthday and thank you. I want to hear all about it on Monday.' I handed her the pastel-coloured gift bag with its crinkle of tissue paper escaping from the top. 'Have a good time all of you.' From the expressions on the four faces who looked up from their desks, they didn't know what to say.

'As you've guessed,' I plunged on, 'life's been pretty shitty for the last year or so and … I've been rubbish at dealing with it. You've all been fantastic and I'm getting there. Slowly, slowly but I am, so I just want you to know … I'm grateful.'

Silence melted into the space. The truth of the words to my own ears felt the same as putting on a warm coat.

Isaac clapped. 'Three cheers for Lily. We love you, darling. Always meet the new day with a smile is what my mother says. Sometimes, she makes sense.'

Saturday dawned with horizontal streaks of orange and peach. A plane's vapour trail dissected the sky like a careless pencil line. All week a damp breath of rain had drizzled from a swollen sky. I'd not seen Asadi or anyone else working on the allotments as I'd hastened home from work. I feared that my seeds would be rotting in the ground before they even had the will to emerge. In the flat, I moved Mum's photo onto the kitchen windowsill so she could watch over my carefully planted pots of marjoram. Each day I searched for signs of life, but only stubborn brown soil remained.

'Be patient.' Asadi laughed when I told him. He found me on the allotment poking at the earth with my finger. 'All this rain will make them grow. Now we need sun and a bit of warmth and soon they will come.'

'I hoped you would be here. I've come to dig over the rest of the plot for you. Please let me. I'm all prepared.' I watched him grapple with emotion, a bent finger worrying his lip.

'That would be a big help. This soil is too claggy for an old man.' He seemed to shrink as he spoke. 'I am glad you have come back. I saw how after last week you began to smile from within. Come, I will show you where to start.'

All morning we worked. Me digging away, the smell of freshly turned earth all around. Asadi pottering, brushing soil off wooden labels and fixing cane supports which he said were for runner beans.

'Just the way my mum used to do it,' I told him.

I could see her now in denim dungarees, her hair tied back with a piece of twine, totally absorbed in her task, oblivious to time and a hungry child. 'I'm hungry, when can we have something to eat?' I'd plead. She would scoop me up, smearing me with mucky fingers. 'Oh my gosh, is it that time already? Why don't we have chips on the beach?' Then the whole day would become fun and we'd sit on damp sand, playing chicken with the waves.

Remembering brought back the taste of hot, fat chips and licking salt and vinegar off my fingers, throwing scraps to seagulls who strutted with attitude. I was used to memories cutting through me, sharp as a new blade, carving hollows beneath my feet for me to drop into. This time it wasn't like that. I didn't try to shake the images from my head or blank them out. Instead, it was like a lost jigsaw piece suddenly found and fitted into place. I looked up to see Asadi watching me.

Being at the allotments with people who had become my friends became the pattern of my weekends. I proudly planted out the marjoram, the leaves already smelling of sunshine. Shoots of chard and marigold greened the earth. I was as excited as a child. Sometimes I would share coffee with Abeke who would sit with her legs apart and regale me with stories of her teenage sons. She had me laughing when she mimicked them, her ample bosom heaving, her arms flapping. Adam's children would always come to see what I was doing. One Saturday Sam brought me a biscuit he'd made at playschool. A random shape with sweets for eyes and a splodgy icing mouth. 'It's for you,' he proudly announced.

'You've scored a hit,' his dad said. 'He's been desperate to bring it to you.'

I wondered about this shy man. Loneliness was something I knew and an air of it surrounded him.

Asadi wasn't always up to staying for more than a couple of hours, but we always found time at the beginning and end of his day to sit for a while on his bench, our favourite spot. He would leave me with instructions as to what I could do.

'What if I'd never met you, Asadi, and not made all these new friends? I still remember how devastated I felt when I found there were only seeds in the box that Mum left me. Did I tell you I threw them away? What if I hadn't retrieved them?' The fragility of chance, fleetingly, filled me with anxiety. He breathed heavily as he spoke. 'I said your mum was a wise woman. She understood the language of growing, of new life, of beauty and peace. Was there nothing else in the box?'

'No, that's the thing. It was just a series of empty glittery boxes one inside the other. If you stack them, they sit on top of each other and form a pyramid. My friend says they're just boxes and I'm making too much of them. I suppose she's right.'

He stared into the distance where perky new leaves fluttered on the trees. 'See, they are dancing in their new clothes,' he said, as we both watched. A sigh settled on his chest. 'Your mum, she wanted you to fill the boxes with memories, happy moments, a lifetime of treasures.'

Through his eyes I saw the boxes spilling with photos, with keepsakes of what has been, waiting for what may still be to come. 'What a lovely idea.' I clapped my hands with a wisp of excitement. 'You always turn my confusion into something positive, something to look forward to. My mum was a collector, a hoarder, she would love that idea. I'm going to do it.'

Asadi shuffled his feet. 'Keep them safe, they are precious.'

'Will you share some of your memories?' I gazed into his uncertainty and stuttered on. 'You must have lots from a long life.'

There was a catch in his breath and I wished I could take back my words. Between us the air hung silent, heavy, as before a thunderstorm. His hand moved to rub his finger stumps in a gesture that had become familiar. I grappled for the courage to continue, whispering into the pause.

'Can I ask you something, Asadi? What do you do with the loudest memories, the ones that bring only pain? They are what torment me.'

'You mean the ones that scream at you in the middle of the night, that hide in corners waiting to surprise you, events so real they could have happened yesterday?' He covered my hand with his. 'Those you keep near to your heart where the pain is only felt by you.'

'You know?'

'Yes, I know.'

I felt the heat of his palm, saw the brown age spots that peppered his hand.

'Your mum was incredibly special. You never talk of your father.' He turned to me searching for something.

'I have no memory of him. He was never part of my life.'

'He left when you were young?'

'Before then. Before I was born, even before conception took place probably.' The thought provoked an ironic chuckle. 'I haven't missed him.'

'I suppose that's the truth of it, isn't it? No one can miss what they don't remember.'

I sensed another conversation was happening here. Asadi was in a different place, far from an allotment in north London, a place beyond our horizon.

'You are a daughter without a father. I am a father without my child.'

9

I grinned at the cheery marigolds in my hand, orange and yellow petals in perfect symmetry around black faces.

'Look, Adam, I'm so chuffed.' I waved the small bunch of flowers above his head. 'My first posy.' He was crouched over a tunnel of netting. I tugged at it, keeping it taut while he pinned it to the ground.

'They're pretty. When I picked my first beans, I was dead proud; they were the best beans I'd ever tasted. Beware of the gardening bug. It strikes when least expected and there's no recognised cure.' He nodded knowingly running a soil-stained hand through his hair. 'Butterflies always find a way in however much I try to keep them off the cabbages. Before you know it, a hundred caterpillars have shredded the leaves.' He stood up. 'Listen to us, we're like a couple of old codgers. What brings you down here on a weekday night?'

'I love these long summer evenings. I often come and just wander. I've never heard of some of the vegetables that are grown here. Bitter gourds, fenugreek; Abeke has told me the names but I'm not sure I'd recognise them, let alone know what to do with them. Sometimes I just sit watching the bees on my marjoram plants; they hum like a choir. Calming like a symphony.'

'Do you fancy a drink in the pub up the hill?' His words rushed out. I must have looked disarmed. 'It's half-term, the boys are with their grandma.' He added the explanation as if to convince himself and me.

'Why not? Sounds a perfect way to finish such a lovely day.'

We sat in the garden of the pub beside a pond. Adam brought out a tray with two packets of crisps, two glasses of lager and one of water. 'For your marigolds,' he said, ceremoniously putting them in the water and positioning them between us. 'Can't have them wilting before you even get them home.'

The moment was interrupted by a blaze of laughter from a

table of young men, followed by the clink of their glasses as they toasted some indiscernible event. Over from us a family ate chips from a basket; a couple held hands across a table.

'Wouldn't you love to know what they're talking about, what their lives are like? We're all here, in the same place, briefly sharing a moment in time.'

'That's very philosophical.' Adam looked bemused at my random wanderings.

'Must be my mood.' I smiled. 'Earlier, I needed thinking space.' I stopped, suddenly remembering, but reluctant to share what Ben had said to me at work today. 'Give me your decision tomorrow,' he'd said. Now I covered my hesitation by crunching on a crisp. Adam was watching me. I shook my head, and he dropped his eyes, giving me space.

'There is something though; it's about Asadi. He seems so frail … and sad. I knew he wouldn't be around this evening, but I just wanted to think about him in the only place I know him. He's been so kind to me. I've become very fond of him. I love his company. What's his history, do you know?'

'I don't. He's very private. He's talked occasionally about India. I think he came over as a young man. I guess all of us have a story to tell.'

'I shouldn't have asked.'

'At the allotments, amongst everyone, there's a tacit agreement to leave the past where it is unless someone wants to share it. Everyone's accepted for who they are now.'

'I didn't mean … to sound nosy. I was worried …'

'It's okay. And you're right, Asadi does seem old. He used always to be busy, now he sits and watches.'

We finished the crisps and Adam very deliberately folded the wrappers and wedged them between the slats of the table. 'The allotment was Rosie's passion … and her refuge. When she died, that quiet acceptance is what helped me most. The fact I had somewhere to go where no one asked questions – or avoided me. They were just there.'

He grasped his glass so tightly I wanted to reach out and touch his hand.

'Adam, I'm sorry.' How had I reduced a nice evening to this? 'You don't need to tell me.'

'Perhaps I do. It feels like I do anyway.

'We knew each other from school. Began as mates but the relationship became more, deeper. We both went off to university but neither of us wanted to let the other go. Her twenty-first birthday was the day we married. Lots of people, like parents, thought we were too young.' His half-laugh ate at the tension and startled me.

'It proved to be a serendipitous decision. Noah came along about a year later. Bad planning. We had both started our first jobs. Still, we were excited, and it was all an adventure.

'Uh huh,' he paused. 'Rosie is shouting in my ear reminding me we were lucky and how I promised to remember it.'

'Lucky!' It slipped out from under my surprise.

'I know. It sounds odd. It was one of the last things she said to me. Most days, and when I look at the boys, I do remember. Then there's a black day when I rage against the world and its cruelness, when I resent every other person their happiness. At those times I'm not good to be around.'

Adam pulled a face, his mouth lifted on one side, the freckles across his nose hunched together.

'Rosie said Noah should have a sibling and along came Sam, cute as a monkey and entirely different to Noah. A happy baby but he knew what he wanted; being put down and sleeping were not on his list.

'Rosie began forgetting things, complaining she couldn't concentrate. She was tired. I was. A new baby, a lack of sleep, who wouldn't be? Then she began to stumble. It was the wet, an icy patch, a muddy track. Excuses to fend off fear.

'Sam was eighteen months when she was given the diagnosis.'

Adam unfolded the crisp packet and smoothed it with his hand, the silver foil like his mirror into the past.

'Huntington's Chorea.' He shook his head.

'Sorry, I don't know what …'

'A regressive condition which robs you of all your faculties. One by one. So you can't walk, can't talk, can't feed yourself. A helpless baby in a wasted body.'

I covered his restless hand with mine.

'We were numb. We couldn't help ourselves and we couldn't

help each other.

'One week after the diagnosis Rosie took her own life.

'She left each of us a card. Said she wanted me and the boys to remember her as she was then.'

He pulled his hand from under mine and drained the last of his pint.

'Every day, I am reminded of what we shared. The kids are her gifts to me. My biggest sorrow is that Sam won't remember his mum. He tells everyone that she's gone to sleep.'

'I think those boys did get lucky with their parents.' I risked the lightest smile.

He tilted his head, his cheek catching the translucent glow of dusk. 'Just look at that sky. An artist's palette. Longest day soon. One day I will have time to paint again. Anyway, sorry to burden you with that. Enough of me, what do you dream of doing?'

I was still with Adam in his story. 'Me?' That I could dream came like an unexpected hand-out. 'It feels a while since I've thought in that way. I don't know what to say.' In the distance the glint of silver wings forged a path through marbled clouds. 'I've never been on a plane. That's a shocking admission at my age, isn't it? We never had enough money for holidays. I think the furthest we went was Morecambe. We stayed in a caravan one year. it was so exciting. I suppose I realised I was missing out when I heard other kids talking at school. I expect I stomped about; told my mum it wasn't fair. I always knew we couldn't afford it.'

Adam followed my stare, and the plane became a dot amongst the clouds. 'Well, that's an achievable dream. So many places to see. I wonder where all those people will find themselves in a few hours.'

We walked back past the station, along streets which in daytime buzzed with commuters. Now quieter, there was space for strollers enjoying the long daylight of a summer's evening. We parted by the High Road, hesitant in our goodbye.

The next morning I sat with Ben in the interview room which gave the meeting a gravity I hadn't expected.

'Had any thoughts, Lily?' He twirled a pen in his fingers. 'The truth is I, we, the whole office would be sorry to lose you but it's an opportunity I had to offer. You have been brilliant to work with and you're deserving and more than capable of a promotion.'

Ben being serious quietened me. All the thoughts that had swirled around in the night clustered together refusing to take form.

'I know Manchester's nearer to home. Head of Recruitment in the new branch. It must feel like a no-brainer.' I realised he was coming to my aid, sensing my discomfort.

Did it? A no-brainer? Nearer to home? Home is an empty seaside town and a council house with new occupants I don't even know. 'Where's home?' I spoke the thought out loud.

Ben clasped his hands together, his index fingers raised.

'I'm flattered you think well of me and it's an exciting opportunity.' I saw myself telling Lou, celebrating with a bottle of bubbly. Maybe we could share a flat together again.

'But … I don't want to go.' I couldn't articulate the reasons, the realisation as sudden as a pan of milk boiling over. Jade, the gang, the bar I can now enter without panicking, Asadi's kindness, his friendship, Abeke's laugh, orange marigolds and … Adam; a collage of images tipping the scales.

Ben gave me time to say more, his pen poised in mid-air. 'I thought you'd jump at the chance. I'd even worked out what to say so you would know you had my full support. Now I'm stumped.' He failed to curb his grin and briefly patted me on the shoulder like one would pat a dog. 'However,' he inhaled sharply, 'I want you to go up there anyway for a couple of days. Advise them on recruitment, get a feel for the department. Help you decide for sure.' He was serious again. 'If you change your mind and want to go for it then that's okay.' His voice dropped like he hoped I wouldn't hear the end of the sentence.

Hi, Lou. Short notice I know, but I'm going to be in central Manchester tomorrow staying at the Premier Inn. Can we meet?

I fired off the text as I packed an overnight bag. Her flat was not far from there. It would be fun to see her, catch up on all the news. Go out somewhere or stay in with a takeaway – like old times. Her reply was almost immediate.

Brilliant. Shall we say, 'A Taste of Thai', at 7pm?

I knew where that was. We'd been before when I'd visited. I held onto the frisson of excitement. It tingled in my toes all the way to my head.

Euston station was full of greetings and goodbyes, passengers with blank expressions and computer cases. A smell of coffee mixed with that of freshly baked croissants and diesel fumes. Anticipation made me fidget. A business trip was beginning to seem like a school outing. The feeling only grew as the scenery changed, became more northern and as comfortable as a much-loved pair of shoes. I'd told Ben I wouldn't take the new post. Would Lou try to dissuade me from my resolution? Would I let her?

10

The new Manchester offices were on the eighth floor of a building that appeared to be made entirely of glass. Inside, angled windows diffused light across shiny new desks with swivel chairs of either lime green or royal blue. Unfamiliar faces for which I had no names watched me as I gave my presentation. A young man flicked through his phone, held surreptitiously in the palm of his hand while a woman in a grey trouser suit and red silk blouse sat at the front taking notes, her hand frequently waving to attract my attention and ask questions. I saw looks exchanged between the two colleagues on either side of her. I guessed all three were probably candidates for the Head of Recruitment post. Tensions were visible, office politics playing out before me. I smiled, thinking of Isaac, seeing him dipping into his bag for a self-deprecating tale to make us all laugh. I hoped this office would have a joker too.

To my relief the last scheduled meeting was put back until the morning; I escaped towards the elevator and stood for a few minutes staring through the glass at the skyline. Gun-metal grey clouds had wiped out the sun, dulling the skyscrapers with a matt finish. The leaves on the street trees hung still and only people scurrying in all directions gave energy to the scene. I gazed towards the north and west where remnants of light lingered. How far to the place I once called home – a hundred, a hundred and fifty miles? In my head, I was there with the brush of the waves on the shingle, the stunted shrubs and Mum's laugh, bright as a vein of gold. Remembering didn't make me sad; I was learning that she was with me wherever I went. But I felt dislocated, unable to recognise the young woman who stared back from the mirror in the lift or to recall the child I'd been, running free in a world that had faded and smudged.

It was too early to go to the restaurant but too late to go back to the hotel. I hesitated outside a wine bar, chatter and warmth filtering onto the pavement; I didn't want to go in alone. I scolded myself, I'm over that now, but anxiety surfaced and tightened my throat.

I passed a man sitting on a sleeping bag in front of a shop. His dog, a straggly brown mongrel with hair as matted as its owner's, lay beside him, its head across the man's lap. I fished in my bag and pulled out the unopened packet of cheese sandwiches left over from the train. The man muttered thanks and shared them with his dog. The tableau they formed had me going back to drop a handful of coins into his paper cup and immediately I wondered if it was the right thing to do. Without raising his eyes, he called, 'Cheers,' lifted a fingerless-gloved hand and slugged from a bottle.

Vodka! The thought gave me an idea. Our student solution. Lou and I, too skint to pay pub prices, used to share a few glasses as we were getting ready to go out. Tonight, feeling silly with fun, I dived into an off-licence and bought a bottle. I had time to go to her flat, surprise her with my gift in its brown paper bag and we'd giggle our way into a good time.

I found her block. I'd only been there once before but I recognised it as soon as I saw it again. An old warehouse, dark and sombre from the outside but converted into modern open-plan apartments. I climbed the stairs hoping I'd identify the floor she was on. All the flats opened onto an outside corridor that formed a square around a courtyard. Two children on roller blades whizzed past me squealing, their arms pumping in time with their legs.

I recalled Lou's place had a blue door and an odd fish-shaped knocker that she had sworn she would change but obviously never had. I rang the bell and it chimed inside. Footsteps came closer. I pulled the vodka from its bag and held it in front of my face.

'Surprise!' I thrust the bottle forward. A hiatus that lasted seconds, or minutes or hours – long enough for *Live Like You're Dying* to blare through my head, to remember the smell of alcohol and vomit and for the bottle of vodka to slip from my hand and smash on the tiles.

'Lily!'

He had the advantage. He knew my name. White-blond hair, eyelashes pale as water and a Celtic knot tattooed on his shoulder. I didn't need a name. I knew who he was.

'Lily.' For the second time my name punctured the pause. Lou pushed aside the man who stood with a towel wrapped around his waist, his hair wet. 'I thought it was the pizza delivery.' He turned away. 'I'll get a mop.'

'You're here? Why? You weren't supposed to ...' She was grabbing at my hand with cold fingers. 'Later – in the restaurant – I was going to tell you – explain. It's ... Oh, Lily, I can't bear that you look like that. Come here.'

Her arms folded around me, and I felt the cool touch of her skin against my burning cheek. I pulled back, my arms locked by my side, my feet crunching on broken glass.

'Wait, don't go. I'm almost ready. I'll grab a jacket.' She shouted something into the apartment, that I couldn't hear. We walked away, towards the stairs, the door gaping open, liquid seeping across the threshold.

I couldn't speak, my throat constricted like a sealed bag. Any words I had were floating, trapped, suffocating in the lack of air.

'We don't have to do this. I'll go back to the hotel.'

'Yes we do, Lily. More so now than ever. I've been looking forward to seeing you so much and ... dreading it at the same time. Whatever you're thinking, it's not like that.'

Thinking anything was beyond me at this moment. My head stuffed with nonsense.

She took my arm and squeezed. 'But hey, what a waste of vodka!' A hint of a smile wavered, expecting to be wiped out.

Her eyes were dark, pleading.

'You're right. What a waste of vodka.' It came out too loudly and the tension imploded. I stopped by the kerb with the traffic lights changing colour, and enveloped her, my breath catching in her hair. 'I was so looking forward to seeing you too.' I wanted to beg her not to elucidate, that we'd pretend I'd never come to the flat, never seen him. That we were just two friends, with lots to say to each other, meeting up after a long time. But it was too late. The past had fingered the evening and wasn't going to go away.

I pushed prawns around my plate, Lou left her rice untouched.

'He came ...'

'Lou, how could ...?'

We began at the same time, the words a conflation.

'Will you hear me out, Lily? Then it's up to you what you do.'

'I feel like I've been thrown off a cliff, Lou. Can you even begin to imagine how it felt to see him like that?' I got in first, I didn't want to make it easy for her.

'After it happened – with you – a few weeks after. He …'

'HE. HE. I don't even know his name.'

'Jake, Lily. His name is Jake.' She spoke it in a way that made its hard edges disappear. 'He came to the house. He'd been trying to find you. Said he wanted to apologise. What occurred had been eating him up. He hadn't seen you around. He didn't know about your mother. I told him she'd died in an accident the day after the party. I was angry. I accused him of raping you, told him he was a despicable bully. I described your bruises, the mess you were in. I took all my rage at what had happened to you out on him. I wasn't going to let him off. I screamed at him so that he would suffer too. I was horrible.' Lou sat with fists clenched. 'He crumpled into that old bucket-chair we used to have, and he cried. He isn't the sort of man you think he is, but I don't expect you to believe me. I didn't know it either then.'

In my hand wine swirled in its glass, the motion mirroring my feelings as I tried to reconcile what Lou was saying.

'Okay,' I sneered. 'So, he's this really nice guy who wouldn't hurt a fly and is eaten up with remorse. How does any of that justify him being in your flat prancing around in just a towel?'

'Sod you, Lily. I don't have to defend myself or seek your approval for my relationships. If I remember the scenario correctly you weren't exactly a paragon of virtue. Fucking-drunk was how I think you described yourself.'

Lou scrunched her serviette into a ball and tossed it onto a plate. 'Jake and I love each other. How or why is none of your business but if you really want to know how it came about, I'll tell you because I still think of you as the best friend I've ever had.'

'Would you like the bill?' A waiter hovered by the table, his downturned mouth and abrupt tone made it clear he'd overheard and wanted us to leave. We paid and walked aimlessly, emotions stewing inside me. I was conscious of Lou swiping at her cheek and knew she was struggling too.

'I feel betrayed.' It wasn't what I meant to say but the raw truth cut like a slash.

'Jake wanted to contact you; he wanted a phone number. I wouldn't give it to him. He used to come round, and we'd talk, he told me lots of things. He never offered excuses for his behaviour but there's always another side isn't there? Other things going on. Most times we can't be arsed to listen.' Her eyes raked my face. 'So we never find out.'

We kept walking, side by side except when noisy groups of revellers pushed us apart. Illuminated shop windows lit up rough sleepers huddled in blankets, their bodies and faces hidden. Sexless, no identity. I didn't see the man and his dog again.

'I couldn't ... dared not, share any of this with you, Lily. You were fragile, more than that – on the edge. I didn't want to be the one to push you over. I could see it, hear it in your voice, you were crazy with grief but couldn't grieve. I had no idea what to do. You say you feel betrayed. I felt helpless. Two people needed me for different reasons, and I was as useless as a paper boat.'

That feeling, and the memories came back taut as a string. She was right. I'd floundered like someone with no destination, handed a map with no markings. I thought I was holding it together if only just. Were my friends, my colleagues, seeing something else? It had felt like crawling out of a tunnel towards a needlepoint of light that was sometimes too faint to see. God, what sort of burden was I?

'Are things any easier?' Lou's question a trigger waiting to be pulled.

No, I thought, my guilt hasn't diminished. I miss Mum like she died yesterday. But yes, I can laugh again, look forward to things. I have new friends. I sometimes even like myself.

I grimaced. 'Three packets of seeds, that's what it took to ... make things easier. I smiled at how stupid that sounded. 'So, you and Jake?' His name tasted like sour milk.

'We got to know each other, to like, then to love, each other. He's a really kind and special bloke.' Her voice dropped to a whisper. 'We're planning to get married next year.' Her whisper faded as the day had done. 'Lily, I hope you will ...'

'NO, Lou — be your bridesmaid? Don't even suggest it.'

'I was going to say ... get to know each other ... in a different way.'

11

When I'd told Ben I didn't want the Manchester job he hadn't tried to hide his delight. I'd explained my rationale but never alluded to the main reason. I knew I'd made the right decision and I had no regrets.

So why did the Lou and Jake situation continue to bug me? I wanted to hate him, or at the very least still feel angry, but now he had a name and a face it was harder to do. Jake, the sound rolled round my mouth. I heard again Lou's plea for understanding. 'He wanted to apologise, wanted to find you.' Her simple 'We love each other.'

An accusatory voice persisted; refusing to be buried like before. When he was anonymous you could blame him for what happened, for everything that transpired that terrible weekend. You didn't have to think about the part you played. I banged my forehead with my fist to dispel the truth of it. Vindication of myself seemed hollow and false.

I hadn't sought *him* out. Why not? It was easier to make him responsible for the appalling state the police found me in when they came to inform me of Mum's accident. It reduced my shame. I'd thought about him, had woken crying in the night, made him the reason anxiety had engulfed me for the past two years. But now, because of this, a layer had peeled off, guilt and grief exposed as anxiety's companions. I'd refused to recognise either of them.

I sighed. Today I had another decision to make. What to wear to the midsummer bash? A heap of discarded clothes lay strewn on the bed like the certainties I'd been clinging to. The jeans looked too casual, the ankle-length dress too formal.

Adam had asked last month if I was coming to the lunch. He'd reminded me two weeks later and looked embarrassed when I laughed at him.

I'd told him he didn't need to persuade me, that I wouldn't miss it for anything. Asadi had shown me the produce that would be ready to pick and cook. He had more faith in my culinary skills than I did.

'The boys want you there,' Adam said. 'They love the stories you tell them of when you were a little girl playing on the beach. Because of you, they want to live at the seaside.' I'd continued to hoe between the rows of onions. He'd lingered, collecting up weeds that missed the bucket I was tossing them into. 'And *I* do — want you to come I mean.' He'd grinned as he left to retrieve his sons who were washing their football under the tap, getting soaked in the process.

I sat on the bed in my bra and pants, clasping my knees, wanting to look forward to today. '*He* is not the reason I can't make up my mind what to wear,' I argued with a beaming Mum. 'I don't know the correct form of dress. It's only because of you and those packets of seed that I'm going to an event like this at all.'

I'd be happy if only I could destroy the reel that seeing Jake had triggered, stop it playing over and over in my head.

'Come home at the weekend,' Mum had said. It was her birthday the following week. 'We'll do something special.' I heard the pitch of her voice holding on to a secret she was trying not to leak.

'It's *your* birthday. Shouldn't *I* be treating you?'

'My surprise.' She was excited. Me too.

But then Friday came. 'Mum, please could we postpone your birthday celebration for a week? Instead of this weekend could we make it next? Only … this guy has invited me to a party. I'm so happy. I really like him, Mum. You don't mind, do you?'

But that's not what I said.

'It's a piece of work I must get finished. An essay that has to be handed in.' I waited for her to say something. I gabbled on, hiding my deceit. 'Look, I'll come next weekend. We'll celebrate after your birthday instead of before.' I didn't want to detect her disappointment.

The beat in time, momentary, imagined perhaps. 'Of course, darling. You work so hard. I'm proud of you.'

Why did I lie? I was letting her down and I knew it. Selfish with a capital S. I didn't need to lie. We could talk about anything. If I'd told her a guy had invited me to a party, she'd have been pleased and curious.

'Come on, what's his name, what's he like, what …?'

Pat, our neighbour, told me after the funeral that mum had booked a table at the 'posh' place in town, bought herself something new to wear. You'd always wanted to go, she said, and you deserved a treat. She was so disappointed when you couldn't make it because you had too much university work to do. But you know your mum, she never let things get her down. You made her so proud with all you achieved, going off to study and the like. She changed the booking to the next weekend and got excited all over again.

The posh place was a hotel with a grand entrance and long windows swathed by curtains held with a gold hoop. We used to walk past arm in arm. 'I'll be wearing a scarlet dress that floats to my ankles. My hair will be flounced back on one side and fastened with a diamond pin,' I'd say, and push my curls behind my ear to demonstrate. 'I'll wear black,' she'd add. 'Chic, sophisticated, with soft folds of material plunging down my back. I'll arrive in a limousine and stretch out an elegant leg, displaying a slim shoe with a six-inch heel. David Bowie, or maybe Orlando Bloom, will take my hand, escort me up the steps and hold open the door as I sweep in.'

The birthday she never got to celebrate, a new dress she never got to wear, the surprise she never got to give.

It seemed a long time ago but felt like yesterday. Don't spoil today, she wouldn't want you to. The voice, kinder now, letting me smile. I settled on a short yellow dress and left my hair loose. 'You look fine.' I grabbed a jacket for later and picked up my precious goat's cheese and spinach pie. Asadi and I had picked the spinach together and I'd proudly swapped some of my wonderful rainbow chard for six newly laid, still-warm eggs from Gulnar's hens. Never had I made anything this exotic even if the filo pastry was bought. I'd pored over the recipe, precisely measuring all the ingredients, watched like an over-protective parent as the pie cooked in the oven. The finished dish actually resembled the picture, and I was chuffed.

'Hello, monkeys in a cage.' I called to the two faces pressed between the railings of the allotments.

'We've been waiting for you.' Sam jumped up and down. Noah was playing it cool, but he let me give him a quick cuddle. 'We've got new shirts and mine's a jungle.' Sam held out the bottom edge of his to show off the tigers and snakes. 'Come and see what we've made.'

'You both look very smart. You'd better show me where I have to put this pie.' They peeped inside the box but neither looked impressed.

'Me and Daddy made a pavlova. It's going to be yummy.' On a table laid with foodstuffs Noah pulled a plate forward on which stood a wonderful cream and fruit-filled confection.

'You are so clever, Noah. That looks fabulous.' His shoulders straightened and a smile crinkled his nose.

'Daddy helped me.'

'And I picked the strawberries and raspberries.' Sam tugged my arm so as not to be upstaged.

'I have something else for you two later, but you can't have it until you've eaten some of these delicious savouries.

'Yuk, I only like cucumber.' Sam helped himself. I picked up the plate and offered it to Noah sensing he knew better than to be diving in like his little brother.

Abeke bustled over; large, hooped earrings swung from her ear lobes and jangling bangles stretched from her wrist to her elbow. She enveloped me in perfume and an embrace. The boys had already spotted her teenage sons and rushed across to them. We watched as the younger boys were swung around, Sam riding piggyback, clinging to a tall gangly youth. 'My lads make such a fuss about coming,' Abeke said. 'So, I say to them, come for half an hour. Look now, just big kids really. They'll play with Adam's two boys and eat a mountain of food, then tell me tonight they were bored.' Her laugh floated over the laden table, and she sailed off to welcome others.

It seemed everyone from the allotments had come. Some of them I didn't know. Conversations were snatched with Adam and precious moments spent with Asadi who nodded off in a picnic chair. I exchanged names with others, listened to talk of carrot fly and learnt the best variety of beans to buy and how to cook okra. World politics, jokes and cultural practices were all thrown into a cauldron of multi-lingual chatter interspersed with peals of gaiety and bursts of music to which Abeke gyrated her hips and shook her sizeable bosom. Bright bunting hung between the trees and the day shone with carnival colours.

Sam and Noah, by now hot and dishevelled, found me sitting on a low breeze-block wall. They flopped dog-tired one on either side. I pulled a packet from my bag. 'Time for snowballs I think.'

'What?'

They giggled when I showed them what they were and even more when I showed them how to eat them. 'That's how I used to do it when I was a little girl, and my mummy would pretend to be cross because my hands and my hair and my face would be all sticky.'

'My mummy's asleep in the sky,' Sam said between finger licks. His brother leant across and pushed him. Noah half stood and cupped his hands round my ear and whispered,

'She's not really asleep. She was poorly and died.' He sank back onto the wall and pressed himself against me.

'I know. Your daddy told me. My mummy went to sleep too.' I softly mouthed 'died' to Noah to show I knew he was grown up. 'Sometimes it makes me sad and I cry. But lots of times I laugh because I think she would want me to.'

'That's funny.' Sam paused. 'Two mummies the same. Do you think they know each other?'

'I think they might. What sort of things did your mummy like doing?'

Sam leaned nearer to his brother. 'She liked making biscuits, didn't she, Noah?'

'She liked making lots of things, craft things, cutting out and drawing.' Noah's hand crept into mine. 'She liked dressing up.'

'In that case, they definitely know each other because my mummy loved dressing up as well. What do you think they dress up as?'

'Princesses?' Noah offered.

'Or pirates?' Sam squealed, his hand over his eye like a patch.

'Or Superwoman and Catwoman?'

The three of us, lost in our game jumped at the new voice.

'It will have to be something incredibly special with glittery costumes and scary masks.' Adam came from behind and crouched in front of us, ruffled Sam's hair, and punched Noah lightly on the arm. 'Sorry, I've been listening.' He squeezed from under the tangle of arms around his neck.

My face flushed and I chewed my lip. I tried to stand, but Adam eased me down again, his hand on my shoulder.

'What are you three up to anyway?'

'We've got snowballs, Daddy.'

'Snowballs. In September?'

'They're not real, they're cakes, silly.'

'And you have to eat them like this. Lily showed us. You make a hole in the top then poke your finger in and cover it with … white gooey stuff.'

'It's called marshmallow,' Noah filled in.

'Then you lick it off your fingers.' Sam demonstrated, managing to smear stickiness around his mouth and under his nose.

'Right, I get it.' Adam laughed out loud as he twisted towards me with one eyebrow raised.

'Perhaps we'd better give Daddy his snowball so he can try it.' I handed him the remaining round coconut-covered chocolate ball. 'Then he can be as sticky as us.'

'And you have to wish a wish when you make the hole. I wished for a blue scooter.'

'Did you, Sam? Good job it's your birthday soon.'

'What are you going to wish for, Daddy?'

'If I tell you, it might not come true so I'm going to keep it a secret.'

I felt Adam's gaze like the beam of a torch. He sat poised with a marshmallow-coated finger in the air, squinting at me from under lowered eyes.

The sumptuous plates of food gradually disappeared; the table lay scattered with crumbs, the cloth damp in one corner where someone's drink had spilt. Lunch over, people were wandering away, their harvest celebrated with laughter and friendship. I found Asadi sitting on his bench in a cone of light, a rolled cigarette between his fingers. Rays from the sun played with quiet shadows across his allotment.

'Your marigolds will self-seed and come again next year.' He nodded towards where orange blooms still shone in the brightness of the day.

'Perhaps I'll grow some different flowers as well. Will you help me to choose? If you don't mind, that is, me sharing your space again.' I'd almost forgotten I was just a visitor. I'd begun to think of us as a team. 'But choosing is for another time.' His grey pallor, the tremble in his hand and the heave of his shoulders with each breath worried me. I wanted to blame today's excitement but I knew it was more than that. 'I'm tired, so you must be too. It's been a long day. I think it's time to go home. We will look forward to Diwali in November. Abeke was telling me how you decorate the area with lights and cook over a brazier.'

'Our festival of light.' His dreamy eyes brightened, his face kind and warm. 'Last year it was especially beautiful.

'Lily, we both know I won't see another Diwali, but it isn't a reason to be afraid. I have a lifetime of happy festivals to remember.' His hand crept over mine and he didn't flinch as I traced the stumps of his fingers affirming a truth we both knew.

'I will miss you.' I stared at the blue-grey sky, cloud shapes blurring as Asadi's words became real.

He patted my hand. 'Thank you for not placating me or pretending the truth is something else. I do not fear death. I have much to be grateful for.'

'Asadi, when I met you in the spring, I was still a mess, stumbling along unable to make sense of my mother dying so … unnecessarily. She fell off a ladder trying to free a pigeon. The pointlessness of it all made me so angry. And there were other things, things I'd done of which I was ashamed. You held my hand, just like this.' I lifted our clasped hands, 'And led me to a place where I could breathe again. I will always remember you as my greatest friend.'

'Grief has many faces, Lily. Sometimes it disguises itself as shame, or anger, sometimes as loneliness. It distracts and confuses but always in the end it grows weak.'

He coughed, the sound as rasping and dry as sand. My chest grew tight, a fist punched at my heart.

'I believe your mother sent you to me. I said she was a wise woman. It is I who should thank you. You have made an old man very happy in his last few months and even when I have gone, I will still be your friend.' A tear teetered on his eyelid then spilt slowly down his cheek.

'I have something I want to ask of you.' His chest hiccupped with trapped breath.

'Of course, anything. I will do anything for you.'

He turned his face to mine and placed a dry finger across my lips.

'Shh, my precious girl. I have much to tell you. You must not give me an answer now or promise anything until you have heard my story. Only then can you decide.'

'But what is it, what do you want me to do?'

Asadi drew his hands together at his heart's centre. 'Namaste, Lily.' He gave the slightest bow. 'I would consider it an honour if when I die, you will carry my ashes home and sprinkle them on the holiest of rivers, the mighty Ganga.'

Asadi
Rajasthan India 1939

In front of the wooden step where I waited, the other boys kicked a can around sending the sand into clouds of fine dust. They soon tired of their game and ran off towards the village. They didn't ask me along.

I peered through the cracks of the green schoolroom door with its flaking paint into the darkness within. When I shook the rusted bolt, the rattle resounded inside. Another day with no lessons. I shoved my bottom against the wood and felt it splinter and crack. A loose plank came away easily in my hand leaving me staring into the empty space.

'What are you doing? Where's the teacher?'

It was Faraz. He was always late. He had to walk three or four miles to get here. Often, he didn't come at all.

'Mr Singh hasn't turned up. He wasn't here yesterday or the day before.' I kicked at the jagged wood, and another panel clattered to the floor. The hole was now wide enough for me to crawl through. All his belongings were gone. The dirty blackboard duster, the chalks, the stick with a frayed end which always stood propped against the wall ready to be used on our knuckles, our backsides or our legs.

Faraz stuck his head through the hole. 'Where are the rest of the boys?' He was small, his dark eyes round and large in his thin face. I'd seen him struck many times with the stick and left to whimper in the corner.

'Gone. They're happy not to be in school today.'

'Aren't you happy then? I hope Mr Singh rots in camel dung.' Faraz jerked his head from side to side. 'Are you sure he's not here?'

'Stop your talk!' My shout was loud enough to hide his lack of respect.

His faded shirt snagged on the damaged door as he pushed through. 'Probably no more school anyway. My father says the British are going to war.' He turned full circle, his hand and arm a gun. 'Bang, bang, bang. Maybe I will be a soldier.' He swigged from a cup of water left on the side, then sputtered the mouthful onto the floor. 'That's disgusting. I'm off. You're going to be in big trouble.' He tossed a piece of split wood towards me, squeezed his way out and ran off, his bare feet slapping the sand.

The room was quiet as I sat with hunched-up knees. I picked at the rush mat that covered the beaten floor. Ten or twelve boys should have been there sitting cross-legged and fidgety, arranged in rows according to age. Mostly they were young. Seven, eight, nine. By ten they had drifted away, needed by their families on the land or for chores that don't involve learning. At fourteen I was the oldest.

My mother was different. She always told me to go to school. To learn well. 'Then you can be whatever you want. Become a great man.' I liked it when she recited poetry to me, learnt in a childhood she never spoke of. Often, she would pause and lift her head, her eyes seeking the horizon. The smile that played on her lips promised me everything. It was the encouragement I needed to make me go to school.

Now, no lessons. For how long? I wrote Asadi in the dust on the blackboard then rubbed it out with the hem of my shirt. I would miss hanging around at the end of school when the other boys had gone home, listening to the stories Mr Singh told of Bombay and what the sea looked like and the big ships. He said he wanted to teach in a college in the town. To teach the children of the British officers, the government people, children who wore uniforms. 'Village children are dull; they don't want to obtain knowledge,' he'd say. I told him I did, but he'd spat on the floor, so I kept quiet. Maybe that's why he's left. To teach in a proper school with books and pens and where the pupils have white faces.

I wandered out, reluctant to go home. The day was succumbing to the heat that dulled even the flies. If the boys had set up a cricket game, they might let me play because my batting made them lots of runs. Or they might shun me, throw stones and hurl abuse. I wished I wasn't the son of the moneylender and have to bear the brunt of every village family's misfortune. Father was needed, but not liked. Any leniency and compassion had long been squeezed out of him. His boss was only interested in profit.

Women in brightly coloured *ghagras* walked the path to the village. One carried firewood on her head, another a pitcher of water. They averted their gaze as I approached, their *odhni* veiling their faces in soft folds. A man patching his house walls with mud called to me. 'Go quick. You must get home, Asadi. Don't dawdle.' He pointed and flicked his arm. Two small children, bare but for vests, ran to their fence. The girl sucked two fingers, the boy copied his father and shouted, 'Go quick,' before crouching on the ground with a giggle.

The command made no sense, but his urgent tone made me obey. I took a shortcut, jumping over low prickly shrubs that scratched my legs, and crossed the wadi where water ran briefly when the monsoons came. Too hot to keep running I slowed, tasting bile. At home, my father would have an errand for me. I could not refuse but I hated doing his dirty work for him. He would give me a message to deliver to some poor family. I would have to stand by as the mother wept and the father sank his head into his hands.

Our house stood away from the rest, on the edge, where the desert began. It was rectangular, made of mud bricks baked in the sun, not round with a grass roof like most of the others in the village. Sheets of corrugated iron protected us when the rains drummed down. Inside we had two rooms. My older brother was adding another on the back for his new wife and himself. From a distance, I could see there was no sign of anyone, but our goats still milled within the compound. Their bleating made me run again.

'Hush her moaning,' my father rasped as he came from inside, tossing the end of a roll-up to the ground. He stopped when he saw me, sputum in the corner of his mouth like a pus-filled spot.

'Take the goats and mind them. Laksha is sick,' he muttered, hitching his dhoti and squatting on his haunches. 'You've been idling.'

'I went to school. I waited for the teacher, but he didn't come.'

'Huh.' He cleared his throat with a wet cough. 'You're done with lessons. It doesn't make money.'

I circled him, tired of his views. Wishing I could fight back without the punishment that would follow.

From the doorway I heard my mother crooning over my sister's agitation. I gagged at the sour smell of sweat and the hot stench of vomit.

'Take the goats,' my father barked. 'Leave the women.'

I was glad to spit out the taste of sickness and herd up the eager animals. The kids jumped and skipped, trailing after their mothers who roamed in all directions, munching at the dry grass and grey-green shrubs. Hollering and using my stick I moved them away from the village to an area where they could graze. The light was fierce and shimmered off the sand. I slumped into a patch of shade offered by a rock. The cries of other young children minding their family's flock drifted across the desert, blurred by heat. Far off I could hear a ring of metal coming from where the smith worked.

I sighed and poured sand through my fingers. This is what my sister did every day. Laksha was sixteen, two years older than me; my brother, Umesh, four years older than her. My mother had told me of another child, a boy born after Umesh. 'His head a crown of soft black hair, his lips as pink as watermelon,' she would say. 'He was born to a full moon but closed his eyes before the sun came up.'

Laksha never complained of boredom. She milked the goats at daybreak, humming to herself as she sat amongst the impatient animals. All day she would follow them as they scoured the hot sands for vegetation. I'd seen her sitting with girls from the village, gossiping and laughing. At night, she would prepare the meal for us. My mother taught her how to cut, clean and cook the vegetables so that one day soon she could be a wife and care for her husband and his family. I asked her if she dreamed of more; I tried to teach her what I had learnt in school. She was a gentle half-girl, half-woman who replied with quiet eyes and a soft shrug of her shoulders. 'I will dream through you, Asadi. Make those dreams come true.' I wasn't sure whether she meant my dreams or hers. I liked when she brought me clean clothes to wear and cool water to drink and for the way she would listen when I told her how one day I would make her proud. Silently I scorned her acceptance of how things were.

My brother was different. He wore his first-born-son status like a badge of right. I called him idle and ignorant because he had no time for learning. He bided his time, caught me off guard on one occasion, and plunged my hand into the fire's embers. I knew better than to tell the truth of what happened. Last year my father had arranged a marriage for him, and Umesh had brought home a wife who spoke little, cowered in his presence and slunk into dark corners like a rodent.

The day wore on. A cramp in my neck woke me from a doze and I jumped to my feet searching with bleary eyes for the goats. They had scattered but not far. Some lay together, resting in hollows, like spotted fabric laid out to dry. Others munched noisily, stretching on their hind legs to reach for higher leaves. By the time I found them all the air had freshend and a lazy breeze stirred the sand into small puffs. The sky signalled night and hinted at the cooling monsoons everyone prayed would come this year.

Smoke from fires rose from the compounds as I shepherded the animals down the single village road. Cows stood tethered to stakes in the ground. Women clanged cooking pots, goats bleated and chickens skittered in the dust. Men squatted in groups shooing off the barefoot children who plagued them. They fell silent as I walked past.

'Is it the fever?' one of them shouted. A woman stood still, her hand poised over a metal bowl. More women lifted their heads from their tasks or retreated into their houses. A small boy running past stopped in his tracks when his mother yelled, 'Get away from him.' He began to walk backwards, tripped, then ran back to her crying.

The village paused, the air sucked from it – and from me. I ran for home.

Freaked by my haste to fence them in, the goats hustled each other. I left them bleating and pushed aside the fabric that draped the doorway of our house, momentarily blind in the dark interior. My mother knelt beside my sister's sleeping mat wiping Laksha's face with a wet cloth. Laksha tossed her head from side to side, her arms flailed like she was batting a swarm of flies.

'Ma, what is wrong with Laksha?'

'Fetch me more water, Asadi. Your sister is very sick. She is screaming with dreams. She does not hear me.' My mother's face was beaded with sweat and she pulled at her clothes. 'It is so hot in here. Bring me the water, then take some gifts to the shrine.' She began to chant, the murmur of a soft wind.

Sita, my brother's wife, squatted outside laying sticks and coaxing a fire into life. She emitted a low wail and curled into herself afraid to meet my eyes. I poured water into the pitcher and took it back inside.

'Leave it there, Asadi. Don't come close.' My mother's weak plea stifled me with fear.

I placed gifts of grain and fruit on the shrine for Divine Mother. Simple offerings to appease. I begged for my prayers to be heard and that Ma and Laksha be saved. A creeping cold began in my stomach and spread to my bones.

Night fell, the blackness chased only by the orange-red flames of the fire. My father returned from his day's business. He washed off the grime of the desert, cursing at the meagre amount of water left for his use. Sita served us a watery mixture of millet, lentils and salt tasteless and weak: not a bit like the one Ma usually cooked. She took a bowl in to my mother but returned with it untouched. Her own food she took to the far corner of the house beside the goats.

'Laksha's fever is no better,' I said.

Baba ate with curled lips. 'The women will attend to her. Where is your brother?'

I shrugged. 'He's not been home in days.' When he was here, we hardly spoke. He chose to spend his time with other young men in the village, talking and smoking. The extra room he had built for himself and Sita was almost finished, but soon the rains would come and seek out every fault.

Baba grunted, tossed his bowl to the ground, the remains slopping onto the sand leaving a dark stain. He glanced toward the house where my mother's crooning had become a moan, then walked off in the direction of the other houses.

I crept inside; a weak shaft of moonlight came through the window space. 'Ma, you must eat. I will sit with Laksha.' They were lying together, their faces turned towards each other. The stale body smell made me bury my nose in my elbow.

'Ma.' I moved closer and touched her burning brow. She tried to flick me away, but her arm dropped to her side. I scrabbled to light a candle. Laksha lay still, her breath short and sudden like it had forgotten its rhythm. I held the candle closer. Her smooth pale skin was blushed with an angry rash. She whimpered as she moved her tongue. It was broken into sores oozing with pus. I lifted her limp hand, the candlelight pooling in her palm.

I thought of my sister, her olive face framed by dark wisps of escaping hair. How she used to love to listen to what I had learnt at school. She would ask me about the world I spoke of that lay outside the confines of our village. How the teacher taught us of fire that shot from the earth and water that spilled over rocks without ceasing. The gods must be speaking to allow such wonders, she would say, her eyes laced with awe, fear lurking in their depth. How proud she made me feel when I drew numbers in the sand and showed her how they could be added together or taken away from each other.

'Go. Let us sleep, Asadi.' Ma's voice fluttered in her throat. 'Be a great man one day.' Her fingers, hot as smouldering twigs, folded over my arm.

I fled into the cool clear air and looked up at the canopy of stars that pockmarked the sky. Where was my father, where was my brother? What should I do? The questions collided in my head, making my heart ache and my legs leaden. I pulled out a blanket and curled against the house wall, the bricks still warm to my touch.

I woke trailing dreams; parings of light flecked the horizon. Baba snored beside the fire. The goats stirred and waited to be released. I grabbed a kid and held it firmly in my arms, its mother protesting loudly.

I knew where *she* lived. We children avoided her and only the braver ones threw stones or called names in her direction. Once I had seen her collecting wood; her back, twisted like a gecko's tail, tufts of hair exposed where her head covering had slipped. I had gasped, almost giving away my hiding place. In my mind she was fierce, with two heads and grasping arms. But she was just an old woman, older than anyone else I had ever seen. She lived beyond where the villagers struggled to cultivate their land. Around her shelter green plants grew, singling her out with a blessing from the gods.

I took the back path to stay away from the village where women would be rising to begin the day. A cow mooed, a lonely sound rolling over the sand. Black beetles scurried from the vibration of my feet. The kid was warm against my chest, its heartbeat rapid next to mine. It struggled in my arms, cried at being restrained. I held it more tightly and inched closer. She slept, a black shape, huddled on the bare ground under a grass roof supported by wooden poles. The embers of a fire had burnt to ash. The goat thrashed free from my arms, wobbling on uncertain legs. She woke and lifted a stick, waving it in my direction. I dared not move. One milky white eye stared up at me, the other looked sideways. She muttered words I didn't understand, and the little goat nuzzled nearer to her, licking at her outstretched knuckles.

'Your mother and sister are stricken.' Her voice was thin like dried grass.

I nodded, afraid of her knowledge, my words dead like the fire. She patted the ground beside her and I sank to my haunches. Her neck was mottled brown, pitted with craters. She reached out and lightly touched my skin, leaving it burning.

'Help me up.' She pulled her veil across her face, but I saw where she was cursed at birth, a red stain on her skin that ran like a bleed from her ear to where it disappeared into folds of material.

My arms stayed by my side as if bound. Her lips parted with a sigh to show a toothless mouth and she used my shoulder to haul herself to standing. When I stood, she was no higher than my chest, so bent she looked only at the floor.

'You are too clever to be afraid. You will grow up to be a great man.'

My mother's words.

'Come.' She beckoned me to walk with her. She plucked leaves from the plants, giving them to me to hold. All the time she recited, a sing-song poem of words, a prayer. We took the leaves back and she mashed them with cinnamon in an earthernware bowl and instructed me to drip a stinking concoction of ghee and milk on top, 'Enough.' She stopped me with a sharp tap.

'It is the pox. It will curse the village. Your Baba will know pain.'

'Will this make Ma and Laksha better? The kid is for you.' I wanted my gift to be enough to make her say yes. Her wayward eyes gave me no answer. 'I have no money to give you.'

'Ha, what is money?' She hawked phlegm into the mixture and stirred it. 'I will take care of the goat. You are kind like your mother. Give this to them, paint it on their lips so they swallow some. It will ease their suffering.

'Go now. Run before you're too late.'

I covered the pot and stumbled away.

'Asadi.' My name like music. 'You will be spared.'

I hurried back with the precious potion. The old woman's predictions, both sweet and sour filled the space in my chest. The sun rose higher, spilling heat and clothing the desert with clear pink light. Still a way off I heard the sound. A wail spiralling into the sky. My stomach contracted, I stopped running and doubled over to find air to breathe. The bitter smell of the medicine in my nostrils forced me on.

Two women squatted outside our compound emitting their fiendish noise. They beat their chests, their wails more piercing as I pushed past.

I thrust the bowl towards my father who sat with his head on his knees on the steps. 'I have medicine to take away the sickness. We must ...'

His shoulders shuddered with the slightest shake of his head. The pot grew heavy, and numbness sapped my grip.

'Ma.' I leant over her and stroked her cheek. Her eyelids fluttered open and I stared into black depths. Her hand crept up and over mine squeezing it with the touch of a butterfly.

'This is for you and Laksha. To make you well again. I smeared the mashed leaves across her mouth allowing the pungent mixture to drip onto her swollen tongue. She recoiled, her body convulsing with tremors, then lay still, exhausted with the effort.

I reached over to Laksha and daubed the green paste on her

cracked lips. Cold lips, her skin waxen, her face beautiful again, her eyes closed as in sleep.

Before the sun arced to its height Ma had joined Laksha on her journey.

My father wept silently, his grief swallowed in the shudder of his chest or the sweep of his fingers through his hair. I watched, learnt how to be a man. What I wanted was for him to fold his arms around me, to speak soft words like Ma would have done. But my brother's name was the one on his lips; my face not the one he wanted to see. I felt as small as a grain of sand amongst the dunes.

It fell to Sita to wash the bodies, to wrap them in their final garments, my mother in red, my sister in white. No one from the village came to help. Incense burnt in our house drifting over the noisy animals restless with hunger.

Outside our compound, women squatted, their heads covered with black scarves, their bare feet grey with dust. Mourners who stalked death for a living. My father gave them money which made them break into action, tossing their heads and wailing to the heavens, beating their chests, and slapping the ground in front of them.

When the bleating of the goats became too much, I took off their milk and walked them away from the house, the sands as familiar as the palm of my hand, parched and barren, the stubby shrubbery like desiccated skeletons.

I railed at the old woman whose foul-smelling paste hadn't worked. *'It will ease their suffering.'* An evil crone. I shouted to the empty sky and the munching goats, 'Without my brother, *I* am the eldest son.' I heard my mother's murmurs. *'Be a doctor or work for the government, Asadi. Be a great man.'* Now it was time to be. But how, Ma? I didn't know how.

No one came to view the corpses, everyone was scared. My beautiful mother and sister waited in peace, their foreheads marked with turmeric, garlands draped around their necks. My father scoured the horizon. He wanted my brother to appear, to be the speck that grew larger, to become Umesh. He waited in vain. The priest fussed, insisting that because of the plague, the prayers and the cremation must be conducted without delay.

Baba and I circled the bodies on the hastily erected pyre and threw flowers. It was I who lobbed the pitcher of water near their heads, praying, who placed sesame seed in my mother's and my sister's mouth and sprinkled the bodies and the dry wood with ghee before lighting the pyre with the burning torch. An exhilarating mixture of pride and sadness surged through me. I felt the heat of the flames as the priest chanted prayers to set their spirits free. Afterwards, I washed, dousing my head with jugs of water; droplets of moisture left on my skin dried in the sun. My father placed his hands on my shoulders, his face so close I could see my reflection in his eyes. The pressure of his hands spoke more than words.

The pox with its evil talons rested in other houses, selected the young girls Laksha had laughed with when she tended the goats. Or sometimes their brothers, or an eldest son, a husband, or another mother. It would make some sick but let them recover, marked with pitted faces and creviced skin. For endless days, up and down the village we would hear the crying of women. Funeral pyres stabbed the black of night with orange-red orbs. I heard the occasional crack of burning wood pierce the desert silence. A camp of Doms had grown up outside the village, 'helpers' who lived by the business of death, sold tinder or ghee or flowers to the bereaved. They would collect the remains for us afterwards.

My father addressed me. 'We will take their ashes to Pushkar Lake, so your mother and sister may attain *Moksha*. It will bring peace and salvation to their souls. Sita will stay here.'

Pushkar Lake, to the south-west of our region. I had no idea how far it was; it was beyond where I had ever travelled before. I knew his reason for scattering the remains in such a place would be to demonstrate his position in the community, to show we had money. Others would have to settle for lesser bodies of water.

Through the following two nights dreams plagued my sleep. I woke, sure that Ma was beside me, her whisper on my cheek. I saw her holding Laksha's hand, two shadows growing fainter in the gloom. After the third day I woke before daybreak and lay listening to Baba's deep snores and the crowing of cockerels. With my eyes closed I imagined Ma rising softly from sleep, humming as she sometimes did, or reciting poetry, the sing-song words cocooning me with love. I brushed away the tears I was too old to shed. We would journey to the lake and set them free. My father and I. Beyond that I could conjure no thoughts on how life might look; to try was like pressing on a bruise.

In preparation for the journey my father organised for camels to be brought to our compound. The lumbering animals lay outside, tied to stakes to prevent them from wandering. Their mouths chewed continually emitting sour breath. Sita took food to their driver who slept under blankets beside the beasts.

The ashes of my mother and sister were safe in our keeping. Incense had been burnt. The camels were ready, their heads held high, their groans and rumbling roars drawing the attention of the villagers despite the pox.

As we moved away a bullock cart rattled down the rutted road between the houses we had left behind. The disturbance made us turn. Dust and litter rose in small flurries from beneath the cart's wheels. Men stepped back to let it pass and women grabbed their children. It stopped beside our house.

A young man wearing the khaki uniform of the British Indian army jumped down. His hair was closely shorn, and he walked with a swagger, chest out and shoulders back. He shouted to Baba. We hesitated, my father putting his hand to his eyes to shield the sun.

'Umesh.' My brother's name leaked from his lips as he ran towards the figure. I watched as Baba embraced him, only to stumble backwards as he was pushed away by Umesh's hand.

The camel owner tutted impatiently, his eyes asking questions. I squatted on the sand and watched. Baba pointed to where I waited. His gestures told the story before voices became raised and my brother, his feet square on the ground, yelled back at him. Sita appeared from the compound and hurried to bring her husband water to drink. The shouting ceased; Umesh with his hands clasped behind his head, turned in a slow circle as though trying to absorb the shock of the news he'd just been given and to orientate himself in this changed world.

Umesh will come with us on our trek. The thought squirrelled past other emotions. My time alone with Baba slunk away like a desert fox. The opportunity to show him I was the son to be proud of faded into haze. If only we had left sooner, if the cart had lost a wheel, if my brother hadn't returned until tomorrow. Ma had always known how to make things well, she could calm Umesh, distract my father, make me feel special. The ache was as piercing as a thorn.

'Asadi.' Baba's voice was loud and firm. 'You will stay here with Sita. Tend the goats. Your brother is here. He will come to Pushkar and fulfil his duty. See. Now he has joined the army. How big and strong he is in his uniform. All the villagers are looking at my son.'

'Baba, let me come too.' My plea became a whine. The camel driver edged closer, leaned in to hear better, his eyes flicking from Baba to me. I knew he would be gathering gossip to spread amongst his friends around a campfire at another time.

'You are disgracing me. You will do as I say,' Baba hissed through clenched teeth. I knew I had lost.

Umesh sauntered up, his face still wet from the water he had splashed on it. He turned his back and peed in the sand.

He shouted to the camel driver telling him he was a lazy good-for-nothing and to hasten before the sun rose too high. He thumped me hard between the shoulder blades and pushed me out of the way. The camels bellowed loudly and ambled off.

I stood until the slow-moving group smudged in the rising heat, until they became small as ants and finally disappeared. Anger scalded my body. I walked head down back to our house ignoring the stares of women working their land. Sita brought me chai; I barked at her to go away.

I couldn't bear to be in the house where memories lurked. I couldn't bear to be outside, to see other families carrying their dead, or stomach the smell of the many burning pyres.

My father and brother had been gone for three days. I tried to picture Pushkar Lake, to see the ashes floating away strewn amongst the flowers. No images formed. When I attempted sleep there was only black behind my eyelids. Sita washed the clothes, made me food and tended to the animals. When her tasks were done, she would sit in the dust, her hands in her lap, staring at nothing.

'You know he will go away again, don't you? Your husband.' I didn't want to give him his name. I was being deliberately cruel, but I continued. 'Now he's joined the army they will send him off to fight. There's going to be a war.' She looked at me with blank eyes. 'He may get killed, then you will be a burden, a widow.' I sneered the last word.

She played with the *mangalsura* fastened round her neck as if to confirm her status as a married woman. Her lip twitched; her shoulders fell. She picked up a small stone and rolled it between her fingers. 'It is the way.'

'You believe that? Accept it? Laksha did too.' Saying her name felt like the lash of a cane. 'Why don't you strive for something different?' I flicked her hand and walked off. I didn't want her company.

In the wadi I followed the tracks of chinkara. The herd of gazelle had passed through recently, their droppings still fresh. High above, an eagle swept the sky. With my back resting against the trunk of an acacia tree I pulled my scarf over my head and covered my mouth, spitting out the gritty wind-blown sand. Grey clouds, backlit by the sinking sun, humped like mountains, bunched together as the day petered out. A few large drops of rain splattered the ground leaving circles of moisture that evaporated in an instant. The forerunner of the monsoons. Will the rainclouds muster, as in recent years, laden with promise, then pass over, leaving crops to wither and people to go hungry? I prayed for rain to fall, to take the temperature down, settle tempers and invoke the gods to release us from the pox.

I saw the man approaching. He carried a staff, at odds somehow with the British-style trousers and shirt that he wore. His way of dressing, and how straight he stood, told me he was someone of importance. I gave him the briefest nod hoping he would pass on by.

'Namaste. You are Asadi? They said I might find you out here.'

The knuckles of his hand holding the staff were smooth, not cracked and chaffed with work; his nails were clean and unbroken.

He smiled. 'I am Mr Chouhan. I am to be the new teacher at the school.'

The man's shirt was white against his light brown skin. Two open buttons at the neck exposed wisps of black curly hair on his chest.

'We have the pox in the village. You shouldn't come here.' It sounded rude even to my own ears. The nod and smile he gave me were understanding and warm, so I hoped he hadn't noticed.

'Mr Singh told me you were the brightest pupil in the school. The potter told me I might find you in the wadi. He saw you walking. Is it a place you like to come?'

'I wanted to be alone.' I said it pointedly. Instead of apologising and leaving, Mr Chouhan sat and wiped his brow with the back of his hand.

'I can't pretend to know how I'd cope if I lost my mother and my sister and I'm sorry it has happened to you when you are so young.'

'They were the first to die. We are being blamed for bringing the pox to the village. My father is the *sahakar*. People owe him money, so no one likes him. He hasn't returned yet from Pushkar Lake. He has gone with my brother to scatter my mother and sister's ashes.' The hurt was a lump in my throat that I couldn't swallow. I felt Mr Chouhan's eyes on me. He paused, then touched my shoulder.

'He says I have to earn money now and that I'm too old to go to school.'

'And is that what you want?'

'No,' I said it so loudly a lizard darted from a rock.

The teacher tightened his lips as if he had anticipated my answer. 'My older brother is a doctor in a research unit in Kasauli. They have a treatment against smallpox. A vaccine. A prick of a needle in the arm. Have you heard of it? He persuaded me to have it. And my wife. He said we needed two doses to stop us from getting ill. It's why I volunteered to come here to this school. My brother sees me as an experiment. My wife was not so pleased!' His half-laugh made me look up and we shared the moment.

I scuffed the ground, making a small hollow. 'There are bad things said about a vaccine. That the British are trying to trick us. I bought medicine from the herbalist. It didn't save them.'

We sat for a few minutes without speaking.

'When you can, after mourning, will you come to the schoolroom, show me around and help me to prepare it?'

In that instant I wanted him to be my teacher and hated even more that my father wouldn't let me go back to school. 'Yes, if you want me to.' It would be better than sitting with the goats or being at home with my father and brother – resenting every moment.

Mr Chouhan jumped up. 'I can see why Mr Singh said what he did. It's been good to talk to you, Asadi.' He looked up at the sky. 'The rains will be here in a few days, I think.' He strode off leaving me with a quiver of warmth in my stomach.

Finish school. Go to college, in Jodhpur perhaps. Escape from here and father's plans for me. I wandered home.

My dreaming was pierced by a splinter of dread.

Baba was back.

He was spreadeagled on the bed, his dhoti streaked with dirt. Sweat had collected where his hairline receded. Through his open mouth he wheezed hot breath. His closed eyelids twitched as though struggling to open. I stood over him seeing the indent on the mat where Ma had lain. The room echoed emptiness, devoid of my mother's songs or my sister's chatter. No aroma of sweet-smelling dishes cooking on the fire tempted me to linger. I looked outside for Umesh or Sita but apart from chickens kicking up sand the place was deserted.

I squatted by the wall. Voices were coming closer from the direction of the village. Men tripped against each other as they carried a shrouded body shoulder high. I couldn't watch. How many more?

I wanted Baba to waken, to ask him about the journey, about Pushkar Lake. To be told that Ma and Laksha's souls have peace and salvation now. I wanted to shout at him, tell him I am his son and should have been there too, to curse the gods who allowed my brother to turn up when he did. I couldn't get rid of my writhing thoughts. Bitterness rooted in my chest.

When he did wake, his mood was sour. He shouted for Sita, cussed at her absence, brushed me aside like an annoying fly. I tried to tell him about the new teacher, but the words wouldn't come. I feared his tongue and stayed silent.

Sita returned with the goats. Her eyes were puffy and she

spun from me as she began to prepare the meal.

'Where is Umesh?' I asked her.

She shook her head. 'He's not here. He didn't come back.'

'Baba, where is Umesh?' My tongue whipped out the words.

'He is a big man; he has an important job in the army now. He had to return. He says the Indian soldiers will win the war for the British.'

'Baba, there is a new teacher. He says ...' I stopped. Baba hadn't heard over the bleating goats and I sensed he wouldn't want to.

The first rain came and ended as quickly as it started. Time hung as heavy as the heaped clouds that shed water in grey sheets. Steam rose lazily from the hot ground.

Our five remaining days of mourning threw us together. We bathed twice a day as tradition demanded and ate a simple meal. I felt Ma flitting amongst us soothing the hurt that shifted between Baba and me. Where were his thoughts, I wondered? How do you feel if you lose your wife and daughter? Did he miss them as I did?

I looked at Sita. Her family were from another village many miles away. Brought here by Umesh she was like a discarded possession. He was gone, at least for now, to a life I could only imagine. Sometimes I saw her crying and wanted to say words to calm her as Ma would have done. I didn't know how, and longing yawned like an empty well inside me.

On the thirteenth day we held *preta-karma*. My father made sacrifices to the gods and to our ancestors so that the souls of Ma and Laksha might be released for reincarnation. Afterwards Sita began the ritual of cleaning all the idols. She pushed back her hair and her shoulders heaved as she settled to the task. I took up a cloth and helped her. She paused, her polishing rag in her hand; her eyes, cupped by purple smudges, met mine and we squeezed a smile, a ray of light after the dark. When we had finished, I placed food and flowers on the shrine, the orange and yellow marigold petals bright with raindrops. Our period of mourning was over. The days stretched before me bleak and barren.

Mr Chouhan pedalled a bicycle past my house heading out of the village towards the school. He beckoned with a wave of his hand. 'I'm going to prepare the classroom. Are you coming?' The bicycle was already propped against the schoolroom wall by the time I caught up with him. Mr Chouhan held a piece of wood in his hand surveying the hole in the door. I flushed as I recalled the foul mood that had led me to break it down.

'I suppose it could have been an animal,' he said, not sounding convinced, but it offered space enough for me to turn away and pick up some of the jagged, broken sections. Sand had blown through and covered the floor and the mat. Small black balls of goat shit showed they had been in here too.

'My brother is building a room for himself and his wife. I can fetch his tools and nails from home,' I said, trying to make amends.

'You must ask your father first, Asadi. Take my bicycle. You will be quicker.'

'Really?'

He laughed at my first attempts to stay upright on the contraption and pulled me up when I toppled sideways onto the ground. I wasn't going to give in and with every try I went a little further.

'You've nearly got it. Going faster will make you steadier.'

I set off again, this time with a whoop, and wobbled off to the village. The wheels bounced over the ruts, but a rush of speed streamed over my face and lifted my hair. I was out of breath when I reached the house, my bottom felt bruised from the hard saddle, but it was the best thing I'd ever done. Baba wasn't around. I didn't want him to ask what I was doing. I stuffed a hammer and nails into a pouch and balanced a strip of wood across the handlebars. The return trip was even better though holding the wood made my arms ache.

'That was brilliant. I want a bike.'

Mr Chouhan had swept the floor with a grass broom and the air danced with motes. It looked odd, him standing with the brush in his hand. I had never seen Baba do anything like that.

We patched the door as best we could. He passed me the nails and I banged them in. 'Good enough for now. At least animals can't get in,' Mr Chouhan said. 'I'll get the carpenter to make a new one. He's been repairing the schoolmaster's house for me. My wife wants everything ready. Our first baby will be here any day now.'

He sat back on his heels and wiped the sweat from his top lip. 'Shall I come and talk with your father, Asadi?'

Excitement hovered for a moment. 'He won't listen. If my mother was here, she could persuade him. Always she wanted me to learn. She said, then I could achieve anything.' I finished with a shrug. 'My Baba is stubborn.'

'I'll try.' He nodded his head several times. 'Now, will you take me to the houses of the other boys and girls. We can tell them school is starting again. You can be my assistant.'

'Sir, it's only boys who come.'

'That is so, but since last year the government is telling us that all children must attend lessons for eight years, to "learn through activities". I know it's not the way in rural areas, but we must see if we can change things, if only slowly. We are told we must teach, not in English, but in the local language.' He laughed, 'What is that? We have so many languages all across India. You have heard of Mahatma Gandhi?' I nodded. 'It is his idea. We must teach handicrafts as well as other subjects.'

What I heard was 'we' and I'm sure I grew two inches. 'Laksha would have wanted to come to school,' I said.

Word of a new teacher and the school reopening had already spread in our village. Mr Chouhan stopped to talk to everyone. He was kind to those who had suffered loss, gentle with others still dealing with the sickness. They listened. Some shook their heads; others fidgeted and shooed their curious children away.

I hung back, said nothing, aware of the glances that were shot in my direction. I acted solely as a guide.

'They show respect, but they are frightened and suspicious, Asadi. I am new here; I have to gain their trust, but it will take time, particularly with the smallpox outbreak. It is good that I am a Muslim and you a Hindu.' He laughed. 'Together we are a team. Everyone feels a connection.'

I felt happy that Mr Chouhan found me useful.

We tramped for miles between the outlying villages, sometimes talking, sometimes walking side by side in friendly silence. Little children ran across the sand to stand and look at us. Dark hair and dark eyes in dust-grimed faces.

'Listen.' Mr Chouhan stopped. Music floated to us through the haze of heat.

'The man who lives there makes musical instruments.' I pointed at a rough collection of huts grouped together. 'He plays for us on festival days. People come from all over to listen to him.'

The man was sitting on baked-mud steps, a musical instrument between his knees. He plucked at the strings and didn't pause as we called a greeting. A curved blade lay at his feet amongst wood shavings. Our arrival brought the women of the house out to look: mothers, aunts and grandmothers, vivid as butterflies in the neutral landscape. Two of the women carried babies on their hips. Washing lay strewn over bushes, drying in the sun. A girl, about my age, squatted with a bucket of water between her knees, wringing out clothes. She smiled from behind the *dupatta* that covered her head and face.

'Brinda.' One of the women called to her. The girl shook dry her wet hands and hurried inside.

'You have many children here.' Mr Chouhan addressed the musician and indicated the ring of faces that had appeared from nowhere and now stood around us in a solemn semi-circle.

'There are six boys and five girls.' The man stopped playing. He spoke names and three of the boys came to stand beside him. The youngest one in a striped shirt began to play with the wood shavings, the other two I knew from school. 'My sons, all fine boys. They will grow up big and strong. These boys,' he pointed to two others, 'are my brother's children.'

'All fine offspring indeed.' Mr Chouhan beamed at them. 'I hope the boys and the girls will come to school when it starts next week.'

The man plucked again at the strings of his instrument. 'They will come.'

'Good, good. I can see you are a wise father who wants his children to do well.'

The girl who had been washing the clothes brought out chai on a tray. She handed one to Mr Chouhan and the man.

'This is my eldest daughter, Brinda.'

'Chai for you?' she asked me in clear English, trying to hide a grin.

I took the glass. Her small breasts pushed at the soft material of her sari.

'She teach herself the English,' her father said.

'I want to be a teacher.' Her voice slipped over my head.

'And I hope you will one day achieve your goal. With your father's permission, I will help you.' Mr Chouhan sipped the chai.

Another man joined our group. I guessed he was Brinda's uncle. 'It will be better when the British are gone, and we have independence. It will come soon enough.' His face was coarse, not smooth like the musician's. He scratched at his groin and shouted for the girl to bring more chai. He said to Mr Chouhan, 'You profess to be an educated man. Let me ask you this question. How can our village industries thrive? All these cheap imports from England being brought in on the railways.' He snarled through broken teeth.

Brinda stood at her father's shoulder. I glanced up and thought I caught her looking. I wasn't sure but I think she rolled her eyes for the briefest second before she looked down at her feet.

Mr Chouhan acknowledged the brother's rant with a polite nod. He spoke to Brinda's father. 'I am wondering if you would come to the school and teach the children how to carve wood, play instruments and make music. They would like that. Perhaps a small payment.'

'Let us see. Your invitation is generous.'

The men's talk buzzed like the flies that hovered round the mouth of the small boy who had grown tired of playing with the wood shavings. He picked up the blade and squealed when he cut his finger. One of the women came and scooped him into her arms with a loud tut.

'We have taken up your time.' Mr Chouhan stood. 'Namaste.'

The man began to play his music again as we took our leave.

'There is much anger in India, Asadi. I have seen it in the towns. I did not expect to find it here in the villages, where more traditional order is maintained.' I saw his forehead crease with worry lines as though his thoughts were troubling him. I flushed with pride that he should speak to me as an adult.

'Is the anger towards the British? Will there be a war?'

'It looks very much like the British will go to war because of events happening a long way from here. But not against us. There is another source of anger. For a while there has been a growing demand for India to break free from British rule and govern itself.' He paused looking into the distance. 'Where I was before, I knew of several illegal youth organisations that have grown up. The young are very angry. I do not approve of these troublemakers. I think we must achieve independence but in a non-violent way. I wonder if that is too much to hope for.'

'My brother, Umesh, has joined the army.' My arms trembled as I said it.

Mr Chouhan stopped. 'I didn't know that. What does your father say?'

'He is proud of Umesh. Baba doesn't talk to me of things, not like you are doing. I need to know what is happening outside of here. I have heard talk.' I wanted Mr Chouhan to think I held an opinion. 'India should be independent.'

'I believe, Asadi, that our country will grow strong under your generation.'

A large drop of rain hit my head, then another. We looked at each other and laughed. A curtain of cloud billowed from the horizon like a herd of bullocks.

'God is good,' Mr Chouhan shouted and jumped like a young boy, his arms outstretched. 'I think we need to run.'

In no time water streamed from our heads and down our faces. I caught it on my tongue and tasted its coolness. It drew streaks on my arms and legs as it washed off the desert dust.

Mr Chouhan waved goodbye and ran up the rough road where the rains had already turned dry ruts into courses of water. Soaked and happy I reached my house.

I heard a cough and saw Faraz, the boy I knew from school, standing outside our compound with a man.

'My father wishes to speak with your father,' he said, their clothes wet from the rain.

I told them to wait and went inside to find Baba.

'There is a man to see you. He is the father of Faraz from

school.'

'Tell him to come back tomorrow.'

'But Baba … they will have come a long way.'

'You heard. Go and do it.' He rolled over on his bed and covered his head with a blanket.

The callers squatted on the edge of the road. The rain had eased.

'My father is very tired. He says you must come back tomorrow.'

The man's head dropped to his knees and Faraz stared at me. His face had grown thin, his eyes squinted above sharp cheekbones.

'Wait,' I said. I spoke to Sita and pointed to the crouching figures. She gave me two bowls of thin dhal and the remains of some baati destined for the chickens.

I offered the bowls to Faraz. He tapped his father on the shoulder and held one out. The man grasped it in both hands and, dipping the bread in the pale liquid, supped noisily. I saw that he was an older man, older than my father. Dirt-ingrained skin on his knuckles bore the scars of hard work.

Heavy rain broke my sleep. It beat on our tin roof with the pace of a heartbeat. The ground in front of the house was torn into strips. Rivulets of water skimmed the sand and the fowl skittered with excited clucks, pecking at the disturbed grubs. The air was fresh and cool. I paid morning respects at the shrine Ma had built long ago in a nook in the wall. I fetched a bowl of clean water and placed it there and prayed to Lord Shiva that he might let the rains fall long and hard.

Faraz and his father were back at first light. I didn't ask where they had sheltered but I could see they wore damp clothes and the rain had plastered their hair flat. I watched as they unrolled prayer mats. They bowed low to where the light was growing, edging off the rain. I took them chai; they received it gratefully as they waited for my father to appear. When he did Faraz helped his baba to stand, and the two men went inside the house.

'There is a new teacher for the school.' I spoke to Faraz. He shrugged.

'I have met him. He's nice. School will start again soon.' Faraz shrugged again.

'Mr Chouhan. He is Muslim, like you.' I tried once more but the blankness of Faraz's eyes told me it was of no concern of his.

I heard my father's raised voice, a tone I recognised as signalling the end to a conversation. Shortly afterwards Faraz's baba appeared. He walked backwards out of the compound inclining his head in the direction of my father. He spoke a few words to Faraz, then the two of them shuffled off into the desert, the boy with his skinny legs supporting his father by the arm.

I looked to Baba, hoping he would give me some explanation, but he lit a roll-up and puffed at his cigarette.

'They are hungry,' I said. 'The rains should make the crops grow and then there will be food.' I wanted Baba to speak to me.

'He owes money. That is all that is of importance to me.' He turned to his ledgers and our conversation was over.

Sita had milked the goats and I took them out to graze, needing to be away from the house that had grown cold and unfamiliar. Grey clouds swelled into the shape of mountains and promised more rain. I stared at the horizon, a clear line in the distance stretching to left and to right. A barrier marking the edge of my world, hemming me in.

I stayed away until the late afternoon and as I returned Mr Chouhan was leaning his bicycle against our fence. Baba was watching him.

'Namaste, Asadi.'

I shouted to Sita to tend to the goats, my day spent idling felt suddenly pointless.

'I have come to speak with your father.' He smiled, smoothed his ruffled hair and straightened the collar of his shirt. A beige dog stopped in front of him and began to lick its underparts. 'Get on with you.' He gave it a nudge with his foot and the dog sauntered off down the road without looking back.

My palms began to feel clammy. I wanted to splash my face with water. I should have prepared Baba for this encounter.

'It will be all right, Asadi. You look like there's a tiger in your path.' He laughed. 'I am here to pay my respects to your father.'

'Baba,' I called. He was no longer in the doorway. I pulled a rickety chair into the shadow cast by the house, straightening its leg to stop it collapsing. Mr Chouhan gave it a shake, pulled a face and squatted instead. I poured water for him to drink.

'Baba,' I called more loudly, 'Mr Chouhan is here to see you. He is the new teacher at the school.' I could see his face, dark in the dimness, his eyebrows knitted together. At first he didn't move, and I wondered if he had heard me. Then he walked slowly outside.

Mr Chouhan stood. He was taller than my father and greeted him with an inclination of the head.

'I have heard much about you. I grieve with you over the loss of your wife and daughter. This smallpox takes many lives and brings hardship.'

A swallow rippled down Baba's throat. I was barely breathing.

'Tell Sita to bring chai, Asadi.'

My breath escaped in a rush. Where was the woman? I didn't want to go looking for her. I found her in the room at the back where she was preparing vegetables.

'We have a visitor. Father wants chai.' Her eyes were still red rimmed. She said nothing. She put down the knife and rose to prepare the tea.

They were talking together. Mr Chouhan was waving his arm, gesticulating up the way. 'Yes, my wife is here. I have been settling her in. We will have our first child in a few days. She is tired after her journey.'

'From Jaipur...'

'The rains are light ...'

'In the army ...'

Snatches of the conversation reached me where I hovered. When Sita brought the chai, I edged closer.

'A bright boy. A promising future.' Mr Chouhan was friendly and respectful giving my father time to speak. My father's head remained bowed, his tongue silent.

I began to hope.

'With a good education he will be able to command a high position and good wages one day.'

Baba crossed his arms. He narrowed his eyes and thrust out

his chin.

'None of which you speak is possible. Asadi has a job in the post office in Jodhpur. He starts next week.'

A car wove down the street, its horn blaring, startling the bony-haunched cows that ambled in its path. I stared at this machine, black and shiny, its motor humming like a swarm of bees. Smoke belched from a pipe that poked from the car's underbelly. I flattened myself against a wall heedless of the puddle of sewage that splashed over my feet. My heart raced as I watched people scatter from the beast that blasted through like an elephant on charge. One day, I vowed, I would own one. My fingertips throbbed as I imagined the power.

I had arrived in Jodhpur after a ride on the same bullock cart that had carried my brother. The driver was a stick-like man who smelt of hooch. He muttered a continual stream of abuse aimed at someone who had given him a black eye. Over the course of the journey it swelled visibly, making me wonder if he could see at all.

In the town I was either staring or scared. People everywhere, walking in all directions paying no attention to each other. Babies clung to mothers while small children played on the roadside inches from rickshaws, bikes and carts going past. Groups of men sat drinking together at rickety tables in front of open shop fronts with dark interiors, old men in dhotis and young men with voices raised in conversation or argument. Washing sprouted from windows and balconies, purple, orange, yellow, items of female clothing that came alive when whipped by the breeze and made me look away. From open windows and roadside fires came the smell of cooking, the rich aroma curling into my nostrils masking the odour of fresh dung dropped by a passing bullock.

Report at eleven o'clock I'd been told. The directions imprinted on my brain seemed to make no sense when translated into actual streets and landmarks. I tapped a man on his shoulder. He chewed paan, and red-stained saliva frothed from his mouth through broken teeth. 'The Post Office?' I asked. He motioned across the road to a sand-coloured building with a stone arch and a panelled door. Small windows were secured with bars where trapped litter blew like torn flags.

Anger at my father for making me do this burnt in my gut but still I felt the quiver of a thrill as I crossed the road. He and I had exchanged bitter words. My pleas were swept aside. It was not about what *I* wanted, it became about respecting him, doing his bidding. I was to work for the Post Office; 'A good job', he yelled at me. He had set it up through a distant cousin whose name I'd never heard before. I could stay in this man's house, I would have the best room, pay him board and lodging. Anything remaining I must take back to Baba. I should be grateful. Get rid of stupid notions of learning. What use were books? How would they earn money for food or support a wife? His thrashing arm had struck me across the cheek and now I touched the yellowing bruise that spilt down the side of my face.

After the argument I had sought out Mr Chouhan in his house. His wife had bathed my swelling with a lotion that stung so keenly I wiped away tears I couldn't hold back. She was gentle with me. A small woman, her stomach swollen with the baby she carried. Afterwards, she busied herself preparing a meal, stopping to rub her back or caress her abdomen. The house smelt of soap. A white cloth lay over a small table and two scrubbed wooden chairs stood beside it.

'Your father is trying to do his best for you.' Mr Chouhan sat across from me in the simple room made bright by the woven rugs on the floor. 'As any father would. You must do as he says, Asadi. Show him respect. He cannot stop you learning. But you must do it on your own. I have books I will lend you. Many boys have to learn that way.' His words healed, made the burning in my chest cool. He gave me the courage to leave my village.

The post office was filled with noise, everyone seemingly trying to shout louder than the next person. People jostled to get to the front of queues. Raised voices were punctuated by frequent thuds as documents were stamped.

I was sent to a small room at the back where a man with a well-ordered moustache and a crisply ironed shirt sat writing in a ledger. He dipped a pen into an inkwell and shook it. The man's skin was white like paper. A bald patch on his head was criss-crossed with strands of hair. I watched with fascination as he ran his fingers over it creating a different pattern.

I waited for him to notice me. Tomorrow, would I be one of those wielding the thudding stamp, controlling the customers, informing them to wait? After a few minutes when the man still hadn't lifted his head, I coughed to politely tell him I was there. He looked up and a weary expression flitted across his face.

'Good morning, sir. My name is Asadi …'

'Yes, yes. Whoever you are if you're here for a job go to the sorting office. Can't you see I'm busy?' He dismissed me with a shake of his head.

Should I tell him my father's cousin had secured a position for me? That I was to be taught the ways of a postal worker. It didn't seem the moment to say it.

'Can you ride a bike?' He threw the question at me as I retreated.

'Yes, sahib. I can ride a bike.' I spluttered the answer, hoping he didn't notice the spray of spittle that flew from my mouth.

'Tell them. Down there and turn left.'

'Can you read and write?' His voice followed me down the green-painted corridor.

I retraced my steps and stood in his doorway. I made myself as tall as I could and pushed my shoulders back. 'Sahib, I can both read and write. I have been educated for seven years.'

He looked up then, his eyes like glass-blue marbles swept over me from head to toe.

'Huh. An Indian who might even be useful.'

The sorting office was a big room that smelt of sour sweat and sweet curried spices. It was so hot that beads of perspiration broke out across my nose. Men and a few women stood in front of benches. Mail was being emptied out of jute sacks by small boys who ran up and down the lines. Letters and parcels were thrust into cubby holes and every now and again a shout rose above the general noise and the contents of an overfull section would be removed and taken off. To my eyes it was chaos, movement everywhere, workers calling, others shouting, a whistle blowing. A man sneezed into his sleeve, and another pinched the end of his nose and blew snot onto the floor.

I tried not to look disgusted when the same man came up to me and asked me what I wanted. 'I am to be employed in the

Post Office. The sahib has instructed me to tell you that I can both read and write … and that I can ride a bicycle. I can also speak English.' I added the extra information hoping he would be impressed enough to allocate me a position in the front hall, not in this teeming frenzy.

The man stared at me as though I had spoken in some foreign tongue. A tic in his cheek twitched, like a fly was crawling inside his mouth. His brown face reddened to puce. 'I can read and write and ride a bike.' He mimicked my words and wiggled his shoulders from side to side.

This is what I thought about as I lay on my charpoy in 'the best room' in my 'uncle's' house. He had told me to call him uncle even though he was my father's cousin, not his brother. He was about the same age as my father and had two sons I had yet to meet. His three daughters, he told me, were married, and moved away, one to Delhi, the other two to places I hadn't heard of. A mouse of a woman flitted in the background. I assumed it was his wife, but he didn't introduce me.

To reach my room he had taken me to the top of the house. Up two flights of brown stairs, to a landing with a leaning balustrade. He had thrown open the door. 'You are fortunate that this room, the best room, is vacant. The man who used to have it, I kicked him out. He would not pay his rent on time.' He made it sound like a warning. Heat trapped for too long escaped along with a smell of unwashed feet. I saw the tiny slit of window hung with limp, orange material that looked like it had been torn from a sari. The room was as small as a cupboard, a wooden bed took up the length of a wall and three steps took me to the stained mattress.

The best room! I swallowed hard to prevent my thoughts leaking out into the sour air.

'In all the other rooms you have to share, sometimes with one or two, maybe three others.'

I wondered if I had actually spoken.

'For family I keep the best.' 'Uncle' had snaked away leaving imprints of his feet on the dusty stairs.

I wasn't allocated a position in the front hall of the post office or given a smart uniform. I wasn't even sent to the sorting office. I'd been given a brown satchel to wear over my shoulder, its leather flap scratched by the fingernails of its many previous owners – and a bike. A heavy bike with a black frame and a saddle that cut into my groin and left my underparts raw and bleeding so that at night I could only lie with my legs wide apart. To stop the contraption I used my feet, scraping the skin off my toes exposing flesh like a plucked chicken. My job was to take the mail to the outlying villages, weekly to some, daily to others. The stone-littered roads were no more than dirt tracks.

I knew better than to complain. I'd seen the foot runners who tramped the streets of the city. Paid less than me, their status was little higher than the stray dogs who roamed in packs.

For the first few weeks the anger in my belly curdled into a fury fiercer than the rains that pelted my body. Sometimes I would travel miles just to give one or two letters or a parcel to someone in a village. They would look at what I had brought, turn it over and stare blankly at the writing that made no sense. If I could be bothered, I might offer to read it for them but more often I would shrug and leave them to it.

At the house there was always a meal of sorts at night. My 'uncle's' wife was not a good cook. The food, the colour of camel dung, always tasted the same. Often it would be a cold congealed mess by the time I got back, left on the side, crawled over by flies. Those nights I would wander the streets, gorge on rotis, dhal and pickles from the street sellers and drink chai on corners where men huddled, swapping gossip.

'It's your home village. You know where it is.' My supervisor, a man with a sharp tongue and a lame eye, had given me a second satchel of letters to deliver, the straps chaffing on my neck. 'The other fellow – bah – killed by a buffalo.'

'It's too far. How can I get round ...?'

He'd kicked at the wheel frame of my bike. 'Leave earlier, pedal faster, idle boy.' He turned away.

I swore at his retreating back, cursing the stupidity of the half-baked boy who'd got himself killed.

I'd been working for the Post Office for three months and in that time had been back home only once. My father's sole interest was the money he made me hand over. He'd rolled the rupees into a bundle and thrust them into his pocket.

'How can I ever be a man when you make me do a lowly job like this? I may as well be a rickshaw walla.' I had stood so close to him I'd seen the open pores on his nose. His eyes narrowed and I sensed the clench of his fist. He hadn't wanted to hear about my work, his cousin, or the sons who slunk from the house in the middle of the night.

Today I pedalled past the discarded metal drum that had rusted by the roadside for as long as I could recall. Familiar landmarks looked different. The monsoon season was ending, too little rain had fallen for the harvest to be good. The water soaked into the earth but cracks as wide as a fist criss-crossed the tracks threatening to unseat me. In the far distance the vegetation that surrounded the herbalist's hut was plush and green against the desert. I turned away not wanting to remember. Hungry dogs scrabbled where the funeral pyres had burnt. Crows and ravens squawked and fought with them over the pickings.

It was market day; people from surrounding villages had brought in their wares and come to buy. A seller beat his metal cooking dishes together. 'Best quality, good price.' A woman sat with her meagre bunches of herbs laid out before her. She raised a bony hand as I passed, imploring me to stop. I scanned the faces for Sita, hoping to avoid her. The potter called out, but I kept my head down and pretended not to hear. Without dismounting I dropped items off at three or four places, tossing them into the compounds and giving the occupants a shout. I pulled my standard issue hat lower over my face and sped on.

'Asadi.' Mr Chouhan shouted my name as I leapt off the saddle outside his house. I willed him not to draw attention and put my finger to my lips. He looked around. 'Is something the matter? It's good to see you. Why so furtive?'

My hands ached from where I had been gripping the handlebars. I pretended to be out of breath so as to have time to calm myself. My apprehension began to leak away.

'Look at you. So tall now. Strong and lean.' He slapped me on the back. 'Come in, come in. You must need refreshment.'

His words were as welcome as water on a hot day. He hadn't

forgotten who I was and, what's more, seemed pleased to see me. I looked at my smooth brown limbs, saw the ripple of the muscles and ran my tongue over the brush of hair that topped my upper lip. I stood up tall.

'What does your father say? He must be proud.'

I took off my sandals and entered his house. 'I haven't seen him. It's better he doesn't know I'm here.'

Mr Chouhan stopped, one hand on the wall. His hair was bushier than I remembered and curled around his ear. He pushed it back as though he knew I'd noticed.

He met my gaze, took my hand and pumped it. 'You are a young man now. You must take responsibility for the decisions you make.'

I nodded and said no more, fearing disapproval.

Mr Chouhan recounted tales of the school like he was reading me a story. He made me laugh as he described the antics of the younger pupils, how they draw on the blackboard behind his back and at the excuses for non-attendance dreamed up by the older boys. 'One told me the sand was hot and he'd lost his shoes when I know he's never owned a pair.'

I asked him about Faraz, the boy whose father Baba had turned away, but he just shook his head. He hadn't seen him. His face became sad when he talked about the small number of girls who had turned up. 'They attend but only occasionally. It is hard to see what I can do. Only Brinda attends every day. She is also coming here to my house for extra lessons. She is determined to be a teacher. Her mother sits with her and listens too.' He smiled. 'I think I have two pupils. I hope one day Brinda's dream will come true.'

My stomach cramped with the pain of jealousy.

'Asadi, you know your father will learn that you have been here today. There are always people watching, ready to gossip. I don't need to tell you that.'

I didn't want Mr Chouhan to think badly of me. Shame at the disrespect for my father made me speak louder than I should have done. 'Baba is not proud of me. He scoffed at the amount of money I brought home last time. What did he expect? That I would be running the Post Office by now? What do I do? Deliver mail that most people can't read. All day, cycling in the heat. Paid a pittance. All I do is work and sleep. I …'

Mr Chouhan's wife came into the house carrying a basket of vegetables. Strapped to her back was a sleeping baby, its black hair just visible under the cover that bound it.

'My son.' Mr Chouhan sprang up and lifted the child free from its mother. 'We call him Irfan. It means knowledgeable. He will grow up to be wise and strong – God willing.'

He cradled the baby in his arms. The smile that lit his eyes reminded me of Ma and I blinked and sniffed to cover my confusion. He handed me the child in such a way that I had no option but to take it. The baby slept on oblivious of its inexperienced handler. My taut muscles made my forearms rigid, but I dared not move. Irfan stretched, arched his back and one small hand, with its perfect fingernails, burst free from the wrap. My gasp startled him, his face crumpled, and he let out a piercing yell. Nadira, Mr Chouhan's wife, prised him from me and the baby quieted.

'One day, Asadi, you will know what it is to have a son.' Mr Chouhan chuckled. 'But not yet.'

A few nights later, back in Jodhpur, I tossed in my bed listening to the scratch of cockroaches on the walls. A rooster crowed, perhaps like me it longed for morning. The talk here was all of war. The man with his sandwich board hanging on his shoulders walked up and down the street with an air of importance at being the conveyor of such momentous news. **British Declare War** straggled in large letters across his board. He shouted the same to anyone who would listen. Indians either cheered him or jeered, depending which side they were on. Most took no notice. I wondered about my brother. What did it mean for him? Where was he now? The heat in my room clung to every surface, the air a polluted fug that invaded my lungs. Whichever way my mind turned it fell into a black well where anger swirled like water. This was not how my life was meant to be. How had all my dreams shrivelled like the balls of an old man?

A stair creaked and my door clicked open. Instantly I was off the bed and onto the floor, my fists bunched to defend myself against the intruder.

'Cousin, cousin.' Two hands pushed down on my shoulders. 'Keep quiet or we will have to make you.' There was a snigger from a shadowy second figure that hovered behind. 'We're family. You have nothing to be afraid of. What are you? A soft-bellied coward? We have come to take you somewhere. You have been cooped up for too long like a tethered goat. It is time we showed you a good time.'

I didn't move and hoped they couldn't hear the thump of my heart as it threatened to break my ribs.

'Get dressed.' It was a command from Gemar, my eldest cousin. I'd heard his name but barely knew him or his brother. I'd seen them as they flitted in and out of the house. I pulled on my pants and long shirt and scrabbled for my sandals in the dark. I was instructed to follow them and we left my 'uncle's' house and walked through a maze of streets. Gemar took charge. He kept turning and beckoning me to move faster. Only the moon gave us light. We circled families sleeping under railway arches, children curled against each other unaware of the dogs that sniffed around their faces. The younger cousin kicked out at the sleeping bodies when they were in his way. They grunted, turned over and slept on. One part of me wanted to ask where we were going but fear of the answer held me back. The other part was excited at being included.

We passed through the backstreets in the shadow of the massive walls below the fort. My cousin threw out an arm and stopped me, then thrust my head down and pushed me through a low entrance. The room I stumbled into was full of men sitting on the floor. Their faces faded in and out of focus as curls of cigarette smoke wafted in the space.

'My cousin, Asadi. I told you about him.'

Eyes stared at me.

'He's very young.'

I wondered what had been said about me to these people and why. I became used to the haze and could see the occupants were mostly young, but two were middle aged. One sat with his feet up on a low table, the butt of his lighted cigarette spreading a dull glow over his cheek. Someone shuffled along and made room, tugged at my trouser leg and suggested I should sit. Any further interest in me seemed to wither and I pushed my back into the wall and tried to make myself as small as possible. The atmosphere felt like the desert before a storm when the air is sucked from the earth and it hurts to breathe. My heart quickened and my throat was dry. I coughed into my hand and the youth next to me nudged my arm and passed me the nub of his cigarette and a glass of liquid that I thought was chai. It tasted bitter and burnt my tongue and the inside of my mouth.

They were talking about trains and the network of lines that connected India's cities. I tried to make sense of their discussion of signals and points and timetables. The conversation flew from person to person. They had to be engineering students I decided, and I could tell by their knowledge and the words they spoke that I was amongst educated people. All Hindus. That my cousins had brought me here to mix in such company touched me with pride and I was beginning to warm to them.

'You work for the Post Office.'

I just nodded to the older man who had spoken as he seemed to be making a statement rather than asking a question. Everyone was attentive. 'You pick up the parcels and goods from the mail train?'

Would I let my cousins down if I admitted that all I did was deliver post to the villages on a bicycle? I wanted to be someone of importance.

'Yes,' I lied. 'Well, sometimes. I ... I do different jobs. Collecting mail from the trains is a responsible task.' I hoped it sounded convincing. 'Are you engineering students from the college?' No one answered, bodies fidgeted, liquid glugged into glasses as a bottle was passed around.

'So you don't.' He looked at me with narrowed eyes pulled together in a frown, a growl rising in his throat.

'You said ...' The man who had spoken leant towards Gemar who pulled back. 'Fix it.'

My younger cousin kicked my foot. I held his glare, tensing every muscle unsure of what had happened there and what I had said wrong.

The talk moved on to the war and the British. 'Why are Indians supporting our oppressors? Leave them to their war.'

'Sikhs and Muslims, they don't have the intelligence to see the ramification of their support for the war. But Hindus? Why are we divided? How will that achieve anything?' A man with hair that fell over his forehead thumped the floor and I jumped. He was waving his arms, mumbling obscenities. 'I hate people with white faces.'

A low cheer frilled around the walls and across the bare floor.

I thought of my brother playing big about being in the army. I thought about the discussions I enjoyed with Mr Chouhan and how he listens to what I have to say with a considered nod of his head. He is a Muslim. To say he lacks intelligence is insulting. I wanted to defend him. I kept quiet.

The discussion and argument rose and fell making me dizzy. I was tired but a buzz stirred my brain, every cell in my body fine-tuned to the shifting mood. A general shuffle seemed to indicate the meeting was over. I found myself included in the communal slapping of shoulders, the earlier tension forgotten. Pieces of paper were distributed; I took one and stuffed it in my pocket. The students slipped out into the darkness. Did I have new friends? I hardly dared to hope.

On the way home I wanted to ask about the young men, who they were, why they met. But by the hunch of my cousins' shoulders and the whispered talk between themselves, with only the occasional glance back at me. I decided to leave my questions for another time.

Back in my room I was buoyed by exhilaration. I had been invited to join them. My cousins had taken me along. My dream of going to college, of mixing with thinking people seemed, for the moment, a little less improbable. Jumbled snippets of the conversation repeated in my head. What must Gemar fix? Why had he spoken of me? I scolded myself for having too vivid an imagination, censored the niggle that wavered at the edge of sleep. Soon I would have to be up for work.

Sleep must have come eventually but it was a sleep disturbed by vivid dreams and I awoke sweating. Remembering the retrieved flyer, I smoothed it out as best I could. The faint light of dawn barely illuminated the scrawly writing. Only the heading jerked into focus. **"Bomb Making"** I curled into a ball, hiding the words from sight, not wanting to face a truth. Images of explosions and maimed bodies flitted behind my closed eyelids.

For the first time, I was late for work. The supervisor cussed in disgust at my unwashed body and crumpled clothes. It was as if my mouth had been raked by a sandstorm and my head pounded with a persistent throb.

Pedalling in the heat towards the villages I felt sick and wearied. I convinced myself that I had read the flyer wrongly, that I must be mistaken, that the conclusion I was reaching was far fetched. There was a simple explanation that my cousins would provide. They would mock my stupidity with laughter and share the joke with their fellow students. I so wanted to be part of their group, to join in again, to feel fresh and alive with excitement. I would suffer the humiliation, laugh with them and it would be forgotten.

My day's work seemed endless. The sun was fierce and every rut and bounce on the road rattled my bones and thrust knives into my skull. I finally reached the depot at the end of my rounds craving sleep and respite from my thoughts.

My boss was waiting for me.

A flush bloomed on my face, proof of guilt. How could he know? Who had seen what I had done? Unable to face the extra miles to the final village I had thrown the small bundle of letters into a festering pool, had poked them with a stick and watched as they became soggy and sank below the surface. My father would beat me for the shame I would bring him. My 'uncle' and cousins, they would all know.

Just as life was beginning it was over.

The boss stared, his lame eye twitching in its effort to remain still. His nose crumpled in distaste.

'You are to come with me.' He squeezed the instruction from between gnashed teeth. I followed him into the post office building and down the green corridor to the sahib's office with its huge wooden desk.

'Wait,' my boss snarled at me, but simpered when he spoke to the sahib. I hated that he did that and the way in which he bowed and shuffled backwards as he retreated from the room. I knew he would loiter to witness my disgrace.

Today the Englishman's hair, which fascinated me before, was greased in straight lines across his bald patch like someone had drawn on his head with a pen. He studied me with hooded eyes, a twitch of his mouth made it look like he was smiling. He took a deep breath and pulled his lips into a thin tight line.

'I remember you. An Indian who can read and write.'

I wasn't going to simper. I stood up straight, pushed back my shoulders and focussed on a point between his eyebrows. That twitch again, the almost-smile, which he covered by clearing his throat.

'I understand you want to move on from being a delivery boy.' His finger tapped on the polished surface of the desk.

I gulped and blinked, not daring to flick at the fly that was buzzing near my ear.

'I like a young man who's ambitious. Reliable, hard-working, honest. That's what's said about you.'

I heard a strangled choke from where my boss was listening.

'Honest. Now there's a thing.' His forced chuckle made me burn inside but I stood still and held my gaze.

'You want to work on the mail trains. Why?' An edge surfaced in his voice.

My hot anger became an icy dribble of fear. *You pick up the parcels and goods from the mail train?* I'm back in the smoke-filled room with the students, the older man rapping the question. *'Fix it,'* he'd said to Gemar.

Saliva pooled in my mouth. I swallowed. 'Yes, sahib. I am proud to work for the Post Office. The railways have brought great advances to India. They have improved communication and …'

'Yes, yes. I know all that. Not many of your sort can see it. Good to find a man who can.

'Singh,' he shouted. 'Stop lurking like a sewer rat and get yourself in here.'

My supervisor shuffled in. I'm sure he would have crawled if he could have.

'Get this employee transferred to the mail trains. As of next week, if not sooner. Got that? Now be gone. I'm busy.'

I gave up my bike and moved to work on the mail train. I didn't understand why or who had arranged it. Was something expected of me? The question whirred in my head like a moth in a spider's web. I'd squeezed the flyer into a crack in the floorboards under my bed. At the meetings its content had never been referred to again. In time I forgot, only being reminded when a thin, quiet student with thick glasses came one evening with his head swathed in a grubby bandage, burnt skin puckering his cheek. That night there was a huddled discussion about chemicals and instability most of which I couldn't understand.

They were my friends now. I'd been coming for months, sometimes with my cousins, but no longer afraid to attend on my own. Looking back, I imagine the other students must have seen a raw youth who hung on their every word, absorbing their proclamations, their apparent wisdom, their worldliness. I got to know who had the loudest voice, who needed to be boosted with flattery, who wouldn't accept criticism or argument. Intense discussion, passion and patriotism flared like flames in a fire. We never used names and the self-elected leaders would bark if one was called. There was plenty I didn't understand; a tension that prickled the hair on my arms, knowing glances, sentences unfinished. I watched and learnt.

At first their general talk had troubled me. Fiery and proud, their free India, anti-British exchanges bubbled from mouth to mouth with an intensity that oozed fear into my bones. My head buzzed with their outspoken views, opinions I'd never considered. Why had I not seen the extent to which our nation had been suppressed and misused when it was staring me in the face?

I found the courage to speak out. 'There is no future for boys in rural areas, no jobs, no opportunities.' They listened as I talked about my life. How stuck the village was in its ways, the poor transport links, the ignorance of my father who allowed himself to be ruled by white bosses.

They had nodded. 'The villages are a site of backwardness and oppression.' A man sitting across the room, his arms clasped around hunched knees, agreed. They wanted to know more, asked questions. I felt big. What I had to say counted, if only in a small way.

'We have to get them out. They exploit our resources, flood our markets with cheap goods. Gandhi's imprisonment was a violation.'

'Indians are made poorer. There is terrible famine in Bengal.

Now they want us to fight their war.'

'Jinnah is demanding a separate homeland for Muslims.'

'It's a bargaining chip.'

Excitement swelled when news of small victories filtered through. Electricity supplies cut off. Telegraph wires severed. Sometimes anger snarled like a rabid dog; the older men, who I took to be tutors, interrupted only if tempers threatened to challenge the group's solidarity.

I turned sixteen, edged closer to seventeen and gone were the sweating palms, the rapid heartbeat that threatened to expose me.

This particular night, the professor, a normally quiet, watchful man with a moustache that covered his upper lip, arrived hardly bothering to hide his excitement.

'The war is not going well for our oppressors. They say France has fallen. The British are in retreat.' The ripple of a cheer was hushed but joyful. 'The Japanese are attacking British territories. India will yet be free.'

Nothing had ever been asked of me. Until now.

'You will hand this to the man who approaches you. He will be on the night train tomorrow. He will ask you if you live in the blue city. You will reply with the words, "It is the city of my birth." Straightforward instructions. Do you understand?'

I wanted to tell him I wasn't an idiot but let the retort die in my throat. I turned the shoebox-sized parcel around in my hands. It looked like many others that I handled every day at work, wrapped in brown paper, the address written in a spidery hand.

'What's in it?' I was aware of the low hum of conversation around me tailing off; I heard breathing.

'Equipment. The man is an engineer, he needs it for his work.'

'How will he know me? What if he doesn't turn up?'

'He will. You ask too many questions. Are you man enough to perform this simple task?'

I took the parcel with a grunt and turned away, rebuffing his scorn. He would learn to trust me. I may have been naive once, but I no longer recognised that boy. My fingers gripped the package while the nature of its contents teased my curiosity.

A black engine puffed into the station, the sound of its whistle echoing to the rafters, sending up clouds of crows chattering and screaming in protest. The platform was crowded; men, some young, some old, squatted on the ground in grubby clothes hoping to be hired in the morning for a day's work. Others already slept, their possessions tied in bundles beside them. Passengers walked between and around. A pretty, white woman wearing a large straw hat pulled her skirt close so as not to have it sullied. She clung to the arm of her stylish, moustached companion as they pushed their way towards the first-class carriages. A group of soldiers laughed and jostled with each other; kit bags strewn at their feet. They broke into occasional boisterous bursts of song interspersed with loud burps and more laughter.

The engine hissed out steam. Dirty smoke plumed veils of soot over people and surfaces alike. How would anyone find me in this melee? I stood close to the mail van looking from side to side, standing on tiptoe. Who was I looking for? The day was fading; the parcel in my satchel, its presence looming larger than its actual size. My chest was tight, the cloying hot air making me wheeze. Don't get this wrong, I berated myself. 'It is the city of my birth. It is the city of my birth,' the words on a reel in my head. A man approached, his hand held out, sunken eyes in a leathered face. A beggar. I pushed him away and he stumbled against the train, issuing a string of curses aimed at me. Others stopped to watch, a diversion from their usual humdrum routine.

'Chai, chai.' Somehow the chaiwala made himself heard as he balanced pot and cups and rapped on the carriage windows. Usually, he would pause briefly to exchange a few words with me but today I shooed him away with a flap of my hands. The tea he offered slopped at my feet and splashed my bare legs.

A tap on my shoulder, light as a breeze, startled me into spinning around. An Indian in a well-cut suit looked me straight in the eye. His skin was smooth, polished by a faint sheen of sweat.

'Good evening.' He greeted me the British way. I sensed heads turn in our direction. 'Do you live in the blue city?'

'It is …,' I began, my voice high and squeaky. What had I expected him to look like? Not like this. I coughed to clear the phlegm that choked my throat. 'It is the city of my birth.' His eyes pulled me in until the leather case he carried bumped sharply against my leg. I scrabbled in my satchel and removed the parcel. He took it with the briefest nod of his head. The moment, worried over, waited for, was gone. No opportunity to talk. The man's cold politeness told me he wanted to be on his way. He moved further up the platform.

My hands shook and my fingers felt thick and clumsy, but I had work to do. Mail was being unloaded and new sacks lifted into the transport. My fellow workers muttered coarse words as I fumbled with the heavy loads. Most days I just collected the post and took it back to the depot. But sometimes, like this week, I got to travel in the train's mail van to and from Munabao, in charge of the parcels and packages. These times were the best and I mustn't mess them up.

The train's hooter bellowed out its warning, the guard's whistle pierced the smoke. The racket made people scramble onto the train. Tired children clung to their mothers and wailed as they were pushed up the iron steps. People hung out of windows and those without tickets clawed their way onto the carriage roofs. My well-dressed friend was almost the last to board. He lifted a small child and passed her to her mother then walked to the next carriage and boarded. He called to the chai seller to bring him tea. That man should be sitting in one of the first-class carriages I thought, but they were not for Indians however smart and important.

The mail van had a split door, and I swung the top half back letting the warm wind wash over my face and through my hair. The rhythmic click of the train on the rails quietened my jangling nerves. I had completed the task, a small cog in the network. The older generation had become weary and apathetic. As the youth of India, it was our duty to stand up for her. Our cause, our future. I remembered the impassioned discussion of the night before. A flush of pride fought with the wind on my face and I smiled at the thought of recounting it all to my cousins.

The light from small fires outlined mud-walled houses as the train chugged through villages. People flitted about like bats. Soon it became too dark to see. I settled down to rest in the corner of the van, my back wedged against the wooden slats, my pillow a sack of letters. The other worker who travelled with me was already asleep, paan-stained saliva dribbling from his mouth with each noisy snore.

I woke to the flicker of a match held close to my face. 'Get off before Barmer.' A man's voice, low and urgent.

I blinked to try and shake myself awake. What had he said? I imagined it to be the voice of the man to whom I'd given the parcel. But why would it be him? He would have had to walk the length of the train to reach the mail van. A trace of sweaty odour lingered. I called out to the retreating shadow. 'I'm not allowed. I must go further, as far as Munabao. My job ...' I saw his shrug as the match went out.

I crawled over bags to the half door and pushed the top open to try and shake off sleep. I needed to think; Barmer a way off yet. Cool air and darkness pulsed in. The train rattled across the flat countryside, the engine a black snake's head up in front. Paan-man slept on, rumpled like a pile of discarded clothes.

White light seared with orange. Purple. Red. A blast I felt. My head exploded; blood gushed from my nose. I turned, twisted, flew. Heard the thumps of raining bodies.

'Asadi *chutki*.' Her voice was warm and soft like honey stolen from the desert bees. My tongue tasted its sweetness. 'Open your eyes.' More urgent now. Her hand brushed over my face, her fingers played on my cheek, the scent of cardamon and spices lingering.

'No, Mama. It's too early. Let me be.' The familiar game. Me curling into a ball, savouring the warmth of my sleeping mat. The lightness of her lips on my hair welcoming me to a new day.

'Asadi. Asadi.' Pulling me back from sleep. 'It isn't time to go. You have much to do.'

Her face faded at the edges, becoming smaller as she backed away from me. I lifted an arm to touch her, but she dissolved into air.

Pain whipped my legs, pounded my ribs and settled in my hand, a pulsating, thwacking beast. I forced my grainy eyes open, spitting out the sand that filled my mouth. I was outside the mail van. The cold of early morning made my limbs twitch and shake. I was a chicken with its head cut off.

'Mama.' The name drivelled from my mouth. Silence, deeper than the darkest night blanketed me. Torn away by a scream. Not one scream, but many. Piercing, high pitched. The crying of a child. The sound of keening spiralling into the breaking sunrise.

At first, I only squatted, the hard sand real under the soles of my feet. A pounding lodged in my head. I stared at my left hand not recognising the pulpy red mess it had become; I wrapped it in the hem of my shirt, disgusted by its betrayal.

I struggled to stand; my head as heavy as a water-filled pitcher. People everywhere. Some sat or lay still, clothes tangled around their limbs. Others crept on all fours as though trying to complete their journey. The stationary black engine panted steam in sporadic bursts no longer being able to pull its load. Behind it a carriage stood intact, silhouetted against apricot clouds. Other carriages lay at angles, one, its front wheels clinging to the rails, its metal distorted into shapes. Another lay on its side like a dead dog in the gutter. Figures, fly-like, crawled from the wounded train.

A man, his dhoti in shreds, was running between heaps haphazardly strewn. Sometimes the heaps moved, mostly they didn't. He came to me. His eyes red, the skin on his cheek burnt away. He thrust a vessel of liquid between my lips then poured the rest over my head and ran on. The water's coldness shocked me. It trickled down my neck leaking onto my chest. I stumbled, stubbing my toe against a rock. The first person I came to was paan-man, still sleeping. Parted lips displayed his red marbled teeth, his hand clutched his chest, the back of his skull a gaping hole of mush.

A small boy clung to his mother's inert body. I eased him away, carried him to where a group of the 'just-living' had begun to huddle. A woman took him clutching him to her bosom as though he were her own.

Fires had sparked, hissing and fizzing; either giving up or bursting into insistent flame fed by toppled samovar pipes. I vainly reached out to retrieve a smouldering mailbag already charred black; orange flame soon consumed the jute. Fire took hold, the wooden mail van and its contents providing dry and ready fuel. Lazily it spread and licked at the toppled carriages, lapped at the human forms that lay folded over shattered windows.

'Help me. Help me. My husband.' A woman clutched my arm pulling me towards the wreckage. With a burst of recognition, I remembered the pretty lady from the station in Jodhpur. Her familiarity a comfort, one small thing that made sense. I let her tug me towards a carriage that leant precariously. Oddly, she paused to right the straw bonnet on her head despite the bodice of her dress being ripped open exposing her undergarments and the curve of a white breast.

We tripped over bodies. I stopped, halted by the sight of my smart-suited friend lying on his back. The expression on his unharmed face seemed to be one of surprise. Blood seeped onto the ground from where his legs once joined his torso. I threw up, spraying his suit with vomit. Globules of food, green bile and my own guilt spewed onto the sand.

The woman pushed me, urged me through a mangled space that was once a door. She didn't follow but called. 'Gerald. Gerald,' louder, ever louder from outside. She was Mama calling my brother and me in from play.

The carriage lurched then settled again. I inched along the aisle littered with debris. A pair of spectacles, a woman's bag, a suitcase, sleeping blankets, a blue and white striped hat box, three fingers and a thumb.

I heard his groan, saw his ashen face plagued by strips of light from the risen sun.

Panic soaked me.

'Help me, boy. Some damn thing has landed on my legs. Can't move the bloody things. I'm so hot.'

A luggage rack, loosed from its fastenings, swayed above him. He was pushing at smashed seats with his hands. A trunk, its contents spilled from the open lid, lay across his chest. His head rested on rich, plush upholstery the like of which I had never felt before.

Agony ripped through my shoulder as I heaved away the

trunk with my one good hand.

He cried out, throwing an arm to stifle the gasp that gurgled in his throat.

'Sorry, sahib.' I waited for his anger to explode.

His wife was banging on a window, mouthing his name.

'Don't mind me, boy. Bloody hurts that's all. Do what you must do. And tell my wife to stop that infernal racket.'

I hesitated over his instruction but stayed silent.

Seat cushions had crumpled inside contorted frames that jammed his legs. I wrenched off his shoes and twisted a floppy ankle to squeeze a leg from the metal that trapped it. He screamed in my ear. His nails dug into my back. I yanked and the leg came free.

'Hell. Do you know what you're doing?' Moisture poured down his face and gathered in his moustache. His lips had turned a purplish blue.

'No, sir. I work in the mail van. But I am strong. Soon I will have you out.'

He lay back, his chest heaving with the effort of breathing.

Another passenger sitting opposite leaned against the neck support and watched with empty eyes. The book he would never finish lay open on his lap.

Noise and shouting increased outside. People running.

'One more pull, sir.' He grabbed my injured arm sending bolts of pain shooting into my head. His second leg came free. Through torn trousers I glimpsed a limb covered with curled blond hairs. Jagged white bone protruded through white skin.

'Get your filthy hands off him.'

Shoved sidewards I bumped against the lifeless passenger who shifted in his seat, his head lolling to his chest. His book fell to the floor.

Men in army uniform swarmed around. 'Sergeant, lift this man out. Careful with him. This other one's a goner.'

'Bloody move.' Spit showered my face. I had scrabbled to retrieve the shoes. He would need them one day. A soldier kicked me in the shin. Shoes in hand, I prised my way through boot-clad legs out of the tilted carriage and sagged to the ground. Blood oozed from my hand. I held my head, my palm cradling the bump that distorted my forehead. The hammers inside threatened to break through my skull.

'Your name? What's your name?' The gentleman whose legs I had freed called out to me and weakly waved a hand from the stretcher on which he was being carried. He struggled to raise himself. His wife fussed by his side, her bonnet clinging rakishly to the side of her head.

'Stop. I order you to stop.' He banged on the edge of the stretcher to get the bearers' attention. His shaky voice held a note of command.

'Here, boy, over here.' He beckoned me.

Remembering I had his shoes I approached the stretcher.

'Your shoes, sahib.' I placed them by his side. His face was grey, tears pooled, ready to fall. His breath rattled.

He pushed the shoes away. 'Keep them. More bloody use to you. 'What are you called?'

'Asadi, sir.'

A clammy hand grazed my arm.

'Thank you, Asadi.'

He lay back against the pillow. His eyes fluttered shut.

If I pressed my palms against the walls of the cell, I felt a coolness, but it didn't last. The sheer numbers of men hounded into the small space meant we almost had to breathe in unison. I shifted when they shifted, lay when others stood. Sometimes I squatted with my face in the corner where a tiny sliver of air could be mine and I could see no one in the blackness. When the sun outside punched higher in the day the heat became more than anyone could bear. One or two lost their minds, screaming, thrashing, yelling, only to be taken out by the jailers and beaten. They were returned bruised, submissive. Others just gave up, stopped breathing. To be discovered only when tempers flared, and a kicking foot failed to get a response. Then the guards would haul them out by their feet, and we would fight over the crust of bread that would have been theirs.

That was bad, but the stink was worse. A bucket overflowed by the door, urine, faeces, diarrhoea. A soup, flavoured with the smell of suppurating wounds. I can't remember when the pain became intense. Perhaps it started with the shock of all the railway employees at the crash scene being forced into carts and taken to the nearby town jail. Or was it on the third, fourth, fifth day – I lost count – when yellow pus seeped through the torn off strip of shirt that bandaged my hand, when the slightest knock made me cry inside like a baby. The burning hotness of my skin spread up my arm and across my chest, lumped beneath my armpit and gave me dreams that had me tearing at the walls with broken fingernails. And all the time I saw the package, the smart man, cool and polite, indelible images that wouldn't leave me. They filed across the ceiling, lodged behind my eyelids and tossed naivety back in my face. You knew what you were doing. You knew all the time. You were trying to be big. Trying to impress.

The train driver, the ticket inspector, the guard, cooks, even the chaiwala. They were all there. At first, I could tell them apart. Now I didn't try. Others arrived, thrown into the ruckus. I recognised two from the underground student group. By silent assent, we didn't acknowledge each other. Did they know of my role? Would they tell? Would they splutter it out when unspeakable things were done to them? Would I – if a confession might make it stop?

A prison guard thrust his face against the small grille in the iron door.

'Asadi?' His lips curled around the name like he was drinking from a sewer. 'Over here. Now.' He rattled at the lock. Two men pushed forward. Let them go. I shrank into myself, a trapped bubble in my chest threatened to suffocate me.

'Not you.' One of the men was pushed back into the cell. 'You're so old your bones should already be bleached. This Asadi is a boy.'

Those of my fellow prisoners who knew my name manoeuvred me forward, only too willing to shove me out, glad it was me, not them.

The first taste of air that hadn't been breathed a dozen times before was like the evening breeze when the monsoon stops. Fresh and clean. The sudden space around me made me shake, my hands trembled, my knees felt like rubber. The other man and I were roughly herded into an empty room. Shadowy figures moved behind a small window.

We were made to step forward in turn.

A high voice, a woman's voice. Muffled, but I heard her words.

'That's him.'

I knew then I had been found out.

The other Asadi was bundled away, silenced with a cuff on the head.

They took me down a dank corridor. Far away I could hear shouting. Prisoners who hadn't yet surrendered.

The guard threw water from a bucket over my head and swiped a towel across my face. He knocked on a brown door and we waited. I stared at my feet. The bindings cut into my wrists as I shuffled forward. I didn't want to see what awaited me.

'Good God. He's disgusting.'

I could see only small feet in pointed leather shoes. A woman's feet.

'Look at me, boy. Even when things aren't good you shouldn't let yourself get in a state like this. Where is your dignity?'

Water from my hair dripped to the floor. What was she talking about?

'Madam, we are carrying out investigations.' This time a pompous voice. 'A bomb destroyed that train. We will find out who planted it.' A fist banged on the blotter with a dull thud.

I lifted my head a fraction. A small, pert Indian sat behind a desk that diminished him further. In front of the desk, I saw a cane chair and gloved hands folded in the lap of a flowery dress.

'It's him, however foul he smells now. And I do remember he had hurt his hand. Has he obtained treatment for it?'

'Of course, madam. The best.'

'You have received the letter my husband wrote. He orders this boy's immediate release.'

I jerked upright and gawked.

Another thump on the table made the inkwell rattle. 'All these men are suspects, madam.'

'Exactly, commissioner. As you will discern, he is not a man. He is a boy. You can't think he has anything to do with it. He saved my husband's life.'

She wore a different straw bonnet, but it was unmistakeably her, pretty as she'd been when I first saw her on the station platform. My glance went to her chest; no undergarments showing, no curve of a breast. Instead, a row of pearly buttons and a frill around her neck.

'How old are you?' she asked me, dabbing a handkerchief to her nose.

'Fifteen,' I muttered. I'd gathered myself enough to realise a couple of years off my true age might be in my best interest.

'There you are then.' I wasn't sure who she was saying this to.

The commissioner puffed out his chest and stood up. 'He can't be released. There are papers that need to be signed before …'

'Then I will sign them.'

'No, madam.' His splutter collected as froth at the corner of his mouth. 'Your husband must … A woman can't …'

His face was glazed with sweat. One hand fumbled to grip the edge of his desk.

'Have you *read* my husband's letter?' she screeched. 'Do you dare to suggest that is not enough? Do you know whose authority you are questioning?'

The officer's face turned purple red.

'Let me assure you, if this boy doesn't leave with me then you will be the one in a cell with those prisoners. Do we understand each other?'

The brightness of the light outside the police station made me blink and cover my eyes. I scuffled against a wall where angled shade cut across the road. The woman was fumbling in her bag.

'Sir Gerald and I are extremely grateful for the help you gave him at the time of the train crash. Your behaviour was exemplary.' She stood in front of me, her nose and mouth covered with a lacy handkerchief. 'We sought you out through the Post Office. I can't tell you how shocked we were to discover they had put you in jail. He would have liked to have come himself but he is unable to walk. His recovery will be slow, and he tires easily. As soon as he is able, we will be leaving this godforsaken country. That time can't come soon enough for me.'

A man on a bike had stopped to stare at us. A girl, wearing a thin red shirt several sizes too big, forgot about the goats she was herding and edged closer. I saw her grubby hand stretch out to feel the silky smoothness of the woman's dress.

'Get away, you urchin.' The woman used her bag to swat away the child. A stallholder shouted obscenities at the goats and the girl as her animals began to munch the green leaves from his vegetables. She ran off.

A black car drew up and stopped beside us. I yearned to touch it. I was a distorted form reflected in the gleaming bodywork.

I was glad the woman's husband had survived; he had been a decent sort. But I didn't want to listen to more of her words even though I knew I should be grateful. I wanted to run as far away as I could from this hellhole. Any minute I expected a guard to appear and haul me back inside.

She was still going on in her preachy voice. 'We would like you to accept this as a token of our thanks.' She held an envelope by one corner.

'I am not a beggar, madam. I …'

'And I'm not treating you as one. Have you seen yourself? You need some new clothes and a good meal. Show me that hand.'

I left it where it was behind my back.

'Show me. Come on, boy.'

I showed her.

She flinched, her jaw collapsing into her neck. She turned her head away, her spreadeagled fingers a shield between us.

'You need to go to the hospital. Do you understand me?' Her voice louder now.

I shrugged.

'Oh, never mind, I'll take you.' She beckoned to the driver. 'Charles.' He opened the door of the automobile. Dark, shiny, green seats glowed in the sun.

'This boy, Ahmed, is to be taken to the hospital.'

The driver recoiled. My heart began to thump.

'Asadi, madam. My name is Asadi.'

'Yes, yes. These Indian names all sound the same.'

I stepped towards the car.

'Not in there.' Her squeal was sharp as a sword. 'Charles, call that rickshaw.'

By now a crowd had gathered and three drivers pushed forward at once, tangling wheels and bruising legs.

The chosen one pedalled fast trying to keep up with the car. I bumped along in the seat behind, my hand held tight against my chest. At the hospital more people thronged. Many sat on the ground beside the gate. Waiting. Hoping that being close would cure them.

The car stopped and the woman fluttered a hand through its window in the direction of a doctor hurrying past. I couldn't hear what she said but the doctor shot a look in my direction and moved aside his stethoscope to pocket the notes she handed him.

'Come with me. This way,' he shouted and headed off up the steps.

'Good luck, boy.' The car was moving off. 'Good gracious, I almost forgot. For you.' She tossed the envelope to me. It fell short.

A nugget of anger took root in my gut and throbbed its way to my heart as I scrabbled on the ground to pick up the envelope.

My bandage stank. The doctor couldn't hide his revulsion and was too rushed to try.

'You've lost two fingers. We may save the hand. If not, you'll probably lose your arm.' I opened my mouth to protest, to tell him I was too young, but he had already retreated. Pain speared my elbow and clamped my shoulder. It was the last thing I remember.

I stayed in the hospital for nine days. Fever ate at my soul. Corpses from the train crash stalked me in a grotesque parade. They beckoned me to follow them. Only cowardice held me back. The lady in the straw bonnet scolded me, then laughed in my face. When the nightmares faded a knot of anger was a spreading tumour.

I reported to the Post Office. They told me I was no use to them with a bandaged hand.

'Go back to your village. Return when you are well.'

'But my pay?'

They dismissed me with a wave of a hand. 'You want pay for no work? Maybe you don't even have a job.'

'Go to your father's house.' My 'uncle' scoffed at my plea to stay in the city. 'Why would I let you lodge when you bring in no money? I can rent out your room. If you come back, we will see.'

I sought out my cousins. Within the house they were furtive. A glance and a nod of a head was the only acknowledgement I received. I needed them to say something. Had I passed the test? Was I trusted now? I wanted to be someone in their eyes.

'Another huge blow for the British.' My older cousin swaggered with pride as he walked with me to the bus station. 'They can imprison our leaders, but the "Quit India" campaign won't stop until they go. *We* have played a part. *Our* group. We must hound them until they leave our country. Dogs defeated in a fight.' He gripped my arm. 'There are more acts planned.'

'What can I do?' I felt the fire in my chest bringing me alive again.

He stopped in the street. 'Go home. Get well. Then return.' His slap on my back felt like a medal for courage.

Mile after mile on the tedious journey home I replayed events. Pride squeezed out shame, excitement at the future drowned out fear.

'I am a man, not a boy. I am his son. He treats me as a servant.' I shouted too loudly in Mr Chouhan's house. He sat at the wooden table. His wife brought us refreshment, gathered up Irfan, their son, and took him outside. 'This village is so backward. Nothing has changed in a hundred years. Gandhi, Nehru and thousands of others are in prison for daring to speak out. No one here cares. Do they even know?' Unable to sit still I walked the floor of the small room. 'My father counts his money and boasts about my brother who fights for our occupiers. They are losing the war. Soon they will run.' My hand throbbed and I sank into the seat opposite the teacher and leaned my head back against the wall.

'You have grown angry, Asadi.' Mr Chouhan's voice was low and even. 'Sometimes it can cloud judgment.'

I gave him no time to go on. 'In the city I hear things. I see things. How can you bear it? To be stuck in this place. As soon as my hand is healed ...' Irfan came running in wanting to clamber onto my knee, his chubby arms extended. I lifted him up and he sat solemnly between us, his thumb in his mouth. He wriggled his warm bottom into my lap and laid his head on my chest.

'He's a proper little boy now.' I traced the curve of Irfan's ear.

'Yes, he's over two years old. So quickly he grows. Asadi, do you not think I want what you want? I want it for my son. But perhaps there are different ways to achieve it. In my experience violence is not productive – it feeds the ego of politicians who use young men as their vehicles. I want my son to live in an independent India, but I want him to live in peace without fear.'

'The suggestion of forming two countries is gaining support. One for Muslims, one for Hindus and Sikhs. Jinnah is insisting on Pakistan being conceded before the British depart. He wants it to come into being immediately.' I flung the political talk across the table.

He glanced sideways, his grim face a reprimand. 'We are not so out of touch here. I have heard those statements. Politics and religion should be kept separate though I fear it may be too late for that. Is it something you would wish for, Asadi? We have lived side by side for ever. We all love India. It is our home.'

I swallowed and sighed, tiredness overwhelming me. I wanted to curl up and sleep like Irfan. To be held.

'You have been through terrible trauma. You are young. You have witnessed horrible scenes, been in prison. Wounds are not always the ones you can see, it's the ones inside that take time to heal. Give yourself that time, Asadi. Rage is always lurking on the sideline awaiting its chance to inhabit a bruised mind.' He took Irfan from me and laid him on a sleeping mat in the cool. 'They say it was a bomb – in a parcel – that destroyed the train.' He held my gaze as he spoke.

The sting of shame inched down my spine.

I leaned towards him. 'Your life is a dead end if you stay here.'

Leaving my chai untouched I walked back to my father's house.

Sita had prepared a meal. I had no appetite for food. My father sat on the step shovelling lentils into his mouth. We had little to say to each other. Even the simplest thing became an argument. The war would soon be over. British victory, he swore, was down to the bravery of the Indian regiments.

'Our oppressors are weak. The war has stripped them of their money and their resources. Their country is in ruins.' I tried to educate him. Make him see why we must take this opportunity to rid our land of their presence – using any means.

He scoffed at my wild ideals. Only ingrained respect made me draw back. I saw him for who he was. An old man who had wasted his life. He had let my mother and sister die.

The insistent ringing of a bicycle bell chased away my churning thoughts. Children ran squealing after its rider. Villagers paused in their tasks, slipped from their houses and began to gather at our gate.

Baba looked up and jerked to his feet. I moved to stand behind him. Sita stopped washing the pots. The boy held out the telegram.

'Namaste,' he muttered in our direction.

My father didn't move, his arms held stiffly at his side. The boy coughed and pressed the paper into my hand.

REGRET INFORM YOU THAT SEPOY UMESH CHOUDHURY DIED BURMA DECEMBER 1944 LETTER FOLLOWS

Official paper, official words. I read them to myself then repeated them softly to my father, faltering over my brother's name. A fly buzzed around my head.

Baba stood like he hadn't heard. I wouldn't put my arm around his rigid shoulders. I let him turn and walk into the gloom of the house. My breath struggled to find a normal rhythm. It exited my lungs in short bursts. Sita's wail broadcast the news and the other gathering women took up the ancient cry.

I ran as I always did. Into the desert, into the wadi where grains of sand, stirred by the breeze, were all that shifted.

The letter came. My father read it and burnt it. He didn't speak to me for days. He left the house early, ate alone. I heard him in the middle of the night thrashing in his bed or walking the floor muttering expletives to the walls. His face was grey, his eyes hooded. His shoulders slumped further each day like the weight of grief was too much to bear.

Mr Chouhan accepted an apology for my previous rudeness with pursed lips. I sought his solace. Sometimes we talked, often we would walk together, beyond the village, allowing a silence between us. Playing with Irfan was my relief. His giggles made me smile; the feel of his soft limbs was ointment to my aching body. My hand was healing and Irfan, with curiosity, would feel the tender new skin that grew over the stumps of my two fingers. He would study his hand, then mine, fascinated and not repelled.

The days passed. I was ready to return to my 'uncle's' house. I was stronger, restless. News of the burning of a telegraph office in Jodhpur had filled me with an excitement that could be shared with no one. I decided to take the next bullock cart out and came home one evening to inform my father only to see a dishevelled soldier leaving our compound. His face, haunted and thin, was vaguely familiar. A childhood friend of Umesh's. Seeing me, he paused and raised a hand, acknowledged my greeting and walked on. His uniform hung off him. He dragged a leg, making his gait uneven.

'Wait. Have you eaten?' I called out. 'Let us offer you a bed for the night.' He ignored me, didn't hesitate, just limped back up the dust road.

'Who was that?'

In the doorway Sita, with the hem of her shawl bunched in a fist, tried to muffle her sobs. My father, still as stone was staring after the man.

Night fell with its cage of darkness and still he didn't move.

'Baba, that soldier …'

'Umesh, my first-born son. Your brother. Died a hero. We will speak only of him in that way.' He turned away and crumpled onto his mat. 'Shut that snivelling woman up,' he bellowed from beneath the blanket that covered his head.

The dhal was cold. I pushed it around the dish with my fingers, struggling to swallow even a mouthful. Sita squatted several feet away. Her eyes swollen with crying; henna smeared across her cheeks.

'What will happen?' Her voice was broken. I hardly heard her above the restless goats.

'About what?' I wasn't in the mood to listen to her woe.

'The soldier. He was a friend, a comrade of Umesh's. He wanted to tell your father how it was. That the conditions were bad, the fighting fierce. He said we should hate the British army.' I looked at her then. Her eyes cast down, her hands fumbling with the folds of her *ghagra*.

'I listened,' she said.

The tremble in her tone banished the scolding she deserved for interfering in men's business.

'What did he say?' I shot it at her, and she flinched. Her eyes flew to the dark interior of the house where my father snored.

'He's asleep. He won't waken until morning. Tell me, woman.'

The sob hiccupped through her chest. 'He did not die a hero as your father said. He was a deserter. Many soldiers have fled. He was caught. Along with five others. They shot him for being a coward.' She stifled the wail that left her throat.

I hid my eyes with my hands, a torrent of anger tore through me. Aimed at Sita for telling me, my father for not. At Umesh and at his killers. Self-pity like a leech sucked at my blood. I curled up in the dust and wept.

I remained in the village at Baba's insistence. My resentment grew with every day.

'Tomorrow I will leave.' I could stand it no longer.

'You will marry Sita.' Father's bloodshot eyes and thrusting finger dared me to argue. I pressed back against the wall, stunned by his announcement.

I pushed at his shoulder to move him out of my face.

'I will not.'

'You will do as I say. You will marry your hero brother's widow as is right and proper.'

'I will not marry Sita. She is a peasant girl and illiterate.' I hawked it out. 'My hand is healed. I will return to my job with the Post Office. I have important business to do.' Though I shrank from his fury, outwardly I stood tall. 'Let us not fight, Baba.' I wanted to calm his heaving shoulders.

'No son of mine will ever defy me.' His eyes slitted like a cat's.

'Why would I marry an adulterer? Do you think I haven't seen you slinking from her room? Not bothering to hide your fumbling fingers scratching at your groin. She couldn't bear my brother a child. She is barren. Or else your seed too is shrivelled like a dried pea.

I am not Umesh. I am not a coward.'

He slapped me, knocking me down. My head hit the floor. The shadow of Sita fled from where she had been lurking unseen. I struggled to my feet and towered over Baba's shrunken figure. Without another word I left the house.

It was hours before I would allow any thought of my father to enter my head.

Mr Chouhan gave me a place to sleep without asking for an explanation. Later I spilt out what had happened.

'Your father is a proud man who loves his sons. He is hurting in a way we can hardly imagine. He needs your respect.'

'He says I must marry my brother's widow. A solution to serve his own ends.' I raged until eventually the teacher's voice of reason calmed me.

'He is trying to do the right thing, Asadi. Maybe if you talk to him without getting angry, he will listen.'

'No, he won't listen. Not now. It has become about me defying him. He will not back down. It is a matter of principle. My father loved my brother, not me. It's convenient if I am married off to Sita. He uses her now. She's an unpaid servant to him. He wants to be looked after in his old age.'

Mr Chouhan drew a swift breath and laid a hand on my shoulder 'Go home and talk. You are a young man now. That is how men conduct their business.'

Back at our house the gate was open. There was no fire and no cooking pot simmered on warm ashes. Our goats wandered in the dust beyond the compound picking at the rubbish and any vegetation they could find. I called to Baba, to Sita; only the chickens came running, fussing around my feet looking for food.

Father was in the house sitting on the floor his back against the wall, his head slumped on his chest. 'You are responsible for this.' His gravelly voice held an undertone of threat.

'What has happened?' Dread poured over me. 'What have you done? Where is Sita?'

He began to cry. I had never seen him do that. I stared at his puckered face as he rocked backwards and forwards. 'Umesh, my son, my son.'

I shook him. 'What have you done?'

'Sita has gone. She left in the middle of the night. A cartman came to tell me he took her back to her home village. The man gloated, wanted money to fetch her back. He said the honour of our family was at stake. I threw him out.'

I didn't believe him. I ran to Sita's room. All her belongings were gone, a pitiful heap of old clothing and a lingering smell of herbs and trapped heat was all that remained.

This wasn't what I'd prepared for. I'd expected his anger, my head filled with retorts. I wouldn't buckle. It was *he* who sent me away to work. Life had offered me a purpose. I had gained a sense of belonging and found a cause. I wasn't about to give it up.

Baba's breath shuddered in his chest. Red-rimmed, tearful eyes sought my face, his hand reached out.

The pathetic sight of this broken man whipped at my conscience. I ached to give him something.

'I will marry Brinda. The musician's daughter.' I heard the declaration as if I was an eavesdropper to the conversation.

Baba's rocking ceased. His head jerked. His shoulders straightened. 'The musician's daughter.' He stroked his lips with a finger. 'His craftmanship has become renowned. He is a rich man.'

I plunged on. 'Should her father agree to the marriage we will not live here. We will live in Jodhpur where I have a job. You can remain in this village, or you can come with us.' I stood above him determined he shouldn't see the terror in my eyes as I pelted the words upon him, all the time wondering where they had come from.

'She is educated. I would be honoured to have her as my wife.'

He nodded, rubbing his hands together. 'The marriage would be a good one — worthy of our family name. She will come with a fine dowry. Perhaps you have spoken well.'

My disgust of him reignited the embers of my fury. I left before it erupted. What had I agreed to? What would Brinda think? Would her father consider me a suitable match? The fetid air of the house suffocated me.

I fled to the desert and clambered down the steep sides of the wadi onto a sand-coloured ledge. As a small boy, I came here to think and to watch the antelope feed. I sat still and silent as I used to. The air chilled. Night clouds billowed my future into shapes of dark and light.

1945

Everyone loved a wedding and especially now when India was troubled and on the brink of change. We had listened to the *pandit* who offered guidance as to how we should live our lives. For three days there had been gaiety and laughter amongst the many rituals. Brinda's fingers now trembled in my palm as we circled the fire four times to signify our friendship. Then showered with blessings from the priest and everyone present we took our seven steps making a vow with each step to symbolise the beginning of our journey together. The whole village celebrated our marriage. Food lined their bellies, music filled the sky, and we danced beneath a bright canopy of cloth. Soon Brinda would return to her family's house for the last time. I would collect her from there, and blessed with fertility, prosperity and happiness we would leave together.

'You are beautiful. The most wonderful thing that has ever happened to me. Tell me it's real.' I whispered, putting my lips to her ear.

She smiled, her dark eyes glistened. She placed hennaed fingers over my mutilated hand.

'I will always keep you safe,' I promised.

'What do you think?' The journey back to Jodhpur by cart and then a rickety bus, had tired us. I watched her wander around the room touching the dull furniture and rubbing at the small window. My father had remained in his village where he had lived all his life. He scoffed at the idea of city life. I had found this place for Brinda and me, the first month's rent paid with the money the English woman had thrown at me. Today it looked shabby, the air stale. I sank to my haunches as Brinda pulled back the curtain to the tiny bedroom with its wooden bed that filled the space. In another part of the boarding house, a door banged and a baby cried. Outside, street sellers vied for attention with their shouts.

'Two rooms,' I had boasted. I wondered if she felt let down, more used to open space and the surrounding desert.

She touched the top of my head. 'It's perfect. So peaceful and – empty. At home, my parents, brothers and sisters, my cousins, my aunts, and uncles always talking, shouting, crying, arguing. There was never anywhere for me to study, always something to do.' I held her in my arms, let her remember, her breath warm and quiet.

'You will realise your dream of becoming a teacher. And one day we will fill the space with the sound of our own children's voices. Two, three, four boys.'

'Five, six.' She giggled and let me brush her lips with my kiss. I led her to the bedroom.

She was shy, holding her discarded clothes against her body. Happiness a fizz inside me. I lifted her onto the bed and stroked every inch of her tender, smooth skin. Our racing hearts settled to the same beat, and we found each other.

'You came for me. I dreamed of it as a girl – when sometimes we met at Mr Chouhan's house.'

Propped on one elbow I traced her eyebrows and the dimple on her cheek. 'That first time I visited your home and saw you washing clothes. That's when you stole my soul. I was fourteen. Our fathers secured the marriage, but for ever we will give prayers to Ganesha. The god of beginnings and good fortune has blessed us.'

The Post Office gave me work. They put me in the front sorting office. I was clumsy, still adjusting to my missing fingers. The place was noisy and hot, my feet ached from standing. Why, when I joined, had it been the place I most wanted to be? A chance to get out came when they needed someone to ride the trains. I volunteered. I knew what to do. They gave me the position.

Brinda was happy. Mr Chouhan had found her a place in a school with a teacher friend of his. She acted as the man's assistant. Each day she would tell me stories of the children, so eager to learn, so bright. All they needed was a chance. She was sad when a child showed promise then was taken out of lessons to work on the street or mind the animals or younger siblings.

'The authorities let it happen. Why do they turn a blind eye? The laws that could prevent it are not enforced, ineffectual. Mostly it's the girls who leave but it's boys as well. Scores of children never come to school at all.'

I pulled her close. 'That's why we fight for an independent India – so we can govern. Make our own rules. Our children can be educated and …'

'And women be given rights?' Her small face creased in determination. 'You dream the dream, Asadi. Before all that can happen, Indians must be educated. Do they know how to build railways or organise an education system? Will women be shown respect? How do you change the way things have always been? Officials, bosses – they serve their own needs first.'

'I love it when you are cross. You are sweeter than the sweetest rice pudding. Do you know how it arouses me?' I cupped her breast in my hand. She pushed it away.

'I haven't finished. The violence is getting worse. Who are these goondas who kill their fellow countrymen, attack the iron roads and the communication lines? These things are our life blood. Don't they see that? Yesterday, two Muslim families left the school. Their homes had been ransacked. A father and a grandfather were beaten up. Where is the sense in that?'

'This is what I get for letting my wife read the newspaper.' I feigned horror as I twirled a piece of her hair around my finger. Inside, with a lick of shame, I remembered the noisy, ardent voices of the student group, the evermore extreme stance that some of them were taking. They had welcomed me back. I mostly relished the evenings spent in their company, the discussion, the singleness of their purpose. Their vision was mine. I buzzed with their excitement. I would come home from a meeting, waken Brinda, and thrust into her until I was satisfied and spent.

'Your cousin has been here.' Brinda was cooking chapatis on the fire. 'He came when you were away.'

I swallowed hard and stripped off the clothes I'd slept in last night on the post train. 'I'll talk to him later.'

'I don't like him, Asadi. What does he want? He is secretive and – sinister. He comes too close. He makes me feel dirty.'

'You are imagining things, woman. Take no notice. It's men's business.' Her stiff shoulders told me she wasn't appeased. 'I'll see him tonight and tell him not to come here again.'

When she turned to me, I saw her brimming eyes. 'Why must you go to those meetings? You say you just smoke and talk politics, but I wonder what else. When you come back you are not my Asadi.' She didn't try to wipe the tears from her cheeks. 'You are high.' She dropped her head. 'You are cruel.'

I put on a clean shirt and left without trying to comfort her. I walked the streets, kicking out at dogs and beggars who impeded my way. The walls of the fort loomed above me and for a while I sat on scrubby grass in their shadow. The Cause was more to me than I would admit. I couldn't let it go. How could I tell Brinda any of this? She wouldn't understand. How could she? Soon India would be independent. Education will become important. Women's roles could change under a new regime. For now, it's men who must attend to matters of importance, take care of things when there is trouble. I hated that Brinda's words and her actions ushered in confusion and pierced the guilt that I refused to analyse. The Cause or Brinda? Brinda or the Cause? Must I make a choice? My anger rose. Just as quickly it fell when I remembered her face and her falling tears.

'Don't you see, Brinda? This is for you. You and me. We are the future. You have to let me be part of the victory. I'm a young man, a Hindu. We are in the majority.' I spoke out loud scaring off the foraging monkeys.

'But people will get hurt,' I whispered to myself.

'Jinnah and his Muslim League want their own country. Let them have it. India will always be bigger, stronger.' The vehemence of the speaker startled me; a usually quiet, earnest participant, he wore glasses that slipped down his nose. He stood, spreading his arms wide in an elaborate gesture. 'It is not enough to hit the infrastructure. We must stir up civil unrest like in West Punjab and other parts of Sindh.'

A pitcher sat on the floor in the middle of our circle. The infusion of sweet-smelling cannabis and spices scented the air. We drank the bhang liberally, refilling our glasses, hailing our God, Shiva, 'Lord of Bhang', the talk getting louder, boastful, more daring.

'We choose a single street. We intimidate them, chase them out, loot what we can, On Friday during prayers or under cover of darkness.'

The same student, becoming more excited, combed the circle with his eyes. 'Gemar, you, me, and two others.' The instruction addressed to my cousin was framed as a challenge. One guy immediately stood up. 'I'm with you.'

Gemar hollered, fisted the air, and turned to his brother who squirmed where he sat, his eyes to the floor. Gemar hawked, a gob landing at my younger cousin's feet.

No one spoke. Cold fingered each knob of my spine.

'Asadi will do it. He won't be known in that part of town.' Gemar laughed, an ugly sound that loosened tongues; a muted cheer became a buzz of conversation. 'In and out in the swish of a donkey's tail,' he claimed. 'Our faces will be covered. We'll be ready to fight.' His gestures grew brutish the more attention he was given.

I lay rigid in bed listening to the voices of the night. The gentle sound of Brinda sleeping, her soft outbreath caressed my face. I dared not touch her, dared not let my hand wander over her fragrant skin for fear of waking the animal in me. The me that hurt her, the me that I despised. My hand rubbed my crotch, feeding the hungry beast until it released its power, and I could sleep.

A pounding on the door woke me. Brinda already up. Early light lanced the gap where the curtain didn't fit the window, bleaching the colours of the room. With a tongue like a furred ball I staggered dishevelled and sweaty from the bed. My dreams had been of prison, that cell, the stink of the occupants. Hands that pinned me down, my cries for help as silent as my scream.

Brinda froze in the act of cutting up vegetables, a knife upright in her hand. Her eyes large in her pale face looked from the racket to me.

'Who can it be, Asadi?' She clutched my arm. 'What do they want that they bang like that?' Her cool fingers were a douse of water that washed away the remnants of my dream. I touched her cheek, moving her away from the noise.

'Who is it?' My voice loud enough to stop the pounding.

'It's over. Get up, man.' Gemar's voice became a shout. He rattled the lock and filled the room with his presence when I swung open the door.

'The war, it's over in Europe. The Germans have surrendered. Now the British will leave India. They are weakened. They will not fight us. We step up the campaign.' He thumped the wall and raised a fist. 'Our plan, Asadi, we carry it out tonight. We are ready.'

A gasp laced with fear escaped Brinda's lips. I moved to cover her, an attempt to stop his words reaching her ears.

'We'll turn their victory sour in their mouths. Independence will be ours. Victory will be ours.' He threw an arm towards Brinda. 'Bring some coffee, woman, some food.' His laugh hit the walls and rebounded like a fist to my jaw.

Brinda didn't move. Her eyes dulled with something more than sadness. She looked at me as though trying to work out who I was. She turned and went into our sleeping room.

'Gemar, let me get dressed. I must go to work. You can walk with me. We will get *kachori* and chai on the street.' I yanked shut the curtain between Gemar and where Brinda sat on the bed.

I crouched and enfolded her hands that lay limply in her lap.

'It is nothing, Brinda. Gemar talks big. It is not for you to worry about.' I squeezed her wrists. 'After tonight. No more. I promise.' She didn't move. My promise shrivelled like a crop with no water.

'I must go to the school. The children will be waiting. They need me.' She rose from the bed and gathered her shawl to shield her face. The door closed; its click more accusing than any words.

Brinda's look had bored into me. My turmoil became

resentment.

Oppressive heat turned my day into a melting pot of bad temper, laziness and mistakes. I yelled at the boy who dropped a mailbag and scattered post across the platform. As he scrambled to pick up the letters and packages, I stamped on his fingers so he wouldn't be careless again. Today I shared no morsel with the feral kids; I shoved them out of the way like pieces of rubbish.

The British war was over. Newspapers told of victory. Indians whose sons were fighting claimed it as theirs; stories of bravery amongst the soldiers became inflated and wilder with each telling.

My war wasn't over. Perhaps it had just begun. My brain churned with ideas, bloomed with visions of how our country could thrive under its own rule. I would be a politician. Make Brinda proud of me again.

'Be a great man, Asadi.' Mama's voice. Clear and distinct above the clatter of the station and the hissing of the locomotive. Steam from the departing engine curled over me, particles of soot fell like gentle rain. I swiped them off my skin leaving a dirty smudge, a black curse on my wrist.

I lay sleepless, waiting for the hour to come. Brinda gripped my arm as I rose and left our bed.

'Don't' go,' she said. 'I have something to tell …'

I shook off her hand and pulled the door shut so as not to see her face. The night was a shadowy void where the people who inhabited the streets were hidden to me. I didn't hear the barking of roaming dogs or the screech of fighting monkeys. Head down, I saw only my feet, the right, then left, passing in front of each other as if not a part of me. I walked alongside Gemar. If he had any misgivings, he hid them behind a stream of meaningless conversation, punctuated with curses when he received no response.

We met the others at the junction of three roads where a smell of dhal lingered around a street seller's cart. The man slept curled against a wheel, one hand outstretched, palm upwards as if begging. In silence we followed our leader as he beckoned us into a dark cleft around the back of the mosque. I stumbled against a pile of rubble, felt the sting on my ankle, a trickle of blood down my foot.

Gemar, pumped up with bravado, circled us. 'So, each of us takes a house. Threaten the occupants, frighten them, rough up any that show resistance. Wreck the place, pocket anything of worth. Then out.' He clapped our shoulders, his eyes darting in all directions. 'Remember, surprise is our weapon. Keep your faces covered.' He thrust an arm out. 'The Cause.' Three of us clasped hands.

'No.' Our self-appointed leader, the student whose idea it had been, expelled the word into the night. 'A change of plan.' Even in the gloom his pupils shone white. His eyes moved slowly around the small group imprinting his stare upon us. I felt sick at the pleasure he was taking from the moment.

'We set fire to the houses.' He paused letting the command sink in. Opening a bag he revealed four staves, cloth doused with fuel and bound around their ends. A pungent smell escaped. 'Once lit, we toss them through a door or window space. These are poor dwellings; they will go up immediately. You three will take the houses, the mosque is mine. Then we run – fast, in different directions – and enjoy the bonfire.' His voice stretched high and thin.

'But ... the families ...'

'The families, Asadi? They are Muslims. It will warn and terrify the rest of the community. Let them all go and live in Jinnah's promised land.'

My hand hovered in mid-air then fell to my side. I thought of Mr Chouhan, his wife and little Irfan.

'But using fire. Is this necessary?' My thumping heart risked breaking through my ribs. Sour sweat leaked into the scarf that covered my face.

'Are you not man enough? Is your country not worth fighting for?' The student forced a stave against each of our chests, his body taut with pent-up fury.

Gemar spluttered, affronted at being upstaged. An angry face shoved up close to his, dared him to question.

'Go.'

Within minutes, under the portal of the mosque, flames began to take hold.

Down the street our fourth man was the first to fling his

flaming torch through a doorway. Then Gemar wheeled his around his head with a roar and flung it with force.

My burning stave threw heat and light into my face. I ran past the others and stopped in front of a miserable dwelling, its windows boarded with wood. The muscles in my legs and arms refused to obey my brain like I was swimming in ghee. Fear racked my chest.

I stood alone in a tunnel of white, deaf to all sound.

Gemar growled behind me and snatched my stick. It arced through the dark, rolled like a kicked ball until the hungry fire grabbed at the material that served as the family's entrance. The blaze illuminated the shapes of sleeping bodies within.

A woman stumbled from the house. Her flaming clothes undressed her. The baby she held at her breast was a burning pyre.

Her piercing scream stabbed my trance and turned it to hysteria.

I fled.

Pushing against those who ran in the opposite direction, I leapt over piles of rotting vegetable leaves, slipping on shit from cattle and goats. Noise drummed in my ears so loud I begged for it to stop. My lungs rasped for air, and I fell, vomiting into a gutter. I inched towards a stinking stream and splashed water over my head, licking at the liquid that wetted my lips. I crawled through that open sewer until my strength ebbed out in my tears and I curled up like a child and prayed for my breath to cease.

Brinda ripped off my clothes and washed me. She scrubbed at my bleeding knees, her lips a straight line, her eyes dull. When I pushed out an arm to stop her, she cast it away and scrubbed harder. All the time she was silent.

'Brinda. I'm ...' I couldn't finish. The words swam in the bowl of water with my blood. She stopped her frantic rubbing and looked me in the eye.

'You're what?' She threw down the cloth so that water slopped onto the bed. She crossed the room to the window and pulled back the drape of brightly coloured material she had so proudly hung a few days ago. There was an orange glow in the distance like dawn lighting up the sky. A dawn at midnight. I buried my face in the sheets and sobbed.

For days Brinda's anger was a grim presence, an impenetrable wall that shame wouldn't let me breach. She made me go to work. She barred the door when Gemar came round leaving him to rant on the landing. I yearned to tell her I loved her, that she was the only reason I wanted to go on living. Cold ran through my veins. I shivered until my limbs shook and my jaw ached. Diarrhoea coursed out of me, the smell always in my nostrils.

Perhaps it was the new moon that eventually lent me courage, my companion as I walked the floor while Brinda slept. The same moon that silvered the edges of the buildings, deepened shadows and crept into our room bathing her pillow in light, touching her hair. I sat beside her on the bed listening to her breathing, watching the small twitches of her lips as she uttered sounds I longed to capture. I let my fingers run feather-light over her body feeling a warmth I had forgotten existed. Over the small mound of her breast, circling the creased skin of her navel, over the curve of her belly. A rounded curve that I cupped in the palm of my hand. Breath jammed in my throat.

The sun chased away the night as I watched her sleep. Could she forgive me? How could I begin to forgive myself? Let me be a great man, I pleaded. Let me be a good father.

'I tried to tell you.' Her murmur was a smile that teased her mouth in sleep. She struggled to open her eyes, her warm hand found mine and nothing else in the world mattered.

Brinda grew pale and tired. Although her belly swelled her arms were thin, her legs barely able to support her. Always she was sick. I would hear her heaving into a bowl she kept beside the bed, see her wiping flecks of vomit from her face.

'Will you take me back home to see my family?' she begged, her eyes dark and sunken.

'How will you manage the journey? You know it's long and rough.'

'I want to see the cloud shadows playing chase across the desert, to feel the wind and the sun on my face before the rains come. My mother, my sisters … It will mean so much, Asadi.'

In her mind I could see she was already there. Her hand caressed her stomach. 'He will be a child of the sands. It will make me well again.'

The roads were uneven; the number of motor cars had increased, but the drivers went too fast, blasting their horns at the animals and pedestrians that littered their path, startling them into panic. A bus took us only part of the way. After it dropped us, I helped Brinda onto the hard seat of a cart and clambered in beside her. She gripped my arm and I stroked her swollen fingers. 'We'll soon be there,' I whispered, wishing I could sponge the green hue from her face and make her pretty again. 'We'll call at Mr Chouhan's, let you rest, take some chai, before we walk the last part of our journey.

'To your father's house?'

'No. I will go there later. You need the care of your mother.' Brinda closed her eyes and laid her head on my shoulder. I rubbed the swell of her abdomen, a gush of warmth spreading over me like the first rays of morning.

Mr Chouhan's door was shut despite the heat. I turned the knob but couldn't open it. I heard the shifting of a lock, and the door opened a fraction.

'Asadi,' he breathed surprise, his smile said welcome.

'Come in. Come in.' He grasped my shoulders and shook me gently. 'You are a man now.' He clapped me on the back as if congratulating me on my new status. Nadira hovered in the back room, her features hidden by the covering she held to her face.

'Don't be afraid. It's Asadi with Brinda. Let Irfan come and greet them.'

Irfan peeped from behind his mother's sari and bowled into the room. I caught him in my arms, lifting him to the ceiling while he wriggled and giggled.

Nadira studied Brinda, holding her at arm's length. 'Tut,' her tongue clicked. 'Tut, tut.' She lifted Brinda's puffy hand then stroked her face dabbing a tear away. Coaxing her into a chair she turned to us.

'Shoo,' she flicked at us. Go for a walk. Take Irfan. He needs fresh air. We have women's business.'

Irfan clapped his hands. 'Yes, yes.' He jumped up and down. 'Lock yourselves in.' Mr Chouhan instructed his wife.

Surprised, I glanced at my friend, the man I had so long admired. He looked older, his face creased, flashes of grey in his hair.

Outside, we turned away from the village towards the desert. I breathed in the hot, dry air, a scent of herbs faint upon the breeze. Irfan ran ahead kicking up the sand.

'Nadira is scared.' He sighed. 'I am too. Maybe it's not good that you walk with me. It seems, in some people's view, we should not mix. There are those who believe all Muslims should leave.' He stared to where the horizon smudged into the sky and a streak of cloud, purple as an aubergine, thinned to a narrow line. 'This is my country. I have never known another. It is my son's too.'

'In towns there is unrest. Not here surely. You are a teacher.' My words sounded hollow as dry bones.

'A teacher, government official, professor or farmer. What does it matter? Suddenly it is our religion that identifies us, Asadi. I fear for the world my son lives in, and the one yours will be born into. They may not recognise the India we have known.'

We watched Irfan draw patterns with a stick in the sand.

'The British are leaving.' Mr Chouhan's voice was low and grave. 'They are fatigued after the war, in no mood to focus on a distant empire. How will we manage independence? It will come at a price. Our politicians – we no longer know who carries the truth. Are we to be divided? Will hatred erupt? Civil disobedience is growing. It will get worse. People are not who we think they are.'

Visions of flaming houses leapt before me. A woman's screams loud in my ears. Shame coloured my cheeks. Sweat trickled between my shoulder blades. No words squeezed through my aching throat. We continued our stroll in heavy silence. Irfan circled back, his bright face dulling as he scanned our faces. He walked beside us, his hand slipping into his father's.

Nadira and Brinda met us on our return. Brinda had a different shawl around her neck the bright colours giving a flush to her skin. She clutched a medicine bottle.

'It will help take away the sickness.' She looked at Nadira for confirmation.

I turned to wave as we left. Mr Chouhan, his wife and Irfan stood together, a sepia tableau shrouded in shadow.

As we approached Brinda's family house, she held up a finger. 'Shush,' she said. Her father was sitting outside on a wooden stool. The notes of his music floated over to us as the day died and darkness stole across the emptiness. She touched her belly and looked at me.

'Our child is dancing.'

I nodded. 'Everything is going to be all right.' We both believed it.

A hoot of joy and a muddle of brothers, sisters and cousins chased away the moment as they ran towards her. A smile transformed her thin face.

When later I walked back to the village in the dark, fires in the compounds gave off tongues of light and the restless sound of tethered animals punctuated the night. Baba was sitting on the step where he had always sat. No goats bleated a greeting. My eyes strayed to the door of our house willing Mama to appear and Laksha to come running to welcome me home. The doorway remained empty, only a black hole beyond.

Baba stood, slowly uncurling his back, his one hand holding a stick, the other rubbing at his hip. He greeted me with a nod.

'Namaste. Are you well?' I asked him. He seemed so diminished, he had shrunk in height, barely reaching my chin. His clothes hung off his body. 'Baba.' I grasped his arm fearing he would fall.

'You've been away a long time. Does the army not need you now?' He shook off my hand. Even his voice sounded cracked and frail. 'What do you want?'

My fists clenched and I swallowed the retort that had come so easily to my lips. I forced myself to put an arm around his shoulder and help him to sit back down.

'Who is taking care of you?' I wanted him to look at me, but his bent neck kept his eyes cast down. He fumbled to roll a cigarette and I took the paper from him, secured the ends, and lit it from the glowing embers of the fire that burnt near his feet. He puffed slowly, the burning stub the only pinpoint of warmth in his face.

'A girl comes. She can't cook. Your mother – her chapattis – no one makes them like her. Fluffy and hot, straight from the fire.' He twisted his hands in his lap.

'Baba, I have brought Brinda to visit her family. I am to become a father.'

He jerked. 'Who is Brinda?'

Saliva turned sour in my mouth. 'My wife, Baba. Brinda is my wife.' Weariness overtook me. 'I am tired. I have been travelling all day. Let us get some sleep then we can talk in the morning.'

He waved towards the house. 'Your mother will see to you.'

I agreed with Brinda that she should stay with her family for a short time. Her uncle would make the return journey with her. He had business he said. I wondered what that might be.

'Already the desert air is putting colour in your cheeks, and you are rested. I will take Baba back with me and try to settle him. He can't look after himself. He thinks I am Umesh. He has forgotten he ever had a second son.'

Brinda brushed my cheek. 'He is an old man, Asadi. He is confused. Perhaps when the baby comes it will give him something to live for.'

I grimaced and wished I could stay here with her.

'Baba, you are to come and live with us in Jodhpur where we can take care of you.'

He sat by the door; a dribble of spit leaked from his lips. He wiped it away with the hem of his lungi. His empty gaze gave no indication as to whether or not he understood.

'Soon you will have a grandchild. Perhaps a grandson. He will need his grandfather to teach him.'

I tried to find more to say, but my words withered in the heat when he uttered no reply.

The girl from the village came asking for money. 'I have looked after him well when you were not here.' The accusation was clear adding another layer to the leaden feeling in my stomach. I paid her generously and asked her to watch over the house. I knew with certainty that before we had even reached Jodhpur some of her family would have moved in.

Baba had few belongings. Under his stare I gathered them together. He stumbled into the room. 'You are a thief. This is my home.'

I stifled a groan and finished what I had to do. He trailed behind me protesting at everything I touched.

'Baba, I can't leave you here. You will die.'

'I will stay here with your mother.'

Each breath I took increased the ache. 'Mama passed away when I was fourteen. And Laksha. They had the pox. Remember?'

Baba raised his hand. I flinched but grabbed his wrist twisting it away from my chest. Sobs racked his shoulders and he sank to the ground. With my hands under his armpits, I lifted him to his feet.

'Baba, is there anything else you want to take?' I forced myself to say it gently.

He shuffled across to our *mandir*, the shrine that my mother had always so lovingly tended, picked up the *murtis* and rubbed each figurine clean on his hip before putting it in a cloth bag. The wilted flowers and shrivelled fruit looked desolate left in the empty niche. With a grunt he pulled his mattress from the corner and scrabbled in the dry, dusty earth removing a tin box which he tried to shield from my view with his body. It was squirrelled into the bag.

'I don't want your money, Baba.'

His face creased into furrows, he brushed me aside with his stick and went outside to sit on the step again, his bag clutched to his chest.

Mr Chouhan came to see us off. He patted Baba's arm and offered me a *dabba* of *dhal* that Nadira had prepared for us.

'For the journey,' he said. He gripped both my hands with a feeling of finality.

'One day, we will meet again, inshallah.' He paused lips pursed. 'India stands at a precarious moment in her history. They speak of night. I don't know how it will turn out. The cry for partition grows ever louder. We must pray that peace prevails, and these extremist thugs don't spread their poison. Namaste, Asadi.'

'Namaste.' I turned from his moist eyes.

The monsoons came, washing Jodhpur's streets clean, sweeping rubbish into piles, and destroying the meagre shelters erected by those who had no homes. Every day clouds banked like juicy bunches of grapes until the sky turned lead grey and the rains fell.

Baba didn't settle when I brought him to the city. Weeks passed and still he stalked around our two rooms, feeling the walls and touching our possessions, moving them into different places. I made a bed for him near the fire, but he was restless and in the night I heard the creak of floorboards. Several times when I came home from work, he'd gone missing. I searched the streets until I found him, usually in the same place, sitting on a broken wall staring over a piece of wasteland clutching his bag to his chest.

'Baba, you will get lost, or worse still beaten up and robbed. Let me put your bag in a safe place.' He slapped my hand as I went to take it from him, his face grey with anger, his eyes hooded with fear.

'You always were a scoundrel.' His harsh words sharp as a butcher's knife.

I fixed a lock on the door so he couldn't wander and asked his cousin's wife to bring him food on the nights I was riding the trains. I had dreaded visiting the boarding house and feared seeing my cousins again. I missed the passion of the student group discussions, but I had no appetite for arson and murder. I was afraid of their scorn and their wrath, of being drawn back into their activities. I imagined the meetings, voices rising and political lines being drawn as our colonisers limped towards retreat. The voices of our politicians, Jinnah, Nehru and Gandhi were becoming more fervent as each vied for power.

A breeze blew into the landing from our partially open door. Inside I heard the rise and fall of voices.

'Baba.' Fists clenched, I pushed it open with my foot. He

was sitting on a chair, his bag on his lap. Brinda's uncle leant against a wall and Brinda was handing round cups of chai. The window covering fluttered like a rising bird. Fresh flowers adorned our small shrine and the room smelt clean.

'Brinda.' I hesitated. My heart skipped. 'You look so ... different. So pretty.'

Her face flushed. 'Pretty? When the size of my belly almost stops me walking and your child kicks day and night and keeps me awake.'

I wanted to hold her, kiss the small odd-shaped mole that I knew blemished the skin between her breasts. I wanted us to be alone.

'Such a good thing that I'm back. Your father all cooped up and this place smelling like a chicken's roost.'

'Come on, woman,' I laughed, 'Refreshment not scolding is what I need. What a day I've had.'

Three pairs of eyes swivelled towards me; Brinda poised with my chai in her hand.

'I am to be made a supervisor. The Englishman who took me on as a lad is leaving, going home. An Indian is taking that position and I am moving up to take on his vacant role.'

A clap on the back from Brinda's uncle and a hug from Brinda. I smelt the oil of her hair and wanted her more.

Our two meagre rooms were too small to accommodate all these people, so I took Brinda's uncle to my father's cousin's house. Perhaps if my old attic room was not in use he could sleep there.

'What is your business in Jodhpur?' I asked as we dodged between people eating from the stalls and groups of men squatting at the roadside talking and sharing hookah pipes.

'We are in the same business, Asadi.' He stopped walking and gripped my arm.

'What? The Post Office?'

The smirk on his face told me that wasn't what he meant. I had never liked this angry man. Now his bullish manner turned me cold inside. I needed rid of him.

'Let us walk.' He pulled me away. 'You know there are Muslims in our village, tilling our land, eating our food. We must cleanse ourselves of them,'

'No.' I hated that my voice was a squeak. 'Those families have lived there for centuries. They are our neighbours. Besides Gandhi preaches non-violence. We must let our politicians sort it out.'

'Baa, politicians.' He gobbed into the dusty road. 'Lost your balls, have you.? Don't think I don't know. The underground movement has many fingers, boy. Word is …'

'Leave it. I want nothing to do with your evil plotting.'

He laughed, showering me with spit. People stopped to stare when his guffaw interrupted the familiar sound of the streets. 'Bit late for that.' He clapped me on the back like we were the best of friends. The bystanders walked on, no longer interested.

'That teacher. I've seen you with him. What poison is he spouting to our children?'

'Mr Chouhan? You're not fit to even speak his name,' I shouted. 'He is a decent man. He has been a friend and mentor to me. He taught your niece, and enabled Brinda to become a teacher.'

'Ah, I see there is still fire in your belly. Good, we may use it one day.'

'Here is my father's cousin's house. I am not coming in. He will look after you. I hope your business is concluded. In future you are not welcome in my home. I will not eat with you.' I didn't wait for a response. I turned from his steely gaze and ducked down an alley. My rudeness and revulsion were bile in my throat; dread made me weak.

'My mother will come soon, Asadi. Our child is almost ready to be born.' I looked at Brinda hoping she couldn't see the panic her words invoked.

'You must rest. Baba claims your time.'

'I rest when I can. Your father is not a burden. When you are not here, he is calmer. I think when our baby comes, he will be proud.'

She screwed her face, her palm on her swollen belly.

'Will I fetch the woman?'

'No,' she smiled. 'It's not time for the *dais* and her helpers.' The tinkle of her laugh slowed the pulse that beat in my neck. 'Come, feel.' She placed my hand close to hers and I felt her belly, hard as a rock. 'See, the baby is telling us that it is preparing.'

'Brinda, how do you know these things?'

She leaned back in her chair and touched my cheek. 'Just as you learnt how to be a man from your father, so I learnt all that a woman needs to know from my mother and my aunts.'

Baba sat beneath the window, his wispy hair ruffled. He lifted his head, his mouth open, as if trying to capture the faint breeze. Had he tried to teach me? Was it me who had rejected him?

'Your uncle ...'

'He has gone home. I think you do not like each other.'

'He ...'

'I know, Asadi.' Her finger traced a vein on my wrist. 'The promise you made ...   after that terrible night. It is more important.'

With my extra wage I secured another room in the house so that Brinda's mother could stay. She was a thin woman who laughed and sang all day. She and Brinda would huddle together giggling at something their eyes told me was not for my ears. She fussed over my father, swept and cooked so that every day I would breathe in the sweet smell of herbs and spices in the hallway when I came home.

But not this day. I opened the door to find the room full of women and Baba huddled in the corner rocking back and forth.

'It is Brinda's time, Asadi. Take your father and leave us to get on with things. The *dais* is here. I fetched her after breakfast.' A straggle of hair had escaped from her bun. Her touch was firm as she eased me out.

'After breakfast! That is hours ago, it is almost night.' A sound like the howl of a desert dog came from the other room. I stepped towards it, held back by Brinda's mother.

'Go,' she said. 'This is no place for a man.'

'But.'

'Go, Asadi. It will be many hours yet. It is normal for a firstborn to be slow. It means the baby will be a thinker, be wise, not a scatterbrain always in a hurry.'

I took Baba into the busy streets, holding on to him as I would a child. I bought dhal, from the cart but it stuck in my throat and Baba finished both bowls. He led me to his broken wall and we sat watching rats scurry amongst the debris, pausing to devour discarded food scraps. Night clouds swept across the sky until morning began to soften the spaces between the buildings and creep across the wasteland.

Baba placed his hand on top of mine and patted it. 'My son. Listen.' I could hear only the caw of the birds as they rose in black flocks.

'It is time. We must hurry back to your home.' A tear escaped from his watery eyes and trickled slowly down his cheek.

The baby, his head a crown of black hair, nestled in the crook of my elbow. He pouted his lips and wriggled a bare arm from beneath the blanket. Brinda's mother watched, her face flushed and mottled red.

'He is strong. He's a fighter,' she said.

I could only nod, not trusting myself to speak. I stroked his palm with my finger, he clasped it tightly in his small fist. The curtain behind which Brinda lay was closed. No sound came from beyond. The *dais* had gone home. We were left in the luminous morning light with a silence broken only by the mewling sounds of the baby as he sucked on his knuckles.

I stared at the blank space. Brinda's mother held me back with a gentle hand on my arm.

'She is tired, Asadi. It has been a difficult birth. Soon she will wake, then you can see her.'

That's when I heard Brinda's faint call of my name. 'Asadi.' She lay still, her face flushed. Her hair, damp and matted, streamed across the pillow. I hesitated, scared to touch her. She seemed as fragile as porcelain.

'I have given you a son.' She held out her arm and I snuggled our baby into her embrace. I kissed her hot, moist forehead.

Her mother brought me honey and using a finger I performed the age-old ritual and wrote the sacred syllable *oum* on his tongue. Startled he opened his eyes, dark pools beneath long lashes.

'We will call him Ravi.' I gave him his name and whispered it in his ear as I offered thanks to the supreme god Shiva, who my own mother had always held dear.

'He's beautiful. I swear as long as I live that harm will never cross his path,' I choked. 'I love him so passionately it hurts like a hot blade.'

Brinda, sighed, her eyelids quivering shut, her warm breath seeping over Ravi's now sleeping form.

'You wear a frown like a headband. What troubles you, Asadi?' Brinda held Ravi to her breast; he sucked fiercely, all the time wriggling his podgy legs. 'This young man is never still. Only three months old and he is already restless, eager to make his way in this world.'

'But what sort of world? I am frightened for him, Brinda. Frightened for us.'

'Why? It is almost certain the British will leave next year, or at least the year after. We are even now preparing for our independence.'

She looked delicate like the petals of a desert flower. The pink of her sari blushed her cheeks with a rosy tinge.

Responsibility weighed on my shoulders. It sometimes woke me in the night, a twist of dread paining my gut.

'The Muslim League have taken seventy per cent of the vote in the elections.'

Baba grunted from across the room. He listened but how much of what I was saying would make any sense? What would he remember?

'What does it mean?' Brinda asked.

I hated that I was the cause of the tremor in her voice.

'It's not for you to worry about. You have enough with little Ravi.'

'Asadi, don't treat me like a village girl with no education.'

My stomach knotted. I leant across and kissed her neck, smelling the milkiness and feeling the warmth of her body.

'The election of the League shows there are increasing numbers of Muslims wanting to have their own country. It's to be called Pakistan. If it happens there will be millions of people uprooted. Muslims going one way, Sikhs and Hindus going in the opposite direction. I can't bear to think about Mr Chouhan. He told me he considers India to be his country. He doesn't want to leave. What if he is driven out? What if it was us? How would we feel?' I trailed a hand through my hair trying to curb my imagination. 'Everything is so tense. The division will not be peaceful.'

Brinda stretched out a hand to hold mine. 'You worry too much. Any trouble will only be in big cities like Bombay, Calcutta and Delhi. Not here in Jodhpur. The authorities will sort it out, clamp down on troublemakers.'

'I want you to be right, but I have this awful sense of foreboding. Your uncle said there were moves back home to drive out the Muslims from our village. Good men, like Mr Chouhan and his family.'

'That cannot be. Don't say such things, Asadi.' Her face creased. Her hand flew to her mouth.

'You're right, I expect. I am making too much of what I read and hear.' I could see my words were not reassuring. Ravi slipped off her breast and his high-pitched wail gave voice to the anxiety that filled the room.

Ravi grew into a happy little boy. Nine months old and his bright smile could lift me from the black despondency that I felt at times. I tried to keep my worries from Brinda but the political situation had become more tense. India's politicians quarrelled amongst themselves. It seemed to me that they had lost sight of the original goal and building their own power base had become more important than the interests of the country and its people.

On a day in July our boss Mr Kapadia strode into the sorting office, mounted the lower steps of the staircase and addressed us from above. We paused in our tasks; the general level of noise sank to a hush. He looked stern, thick eyebrows knitted together, lips tight.

'Our duty is to keep our Post Office running. You will no doubt have heard that Mohammed Ali Jinnah has called for the sixteenth of August to be observed as a Direct Action Day. He has called for meetings to be held in towns all over India. I remind you that in Jodhpur it is not an official holiday.' His even tone became a shout. 'You will attend work as usual. If you do not, you will be sacked.' At that, he descended the steps, pushed through the workers and returned to his office.

A murmur stole into the quiet. Workers turned to mutter to each other. A box of mail crashed to the floor causing a diversion I suspected was deliberate.

'Get on with your work,' I barked above the growing disturbance. I marched along the aisles urging people back to their posts and splitting up small groups, mainly Muslims who had huddled together. A man pushed forward. I knew Mirza. A loudmouth my boss had called him. Always ready with some quip that made his fellow workers laugh and fed his ego. His work rate was poor compared to others. He stood in front of me, so close that I could see the gap where his front teeth should be. A tight scar pulled his mouth to one side.

'*Our* leader wants us to hold demonstrations.' His emphasis was not lost on me. 'It's *our* right. To show we are behind him. Muslims *will* have their own country.' He pushed his shoulders back and sneered.

I swallowed the lump of dread his words brought. I would deal with him later. It being the holy month of Ramadan I was wary: tempers were often short and the Muslims tended to be either languid or lazy, fasting during the day and eating only after dusk.

'You heard what the boss said. Your choice.' I turned from his smirk. A muffle of cheers and jeers trailed me to my office where I shut the door and inhaled deeply. I swirled a swig of water around my mouth to try to get rid of the sour taste that lingered. I was not afraid of the man, only the reason behind his outburst.

As the sixteenth of August broke, I warned Brinda to stay at home. 'Do not let my father out. Be sure Ravi is safe,' I told her. Though the storms had been fewer this season I prayed for a monsoon downpour that would keep the streets clear of demonstrators.

The night staff were still handing over when I arrived early to work. I sensed a restlessness, a fidgeting amongst the men reporting for the day shift. Furtive glances were cast in my direction, conversations halted when I drew near. Mirza's station was empty. Most of the other Muslims were missing too. I didn't ask where they were. No one offered an explanation. I knew they were waiting to see what action I would take.

Around midday noise levels increased and a few of the men gathered around the entrance peering into the street. I climbed the stairs to a small landing from where I could see a column of marchers filing between the buildings carrying aloft the flag of the Muslim League. They carried posters bearing Jinnah's face and congregated in the square. A holler came from an onlooker, 'Go to your own country.' A few of the marchers turned on him, hurling abuse and he melted into the side streets. I couldn't see how many more had gathered at the rally. A speaker shouted into a megaphone, his voice rising and falling riding the roars of the crowd. I didn't hover to watch. I urged people back to work and closed the heavy Post Office doors. The distant drone of the megaphone went on for about an hour. When I next looked the crowds had dispersed and the streets were filling up again with the humdrum of normal life. Cows had wandered back; a camel slept in the middle of the road. I heard the familiar sound of bicycle bells rung as their impatient riders wove amongst animals and people. I began to breathe more easily, the workforce chatter quietened, the tension dissipating as the heat of the day clung to their skin.

In the early afternoon Mr Kapadia beckoned me to his office. He tugged at his sweat-stained kurta, his brow beaded with moisture. Even the flies were still in the stultifying heat.

'A storm will break soon and clear the air,' I said in an attempt to ease the tautness from his body.

He wiped a cloth across the back of his neck. 'The telegraph office is getting word of escalating riots in Calcutta. Street fights between Muslims and Hindus. Men armed with weapons have rampaged through the streets.' He thrust a telegram into my hands. The words swam before my eyes, but they confirmed what he had told me.

I sought to reassure him. 'It's peaceful here. The demonstration and the meeting passed off without incident. A few of the men failed to turn up this morning. I will deal with them when they return.' I stood straight to show him I accepted my responsibilities and to seek his respect.

'It's bad, Asadi.' He didn't appear to hear what I'd said, his mind elsewhere.

I blinked at his use of my first name; he so rarely addressed me in that way. I sat down on the chair beside his desk. Instinctively I felt he needed my presence, but I was at a loss as to know what to say. The supervisor from the telegraph office interrupted our silence when he barged in waving another telegram in his hand.

'My brother in the communications office in Calcutta just sent this.'

VIOLENT CLASHES BROKEN OUT ALL OVER CITY STOP MUSLIM GOONDAS RANSACKING HINDU BAZAARS STOP ORGANISED RETALIATION BY HINDUS AND SIKHS STOP FIERCE FIGHTING STOP LOOTING RIFE STOP

Neither of us spoke as the seriousness of the situation seeped into even the darkest corner of the room.

'Jinnah said he wanted either India divided, or India destroyed. He may have sealed our country's fate.' There was no rancour in my boss's tone, just resignation. Deflation hunched our backs.

My eyes smarted. How had it come to this? The struggle for an independent India. The fight that once had stirred my soul and roused my passion now left me filled with horror. Had those rioters in Calcutta felt that same passion? Would they come to feel like I did, forever steeped in disgrace?

'I'll return to the floor, keep the workers on task.' I needed to get out of the room before my shame exposed me.

'Asadi, this news must not reach the men. It will break soon enough in the newspapers.' My boss thumped his desk making the inkwell overflow; the black spillage spreading into a widening stain.

At the end of the shift the men left. Mirza had not returned. I hoped I wouldn't see his face again. I knew I would have to fire him but feared the unrest it would cause. I hurried home scouring the faces of passers-by who mercifully seemed oblivious to the riots happening a thousand miles away. To my relief I found Brinda and Baba secure in our rooms. Ravi crawled across the floor to me, and I buried my lips in his soft, warm neck, his giggle bursting the taut bubble of strain the day had left.

I quickly ate the food Brinda had prepared. I couldn't settle.

'I'm going back into work.' I said this as I laced up my shoes and grabbed a jacket.

A frown of suspicion flitted across her face. I thought her mistrust had diminished but at moments like this I knew she had only buried it. 'There have been serious riots in Calcutta. Our telegraph office is buzzing. I can't just sit here. I need to know what's happening.'

'Why, why must you go? What difference can you make?' She pulled back the curtain and looked into the blackness of the cloudy night.

I shook my head. She couldn't be expected to understand.

'What is the news?' I asked of the man whose brother was in Calcutta. He looked gaunt, his hair a greasy trail when he raked his fingers through it for the second or third time in quick succession.

'The violence has subsided ... a thunderstorm has emptied the streets. They've imposed a curfew – my brother says the police will soon have the city under control.' His broken sentences didn't convince me he believed it.

We sat around drinking chai, the room a fug of cigarette smoke. Everyone seemed reluctant to go home, eyes flicking to the telegraph receiver whenever any new telegram came through. I must have dozed because it was after midnight when a colleague woke me, knocking my elbows from under my head.

Snatches of conversation whirred within the room.

'Armed killers.'

'Marauding mobs.'

'Hindus killing Muslims. Muslims killing Hindus.'

'The slums alight.'

Men crowded around the central desk, anger and shock barely contained. We waited, each with our own thoughts.

Nothing more came through. The telegraph system fell silent. We slept on the floor snoring into someone else's face. Groans and gripes met the cool air of early morning, the stale smell of disquiet surrounded us all.

Someone said, 'Reports were probably exaggerated. The

police will have dispersed the mobs.' No one answered him. I hoped he was right. At that moment the telegraph printer sprang into action. Breath trapped in my chest wheezed from between my clenched lips.

HUNDREDS OF CORPSES LITTER THE STREETS STOP CARNAGE UNABATING STOP

The operator adjusted his earphones and yelled for quiet. The tick of the clock on the wall became the only sound.

We waited. But that was it. There was no more.

I crossed to the sorting office with weariness hanging from me like a limp rag, nausea gagging my throat.

Worse news filtered through. Slaughter on a huge scale. Women raped, and children torn limb from limb. Complete chaos.

Over the next four days the bloodbath raged. The newspapers talked of a pall of smoke and had pictures of piles of bodies with vultures and dogs ripping at the flesh. Stories of ordinary Calcuttans joining the goondas, of local police taking sides and standing by whilst citizens were hacked down and beaten to death with staves.

I devoured every word of print. 'Brinda, listen to this. It says, *'Calcutta is under mob rule. Swathes of the city have become no-go areas. The police were conspicuous by their absence. Troops have been moved in. The rioters were equipped with knives, swords, cleavers and metal rods resulting in heavy casualties. They estimate between 4,000 and 10,000 people have died with up to 100,000 wounded. There are reports of mass rape and baby killings'*

'Asadi, stop. I don't want to hear these things.'

She plucked Ravi from the floor and clutched him to her chest.

I tossed aside the newspaper. 'I'm sorry, I thought you wanted to know.'

'I do, but not the detail. Is it ... is it under control?'

'They are calling it the Week of the Long Knives. Now politicians are blaming each other.' I gathered Brinda and Ravi into a huddle. I stroked her hair and felt the shudder of her shoulders as she cried silent tears. Ravi, thinking it all a game, squealed with delight piercing the anguish of our misery.

1947

The Hindu press had been full of the massacre of the Hindu population and the atrocities inflicted on women in the district of Noakhali in Bengal. Further violent riots in other towns littered the last few months of 1946. I chose carefully what I told Brinda.

At least work was going well. Being a supervisor suited me. Ever since that night of carnage when news of the Calcutta killings had broken, Mr Kapadia had taken me into his confidence and made it apparent he valued my opinions. He was a focused man, fiercely proud of his job and his position. We discussed the worsening situation in the east and the deepening animosity between different religious groups, but always in relation to the workers and the service.

'At all costs we must ensure the mail gets through uninterrupted. That must be our priority.' He would pace the floor of his office, fists clenched, as if warning anyone who prevented it would have to deal with him. 'There may be occasions when you have to take charge at the rail station, Asadi.'

He would squint at me and nod as I muttered my assurances.

I told Baba I was a man of importance. I wanted him to be proud. Any boasts shrivelled to nothing under his blank stare. Only Ravi could reach him and bring a smile to his lips. Baba used to lift him onto his knee and rock him to sleep, then as he had learnt to walk, the two of them would sit side by side murmuring away in a language only they seemed to understand.

My son was a beautiful little boy. His skin soft and unblemished, pale like the first paring of a waxing moon. We took him to see the desert on the edge of town. He cried with excitement and toddled with arms outstretched towards the fiery red ball of the sun as it slipped below the horizon. We marvelled at the child we had produced.

'One day he will be a professor,' Brinda exclaimed as we watched him scrabble in the sand chasing a burrowing spider.

'Listen to this.' My excitement made Brinda look up from her sewing and startled Baba into wakefulness.

'What is it, Asadi ? You always have your head buried in a

newspaper.'

'The British Prime Minister, Clement Attlee, has appointed a man by the name of Viscount Louis Mountbatten as Viceroy of India who is to oversee the transfer of power to India – not later than June 1948.' I waved the newspaper in the air. 'Next year, Brinda. Nineteen forty-eight and India will have her independence.' My voice spiralled into a cheer.

'Hush,' she laughed and then scolded, 'You will waken Ravi.'

I relished the part of my job that enabled me to oversee the postal staff who worked the trains. I had missed my overnight trips, remembering the power of the iron monsters as they sped through sleeping villages and towns, the smell of the desert air and the sight of the sun as it spread shifting rays over a brightening sky. But recollection brought other visions too: of toppled carriages, torn limbs and lifeless bodies. I would remember and regret. Always praying for forgiveness. The boy I was then had inhabited a different body, one I no longer recognised.

I told Ravi about the big trains. He sat still his eyes fixed on mine. 'There are big black engines that puff smoke from their funnels. And a man who is hot and sweaty, as mucky as coal, who stokes the fire to make the engines strong enough to pull twenty carriages.'

'This big,' he would squeal, his arms open wide.

The day I took him to see the trains started early. He shook me awake. 'It's morning.' He puffed round our small room pretending to be a train.

The station was a cram of people. I held Ravi's hand but still he was jostled and bumped by people's baggage.

'Up, up.' He raised his hands. I scooped him into my arms and wove through the crowd to the puffing engine that stood at the end of the platform.

Ravi watched, silent beside the engine's size and its might. I felt his small heart pounding as he pressed closer to me. We peered into the cab and saw the fire being fed, felt the white-hot heat from the open hole. The stoker wiped the sweat from his chin with a coal-black hand leaving finger streaks across his nose.

Ravi pointed at the man. 'Tiger,' he giggled. The train let out a loud hoot. He clasped his hands over his ears, his eyes wide and staring.

'It's very busy today.' I shouted to the train driver as he mounted the steps to the footplate.

'Every day, sir. People leaving.'

'From here? Why?'

He shrugged. 'A sahib tell me it is knowing which side their bread is buttered. I not understand what he means.'

'But these passengers are not British. They are Indian.' Reality hit me in an instant – 'Muslims.'

The driver raised his hands in a gesture of helplessness.

Angry shouts coming from the far end of the platform stopped any further conversation. A horde of youths wielding sticks ran between passengers who were trying to board the train. They randomly banged on the train windows, frightened people with their noise, struck out at men, women and children, hurting them as they barged through the crowds. Bags were ripped from hands and possessions strewn over the ground. They punched a chai-walla sending him sprawling, cups shattered, tea spilt.

I ran from the station, Ravi's face buried in my shoulder, his body quivering.

'No like trains,' he told his mother when we got home. He climbed onto my father's knee, curled into a tight ball and sucked his fingers with noisy guzzles.

I sat with my head in my hands. Scenes flashed behind my closed eyelids. I became aware of Brinda standing beside me, of her hand on my shoulder.

'What is it, Asadi? What has happened?'

I swallowed hard trying to form the words. 'It's started here, Brinda. It's started in Jodhpur.'

'What has? Tell me.' She crouched down and prised my fingers from my face.

'It was horrible. A gang of young men – they attacked passengers at the station. 'I paused, struggling to make sense of what I'd witnessed.

'Who were they? Why were they attacking passengers?'

'The mob: Hindus and Sikhs, Brinda. Prowling together, looting. The passengers – were mostly Muslims.

'Leaving India their home.

'Brinda, what have we done?'

Unrest seeped like spilt ghee into conversations I overheard in the street: amongst the food sellers, in the cafés where men sat in huddles, between women who gossiped over the vegetables. The banter that usually produced laughter in the sorting office, shrivelled into sullen silence. Workers were guarded, eyeing each other with suspicion and distrust. Tempers frayed and arguments erupted. Most of the Muslims left, disappearing one by one overnight without a word. The next day their bench would be empty. No one asked why or where they'd gone.

I liked to leave early for work, when the air was cool. Outside the building where we lived, I found a woman sitting in the dust her face covered with a hijab, her bare feet bloodied and cut, the soles like raw meat. Two children stood silently by her side; a baby cried in her lap. I tossed her a few rupees and ran back upstairs. Brinda gave me water and a crust to take to the hapless group. When I returned, they'd gone, the empty space filled with their desolation.

I saw them again later at the station curled up at the foot of a pillar. All asleep but for one child. He shrank into his mother's body when I approached.

'Where are you going? Are you waiting for a train?' I bent down to talk to him.

The boy shrugged.

'This train is going to Karachi.' I pointed at the carriages where people were pushing and shoving to get on. Children cried, women wailed, men flung out their arms or grappled with footholds to climb onto the crowded roof already jampacked with individuals including a goat.

The child shook his mother's shoulder. She woke to find me peering at her. She pulled her son closer and shielded her head with her other arm.

I beckoned and smiled trying to allay her fear. What had she been through to infuse her eyes with such terror?

'Your husband?'

She shook her head.

'They killed him,' the small boy said, his voice flat, defeated.

I picked up the boy and his sleeping sister. The mother scrambled to her feet ready to protect her children.

'Come.' I pulled her sleeve.

I bellowed at the top of my voice using the authority of my uniform to push through the crowd. People parted, frightened by my yells. I lifted the children into a carriage seething with families and their belongings. I laid my hand beneath the woman's elbow to help her up the steps with the baby. She jerked her arm away as though stabbed. The swarm closed in, and the little family were consumed by the chaos.

Overseeing the mail that day seemed so futile. I couldn't get the woman's face out of my mind. I went home, held Brinda's hand and cried.

Every day it was the same. Desperate families escaping. Fleeing in panic, their fears fed by what they saw all around them and by the rumours of random killings and rapes. Indians slaughtering Indians.

I was used to the same newspaper seller greeting me every morning by waving a paper in my face. He was no more than a young boy. Calloused, bare feet with a grubby shirt and torn shorts he had the loudest voice on the street.

'Slaughter in Punjab. Hindus retaliate. Villages burning. Read it here.' He paused to sell a paper to another passer-by then stuffed the rupees into a pouch around his waist.

'How do you know?' I asked him. 'Can you even read?'

The boy grinned. 'No, sahib, I cannot read but I have big ears.' He flapped at the side of his head with his free hand. 'Balvinder smart. I listen plenty, so I know what to say. Bad trouble in the Punjab means I sell lots of newspapers.' He squeezed his bag of money and jigged on skinny legs.

'Do you know where the Punjab is?'

He pouted. 'I do, sahib. It is many miles – over there.' He waved in no particular direction. 'Sir, my family very poor.' He rubbed his belly. 'One day I will be an important man like you, earn lots of money. I will give it all to my mother. Then she can feed my many brothers and sisters ...'

'You cheeky scoundrel.' I laughed at his big cow-eyes in his grimy face. I bought the paper and added a few extra anna coins.

'Tomorrow, I keep a newspaper for you, sahib.' he called after me as he did every morning. 'You are my best customer.' He made me smile. It lasted only until I read the headlines.

Local civil war breaks out close to Delhi

Hindus break truce. Twenty Muslims killed in the village of Naurangpur. Organised mobs retaliated. Four Hindu villages alight after skirmishes escalate along a 50-mile front.

I hurried to share these facts with Mr Kapadia at our morning meeting. Sometimes he would want to talk, at other times he was too distracted, shuffling piles of papers on his desk. Weariness etched his features.

'Where are the British soldiers?' I moaned. 'Why are they not sent to quell the riots? They are always too late.'

Mr Kapadia shook his head. 'The British are going to leave. The officials are worn out and cynical. What's it to them if India tears itself to pieces?'

Mountbatten, the British viceroy, announced that he would speak to the nation on the third of June, and he invited each of the Indian leaders to follow him. The day was unbearably hot, the sun a sizzling sphere of heat in a bleached sky. Sweat gathered under my armpits and trickled down my ribs.

Anyone who could get near a radio did so. Employees crammed around work benches. Will there be one India or two? Most thought they already knew the answer but here was the opportunity for the politicians to confirm it.

The door of the boss's office was ajar, and he shouted, 'Come in, come in' as he reached up to a small window, high in the wall, trying in vain to push it open to find some cooler air. He gave up and wiped the moisture from his upper lip with a white handkerchief.

'Mr Kapadia, the men have a wireless. Shall I tell them to get back to work?'

'No, no. Sit down, Asadi. It would only antagonise them. It's everyone's future after all. Let them listen.' He gulped a mouthful of water. It glugged as it passed down his throat.

The voices of the leaders dropped into the stuffy room from

the brown Bakelite radio on the boss's desk. He twiddled the knobs to increase the volume, a whine of static foiling his attempt. First to speak was Mountbatten who asked the leaders to convince their followers to accept partition and move forward.

Baldev Singh spoke for the Sikhs.

Jinnah followed him, his tone glum. *'The plan does not meet, in some important respects, our point of view.'*

'What else does he want?' Mr Kapadia groaned. His foot tapped incessantly on the floor.

Then Nehru.

'It is with no joy in my heart that I commend these proposals to you though I have no doubt in my mind that this is the right course ... We stand on a watershed dividing the past from the future. Let us bury this past in so far as it is dead and forget all bitterness and recriminations. Let there be moderation in speech and writing ... There has been violence – shameful, degrading, and revolting violence – in various parts of the country. This must end. We are determined to end it. We must make it clear that political ends are not to be achieved by methods of violence now or in the future.'

We sat in silence. The clock marked every second.

Mr Kapadia exhaled loudly as if with relief. 'So, India will have its independence but without its north-western and north-eastern lands.'

'And it will lose the tens of millions of its citizens who live in those areas,' I said, my voice stretched. 'But will the madness stop?'

He poured a glass of water for us both and pushed mine across to me sending a sheaf of papers fluttering to the floor.

I stood in the shadow of our rooming house wall watching Brinda as she squatted on the dry earth winnowing the rice. 'After our politicians spoke to the nation, we all breathed a sigh of relief,' I said, addressing the top of her head. 'We had certainty. Now there are reports of bombings in the Punjab. Not too many have been killed but there are hundreds injured. Imagine the terror.' I hesitated, reluctant to go on. 'I've been thinking, Brinda – you should go back to the village, take Ravi and my father – at least until after Independence Day. There you would have your family for support.'

She paused, with the winnowing fan clutched in her hands. 'And who would look after you, Asadi?' She lifted her head, her unblinking eyes held mine. 'We will stay with you.'

My stomach cramped, shrinking from the sudden wash of panic that coursed through me. I crouched beside her and brushed back the hair that had fallen across her face. 'Promise me, Brinda. If you are ever afraid … if anything should happen to … You will take Ravi, keep him safe.' I eased the tray from her hands so I could hold them. 'Promise me, Brinda. Promise me.'

She nodded and shook her hands from my grasp. 'You are scaring me with your talk. We are just an ordinary family. Nothing is going …'

'That's just it. It's ordinary people who are …' I held my head between my hands. Ravi's cry from our room upstairs told us he had woken.

'I need to go for a walk. I need time to think,' I said as heat flushed my face. Brinda straightened her *ghagra* and collected up the rice. Her cool hand brushed my cheek and she went indoors.

June faded with no let-up to the torrent of horror stories reported in the press. Rumours spread like the flash floods of the monsoon. They took root and grew in the strangling heat between the storms.

'The telegraph office has been chattering all night.' Mr Kapadia shook a sheaf of telegrams then laid them on his desk and stamped a heavy paperweight on top. 'The British parliament have approved the Independence Bill. We have a date, the fifteenth of August.' He stood up then sat down again abruptly. 'Only twenty-nine days away.'

'So soon.' The words escaped my lips. How long had I dreamed of the day we would gain independence? Now it felt like a runaway train hurtling towards us without a driver to halt its motion or slow it down.

Mr Kapadia nodded. 'Already there's disruption. Twice this week the mail's either been delayed or not got through at all. I want you to go and check what's happening, Asadi. Find out where the problem is. Sort it out.'

'I'm hearing from the men that there's chaos at some of the

stations on the route to Karachi. They tell me the flood of migrants has become a surge. Muslims heading either west or east and the minorities in those areas coming the other way. People are fighting to board the trains. Everyone's scared. There is more talk of random attacks and killings.'

'Go and check for yourself, Asadi. Travel as far as Munabao. See if the problem lies before or after there. If we need armed guards in the mail van, we will get them.

'There's something else I want to talk to you about.' Mr Kapadia came to the front of his desk, so we were only feet apart. 'When all the hullabaloo of independence has settled, I am to take charge of a bigger area. I am to move to Jaipur or Delhi. I have recommended that you succeed me here.' He paused and placed a hand on my shoulder. 'You are a good man.'

'We'll be able to get a better place, Brinda. We can have our own front door. More space for Ravi to play. A room for Baba.' I grabbed her waist and whirled her around.

'You need to get the position first,' she said with shining, laughing eyes.

'I will, I will. He as much as said so. He said I was a good man.' I turned to Baba, knelt and held his cold, bony hands. 'Do you remember Ma used to tell me to be a great man? I will be one day.' His rheumy eyes stared blankly. Perhaps he sensed my excitement because he clasped both his hands around mine and squeezed.

To hide my emotion, I turned to Brinda. 'Tonight, Mr Kapadia wants me to travel overnight with the mail on the train, find out what's happening. Why it's not getting through. He trusts me, I can't let him down.'

'Of course you must go but I will worry about you. I hear such terrible stories.' Her beautiful forehead furrowed.

I kissed the top of her nose. 'I'll be home before you notice I've gone.'

'When you're not here your son misses you. And I do.' She peeled Ravi off my leg, lifted him up and held us both. 'Be careful,' she whispered in my ear.

At Jodhpur station mayhem greeted every train. I was relieved when the guard blew his whistle and we pulled away from the ever-growing crowds. The carriages bulged with passengers; many clung to handrails on the outside or balanced on the roof. The train, like a snake bloated with parasites, wove through the desert. In the mail van, parcels and letters had been tied up in sacks, labelled with the name of the station where they would be unloaded and set in piles. My three fellow mailmen opened their *tiffins*. The smell of warm samosas, subji and chai filled the van. Their conversation became a hum. Everything felt orderly and predictable. The pulse in my neck slowed. I experienced a guilty thrill of pleasure as the train thrummed over the rails.

It didn't last. As we travelled through the night, I saw houses burning, tongues of orange flame leaping into the dark or curls of smoke winding above charred piles.

Crumpled shapes lay beside the track. I saw a child spreadeagled on the sand. A rush of memories thundered in. 'There are corpses,' I shouted over the engine noise into the gloom of the mail van. One of the workers was still awake. He lifted his head, a shoulder twitched. 'They fall off.' He went back to picking his nose.

Stop after stop the train was delayed by the chaos. Hordes of miserable peasants clutched their ragged possessions. Sometimes they dragged along a goat or a sheep, or a bellowing cow, its eyes wide with fear, froth dripping from its mouth. Everywhere, fathers, mothers or children carrying siblings. They clogged the surrounding roads and filled the platforms with their stinking bodies and excrement. They were a hungry mob. Wails, cries and screams rose to a cacophony.

At Munabao people teemed around the van as we tried to unload it. 'Get out the way,' I screeched. 'It's not a carriage. You can't board here. Let the mail through.' I batted at people's heads sending them stumbling backwards. Others swarmed over the fallen to fill the empty space. We pushed the heavy, cumbersome trolleys laden with mail sacks; the wheels damaged legs and crushed arms. Nothing it seemed had value anymore. By the end I didn't care.

The train departed and continued its journey to Karachi with its load of human misery. It grew smaller until it curved away and all I could see was a plume of smoke. The first streaks of morning lightened the sky and the mounds of bodies cluttering the platform began to stir. I bought *chaat* from a street vendor. A girl followed me and stood watching. She thrust out her flat chest and wiggled a hip. 'Two rupees, sahib.' The food clogged my throat, and I gave it to the child. She sat in the gutter and ate every scrap.

The train on which I planned to return was already late, first by minutes then an hour which became two.

'Every day it's the same,' the station manager told me. His eyes were bloodshot, his tone weary.

'I'm here to find out why the mail's not always getting through. To discover where the problem lies.'

He stared at my uniform then at my face. 'The mail.' He shook his head. 'Some trains scheduled to stop here don't. They slow down, see the madness, go straight through. People still try to jump them. Body parts strewn all over the tracks. That's what I have to deal with. And you're bothered about the mail.' He walked off, leaving me to swallow hard.

Beside me a woman tried to stem a flow of blood from her head. A teenage girl flew past, hounded by rampaging men. She sobbed and pleaded, her clothes in disarray.

I screamed at a soldier who stood and watched. 'These goondas are running riot. Molesting, stealing.' I snatched at his jacket and shook him. 'Do something.'

He shoved me away. 'What?' He threw up his hands. 'I'm only one. We are too few.' He melted away, choosing to save his own skin.

I felt helpless. Defeat crawled like a fly over my skin. The train arrived. It looked like the one I'd left earlier only this time with a different set of refugees, fleeing in the opposite direction. I pushed my way towards the mail van, reaching it just as a thug threw a lighted stick into bags of unloaded mail. He ran off, lost in the commotion. The mail workers stood and watched.

'Get brushes, water. Use your feet,' I yelled at them. We put out the fire eventually. The contents were a blackened heap.

'You stood by. What if I hadn't come along? You represent the Post Office. Where is the pride in your job?'

The three men shuffled their feet. 'Sahib. It's every day.

Trouble all the time.' One of the men gestured with his hands. Another scoffed and turned away kicking at the charred remains. 'What do you officials know stuck in your safe offices?'

I should have sacked him for his insolence. I let it go. He was right. What did we know?

I sat apart from them on the return journey. Whenever the train stopped, I offered to help. They clearly resented my interference, so I let them get on with it. The disorder didn't let up. At least there were no more fires. What was I to tell Mr Kapadia? A loud hoot from the engine vibrated in my ears and shook me from my anxious thoughts. Reading of the chaos in the newspapers was nothing like seeing it. Those empty eyes, the futility of it all. How did any mail get through at all? Lack of sleep numbed me, my head pounded, my chest ached with shrivelled hope.

At Jodhpur station, in an attempt at conciliation, I called out, 'Let's get this job done, then we can all go home.' The men gave a grudging nod and together we hauled the undamaged sacks of mail onto a trolley.

A jeer came from behind. A shoulder thrust into my back.

'No longer the big manager then. You stack the mail now.' A stick struck me across my legs. I wheeled about and recognised my assailant as an idle man I'd sacked from the post office. A Hindu. I'd seen him at the temple.

'You're an ignorant fool,' I yelled in his face. His eyes were sickly yellow, his mouth curled into a sneer.

He swung at a young girl of about ten who ducked under his arm. He grabbed her by the hair yanking her to him, pressing her into himself; his hands roamed over her body.

I caught him full in the face with my fist. His nose exploded into fragments; blood spurted over the terrified girl. She squirmed from his grasp as he tried to protect himself. I threw him to the ground and kicked him hard. Again and again. A few of his gang closed in. I picked up a metal bar lying inside the railway van and wielded it in arcs to fend them off. The man lay bleeding on the ground.

'You're marked.'

I heard the threat but couldn't tell who bawled it. They hauled their groaning friend upright and staggered away, his arms around their necks, his head lolling.

'Cowards,' I shrieked after them, then I vomited over my shoes – my throat burnt by the caustic food.

My boss flipped his paperweight from one hand to the other as he listened to what I had to tell him about the disruption to the mail. His frown deepened when I recounted the story of the mob setting fire to the sacks of letters. The mole on his nose moved up and down with every crease of his face. My hot, bruised knuckles were a reminder of my fury, but I made no mention of the fight.

He groaned like a man in pain. 'This is terrible, terrible. It will get worse, and we will be held responsible.' He fumbled to light a *beedi* and drew deeply on the cheap cigarette. The smell wafted across the room. He tossed me the packet. I refused with a shake of my head.

'You look tired, Asadi. It has been a long journey and an upsetting one I'll warrant. Go home.' He sank his head into his hands, the red tip of the cigarette close to his ear. 'Only the Gods know what will happen when the borders are drawn up. What then?'

I slid out quietly, the door shut with a sharp click. Outside, heat shimmered off the road. I ducked into the bazaar, its narrow alleyways creating their own shade. The air was sweet with the fragrance of incense and cinnamon. Brightly coloured spice powder was moulded into cone shapes and arranged in rows on shallow dishes. I bought mango *lasse* and let the cold yoghurt drink slide down my throat. The horrors of the night felt like something I'd imagined. I longed to sleep but feared they would reappear if I closed my eyes.

Across the alley, two women, one young, the other old, sat on stools in front of bales of vibrant cloth and saris. The younger of the two, wearing a turquoise garment edged with silver thread, was pale skinned, kohl deepened her eyes, emphasising her high cheekbones. Her perfect face with its ruby lips made me want to stare. In contrast, the older woman wore widow's white. Wisps of hair escaped from her head covering. She beckoned me over.

'Buy for your wife. She will look so beautiful you will not be able to stay away from her bed.' She cackled with delight and

pressed a hem of a purple sari into my hand. 'Silk, the finest.'
The cool material glided through my fingers. 'Or you prefer
orange like a marigold, or blue the colour of midnight?'

'Auntie. Sahib-ji's wife will not be a village peasant dressed in
dazzling colours,' the girl softly scolded, her voice as tinkly as
water from a fountain. 'She would like pale shades, the colour of
blossom or the tinged petals of a lotus flower.' She pointed a tiny
foot in a jewelled slipper as she reached for more saris.

'No, no, not today.' I held up my hands. 'I will bring my wife
so she can choose.'

Other women crowded round fingering the multi-coloured
lengths. Their excited chatter let me slip away unnoticed.

A gift for Brinda. The idea grew in my mind. What would
please her? I saw wall hangings and pillowcases, bright fresh
vegetables, plump tomatoes and long emerald beans. I couldn't
decide. Too jaded to think I left the bazaar only to be confronted
by a boy with a string of jangling bangles looped over his
shoulder. He looked like my newspaper seller. Similar faded
shorts with ragged edges and a shirt too small, tight across his
chest. In his upturned palm he displayed ear studs, rings and
brooches. It wasn't the cheap jewellery I noticed but his fingers.
Two of them were missing.

'Like mine.' I held up my hand and showed him my stumps.
He leant towards me and stroked the top of them as though he
wasn't sure they were real. He grinned. Touching each of my
thumbs and fingers in turn he counted to eight then did the same
with his own hands. He laughed so loudly a blind woman sitting
in the dust shouted 'Jiji'. She waved a white stick, alarm in her
voice.

'Maa, it's all right.' The boy placed his hand on top of the
woman's head. He was still laughing and splaying his fingers. I
pulled out two rupees and dropped them into the woman's lap. I
touched the boy's shoulder and walked away. Before I'd even
gone the length of a building, I heard a slap of feet. 'Namaste,
sahib-ji.' The boy caught up with me. 'For you.' He held out a
glass bangle, gold in colour, set with a crimson stone as red as
the setting sun. He pushed it forward, forcing me to take it. I
scrabbled for coins, but he tossed his head and held up his
two-fingered hand. 'Same, same.' A grin split his dirt-smeared

face and he ran back to his mother.

Brinda stopped chopping vegetables when I pushed open the door. Her hand flew to her breast. 'What has happened?'

'Nothing has happened. Mr Kapadia sent me home to sleep. I have been up all night. Where is Ravi?'

'He and your father are napping.' She crossed the room and placed her hands on my arms pinning them to my sides. 'You look so tired. Tell me, was it bad?'

'Worse than I imagined. So many refugees, the trains are bursting with them. There is violence. People are dying.'

She rested her head against my chest and for a moment we stood unmoving.

'I have a present for you,' I said, laughing as I reached into my pocket and produced the bracelet. 'An urchin gave it to me. He was happy because he had found someone who had lost two fingers like he had.'

'It's pretty.' Brinda twisted it around, then eased it over her wrist so it lay with her other bangles.

'I wish it were gold.' I touched the red stone. 'You are my jewel, always in my heart.' I pulled her close and let my tears fall.

Independence Day loomed closer. Excitement and fear a deadly potion we all imbibed. Twenty-nine days became twenty-one, then fourteen. The town filled with people arriving from the outlying areas by whatever means of transport they could find. Bullock carts brimmed with families. Mothers with new borns, grandparents staggering. Others being lifted. The young carrying the old. All were headed for the station.

'Mr Kapadia-Ji.' I knocked on his open door, reluctant to disturb him. His mood these days was unpredictable. Sometimes he would call me in and we would talk, other times he would shout, his face dark with fury and exhaustion. The piles of paper grew on his desk dwarfing him. 'This Englishman, Radcliffe. When will he complete the work of dividing Bengal and Punjab?' He held his head, his fingers in his hair. 'Who is he anyway? They say he has never been to India.' He muttered expletives I hadn't heard him use before.

'There's a man outside asking for a job.' I tried to draw the boss away from his black thoughts. 'He says his name is Rabin Singh. He is smartly dressed and speaks well. He says he worked as a civil servant in east Punjab.' I omitted to say I'd seen the tremor in the man's hands, or that his turban failed to hide the gash above his swollen, purple-yellow eye.

'Hire him, Asadi, if we have a vacancy. But tell him to keep it quiet or we'll have hordes more refugees wanting jobs too.' Mr Singh had already asked on behalf of his brother and his nephew who also needed work, but I decided not to mention that.

'I am profoundly grateful,' the man said when I told him he could start tomorrow. 'Our family numbers fifteen in all. If I at least have a job it will help.'

'Where are you living?'

He looked down at his feet. 'We are managing, sahib.'

'And your face?' I pointed to his eye.

He ran his hand over his beard and closed his good eye. His chest heaved. 'I will be here tomorrow.' He squeezed the words from between tight lips. 'I am a good worker. Namaste.'

'I have baked pakoras, Asadi. Take them.' Brinda pressed a bag into my hand. 'Give them to some children. I can't bear to think of so many going hungry. We have so much. When I see such misery everywhere I thank the gods for our good fortune.'

'Ravi,' I called to him with my arms open wide. He came running, his giggles swirled as I swung him round. 'Be a good boy.' I kissed Brinda on the cheek and squeezed Baba's shoulder.

I joined the hordes who headed for either the bus station or the railway. I needed to hurry if I was to meet the train from Hyderabad, but it was difficult in the congested streets. Ahead, a bullock cart lay toppled on its side, one wheel still slowly spinning. Bowls and cooking utensils, people and bundles of clothes were spread across the road. The driver yelled at the bullock and hit the bony-haunched animal with a stick. Its eyes rolled back, nostrils flared. The panicked beast pulled frantically between the shafts before falling to its knees.

I pushed past the crowd that gathered around the stricken group. I heard the screech of the train and the hiss of its brakes as it approached a platform. The mail van was at the back; I reached it as the wooden door slid back and two men jumped out.

'Any trouble on the journey?' I shouted over the clamour of passengers trying to get off at the same time as others were desperate to board. One of the mail carriers shook his head. 'Sahib, it is crazy.' He began to unload parcels onto a trolley while I and the other man tried to fend off the crowd and keep looters at bay.

The sound of a gunshot bounced off the vaulted roof of the station scaring the rooks and crows into flight. A scream rent the air. I craned to see what had happened. A terrified mass was scattering in all directions. Fear shuddered down my spine. 'Imbeciles,' I yelled.

'Get this lot off.' We threw the bags out of the van in a frenzy of activity to a backdrop of rising wails.

'Sahib.' A Muslim man with a beaten face gripped my arm and thrust a baby at me. 'You buy? Girl child. My granddaughter. Very quiet.' He laid the bundle on top of the parcels like she was a piece of discarded rubbish.

I seized his *thobe* and lifted him off his feet. His head jerked back in shock; I threw him against the train banging his head against a carriage door. I hauled him to his feet and shoved the now crying infant against his chest. He took it and fled. More wrenching cries from further down the platform. Raging, I tore towards the noise. Came closer. The primitive howl I heard was mine. A woman lay on the ground, her red wedding sari bright between men's legs. Leering eyes turned towards me, the stink of men's body odour like vomit in my nose.

'Hey. It's him. Get him.' The screech hurt my eardrum.

Thugs grabbed me, tore the buttons off my shirt and ripped it from my chest. Yanked me aloft.

'Aargh. Let go of me.' I wrenched at a man's hair pulling loose a handful.

'Get some of this, mail man. We've had our fun.' Held horizontal I bumped over heads. Hands tugged at my trousers, and pants, stripping them to my ankles.

'*Gaandus.*' I spat and kicked. The chants and jeers grew louder as I heaped on insults.

My feet thudded to the ground. I stood astride the Muslim bride, her sari open, like a gutted fish, her legs apart. A breast. A fuzz of black hair. Shredded skin. Blood seeping.

Already dead. Her staring eyes faced her husband who lay nearby, half his head blown off, an arm reaching out for her.

That's when I heard it.

'Asadi, Asadiii …'

A drawn-out shriek. Its abrupt end. I jerked towards the yell. The crowd blurred. The margins dissolved. A cone of white light. Clearly I saw Mr Chouhan, yards away on top of a carriage roof, bent over. Irfan dangling. Nadira, her swollen stomach silhouetted. I heard her unceasing howl.

The blast of a whistle.

The train lurched.

Irfan slipping – slipping – slipping into the gap, onto the rails.

The locomotive gathered pace.

Time ceased. Everything in slow motion.

Me – Mr Chouhan. Mr Chouhan – me. Shame a thrusting dagger.

I yanked up my trousers. Pushed, shoved, bawled a way out of there.

Another platform. Another train. Hands snatched at me, hauled me in. The train door slammed. I buckled. Hit the carriage floor between a sea of legs. Irfan slipping … slipping. My mind shut off.

'Here. Have this.' A man squeezed a wet cloth between my lips. 'Suck it.'

I thrust his arm away, banged my forehead with a fist. A scream. Who was screaming? On and on, never-ending. Strangling my brain. There's something I should remember. No, no, don't let me. My heart a gong inside my chest.

Minutes, hours, daylight, darkness. Stale air, urine, vomit on my chest, kicking feet, crying.

'Put this on.' A man, maybe the same man, urged my arm through the sleeve of a jumper. 'We're nearly there.'

His words made no sense.

'Come on. You can't give up now. Bombay. We're in Bombay. I can see the docks.' With my arm over his shoulder, he dragged me. Someone else helped him for a while then let me go.

The slap of water. A smell of fish. Shouts. A ship. Smoke. People everywhere, milling about.

Stumbling up a gangplank.

'Stay there. I'll come back.'

The man rammed me into a black space underneath a boat. A boat? I didn't care. I begged only to die.

12

'And so I came to England, Lily.'

'But …' I gripped his hand, emotion smothering the questions I was scared to ask. I thought I couldn't cry any more tears yet still they slipped down my cheeks.

'I have upset you. Forgive me.' He took a shuddering breath which made him cough. 'I hold a great sadness which never goes away. It is buried deep in my heart together with the love I once knew. That I keep safe. I am fortunate to have known such love. Not everyone can say that.'

'Brinda and Ravi …?'

'Did they find me; you want to ask?' His chin lifted as he followed the flight of two brightly coloured leaves that twirled slowly to the ground. 'They say if you catch a falling leaf in autumn you must make a wish,' he said and smiled at me. 'I pretended that one day they would come to England. I wrote letters. The first few I posted. There was never any reply. After a while I still wrote but never sent them. I had brought dishonour on Brinda too, on my family. How could I have faced her? Nothing I could have said would have caused her to despise me less. My son deserved a better father.

'Always I returned to that day. Even now I see it clear in my mind. Mr Chouhan, his yell for help. I see Irfan's blue shirt. Him slipping. If I'd run – if I'd run, I might have saved him – I didn't even try. I didn't move, Lily. Disgrace is like a layer of skin, wrapped so tightly around me that there are times when I can barely breathe.

'Nadira's scream … still wakens me.' He stared into the distance. 'I am haunted by what Mr Chouhan saw. His last sight of me … It's my punishment to be shackled with shame. I let them down in an unforgivable way. Time passed and then it became too late.'

I ached to hold him. 'Would it be all right if I hugged you?'

'I think I would like that.'

I drew his bony frame close, cradling his head, trying to

squeeze out the sorrow he'd shared.

'For a long time, I wouldn't let myself remember anything. Later, a memory would occasionally sneak in unbidden, like a slap on the head.'

'A flashback.'

'Yes.' He nodded, stroking the stumps on his left hand.

'I was on that ship for about three weeks. I had no papers, nothing. Many Indians were the same, desperate to escape the violence. The boats were crammed. The authorities had lost control. It is hard to describe the chaos. I didn't utter a word even to the man who kept me alive. I never knew his name. He brought me rice, dipped my fingers into it and guided them to my mouth; he made me drink. I surrendered to exhaustion. Confusion and panic the alternative. I blocked out all thoughts.'

Asadi trembled. 'The days were stifling. The ship packed. The decks teemed with every kind of Indian, all running away from something. Soldiers too. Noisy British soldiers. I didn't sleep. Hot nights, thick with stars. Seething ports. The man brought me blankets when it became cold. I still shivered; the chill crept into every bone. Grey skies. Rain. Endless heaving sea.'

'You don't have to tell me more. You are distressing yourself.' I don't think Asadi even heard me.

'One day the man forced me to my feet, held me upright against the ship's rails. Everyone on deck was silent, watching land appear. White cliffs, green fields. He pointed to them like I was a child. I was more helpless than a child.'

A smile brightened Asadi's face.

'For a brief moment the cliffs sparkled, the fields flooded pink and gold by the sun. Brinda appeared to me, as beautiful as she looked on our wedding day. It helped me to go on.'

'You two look deep in conversation.' Adam stood in front of us looking from one to the other. 'I'm interrupting. Sorry, I'll come back later. I ... I was just wanting some advice.' A trouser leg had edged out of one wellie; he tried to tame his hair and streaked a smudge of dirt across his forehead.

'Asadi was telling me how he came to England.' I felt compelled to fill the clumsy silence.

The old man squinted up at Adam. 'It was 1947. Only days

before India finally gained her independence. My dream for many years, and I missed it.'

Adam grimaced. 'Britain wasn't very welcoming to foreigners back then, was it?'

'No, there were many prejudices, but also some kindnesses.' He sighed. 'That story will have to keep for another day. I am very tired. This lovely young lady has indulged an old fool for long enough.' He took my hands. 'Thank you for listening. You may not wish to even consider my request … now that you know me better.'

'Oh, Asadi …' I couldn't finish the sentence. I didn't know what to say.

'You wanted to ask me something, Adam.'

'Only, when to plant my broad beans? Not important right now.'

Asadi stood up, slowly gathering his breath. He left us and faltered towards the gate. He turned, recovered his balance and waved.

'Are you all right, Lily?'

'I saw him as just an old man … I never imagined … His story is shocking, frightening, and full of sadness. It was hard to listen to parts of it. The things he has done, what he has seen, what he was part of.'

We looked on as Asadi's form faded into the chequered half-light.

Adam's arms folded around me and held me tight until I calmed. He smelt of soil and fresh air.

Sleep hid from me that night. It sneaked into the shadows of my bedroom. In the end I gave up trying. I went and sat on the sofa, hugged a cushion and let events from Asadi's life parade through my mind. I threw the cushion across the room. He shouldn't have asked. It wasn't fair. What was I supposed to say to him?

'What would you do, Mum?' I pulled her photograph onto my knee, then turned it face down. I knew what she would do. 'Yes, but you don't have to do it, do you? I've never even been to France. What do I know of India?'

She still smiled when I turned the photo over again. I traced the shape of her head, and stroked the strand of hair that blew in the wind. I heard her voice.

'You used to beg me to go on an adventure? Remember? We went all over the world; to hot places, cold places, to remote islands and other planets. What's so different about this?'

Her laugh chimed. 'You will make an old man happy. I'll come with you, Lily.'

September was full of those golden days when the light is clear. People's faces and even London's pavements appeared gilded. I looked forward to the weekends. If I passed the allotments and Asadi was sitting on his bench in the sunshine I would go and sit beside him and share a glass of tea from his flask. He hardly ever worked on his patch now. 'I love to come and sit,' he said. 'It is a place where I am happy and at peace. And I like your company.'

Walking halfway home with him one Saturday morning I suggested we have a bowl of soup in the café on the High Road. I made out it was for my convenience, but I wanted to make sure he was eating something. He seemed to be losing weight so quickly, exertion made him splutter and wheeze. 'Besides,' I said, 'will you tell me what happened when you reached England?' We linked arms and I guided him in.

The café had a warm air of comfort. Steam rose from the coffee machine and the smell of roasted beans and sausage rolls mingled with the chatter.

He looked around seemingly fascinated by the shoppers with their bags between their feet, by the two little girls in pink ballet slips tucking into cake and giggling while their mothers talked. A young lad appeared in full football kit, complete with muddy knees and a wide grin. 'We won,' he shouted to one of the mums, 'and I scored.'

'You should be here with Adam and his two boys, not with a wizened soul like me.' He said it with a twinkle in his eye. 'I've been watching the two of you ...'

I felt the heat rise up my neck and passed him the menu to distract him from where this might be going. 'Don't you be matchmaking,' I chided him, but my lips gave away the smile I failed to hide.

'Two lovely people in need of happiness. It warms my heart.' He patted my hand, his veins blue and prominent like ridges on a brow.

'About what you asked me to do, Asadi … to take your ashes to the Ganges … I'll do it. It will be humbling, scary and amazing but most of all a privilege.' Where did that come from? I'd intended to reassure him that I hadn't forgotten about his request, tell him I was thinking about it.

I swear I heard Mum clapping behind me and a sudden twist of happiness spiralled in my chest.

He made a sound like a breeze sighing through long grass. 'Lily, you can never know how joyful that makes me. There is no one else in the world I would rather entrust my remains to.' He chuckled until it became a gurgle in his throat. 'You and I were destined to meet. I have so much to thank your mother for.

'I must finish telling you my story. England was a frightening place for a long time. I wasn't well. I hardly spoke. Foul dark moods. There's a fancy medical name for it now, I believe. They took me to London along with others. We were put up in the basement of a church. We slept on iron cots.' He shook his head. 'There was only one light, a bare bulb that swung on a frayed cord whenever the door opened and let a blast of freezing cold air shoot in.' Asadi pulled his jacket tight like he was feeling that cold again. 'We didn't have enough warm clothing and I spent most days hunched beneath a blanket, keeping the world out.'

'Did no one try to help you?'

'They probably did, but I didn't want to be helped. For many months, even years I was traumatised, unable to gather thoughts or find the energy to do any other than the most basic tasks.' A quivering gasp shook his lungs and he rubbed his temple with trembling fingers. 'London was in ruins after the war, the population sapped of energy. At street level, I saw bombed-out buildings, piles of bricks, pinched faces and all the time people stared. Some mocked and jeered. Mothers hurried children into shop doorways or crossed the road so as not to pass near me. Not just me. Anyone with a black face. There were lots of West Indians too brought over to work. I remember the women wore hats and bright clothes, like peacocks in a fog. The colours reminded me of home. No one would rent to blacks so if they did find a room, then ten, sometimes twelve people shared it which only gave them a worse reputation.

170

'Spring came then summer. I began to walk for hours through the streets. I recall sitting in a pool of light on a piece of wasteland, a broken chimney pot lying at my feet alongside the severed head of a little girl's doll and a child's red shoe. I lifted my face and felt the merest hint of warmth from the sun's rays. That same day I walked past a sorting office. Maybe I'd passed it lots of times before and it was only feeling that hint of warmth that opened my eyes to it.'

A woman wiped our table with a damp cloth sweeping the crumbs onto the floor. 'Order at the counter, love.' She gave me a strange look and glanced at Asadi. I nodded wanting her to go away.

'Anyway, I took to going there every day. Just standing at the rails looking through. It was a comfort. Something familiar. I saw men loading and unloading mail, tossing parcels to each other, packing them into vans or onto trolleys. I smelt the jute of the sacks and breathed it in like it was perfume. Some of the workers shouted things like "Hey, darkie, say something," or, "We left India to you Indians, didn't we? Why don't you go home?" Often crueller things. After a while, they got used to me being there.' Asadi took out a handkerchief and dabbed his face. 'Please, Lily, will you get me a glass of water while we wait for our food.'

'Of course, I'll get it now when I order. I'm sorry, I shouldn't have asked about ...'

'But I want to tell you and there isn't much more.' He took a long drink from the glass when I placed it in front of him, then continued. 'You see, one day a man, a supervisor, I learnt later, brought me hot tea. I think it was raining. He wanted to know why I kept hanging around. I told him I used to be a postman. That I worked in a sorting office in India. I said I liked to come and watch. Well, after that the men were nicer to me. One even brought me a stool to sit on.

'In the end I was given a job. They warned me about causing trouble. I kept my head down, worked hard, covered for those men who were sometimes late or who struggled with their workload. They grudgingly accepted me, or most of them did.'

He sipped at his water and crumbled his bread into his tomato soup when it came. 'I worked on that post office floor for nearly five years. Found a room to share. Frost on the inside of the window in winter, plaster missing and a door that only tied shut with string; it was somewhere, better than a church crypt. But the pain never left me. If anything, I loathed myself more over time.

'Then out of the blue I was given the opportunity to become a postman on the district, to have my own round.' He laughed, a cracked throaty sound which made other customers turn and stare. 'I had that same round for forty years. Saw some changes I can tell you. My householders became used to me, loved me even, especially the old folk. I used to bring them eggs or do a bit of shopping or repairing for them. Many had lost their men in the war. They used to tell me everything. I knew all about their sons and daughters. What their husbands were up to.' He shook his head. 'Folk had time to talk in those days. They gave me much more than I gave them.'

His eyes teared over and he dabbed them with his sleeve. 'Next time I see you, Lily, I will show you something.' He pulled himself to standing. 'Too much talking. I'm going home for an afternoon nap. I have enjoyed my lunch.'

I noticed he had only eaten half of it. He inclined his head. 'You will be doing me a great honour and I thank you.' He shuffled out the door.

13

'Lily. Hi.'

I looked up from pulling at a bramble that seemed to have grown up overnight. Adam was hovering, one hand in his pocket, the other fluttering like a wary sparrow.

'Oh, hi. Good to see you. No boys today?'

'They're at football coaching. Sam's already playing for Spurs! Noah's so serious these days, like he has to be all grown up, and he's only just seven. I wish it was him having those crazy dreams.'

I nodded, trying to imagine how a child understands death. 'Hey, why don't we take them to a football match. I've never been to one. It would be fun.'

Adam blinked and took a step back.

'Sorry, maybe that's insensitive.' I blew air up my face to cool the rush of blood. 'A bit like a bull in a china shop as they say.'

He grinned and dropped to his haunches. 'I came hoping you'd be here. I've been watching you for the last ten minutes, feeling like a bloody teenager.'

'Really. Why?'

'I've been given two tickets to a play next Friday, and I wondered if you'd like to come with me. No idea what it'll be like. It's in a theatre south of the river.'

'Oh, Adam, I'd love to. Thank you.'

He let out a long breath. 'Phew, why was that so hard?'

We both sat back on the gravel path and beamed. I chucked a pebble at him. 'It's quite fun being a teenager again.'

'It sure is. And yes, let's take the boys to a football match. You're already their hero. That would elevate you to super-hero status.' He took my hand and pulled me up. 'Leave it with me.' He glanced at his phone. 'I must go. My two budding Wayne Rooneys will be almost finished, and I can't be late.' He ran towards the gate. 'I'll text you with the details.' I probably wasn't meant to hear the 'Yeah'. Or see his arm in the air, but I did.

'It's Friday. Wine bar after work as usual everyone?' Isaac called across the office. I love that I'm included, their assumption now that I'll be there.

'I can't make it tonight. Sorry.'

Four heads looked up in unison.

'I … I'm going to the theatre.' The hush was like a church. 'What?'

Amir twirled his chair in a circle. 'I do believe Lily has a date?'

I shook my head at them but couldn't hide my grin.

Isaac grabbed a clipboard and Amir tossed him a pen as they came and perched on the corner of my desk. 'Name, age, intentions … let's begin there.' Isaac pulled his glasses to the end of his nose and peered over the top.

'Leave her alone,' Jade shouted.

'Yes, get on with your work.' Ben banged an empty mug on his desk. 'Is that new advertisement ready yet, Isaac?'

'Winging it across to you now, boss.'

Amir winked and stuck up both thumbs. 'We're glad for you, Lily.'

I knew they meant it. They were such good colleagues and friends, always fun. Not going to Manchester had been the right decision. Lou and Jake drifted into my mind. I could say his name now even if remembering that night still made me recoil with embarrassment and disgust. Perhaps if I were to meet him. Talk. A shiver rippled through me. To have even considered it felt like progress.

Over lunch, as we shared a plate of nachos, I told Jade, 'His name's Adam, he's just a guy I met at the allotments. He happened to have two theatre tickets. No big deal.'

'He has an allotment. A gardener-type?' She looked sceptical.

I wound a thread of stringy cheese around a crisp and popped it in my mouth.

'It's not like that. The allotment was his …' Suddenly I didn't want to say more. It was Adam's story to tell, not mine. 'It's a night out – and he's nice. I promise to tell you all about it on Monday. Now can we talk about something else?'

Friday afternoon and I kept glancing at my phone and reading Adam's text over as if I might have missed something.

Can we meet at the station at 7pm? My sister's going to babysit and stay the night so if you like we can grab something to eat after the show. A xx

Ben must have noticed because in the end he said, 'Lily, why don't you pack up early and go home. We owe you loads of time anyway.'

'Can I? Thanks, Ben. I might just do that.'

'Enjoy.' It was a chorus as I headed for the door.

Adam had arrived before me. He wore smart jeans with a jacket over an open-necked shirt. I must have looked impressed.

'Did you think I'd turn up in my dirty clothes with soil on my face? You look different too – lovely.'

I'd teamed a red blouse with black trousers and let my hair fall loose, the curls corkscrewing around my face.

'Come on, let's enjoy ourselves.' Laughing, I pecked him on the cheek; he took my hand, and we raced down the steps as a train came in.

The streets around the Elephant and Castle were dark and quiet. The offices were shut, all the workers gone. The rough sleepers were already bedded down on the pavement, sleeping bags pulled over their heads. The theatre was under the archways of the railway, small with black painted walls and low ceilings. The haunt of art students: girls in outlandish dresses, all mismatched colours; men with long hair tied back in ponytails or wearing beanies.

'Do you feel over-dressed?' Adam whispered as we took our places.

'I feel as though I'm a cast member. We're that close to the stage,' I whispered back. 'Can you smell cannabis? It takes me back to uni days.'

He lifted an eyebrow. 'Shh. Best not to say it out loud. Cheers,' he raised his beer. The unsatisfactory plonk of our plastic glasses made us quiver with laughter.

Two hours later we were back on the street. 'Well, that was different. I got the play, the different relationships between sons and their fathers, but who on earth were those weird characters who came on at the beginning of each act? They looked like something from the witch's scene in Macbeth.'

175

'I suppose every director wants to add his own take. A desire to be unique.'

'Let's find something to eat.' Adam stopped outside a restaurant and was reading a menu. 'Do you like Colombian? It looks all right.'

A pencil-thin young man dressed all in black showed us to a table in an alcove tucked away from the gaze of other diners. Like the theatre it was beneath the arches and when a train thundered overhead we briefly stopped talking as the room shook.

The food came, hot and aromatic. 'This is completely new to me. The seafood in the coconut and cream is yummy.' I paused. 'It's been such a good evening, Adam. I've been looking forward to it all week. After my mum died, I fled to London to get away from grief … and other things. It was the best decision I ever made.'

'I'm glad you did.' He tilted his glass in my direction and we both smiled.

'You know, the other day Asadi told me the story of his life. I fled from the north of England, he came from India, traumatised, ill. Knowing no one. He had to make a completely new life for himself. What must that have been like? Did you know he left a wife and child back in Rajasthan?'

'You're kidding.'

'He never saw them again. It's such a sad story.' I hesitated, 'Can I share something with you?'

'Anything.' His face grew serious.

'It's about Asadi … he has asked if, when he dies, I would take his ashes back to India. I think he fears he's not going to live much longer. He wanted me to understand who he was, to hear the story of his life, the bad bits too. To give me the choice of saying no.'

'Wow.' Adam stared at me. 'I would never have guessed that was what you were going to say. It's some request.' He put his fork down. a frown creasing his forehead. 'And how do you feel about it? What does he want you to do with them?'

'To scatter them on the River Ganges. He has no family. The thing is, I've said I'll do it, and to be honest I'm petrified.' I pulled a face as the size of the task hit me.

He nodded. 'Of course, the wish of every Hindu.' He fell silent. I could tell he was mulling it over. 'What a huge compliment to you that he should even ask. He loves you for your compassion and empathy just as I do. I mean …'

'That's a nice thing to say, thank you.' I crumpled my serviette and put it beside my empty plate, feeling suddenly shy and allowing Adam's blush to subside. 'Thing is, I've never been out of the UK. I feel so naive.'

He grinned and threw open his hands. 'Maybe life is about taking risks, Lily. After all, what's the worst that can happen.'

'Delhi belly for a start.' The absurdity of it punctured the gravity and we both laughed.

'Thank you for a fun evening and a lovely meal. Can I offer you a coffee?' We stood outside the darkened shop, a residual smell of pizza seeping from the interior. In my flat above, a lamp glowed behind the closed curtains. He tensed; I saw him hesitate. Fighting what?

'Thanks, but I'd better get back. You know – the boys. Thanks, Lily. For everything.' His hug was warm. He brushed my lips with a gentle, fleeting kiss.

I stood inches from him, sensing we both wanted more.

'If you meant it, Noah and Sam are definitely up for that football match.' He searched my face.

'I did. Let's do it. I can't wait to see their excitement.'

I waved from my window as Adam walked away down the street. 'We're both scared,' I whispered in the dark. He grew smaller and smaller before disappearing around a corner.

'Are all these people going to watch the football?' Sam sneaked his hand into mine while Noah bounced along in front beside his dad. Sam's eyes were wide as streams of supporters passed in all directions. 'They are. The Spurs supporters have navy blue and white scarves, and Southampton fans have red and white. Would you like a scarf?' We stopped at a stall and the two of them spent forever choosing which one to have.

'Good on you, boys. Come on you Spurs.' The stallholder, his face painted in the club colours, wore a Spurs hat and an array of brooches on his lapel, depicting the players. Sam looked at him in awe. 'What's the score going to be today then, boys?'

Noah screwed up his face. 'Two-nil to Spurs.'

'No, six-nil,' Sam piped in.

'That's what I like to hear.' The man high-fived both of them and winked at us.

Adam bought hot dogs and we sat in a row. Tomato ketchup and onions oozed from the rolls and smeared our fingers. I looked across the boys' heads at Adam. He was laughing and joking with the man behind. It was good to see his high spirits. He caught me looking and returned my smile.

The boys stood on their seats swinging their scarves from side to side as the teams came out. They were hardly able to contain themselves when early in the game Spurs hit the bar, but their excitement reached new levels after Gareth Bale scored in the second half. They copied the other fans and sang, *Glory, glory Tottenham Hotspur*. Noah jumped up and down. I lifted a cheering Sam so that he could see the celebrations. He put his hands over his ears as the deafening sound reverberated around the stand.

'That's my best day ever,' Noah declared as we bundled into the car to go home. 'Can we go again, pleeease.'

'Mine too,' said a sleepy Sam. 'Lily, can you be our new mummy?'

Adam flinched; I saw pain flick across his face. A man dodging between the jammed traffic banged on the car window and yelled, 'Spurs forever.' He put both fists in the air and cheered to the boys in the back seat. The moment passed.

'Lily, look, about what Sam said earlier …' The boys were in the bath after we'd shared a supper of pizza and chips. Adam had opened a bottle of wine.

'It's all right. He's too young to understand.' I longed to kiss away the sorrow in Adam's eyes. 'Besides I think it's been my best day ever too.'

'Don't, Lily.' He was picking at a quick on his nail. 'I'm afraid — for me, for you. Of you going off to India. Maybe this — I mean us — it's not a good idea.'

Cold wrapped itself around my throat.

'And particularly for the boys. They've been hurt too much already, especially Noah. I couldn't bear it if they were hurt again.' His voice almost a sob.

'Daddy.' The squeal came from the bathroom.

Crouching in front of Adam I took both his hands in mine. 'We can't know what's in the future. Hey, Asadi will probably live for ages yet. Do you remember what you said to me? You said sometimes we have to take risks. Maybe this is one of those times.'

14

'How was the football match?' Asadi was sitting hunched on his bench with a scarf around his neck.

'Maybe you should be at home in the warm.' I poured him hot chai from his flask and he breathed in the spicy tang.

'Coming here is still my greatest pleasure. When I was a boy, I used to run to the wadi to get away from everyone, to feel the breeze and trickle the sand through my fingers. If you sit still for long enough in the desert, you will see all sorts. Beetles, spiders and even the small desert fox. People think it's a dead place but it's not. Even the deer were used to me and would graze close by.'

I let him sip his tea and watched the colour come back into his face. 'Do you think about India a lot?'

'More and more it seems. Sometimes the memories are so vivid I forget I'm in England until I see the grey, heavy skies.'

'Do you wish you'd tried to contact Brinda somehow? To have gone back. To have seen her, even at a distance if you weren't able to face her.' I said it in a rush with a realisation of how much it had been troubling me.

'What happened, it upsets you. Even makes you angry, doesn't it?'

'Because it's so sad, but I shouldn't have asked.'

'You have to understand, Lily. Things were very different in 1947. Communications in any form weren't easy then. People were poor. Here there was still food rationing.' He looked up at the clouds that were smothering the weak sun. 'I think it's going to rain.' He rubbed his hands. 'I had no money. Wages were low and for people like me, they were even lower. In India too. After independence there was chaos. The very next year, their appointed prime minister, Mahatma Gandhi, was assassinated, shot by a Hindu fanatic. Times were bad.'

'What do you think became of Brinda and Ravi?' I had to ask.

He stroked the stumps of his fingers. 'After a time, when I

didn't come back, I would be presumed dead. Thousands, millions died when the country was partitioned. Many unrecorded, buried in mass graves. Brinda would have been deemed a widow. Widows have no status in our culture. Sometimes they will be married to another brother …' He shrugged. 'I had no brothers. For widows … it's a struggle. They are vulnerable to … men. Some resort to desperate means. I can't bear to think of crabby hands touching her beautiful body.' He turned his own palms upwards. 'Calloused, rough hands like these. To have witnessed that would have broken my heart. I was helpless. And a coward. Time passed … it became too late …' His voice faded to nothing.

I shook my head, struggling to picture Brinda's life and to chase away my scary thoughts. How was I going to cope in India, with its strange customs and beliefs? What if I did or said the wrong thing? 'Last time I saw you, you said you wanted to show me something, did you remember to bring it? What is it?'

'Dear girl, thank you for reminding me. In the shed on the shelf, there's a white envelope.'

The shed smelt of wood and soil. Asadi's polished tools and his old, frayed coat hanging on hooks made me want to cry.

He fumbled with the envelope and extracted a card. 'When I retired from my post round – I was well over seventy but pretended to be less.' He chortled. 'They held a street party. The residents made cakes and sandwiches and Indian food too. Even the children had kept the secret. It was a complete surprise to me. They gave me a new garden fork and spade. That's them in there.' He pointed towards the shed. 'All tied up with a blue ribbon they were. But that's not what I want to show you.' He passed the card to me. I could see it was covered with dozens of names, spidery writing, neat writing, bold writing, messages in childish hands.

'Read it,' he said.

Dear Asadi,

We love you. Not only have you been our wonderful postman and friend, but you are also a great man.

Enjoy your retirement. We will miss you.

His laugh made his shoulders shake. 'So, you see, Lily, I fulfilled my mama's wish in the end. "Be a great man," she always used to tell me.'

'She would be very proud of you.' I found it difficult to speak, the signatures blurring on the card.

He took it from me and held it close. 'It seems there are many ways to be great.' He coughed, the deep racking cough turned his lips blue and left him wheezing. 'It's this cold wind,' he said, looking up at me with watery eyes.

I put a steadying arm around him and swallowed hard. 'I think you're a great man too. And to answer your original question, the football match was lots of fun.'

'I know, the boys have been telling me all about it. They are very fond of you. That makes me happy.' He tucked the card back into its envelope. 'You will be all right when I've gone, Lily. You will be all right.'

My phone rang at work. It was Lou. I rushed out of the office and perched on the top step of the stairway.

'Lou. What's wrong?'

'Nothing's wrong. I thought I might catch you at lunchtime. We're coming to London, Lily. I want to see Yoyoi Kusama's exhibition in the Tate Modern.'

I heard the *we* and lost the rest of the sentence.

'I wondered if you'd like to come along?' Lou's voice was full of hesitation.

With the phone to my ear, I watched snarled-up traffic crawl along the main road.

'Jake says it's not his thing. He's going to meet up with some old university mates. Lily, are you still there?'

'Yes, I'm still here. Whose exhibition?'

'Yoyoi Kusama's, you know, the Japanese artist. We studied her as part of our course. Please say you'll come.'

Lou has always been my best friend. She stood by me when I needed her most. I knew she was trying to keep our friendship alive. If I said no, the fallout would be my own doing.

'I'd like that, Lou. We've always had fun, mooching around exhibitions, even the way-out weird ones.'

'That's great. Saturday morning then. I'll get two tickets —

Jake says he'll have a coffee with us first, then he'll bugger off.'

I took a huge gasping breath, covering the phone, hoping Lou wouldn't hear.

'Okay.' It was all I could manage.

'Thanks, Lily.' Lou sounded like she wanted to weep.

I sat for several minutes on the step practising yoga breaths before being able to face the office again.

'You, all right?' It was Amir, always looking after me.

'Yes,' I said. And to my surprise I meant it. 'I'm fine.'

The city on a late autumn day wore its clothes like a Romany at a fair; the low sun reflected on the water in a thousand sparkling mirrors. I walked across London Bridge with the wind tugging at my hair. People were laughing together, couples hand in hand leant against the parapet to gaze into the murky, rolling Thames. My mum would have called it a 'good-to-be-alive day.'

How to play this? What to say? Those questions had been stalking me since Lou's phone call. I'd rehearsed the answers, I'd tweaked words, emphasised others. Now they all seemed to have jumbled together like a broken jigsaw. The South Bank bustled with people having late breakfast or early lunch. A tantalising smell of bacon and coffee tinged the air, seagulls squawked as they fought for crumbs, heedless of the feet of passers-by.

I hesitated outside the glass doors of the art gallery. I hoped I would be there first; give my thumping heart time to slow down. 'Come on, Lily you can do this.' I spoke to the red boots on my feet. I loved these boots; they made me feel bold and frivolous. They were having to work extra hard today.

I wasn't first. Lou saw me as I entered the café. She leapt up and rushed between the tables to wrap me in her arms, crushing our cheeks together and releasing the familiar smell of her perfume.

'You look fabulous,' she said, holding me at arm's length. 'Much better. I don't mean ...'

I couldn't help but laugh at her agonised frown. 'I know what you mean. It's okay. I am better.'

She squeezed my arm and led me like a small child to where Jake sat waiting. 'I'm not going to run away,' I said, shaking off her grip. We grinned at each other.

'Sorry,' she mouthed.

Jake stood up, clumsily bumping the edge of the table. His hand hovered towards me before he began picking up the sachets of sugar that he'd spilt from a dish.

I wasn't the only one who was nervous.

'Good to see you, Lily.' He coughed. 'What can I get you girls? Cappuccino, Lou?'

'For me as well please.' I met his eyes. It felt like we acknowledged each other.

Conversation was stilted at first. Jake and I skirted around each other. Lou gamely filled in the awkward pauses. Gradually, over coffee we began to calm down and chat about the usual stuff, life in London and how was work. I asked Jake what he was doing. 'Working for Greater Manchester Council. That's where you end up if you do a geography degree at uni. It's fine though, for now anyway. Just doesn't match the wild-boy image of my university days.' His face flushed scarlet. He looked at his watch. 'I'd better be off soon. To meet my mates. Haven't seen them for yonks.'

'Hang on a minute. I'll just pop to the toilet before we hit this exhibition.' Lou gathered her bag and headed for the cloakroom.

Jake and I looked across the table at each other. I know this man intimately, I thought, yet I know nothing about him.

'A tumbleweed moment, I think,' he said, half smiling. 'Lou's not very subtle, is she?'

'Lou was never known for her subtlety.' The shared joke dispelled some of the tension.

'Lily, I'm sorry for that night. There's no more I can say. No excuses.'

I turned my empty cup around on its saucer. 'It shouldn't have happened, Jake. We were both stupid, irresponsible, *and drunk*.' I twizzled the cup back again and gazed into its depths. 'Sexual assault is wrong in any circumstance. I was too smashed to know what was going on. And so were you. A hard lesson for both of us.' I stole a look at him. He was staring at the table. 'Afterwards, with Mum dying – everything got lumped together. I was in a bad place. You tried to find me. I appreciate that.'

His mouth hovered between a smile and a grimace. 'Lou and

I – are you okay with it?'

'You don't have to ask my permission. But yes, I am. I can see how happy you both are.'

Lou returned, her eyes flicking between us before she gave us each a hug.

'I really must go. Otherwise, the guys will be onto the next pub before I've even reached the first.' Jake kissed Lou and turned to me. 'See you, Lily.' His hand fluttered aimlessly. 'It's good to have met you … again. Have a great time at the exhibition.' With that, he loped from the café to be lost in a sea of heads.

'Come on, this should be good.' I didn't want to be quizzed by Lou, but I could see her visibly relax. She took my arm as we walked up the stairs and it was enough to tell me she was relieved.

Two hours later our feet ached, and the intimacy of the rooms began to suffocate. We had stood in awe in front of Kusama's postage-stamp-sized collages. Polka dots and lights spun us into infinity, and we giggled like schoolgirls at some of the installations.

'I think I'm exhibitioned out, Lou. I'm too tired to figure the meaning behind this penis-covered rowing boat.' I stared at the work in front of me and listened to an earnest young woman trying to explain to her doubting mother what it was all about.

'Me too. Let's go.'

We found a sheltered bar on the South Bank, where we sat outside overlooking the river. Fresh air and white wine soon lifted our weariness. Lou was excited about the early plans for her wedding. 'When I choose a dress will you come with me?' she asked.

'Yes, please. I'd love to. What fun. Are you going simple and sophisticated or is it frills and bows?'

'Hardly the latter. Do you think that's me?' She paused, her glass halfway to her lips. 'And you, Lily. Have you met anyone?' She sipped her wine, her eyes curious above the rim of her glass.

My hesitation was enough.

'You have, haven't you? Tell me all,' she said, picking up a handful of peanuts and leaning forward in her seat.

'Sort of, but it's complicated.'

'Oh God, Lily. He's not married, is he?'

I didn't know how to begin.

'Or it's a woman. That's cool.'

'Are you going to give me a chance to tell you?' I laughed and watched a police boat speeding over the water carving out an arced bow wave. 'It's not a woman and he's not married but …'

Later, on the way home I bought postcards and T-shirts for Noah and Sam. Noah's sported a Union Jack and Sam's a bright red London bus. I hadn't seen Adam for two weeks, not since the football match. We'd texted, avoiding anything difficult. He'd suggested we might take the children to Hampstead Heath or Hyde Park; pack a picnic, so it felt like we were on track.

Buoyed by my happy day with Lou, I decided to take the boys their gifts. Adam opened the door; his face went from surprise to delight in a moment. He came closer. 'I was afraid …' I didn't hear the rest because Sam steamrollered into my legs almost knocking me off the step. 'Sam.' Adam scolded his son but with laughter in his tone.

'I wanted to be first,' Sam said, his lip quivering.

I picked him up and his skinny arms squeezed my neck.

'Now it's Daddy's turn,' I said peeling him from me.

I held Adam, his breath warm on my ear.

I gave the boys their presents and they stripped off their tops and insisted on wearing the T-shirts until they went to bed.

'I'll go and leave you in peace,' I said, as Adam picked up cushions and put away toys. Maybe the way I said it wasn't convincing. Adam squinted at me from his position on the floor.

'Peace is what I've had too much of, Lily. Company, your company is what I want. Please don't go.' I recognised how hard it was for him to say that aloud and I let him finish his tidying before I nodded my agreement.

'I can rustle up pasta with vegetables or we've always got sausages — there are always sausages in this house,' he said with a wry grimace.

'Pasta would be lovely, and I'll come and tell you all about the exhibition I've been to.'

The kitchen was small, white and bright despite the rain that now spattered the window. I leaned against the work surface, a glass of wine in my hand.

'At the time we couldn't afford anything bigger,' Adam told me, as though reading my thoughts. 'I should move but somehow I've never got round to it.'

He took a photograph down from a shelf. 'That's Rosie,' he said.

'She was very pretty.' A petite heart-shaped face with straight blonde hair smiled back at me. 'I have a photograph of my mum in my kitchen. I talk to her all the time.'

'I talk to Rosie too. It helps. She would have liked you.' He put the photograph back in its place and faced me. 'I loved her, Lily, but I have a whole life ahead of me. I have to live it.' He touched my cheek. 'Say you'll stay.' It was a statement, a request and a longing all wrapped together. We kissed, needing to say no more.

I woke in the early morning and lay listening to the quiet rhythm of Adam's breathing. His arm was across my stomach and a bare foot protruded from the bedcovers. A sliver of pale light squeezed between the curtains and played shadows on the opposite wall.

We had been gentle with each other, letting our ghosts settle and fade. Then more fervent, pent-up emotions spilt like water over rocks.

I eased myself from the bed. Adam murmured and turned over. I collected my clothes and sneaked downstairs to put them on. The door to the children's room lay slightly open but all was quiet. I wrote Adam a note and slipped out into the chill of a day not yet fully born.

I walked the near-deserted streets. There was little traffic to disturb my thoughts. A helmeted cyclist, head down against the wind, risked the red traffic light and pedalled on. Leaves blew along the pavement; I kicked them into a yellow shower. I hoped Adam would understand why I'd gone. I would go round later if he wanted me to. But the boys – I hadn't wanted them to waken and find me where their mummy used to be. Adam told me how in the morning, they still liked to pile into his bed and listen to stories. I didn't want to be an intruder.

'Slowly, slowly, Adam. Let's find our way together. This is new to both of us,' I whispered to the trees as they bent towards me.

I crept into my own bed, clutched my pillow and snuggled down, reliving each beautiful moment of our first night together.

'You would approve, Mum,' I told her later. 'I'm happy, happy, happy.' I sang in the shower, letting the water pelt over my head and stream over my tingling skin. Only when I turned off the shower did I hear it. An insistent knocking on my apartment door. 'Drat,' I said pulling on a robe and wrapping a towel around my dripping hair.

I opened the door. It was Abeke – with Adam. Abeke's bright orange headgear lit up the gloomy stairwell. My smile died when I registered her tear-stained face. She enveloped me in a body-hugging embrace then pushed me gently away.

'Lily, I'm so sorry. It's Asadi. I found him this morning, sitting on his bench, his head against the shed.' She whimpered like a child. 'I thought he was asleep.'

15

We fell quiet as we approached the house in the late afternoon. I took Adam's hand; his comforting squeeze slowed my racing heart. Abeke walked in front, her ample hips swaying with each step. I'd wanted to bring flowers, but Abeke had shaken her head. 'Now is not the time for gifts. Later perhaps. Now we will just sit, listen and remember.'

It was an ordinary house in the middle of a terrace. A low wall separated the tiny front garden from the street. The red door stood slightly ajar. Red for a postman. The thought brought a flake of warmth to my icy core. We looked at each other wondering if we should go in. The tap of a walking stick sounded in the hallway and a bent, grey-haired man opened the door wider. His smile and nodding head suggested he was not surprised to see us.

'Asadi's friends. Welcome,' he whispered.

Asadi lay waxen white in his open coffin, a wisp of hair curled towards the sandalwood mark in the centre of his forehead. I wanted to push the hair aside with my finger. He looked peaceful, the lines of his face smoother. He wore a necklace of wooden beads and at his feet a garland of orange marigolds, vibrant against the plain white sheet in which he was wrapped. Marigolds. One of the packets of seeds my mum had left me. The seeds that had led me to Asadi all those months ago. The sight of the bright petals punctured my pent-up emotion; tears slid silently over my cheeks.

The mourners made space and revealed floor cushions for us to sit on. Who were these people? I knew from Asadi that he had no family. Friends from the temple, from the community? Most were elderly. The men in *shalwar kameez*, the women sitting together, tiny and shrunken, wore saris. Their silver-grey hair and the whiteness of their garments shone in the dim light provided by an oil lamp. Abeke had told us to wear white. She said it was the colour of purity and would aid the deceased's soul through the ghost world. It had felt strange dressing in my light trousers and white blouse. Now I felt calm; welcomed by all the kind faces around us. I sensed the room was filled with love.

But Asadi wasn't here. It was both an empty thought and a comforting one. I pictured him flitting through the wilted stems of the beans on his allotment then soaring high above the bare trees, blown by the winds that would take him home at last.

The low murmur of prayers and rhythmic chants drew me back. We stayed until Abeke signalled we should leave.

I glanced one last time at the face I had come to love.

We were ushered out with more silent nods and quiet thanks. The same man who had greeted us stepped outside leaning heavily on his stick. 'Please, I hope you can return on the ninth day. It will be a more joyful occasion. We will eat Asadi's favourite foods. We will free his soul.' His deeply lined face folded into a smile. 'Lily,' he almost sang my name. 'I am Santosh, Asadi's oldest friend. He has told me about you. I will have his ashes for you to take back to his beloved Rajasthan and then to the sacred River Ganges.'

'I'm not sure I'm the right person to …' I gestured towards the house.

'You are the right person because you are the one he most wanted to do it.' He chuckled. 'And I am too old. These legs can barely take me upstairs these days.'

Beside the door, a single dusky-pink rose bloomed in the dark of the evening.

'Look, Adam.' I touched his sleeve. 'So perfect and in November.' I bent closer to inhale its faint perfume. 'I think Asadi is here amongst these curved petals and those of every flower that will ever bloom.' Adam put his arm around my shoulders and drew me closer.

'Let's have cake and a very English cup of tea.' Abeke suggested and headed for a café.

'You appear to understand all the different cultures,' I said as we sat indoors drinking steaming mugs of tea and eating chocolate cake.

She laughed her deep belly laugh. 'I have been here a long time. In the street where I live, we are a hotpot of religions and cultures.'

'A hotchpotch you mean.'

'Yes, that funny word,' and she gave another table-shaking laugh. 'I need to go. My sons will be hungry, and they'll empty the fridge if I don't get back soon.' She left with a wave that embraced all the diners.

'Will you come back with me; wait for my friends to bring the children home?' Adam asked. I shook my head. 'There's something I want to do.' I loved that he didn't probe but leant over and kissed the top of my head as we parted.

The allotment fence stood black and sombre, the iron bars like a row of soldiers standing guard. I opened the solid gate with my key. No one was around this damp November evening. Our allotment looked bleak. Canes of straggly sweet peas hung limp and brown, foliage from spent vegetables and flowers lay spreadeagled on the earth. There were other patches where the autumn harvest had been collected and tidied away, the soil freshly tilled. Cabbages and leeks awaited their season to be picked. I resolved to return tomorrow and make our plot something Asadi would be proud of. Tonight, I wanted to sit on his bench. I stroked the place where he always sat; imagined it felt warm as though he had recently risen from it. The night was heavy, only a few stars shone through. Gathering clouds skimmed across the splinter of white moon. I could have felt afraid, but I didn't. A shawl of peace wrapped itself around my shoulders. A gust of wind blew my hair and stirred the few remaining leaves on the big oak tree by the fence. The shed door creaked on its hinges and banged shut.

'Goodbye, great man,' I whispered as the air stilled and drops of rain splashed on the gravel path.

The three of us went back to Asadi's house on the ninth day. It was full of chatter but empty without his presence. In the corner of the room, an old man wheezed out an Indian song. Others joined in, so the small room filled with notes. We'd brought nuts and fruits and laid them on a table already piled with dishes of food, most of which I couldn't name. A lady who introduced herself as Asadi's neighbour sat us beside her mother who gave a toothless grin and patted my hand. The daughter brought plates of food, pointing out Asadi's favourites. 'He used to bring fresh produce from his allotment, and I would cook it for us all to eat. He would be so pleased that you are here. Tonight, we set him free to be reborn.'

'Lily, the young lady with the beautiful name.' It was Santosh whom we'd met before. 'Asadi talked so fondly of you.' He held out a tortoiseshell-patterned urn. 'We entrust our friend to you.' The room had fallen silent. I felt many eyes watching.

I rose softly to my feet, glad of the pressure of Adam's knee against mine. 'It is an honour and a privilege. Asadi was a true friend. He befriended me – when I most needed it. I loved him.' I closed my eyes to the murmur of a chanted prayer. In my head I heard the buzz of bees and my nose filled with the scent of marjoram. I reached out and took the urn.

Applause rippled around the room; the singer began again, and a hum of voices rose and fell.

I placed the urn on my kitchen windowsill in a ribbon of sunlight. Mum smiled from the photo frame. I swear her smile was wider, mischief lighting up her eyes.

'What have you got me into?' I laughed with her. Suddenly it seemed the most normal thing in the world that I should be setting out on a journey that would take me halfway across the world. 'Asadi will be with me. And you will,' I told her. 'Everything will be all right.'

16

Ben swivelled in his office chair. 'India! That was not what I expected you to say.' His eyes opened wide as he jerked his head back. A twitch of his mouth became a beam. 'Italy, Rome maybe, or even Greece ... but India. Where did that come from, Lily?'

I was thankful he listened without interruption. Even as I gave it my explanation sounded bizarre. I heard myself say I was going first to Rajasthan, to Jodhpur then across to the River Ganges, to Varanasi where I would scatter Asadi's ashes. Until that moment I hadn't been certain of my plan. Telling Ben made it real. Trepidation, or even excitement, shivered through me.

'Of course you can have two weeks off. You're due leave before the end of the year anyway.' His expression morphed from surprise to concern. 'If you're sure it's what you want to do?'

'It is. It really is.' I knew then that I meant it. 'Thanks, Ben.'

'India. On your own?' The buzz of our Friday night crowd in the wine bar hushed. Five heads turned towards me.

'Why is that everyone's reaction?' I said, laughing and raising a glass. 'To India.' To Asadi I whispered in my head.

Amir shuffled across to sit next to me on the bench. 'Tell me more, Lily.' He nodded gravely as I outlined my trip and its purpose. Jade listened in; her hand crept into mine and she squeezed my fingers. I wasn't sure if it was out of fear or encouragement.

'Right. I can help.' Amir grinned. 'I will be your self-appointed travel agent. As it happens my sister's brother-in-law's sister and her husband run a small hotel in Delhi.'

'Who?' I said shaking my head.

'Your first lesson about India. Everyone knows someone who has a taxi, a place to stay, where to eat the best food. You get the picture. This hotel, it's called Green Meadow Park. Quite delightful. You'll love it.'

'Have you been?'

'Good God, no. The last time I was in India I was about six years old. I don't remember much about it except it was hot and I got to drink more Cola and Sprite than I've ever been allowed to since. Something to do with fending off Delhi belly.'

'As a travel agent, you're not selling this.'

'Seriously. My sister's been and she said it was lovely. A couple of nights there to recover from the flight then you can take the train to Jodhpur. Indian trains – best in the world – thank the British for that. Then fly back to Delhi and on to Varanasi. There, you are all sorted.' He sat back. 'I think I have a talent for this.'

The next day at Adam's, Sam walked around the sofa waving his arm like a trunk. 'Will there be elephants?'

'Yes, lots of them,' Noah said, 'and tigers. Tigers eat people. They carry them off into the jungle.' He pounced on his brother and hauled him squealing to the floor.

'Stop it, you two. Lily won't stay and read you a bedtime story if you're going to fight.'

'I don't want Lily to be eaten,' Sam sniffled. 'Daddy, don't let her go to that place.'

'It's all right, Sam. Noah's teasing you.' I snuggled him onto my knee. 'I won't get eaten by a tiger. Maybe I can find a toy one to bring home to you as well as something for Noah.' Their faces brightened, and they disappeared upstairs to choose a book for me to read to them.

Adam leaned across and tilted my chin. 'I wish I could come with you.'

I took a deep breath determined not to let my niggling worries surface. 'Even if it were possible for you to come …' the boys hurtled into the room. 'and clearly it's not,' I laughed, indicating the two whirlwinds – 'it feels like I should accomplish this alone. Sometimes I think it's a plan my mum and Asadi have cooked up together. A journey I'm meant to take.' Adam didn't look convinced, I pulled him closer and kissed the tip of his nose. 'There will be time for us to have adventures.'

Later we made love on the rug in front of the log burner. Warm, tender love, clinging to each other, memorizing the touch of skin, the curves of our bodies. The orange glow from the burning wood threw dancing shadows across our faces.

'Promise you'll come back to me, Lily.' Adam's voice a sob in my ear.

'It's only two weeks,' I whispered. At that moment two weeks yawned ahead of me. A void waiting to be filled. I perched on my elbow, cherishing his finger tracing words on my stomach. 'My mum left me a series of glittery boxes, all of which were empty except one. Asadi suggested she wanted me to fill them with memories. That's what I'm going to do, starting with this trip. In fact, starting right now.' I reached for my phone and took a selfie of the two of us grinning into the camera.

I walked home along the High Road with the light from the streetlamps blanching the dark. This time tomorrow I would be high above the clouds racing towards a country that to me had only ever been a name on a map. I pulled my scarf tighter around my neck and ran the last few yards to my flat.

17

Beyond the window with its patterned wood surround, the sky was a faint purple. Turquoise, voile curtains stirred in an unseen breeze. A matching throw lay skewed across my bed. Everything felt surreal, like I was living in someone else's story. Sounds reached me from the street below. Men hollering, the harsh honk of a horn, then quiet, so that all I could hear was a clink of cups. The tantalizing smell of freshly baked bread crept in.

A light tap on the door and it opened slowly. A young girl of about fifteen or sixteen entered. 'Bed tea for our visitor.' Steam from a gold-rimmed glass of amber liquid curled in front of her face. She laid the tray on the small round table beside me.

'Thank you, that's so kind.'

The girl smiled; a tiny diamond nose stud sparkled in her brown face. 'I am Aisha. This is my father's guesthouse. I help out before I go to school. When you are ready you can come through for breakfast.'

Her features appeared so sculpted I couldn't stop looking. Black hair fell down her back, matched in colour by her eyes and long eyelashes.

'You are kept busy with all the guests.'

'Not really. We have only five rooms. I like talking to our visitors. They tell me of exotic places.' She turned as she went out. 'One day I hope to go.'

I sipped the ginger chai. Already the heat of the day was creeping into the corners of the room. My suitcase lay open and on top of my clothes was the shiny box with its gold, glittery diamond pattern. 'We're here, Asadi.' I whispered from my bed.

I had opened each box in the stack my mother had left me until I found the one into which Asadi's urn of ashes fitted snuggly. Around it I had packed tissue paper and carried it in my hand luggage as instructed by the airline. It felt important to keep Asadi close, to take care of him. A wisp of sadness touched me as I remembered how his face would light up and a mischievous glint brighten his eyes.

Don't be sad. Welcome to India.

'You're right,' I answered the voice in my head. 'I know you want me to enjoy it all. See everything for you, hear everything for you.' I sat for a moment on the edge of my bed before stepping into the shower to let the water wash away the weariness of travelling.

I chose eggs for breakfast, not yet ready to face anything spicy so early in the day, although it smelt delicious.

'You will sit on the balcony?' Aisha, in a blue dress, was ready for school now, her hair covered with a white hijab. She took me through. 'Here it is cool.' From below I heard her name being called. She leant over the balustrade; two girls dressed in identical uniforms stood waiting. 'Coming,' she shouted to them.

'Perhaps I will see you later. Welcome to Delhi.' She flew down the stairs and I watched as the three of them linked arms and walked off down the street.

Foliage draped the balcony. Plants in all shades of green reached from floor to roof. Some with leaves as big as paddles, others bearing small white flowers which gave off an exquisite fragrance.

'Namaste, Lily. I see you like our flora.' A man with Aisha's smile set down my tray of food. 'We are so pleased to have you here as our guest. I am Latif, Aisha's father. How is London? I was there many years ago. It is where I learnt how to run a hotel.' He pulled a face. 'But this is not like the grand hotels you have there.'

The sun filtered through the greenery and dappled gold onto my breakfast tray. 'This is much more attractive. My friend Amir said I would love it. Do you have other guests?'

'Of course, yes. But they are businessmen. They leave early for work. They come often, whenever they are in Delhi. They are more like family. I hope soon you will feel the same.'

'I already do. Thank you. I wish I had longer here.'

Latif's face became serious. 'Yes, I know of your purpose in India. It is not entirely holiday.' He smiled. 'You look surprised. What is it they call it, Chinese whispers?'

I nodded, 'I am getting used to those. I wondered if today I would have the opportunity to see a little of Delhi. Where do you suggest I start?'

'You must eat your omelette and drink your coffee. Excuse me a moment.' He pulled out his phone, sat down opposite me and began talking rapidly to whoever was on the other end. At one point he slapped his thigh. 'Yes, yes, perfect.' The only words I understood.

He concluded his conversation and beamed at me. 'Mohammed will pick you up in one hour. He will show you our city of two halves, the old and the new,'

'I feel overwhelmed by everyone's kindness.' I think Latif sensed my excitement. He lightly touched my fingers with his cool hand and left me to absorb the strangeness of my surroundings.

'You like India?' Mohammed swivelled his head to address me from the driving seat.

'This is my first day.' I laughed and clung to the strap as we swerved around a lorry into a gap. 'It's very manic.'

He banged the steering wheel. 'This is new Delhi, wide roads, much space. I show you the parliament buildings and India Gate, our war memorial. All designed by a British man. Edward Lutyens.' He pronounced the name proudly. 'Seventy thousand soldiers from the British Indian army die in World War I.'

I thought of Umesh, Asadi's brother and wondered if just as many died in the second world war.

Tourists taking photographs crowded the pavements around the memorial. Beggars asked for money. Hawkers sold every kind of street food. One vendor struggled to hold an enormous bunch of brightly coloured balloons and occasionally one would escape his clutches and sail into the sky accompanied by cheering from the onlookers. Mohammed bought a snack from a woman with a metal tray on her head. He gave me a piece. It was a sticky, sugar hit that I pulled a face at but pretended to enjoy.

'It is called *Jalebi*. Sweet, yes?' His laugh bubbled into the air. 'Now we go to the old town. Then you see manic!' He turned up the radio and began to sing along to the Indian song that filled the car.

The roads grew busier and petrol fumes made me cough. We screeched to a stop beside other taxis parked three deep. Buses, bikes and trucks manoeuvred around the obstruction with horns blaring and arms waving. Mohammed indicated for me to get out.

'Here? But aren't we blocking the road?' Other tourists, looking as confused as I felt, hovered like vivid dragonflies between the parked cars.

Mohammed clapped his hands, a row of perfect white teeth split his face. He shrugged. 'It is always like this.'

I cringed as a long blast of a horn sounded close by.

'The other drivers, they like the sound of their hooters, they are not angry. In India we have one hand on the steering wheel, the other on the horn.' He laughed again, obviously enjoying my discomfort.

A brightly painted lorry thundered past inches from my window, and I scrambled to the other side of the seat and out the door he had opened for me. Heat and diesel fumes swirled around making me gasp.

'This is the Red Fort. You want a photo?' Mohammed steered me to where I could get a good view of the impressive sandstone building. Sun gilded the crenelations, deep shade reflected the building's shape on the wide forecourt. 'Very big inside.' He opened his arms wide. 'It was the home of Mughal emperors for over two hundred years. To see it properly would take all day. When you come back to Delhi another time, I will take you.'

Sweat trickled down my forehead.

'On top of the fort the air is cool. It is peaceful. But we have no time today. Come, let's go. I will show you Chandni Chowk, Delhi's busiest market.'

I slumped back into the hot taxi seat, and we roared off, cutting across the lines of traffic. 'You know so much and have incredibly good English, Mohammed.'

'Five languages, I speak,' he said, turning to look at me. I wished he wouldn't do that, given the driving conditions. 'Tourists, they love Mohammed.' He waggled his head in time with the fluffy dice that dangled from his mirror. 'My son too is learning. I tell him if he want to be a rich taxi driver, he must be able to say, good morning, buongiorno, guten morgen.' His words dissolved to a tinkle. 'My Russian, it is not so good yet.'

The car stopped and Mohammed jumped out to talk to a man who stood smoking beside the road. They both looked towards the taxi, I guessed they were talking about me.

'I will wait for you here. My friend Talal will take you into the market on his rickshaw.'

'But ...' a flicker of fear slid under my skin.

'I would trust him with my life – and yours,' he teased, whilst giving me a reassuring wink.

The ceiling of hazy blue sky gave way to shadow as the sun was squeezed from the maze of narrow alleyways we hurtled down. Talal's legs rhythmically turned the pedals of the rickshaw, his calves bulging above flip-flop-clad feet. A faded yellow shirt, with a frayed hem, streamed in the breeze giving scant cover to his lean arms and torso.

People everywhere. Men loitered in groups or criss-crossed in front of us. There were veiled women, women in bright saris, others in jeans, T-shirts and sun hats. Some carried baskets of vegetables on their heads, others balanced babies on their hips while more small children trailed behind. A smell of cooked food and warm cow dung mingled with swirls of dust thrown up by the rickshaws. We slowed beside the fabric stalls; an embroidery of colours lit up the street in stark contrast to the dingy, mud-coloured buildings behind. Women chattered loudly as they pulled length after length of material out and stretched them across the stall. I smiled as they held first one piece then another in front of them. The stallholder saw me looking and called out. 'For a bride,' he shouted, holding up a rich red fabric. 'You are looking for a husband?' The women's chatter grew louder; they dissolved into giggles and waved.

Excitement trembled through my shoulders and down my arms. I'm happy, I thought. Overwhelmed and bewildered, my senses buffeted, but I'm happy. The acknowledgement made me want to shout it to the world. Instead, I gripped the arms of the rickshaw as Talal swerved around another corner and stopped beside tables where men sat drinking chai and playing cards.

'You want drink?' It wasn't really a question as Talal was already grabbing a bottle of cola from the cafe counter and opening it for me with his teeth. I wasn't sure I wanted anything but fumbled for some money anyway.

'No, no, me buy.' He dismissed my gesture with a flick of his head and at once began an animated discussion with a fellow rickshaw driver.

The fizzy, lukewarm drink bubbled in my nose, its sweetness cloying my throat. A young boy, his bare feet grey with dirt, stared up at me with pooled black eyes. I held out the bottle; he took it and ran, dodging between the legs of the masses. The raised voices and excited hand movements of Talal and the other driver suggested they were having some sort of argument, but they finished with back-slapping and clinches forcing me to wonder if it was in fact a display of friendship. There was so much I didn't understand.

'You ready?' Talal stood in front of me picking at a piece of loose skin on his betel-stained lips. A pinprick of blood oozed out and he smeared it down his chin.

The streets became ever narrower. The buildings leant in, and tangles of cable and loose wires hung from them like skeins of wool. At junctions, trucks vied with rickshaws and tuk-tuks for every inch of space. Buffalo ambled between the traffic and thin dogs fought over scraps of bread. Grubby children waved and held out their hands as we passed. The sights and sounds seeped into my head until it began to pound.

Mohammed was lying on the ground in the shade of his vehicle, with a scarf over his head when Talal returned me to the taxi.

'I think I'm ready to go back to the hotel now,' I told Mohammed.

'I take you one more place. All my English passengers, they love it.'

I couldn't imagine what kind of place that might be but by now I was too hot and weary to argue.

It turned out to be gardens with grass so green I sank thankfully into the shade. Irrigation systems fountained water in arcs, reflecting rainbows in the droplets. The grass had a coarse texture, but its colour was restful. I brushed away a persistent fly and closed my eyes. The day with all its complexity and newness receded until all I could hear was a bird singing, hidden in a canopy of leaves. I must have dozed because I woke to Mohammed gently shaking my shoulder. My eyes flew open, and

I gripped his arm, an involuntary squeal parting my dry lips.

'Sorry if I frighten you. It is time to go.'

I shook my head as the remnants of images slipped from my grasp and faded into the now rose-pink sky.

'You having troublesome thoughts?' Mohammed's eyes narrowed with concern. 'You not worry. I was watching over you, from there.' He pointed to the gateway to the gardens where other drivers waited.

'You not like Mohammed's tour? You not like Delhi?' He struggled with the words as he helped me to my feet.

I trembled and sighed, repelling the fragments of my dream.

I tried to smile away the hurt look on his face. 'I like *your* Delhi, Mohammed. I think my dream was of a different Delhi, a time of violence that was once described to me.'

18

Latif dropped me off at the station and showed me where to catch the night train to Jodhpur.

'Next stop Rajasthan. Good luck,' he said before leaving. I hoped my forced grin disguised the knot of apprehension that made a response impossible,

Swarms of people stood or squatted as they waited for the train. Everyone seemed to be moving house. Suitcases, plastic bowls and kitchen utensils rattled against each other.

Heat from the day hung in the darkness. Sweat trickled between my breasts; my shirt stuck to my arms. Behind me the lights of Delhi pierced the night. The city was still alive with traffic and the sound of sirens. Moths flew in frenzies and flung themselves against the naked bulbs slung in loops over gantries. A sleepy child, bound in a sling on her mother's back, stared at me without blinking. The woman put out a hand and touched my hair. 'Very pretty,' she said. I smiled not knowing how to reply except to say thank you.

The train pulled in. The mass surged forward, space cleared ahead of me and I was confronted with the sight of parcels and post being loaded from a trolley into the mail car. The job Asadi used to do. My stomach constricted with a stab of pain. A worker, his skinny arms protruding from a T-shirt with 'Texas' emblazoned across the front, stopped what he was doing and called across.

'Passengers.' He pointed up the platform and repeated it more loudly when I didn't move.

A man wheeling a bike touched my arm. 'You need to find your carriage. It will be in the front portion of the train. It's easy to get confused in Indian stations, isn't it?' From his accent I guessed he might be German or Dutch and his pale skin marked him out as a tourist. I looked from his face to his bike. 'I'm on a cycling holiday. I know. It's crazy. So far, I've suffered nothing more than grazed limbs when I tangled with a herd of goats.'

His friendliness broke my reverie, and I began to breathe

more easily. We walked along the platform together before he peeled off to lift his bike onto the train. I slipped into my reserved window seat and rubbed at the dusty glass with a tissue. The compartment soon filled up. A businessman in a suit pulled a laptop from his briefcase and began to type. Across from him there was someone already asleep, soughing with each breath. Two small boys played with marbles on the floor until their mother pulled down the top bunk. She lifted them up, tucked them under the sheet and scrambled up beside them. The man closed his computer, climbed onto the bunk above me and was soon snoring gently. I spread out my bedding and lay in the dark.

The train sang on the rails as it ate up the miles.

I don't know what time it was when I woke. I tried to look but the light on my phone was so bright I quickly closed it. The smell of sleeping bodies and hot breath wrapped around me. I eased my feet over the edge of the bunk, glad of the feel of the cool floor. I fumbled into my sandals and felt my way out of the compartment and along the bed-lined corridor. One or two passengers were awake, their eyes showing white under the dim lights. Whispers sounded loud. I reached a doorway and opened the window. A rush of air buffeted my face. I relished the fresh wind tugging at my hair and slipping beneath my clothing. The flat countryside slid by; the glow of small fires amongst dwellings occasionally illuminated the emptiness. A time long past hovered in the wind and segued into now. Asadi's stories: the bomb, the crash. People slipping from the roof of the train. Bodies beside the track, burnt limbs, gaping wounds. Dead children. He's beside me asking me to see what he saw. I yanked the window shut and found my way back to my bunk. Memories and history refusing to be extinguished.

'Chai, chai.' The compartment door flew open. A chaiwala poured tea into plastic cups and offered them around. The hot liquid, sweet as honey, soothed my parched throat. My fellow passengers were rousing. The mother took her two sleepy boys to the toilet. Belongings were gathered together. We sat bleary-eyed and quiet waiting for the train to reach its destination.

The tannoy blared, the words a jumble.

'Jodhpur.' The man in the suit translated for me. 'Go safely,' he said as he left the compartment. He was first off the train; I watched his back as he strode along the platform.

Jodhpur. I had heard it so often from Asadi's lips, but it felt unfamiliar as I rolled the name around my own tongue.

The temptation to find a hotel and a comfortable bed to sleep in was strong. Stick to the plan I told myself and settled for a splash of cold water on my face in the restroom and a strong coffee bought from a vendor outside the station. Taxi drivers were easy to find, all vying for trade. I showed the address I had written on a piece of paper to one of them. He wiped a hand through his greased hair and pursed his lips. 'Very far.' He took it to another who studied me. I cringed, realizing my crumpled clothing and tousled hair were a source of amusement. 'Wait,' he grinned. 'I fix driver for you.' He disappeared and I hovered in front of a recruitment poster advertising for nurses to go and work in the UK. By the time he returned I felt I knew the clean, bright-eyed, uniform-clad girl in the picture who beamed her smile at me.

'This man, he take you. Long way, Madam. Big price.' He named a figure, I halved it. We haggled for a few minutes until eventually all parties seemed satisfied. The taxi driver who was to take me picked up my case. I hurried after him to his car which stood at the kerb with the engine running. The long night, my weariness and longing for a shower overruled the spits of worry that flickered in my head. I retrieved an energy bar from my rucksack and settled into the back seat.

We arrived after an hour and a half of being shaken like a lettuce leaf in a colander, of dozing, only to be woken by my head bumping against the window as we hit another pothole. The endless whine of Indian music from the radio rung in my ears.

I eased my aching body from the car. Hot desert air seared my lungs. The sun's glare was fierce; I retrieved my sunglasses from the foot well where they'd fallen. The taxi driver turned his back to me and peed in the sand.

'Namaste.' A gate in the rattan fence opened. A man in a grey safari suit stepped out. 'Namaste,' he repeated inclining his head towards me. 'I am Jahan, Jahan Singh. And you will be Lily, our guest from England. You must be hot and tired. Please come in. We have a cold drink to welcome you with.'

I paid the taxi driver who must have been happy with his tip because he showered me effusively with the blessing of the gods. Like a zombie I followed Jahan through the gate into the compound. He led me to an open-sided thatched structure and bade me sit at the long wooden table. He called across the yard and a woman appeared carrying a tray with glasses and a jug of pink juice. The ice cubes in it rattled invitingly.

'This is my wife,' Jahan said with pride in his voice. The petite woman wore a lemon-yellow sari. Flowers decorated the edges and wound like a garland across her chest to drape over her shoulder. A sparkly hair comb held her hair behind one gold-studded ear. She smiled from beneath long eyelashes and set down the tray in front of me. Her bangles jingled. Beside her I felt clumsy, the creases in my clothes more obvious. I was sure my sweaty face must be streaked with dust, and I ran a clammy hand through my wild curls.

'You have had a long journey,' my host offered in response. 'You must take refreshment, then I will show you to your hut and supply you with water to wash with.

'Thank you.' I sounded feeble. The cool sweet juice slipped down my throat, slowly quenching my thirst. I gazed from the shade of the building over to where three round mud-walled structures stood bathed in sun. A large tree, its leaves hanging still, cast a circle of shade on the sandy ground. Beneath the tree, chairs yawned empty. The merest breeze blew puffs of dust into tiny swirls. 'This is beautiful and peaceful. It is so different from Delhi. London feels a million miles away.'

'I'm glad you like our place. The Thar desert is special, but the people are poor. The tourists go to the cities, to the palaces and forts and to Agra to see the Taj Mahal. Here we offer something different, and it gives work to local people. When you are rested, I will tell you more.'

Jahan provided me with a bucket of water and a jug. I poured the tepid water over my head, each drop washing away the grime and restoring my energy until I laughed aloud with the sheer pleasure of it. Dry and clean I lay down on the wide bed and stared at the conical ceiling of my grass-roofed hut. The sheets were cool, the pillow soft, my breathing loud in the silence. I wished Adam could be here to share it. I closed my eyes and slept.

The next morning I woke early to the sound of a bird's call. A high, insistent note urged me awake. For a moment I couldn't remember where I was, but the round walls came into focus and realization brought excitement. I whispered into the fresh, cool air, 'Asadi, are you pleased I've come? To your village, to the place you roamed as a boy.' Outside a cow mooed long and dolefully. A cockerel crowed; others joined the chorus.

Jahan was already about and beckoned me over to the open building.

'You are refreshed?' he asked, as he poured coffee. 'You have visited my country before?'

'No, this is my first time in India.' But I half wanted to say that I knew this village: the schoolmaster's dwelling, the street down the middle with its dirt track, and the house at the end with its extension made of brick. 'And a wadi where the breezes blow, and the deer roam unafraid.' Without thinking I voiced Asadi's description.

Jahan paused, his hand hovering over the breakfast he was serving.

'You would like to see the desert? I can arrange a camel ride.'

I sipped the rich strong liquid. 'First, I would like to walk to the village — if that's possible? See how it has altered. I mean …' I stuttered, 'it must have changed, grown bigger over time. The school … is there a school?'

'Yes.' He glanced across, a question in his eyes. His hesitation hung between us. 'You know of the school? It is very small — maybe fifteen children. It serves the village and the outlying areas. Some pupils walk a long distance each day to get there.' He laughed. 'I suspect you will get to meet a few of them. My son attends. He will be excited to tell his friends about our English guest. I'm afraid you may be regarded as something of a novelty.'

Jahan placed my breakfast in front of me. Fragrant vegetables whetted my appetite. 'This looks delicious and smells divine.' I bit into a crisp roti.

'My wife, she is a good cook. I am a lucky man. We don't eat meat,' he added almost as an apology.

'That's no problem,' I said tucking in, suddenly realising how hungry I was.

After breakfast, before the heat became too strong, I set off for the village. Beige desert surrounded me, a sea of sand. Cloud shadows were languid moving shapes. I pulled my hat further down my forehead; my sunglasses already slipping on my sweaty nose. Jahan had shown me the way. He'd offered to accompany me, but I wanted to go alone. He'd given me water to drink and put his number into my phone.

'You are safe here,' he assured me. 'It is only the sun that will be your enemy. Don't stay out too long.' He had watched as I set off, hovering as would an anxious parent.

I could see the distorted outline of habitation shimmering in the distance. The closer I got the more my heart tapped against my ribs. I had no plan, no expectations, no reason to be so apprehensive. I felt Asadi walking beside me, the sand shifting with our footsteps. I have brought you home... Show me what you want me to see.

I was drawn immediately to the position of the first abode I reached. It faced the track that wound its way between other crude houses. They seem to have been put together with sheets of corrugated iron interspersed with breeze blocks and wood. This house was a low-slung, single-storey place, with mud walls the same colour as the ground. A rough-hewn fence of dry branches surrounded it and within the area two tethered goats strained to reach the blades of dried grass that grew at its edge.

I knew with certainty it was Mr Chouhan's house.

While I stared, a small boy about three years old emerged. He wore only a blue T-shirt. He squatted in the dust and began to pile up stones until the stack grew tall. With a yell, he demolished them and began again.

'Irfan.' The name escaped in a gasp of breath. The boy looked up. He stood on spindly legs greyed with dust and stared at me. Solemn eyes in a solemn face.

'Hello,' I said to break the spell. A woman came from behind the house steadying a pitcher on her shoulder. She drew her head covering closer around her face and called to the boy who ran quickly to her side.

'Hello. Namaste.' I garbled, trying to smile as I mustered my wildly racing thoughts. She smiled back. A shy smile. She took the boy's hand, and we stood regarding each other.

'This is … was the schoolmaster's house?' I asked.

The stud in her nose caught the light. Her smile widened but she didn't reply.

'Your son?' I said trying again, pointing to the boy. He had shaken himself free and stepped closer to me. The woman nodded and disappeared into the house. She returned carrying a sleeping baby. 'Two,' she said holding up her fingers so that I would understand.

Across the fence I stretched out my hand and touched soft warm skin. The baby's finger curled around mine.

'Chai? Water?' She opened the rickety gate, gesturing me in. I hesitated but she looked pleased when I accepted her invitation. She hurried indoors with the baby and brought out a cushion which she placed on the step indicating that I should sit. The little boy brought me some of his stones. Seeing I was happy to receive his gifts he ran around the yard bringing me more, a brown twig, smooth and shiny, and a bleached white bone. Just as his mother brought out cups of chai he was chuckling, flattening out my hand and tipping several pellets of dried goat's poo into it. I laughed with him, but his face crumpled at the scolding he received. It seemed quickly forgotten when scraggy chickens fussed around our feet and he delighted in trying to chase them off.

We sat quietly watching the boy play. I didn't stop the tears that gathered and spilled. Asadi's tears, his regrets, his shame. His love circled the house and found its place in the little boy's happy giggles. Contentment spread over me like sunshine after rain. I thought of all the time I had spent with the old man on his bench, when there was no need to talk, when listening to the birds or the rustle of leaves had been enough. Today the sounds were different; the cluck of a hen, a small boy's squeal, a dog's bark, and the harsh cough of a scooter as it bumped down the road.

Thank you. You taught me to be. Happiness and sadness are

part of that.

The child's mother squatting beside me squeezed my hand as though reading my thoughts.

19

I thanked the woman for my tea and waved goodbye to her son. The road became a concrete strip that stretched between the dwellings. Plastic bottles, paper, vegetable matter and shredded tyres littered the edges. This is where Asadi played, where he walked. Did he look on these same sights? A hot, sour smell of rotting food and animal dung hung in the air. My presence attracted curious stares. Children stopped playing, mothers looked on. I felt eyes following me. A group of men building a wall paused to watch me walk by. I heard loud talk and laughter from them. I didn't look back to see if they resumed their work. A teenage girl was pumping water into a shiny container while a bare-footed, bare-bottomed child played in the puddles beneath the pump. He tossed muddy water over his head.

The sound of running footsteps from behind made me step aside to let the person pass. A young man drew level. He bent over, breathing heavily.

When he regained his breath he asked, 'How are you?' each word formally articulated. Taller than me, he had thin shoulders and a shadow of facial hair. He flapped at the hem of his white polo shirt to cool himself.

'I am well, thank you.'

'You are lost?'

'No. I'm not lost. I wanted to see the village. I'm staying …' I stopped, hesitant to give too much detail.

'You are staying at Jahan's place. I know. Everyone knows.' He grinned. 'I talk with you? The English. One day I come to your country. My cousin from Mumbai, he lives in Man-chest-er now. He tell me when I speak the language, then I can come.'

'Your English is good. My name is Lily.' I held out my hand feeling surer of myself. He shook it with a slight bow of his head.

'You live here?' I glanced around. Several of the women had gathered together and were watching us. Their saris, yellow, turquoise, purple, blue, were patches of colour in the sepia landscape.

'Outside,' my new companion said waving his hand in the direction of the desert. 'One miles, maybe two. I run to meet you. To practise the English.' He took a deep breath and puffed out his chest.

I couldn't help but like him. 'What is your name?'

'Sahil.'

'I'm pleased to meet you, Sahil. And flattered that you should run so far to talk to me.'

We fell into step. He gave me the names of the people who lived in the places we passed. Rough huts cobbled together with any available building material stood beside more adequate constructions. One or two even had a second storey. With each name came a comment. '*He* has many goats. *Three* brothers live here. They own two buffalo and a buffalo baby. Plenty rich.' His low whistle turned into an impressed smirk. 'One day – I be plenty rich too.'

'I hope so, Sahil.'

He leaned closer. 'This man.' His hand tapped a sagging gate. 'Six children – all girls.' He shook his head. 'Too many.' His mouth turned down; his brows knitted together. 'He not rich.'

I laughed aloud, and the gang of small children who had accumulated around us tittered.

'Shoo, Shoo.' Sahil fluttered his hands at them. They retreated a few steps and then resumed walking behind us in a train.

'Why you come?' Sahil's question took me by surprise. He searched my face, his head tipped to one side.

Why had I come? A cart rumbled past; the donkey stopped to defaecate in the road. The driver whipped the animal's flank. It plodded on at the same slow pace.

Stalling, I banged my foot to rid my sandal of a pebble.

'In England, in London, I knew an old gentleman.' I hesitated still unsure whether to go on.

'Yes.' Sahil nodded as he listened.

'He was a good friend to me. Truly kind. He helped me – my mother had died.' Caught out by the catch in my voice I swigged at my bottle of water so that Sahil wouldn't notice.

'His name was Asadi. He was born here. He lived here until he was fifteen.'

Sahil stopped abruptly. Our group of followers almost crashed into him. 'Lived here? In this village? He went to London?'

I held my breath wishing I'd kept quiet.

'He from this small place. Perhaps I too go to London.' He shrugged. 'I not know him, this Asadi.'

'No. Long before your time. He was almost ninety when he died.'

Sahil whistled again and chewed at his thumbnail. He grabbed the biggest boy from the crowd around us, held him by the shoulders and rattled off words. The boy ran off down the street pursued by the others.

'Did you go to the local school?' I asked, wanting to restore the congenial atmosphere.

'Yes. I have certificates. You come to my house; I show you them. Top pupil.' He prodded at his breastbone.

'And you have brothers and sisters?'

'My brother, he is lazy. He doesn't work hard at school. He dream all day. I tell him he will end up cleaning streets. I have two baby sisters. Same faces.' He traced a circle around his own face.

'They are twins you mean?'

'Twins.' He tried out the word. 'See I learn from you. Twins,' he repeated. 'I will tell them.'

A herd of goats, led by a girl, milled in the road in front of us. Their bells tinkled. One or two stood on hind legs pulling at leaves from a bush. The girl whacked them on their rumps and they ran off bleating.

'Sahil,' a man hollered, pushing through the goats. The boy Sahil had shouted at earlier was with him. I walked on not wanting to be witness to a row.

Here the houses were more colourful, painted white with the top halves blue, or vivid pink. Another was sea green. Open thatched structures supported on cut tree trunks stood beyond each compound and housed a sleeping bullock or a fat sow. This clearly was the better end of the village. I wondered if Asadi's house was here. If it still existed. I reached the last house where the road ended and the desert encroached. Sand had blown into piles against the house wall. A curtain hung over the doorway and a pot steamed on an open fire. Washing like bright blooms lay strewn over bushes to dry.

'Miss Lily, wait,' Sahil called. He took my arm, turned me round and pointed. 'This person. I fetch him. He say he know your friend.'

I shook my head. 'My friend came to England in 1947. A long time ago.'

The man came closer. He wheezed from tight lungs. He was older than I'd first thought, his skin freckled with age spots. His trousers, ragged at the hems, drooped over dirty feet. He was much younger than Asadi had been, too young to have known him. He began to talk quickly. Sweat oozed from the pores on his nose. I turned away from the rancid smell of his breath.

'He says his father knew Asadi. They went to school together.'

'Asadi's father was the moneylender, the *sahakar*.' I offered in clarification.

The man's head jerked. A noise erupted from his throat; he directed a frothy globule of sputum in the direction of the house with the washing outside.

I gaped.

The fellow gabbled on. White saliva collected in the corner of his mouth.

'He says his father died because of the moneylender. That his father was broken, and poorer than dirt.' Sahil looked unhappy, like he wanted the conversation to end.

The man gesticulated towards the house. He kicked the wall, anger bubbling over.

'The family still live there?' I shivered despite the heat.

'No. No. Long gone.' Sahil and I stared at the house which was raked in sunshine. 'He tell me the moneylender's sons died. Both of them. In the war. He says when he heard that he was glad.' Sahil's shoulders drooped under the weight of the translation.

I swallowed and stepped back from the hatred that contorted our companion's features.

'It's all right, Sahil. You meant well. Thank you for walking with me. I'm going to go back to Jahan's now. It's ridiculously hot.' I used my hand as a fan. 'I hope one day you make it to

England.' I turned away trying not to give in to nausea that churned my stomach.

Jahan was preparing the other hut. He didn't see me return. I collected my book and sat in the shade of the big tree. A limp breeze ruffled the leaves allowing light like transparent gold to filter through. I recalled the loathing in the villager's voice, felt his anger. My hurt was for Asadi. For him as a boy growing up — being despised for what his father did. Losing his mother and sister in the smallpox outbreak, the family blamed by the village for being the cause. Scene by scene the story he told me was becoming tangible. He wanted me to know him. I was beginning to.

Loud whispers and muffled sniggers woke me. Several children stood grinning in a semi-circle in front of my chair. They clapped when I opened my eyes.

'Hello,' I said trying to gather my thoughts.

'Hello,' they repeated in unison and fell about with more titters.

Jahan arrived with a cold drink for me.

'I said you were not to waken Miss Lily.' He admonished the group, but his voice smiled.

'This is my son, Rishi.' Jahan's hand rested on the shoulder of a boy in shorts and a checked shirt. The other children called out their names. A little girl of about five came closer and stood by my chair.

'Have you come from school? It's lovely to meet you all.'

'Yes. School,' the tallest boy said. Lots of heads nodded.

'You like school?'

Some smiled, some pulled faces. 'School is too long. It is ...' The boy struggled for a word. He put his hands together by his cheek and shut his eyes.

'Tiring?' I tried to help him out.

He shook his head then held up a finger. 'Baw-ring,' he drew the sound out.

I burst into laughter and so did Jahan. One of the girls punched her schoolmate on the arm.

Jahan flicked his fingers at the group. 'Go and play.' The

boys began to kick a ball around; the girls sat at my feet talking amongst themselves.

I asked them, 'Do you know how to play hopscotch?' They watched with solemn concentration as I drew large squares in the sand and searched around for a smooth stone. I threw the stone into each square in turn showing them how to pick it up standing on one leg. They soon got the hang of it and the air was full of happy laughter. Even the boys joined in, tumbling to the ground when they lost their balance.

Engrossed in our game I didn't notice the stranger until he spoke to the children. Dressed head to toe in orange his presence startled me. A diminutive figure, he sat cross-legged on the wall that surrounded the tree. His loose robes exposed a bony, bare, brown shoulder. Beside him lay a whittled staff. The children seemed untroubled and soon resumed their games. With his shrivelled skin and orange scarf wound around his head like a turban, he looked like a garden gnome. A white beard stretched from chin to chest. His cloudy, sunken eyes followed me. He watched as I skipped and jumped with the kids. He made me feel uncomfortable. I sat back down in my chair.

Jahan's wife sent the children home when she brought the man a plate of rice and vegetables. He ate with his fingers, rolling the food into balls. A younger male came to join him, greeting him with a slap of the hand. Their talk was earnest, their heads close together. I tried to concentrate on my book but each time I looked up I encountered the old man's gaze.

'My son has something he wishes to ask you.' Rishi, his shirt now streaked with dusty finger marks, stood beside his father. Jahan eased his son forward.

'Please you visit our school tomorrow?'

'I would love to come to your school. Thank you for the invitation.' Asadi's school. Where Mr Chouhan had taught.

His father patted his shoulder. Rishi looked happy and ran off. 'I like him to practise the English whenever he can, but he is shy.'

'He does very well. You must be proud of him.

'Jahan, can I ask, who is this man?' I said it softly, not wanting to appear rude.

'Ah.' Jahan squatted beside me. 'He is a holy man. A sadhu. He wanders many miles each day. People give him food. He is, how do you say it – a wise man. He gives counsel. This man.' He gestured towards the younger of the two. 'He is a student. They are discussing religion. Sometimes for many hours.' He gave the slightest shake of his head.

'The holy man looks ancient. I think in India age is revered.'

'It is. No one knows how old he is. He has been around all my life.'

Night fell with a suddenness that still surprised me. Moths flew around the Tilley lamp Jahan had hung in the tree. I felt the nip of biting insects on my ankles. The holy man stood up, his scrawny, bowed legs looked barely strong enough to support him. His companion acknowledged me as they left together, still deep in conversation.

When I went across for dinner there was another guest already eating. He peered at me through thick glasses, smiled briefly, then continued to read the book he had propped up against a glass.

'Mr Sultanov is an entomologist. From Kazakhstan. He comes every year.' Jahan placed dishes of steaming food in front of me. He leaned closer. 'He collects insect specimens from the desert.' His eyebrow lifted a fraction as his lip twitched in a smile.

'You must meet such fascinating people.'

'Yes, from many places in the world. I am very fortunate.'

As I ate, I envied Jahan his apparent contentment. What would be the future for his little son I wondered.

After the meal, I sat staring into the darkness. A million stars shone like fireflies. The warning call of a deer pierced the quiet and bats swooped, blacker than the night.

Jahan came to sit beside me. He coughed and fiddled with a place mat on the table.

'Is something wrong?' I asked, trying to ease his discomfort.

He glanced at me. 'The sadhu, who was here earlier.' He hesitated. 'He said you have been asking about someone who used to live in the village.'

Surprise made me start. I felt a bristle of irritation that

dissolved when I saw Jahan's worried look.

'I am sorry to ask,' he said.

'It's not a problem. I'll tell you. I wanted to come here because, in England, I knew someone who came from here. His name was Asadi Bai. He was a dear friend. He told me so much about this village, about India. When he died, he asked ...' I steepled my fingers. 'I decided to see it for myself.' Loyalty or caution made me reluctant to tell Jahan what Asadi had asked of me. I sighed. 'That's all. You can explain it to the holy man when he next appears.'

'Please forgive. This is India ...' Jahan gave me a warm smile. 'Sleep well.'

'Good morning, Miss Lily,' the children chorused. The little girl who had attached herself to me yesterday sat in the front row grinning. A pink bow lay on her wild hair like a nesting bird.

'Namaste, children. Thank you for inviting me to your school.'

I laid my cloth bag carefully on the floor. In it was Asadi's urn which I had brought on impulse. Now I imagined him moving around the room, squatting on the floor, touching the walls.

The pupils shuffled about on the rattan mat. I counted fourteen of them sitting in rows, the older ones at the back. The teacher, a youngish man who wore a startlingly white shirt, apologised. 'Not all of our students attend every day.' He grimaced. 'There are lots of reasons. We are honoured that you have come.'

I looked around. A table with exercise books and pencils stood to one side. Peeling blue paint covered the lower half of the walls, a grass brush stood in the corner. I turned to the open door knowing it would be green, half expecting to see where Asadi and Mr Chouhan had patched it up.

'One day we hope to have a new school.' A bead of sweat trickled down the teacher's forehead. 'But there is no money.' He held up a hand and pointed to a boy of about eleven who stood up and recited his nine times table. Everyone applauded when he finished. Then it was the turn of two girls who read a passage from an English reading book, a series outdated even when I was at school.

'You have clever children here,' I said. 'I met some of them yesterday, they are all so polite.'

The teacher beamed.

'Work hard,' I addressed them, 'and I'm sure you will do very well. When you grow up you can be doctors and lawyers. Anything you want to be.'

'I tell them that, miss, all the time.'

An arm shot up. A boy struggled to stand. One foot turned inward making him lean to the side. 'I want to be an engineer. Build machinery that will bring water to our village.'

'Wouldn't that be wonderful?' The constriction in my throat made it impossible to say more.

'We are very happy that you have visited us today.' The teacher showed me out. 'It is good for them to meet people from other countries.'

'Goodbye, children.' I waved.

'Goodbye, miss.' A ragged chant of voices followed me down the outside steps.

It was still early with a freshness that would burn off as the heat grew fiercer. I had brought the urn with me for another reason. I'd asked Jahan about the wadi. He'd looked worried when I said I wanted to go there.

'Be careful. The sun, snakes ...' He shrugged and pushed a bottle of water into my hand. 'You not stay long.'

I'd promised him I wouldn't and with the sun beginning to whiten the light I understood his concern.

Dry shrubby plants and bleached stones marked the track where the desert rose into low hills. A train of camels ambled past, led by a driver in a grey robe with a scarf bound round his head and face so that only his eyes were visible. I waved my phone and asked if I could take a photo. The man stood upright beside the lead camel and then walked on when I uttered my thanks. Fresh dung steamed on the path.

Sam and Noah would like the picture; I winged it off to them. Adam and the boys. Work — everything seemed so far away, so long ago. Homesickness like a flush of fever made me stop walking. I scrambled up the slope into the sparse shade of a stunted tree and let the ache recede. I'll be home soon. Suddenly I wanted to be.

Silence echoed around me. So heavy it pinned me to the ground. No birdsong, no flap of wings or bleat of a goat penetrated the peace. A waft of wind lifted my hair. A yellowed leaf spiralled slowly down from the tree to rest by my foot.

This is the peace you spoke of Asadi. The peace you sought when your mother and sister died and when life became even more lonely and hard.

I felt it. I understood.

I took the urn from my bag, placed it between my knees and unscrewed the lid.

'Breathe again, Asadi,' I whispered. The breeze, softer than the brush of a feather, lifted the surface and blew some of the powdered dust across the sand. I quickly screwed the top back on. Was it disrespectful? I had been entrusted to take the urn to the Ganges. The freed ash stirred and moved in the warm wind. The quiet returned. I smiled and knew Asadi was smiling too

The strange, wizened holy man was eating fruit, deep in conversation with Jahan when I returned to the complex.

'Namaste,' I called, bending my head to my raised hands. He soundlessly returned the greeting. I felt clumsy and awkward under the probe of his eyes. I retired to my hut, glad of the cool familiar space.

That night it was Jahan's wife who served the meal. She looked pleased when I told her how delicious it was.

'We have lots of Indian restaurants in England, the dishes are nothing like this.' I'm not sure if she understood what I said, but she offered me more food.

My fellow guest, the entomologist sat with me keen to show me the drawings he had done that day. Of beetles and spiders, every detail exquisite. His enthusiasm was palpable as he turned the pages of his sketchbook. Afterwards, like a busy spider himself, he scurried off to bed.

'He is an expert in his field.' Jahan brought me chai. He hovered at the table, his head blocking the light from the lamp.

'You have enjoyed your stay here?' He fiddled with the

button on his shirt.

'I certainly have. It has been very special. I will never forget my few days in this corner of India.'

He grew serious. Two creases formed between his eyes. 'You liked your visit to the school? My son was very proud. The building, it is old.'

He seemed embarrassed.

I pushed aside my teacup. 'Will you sit down?'

He hesitated but pulled out a chair and sat opposite. Light pooled onto the table holding back the warm blanket of night. He took a scrap of folded paper from his breast pocket and spread it on the table. He pushed it towards me.

'There is a man – he lives in Jodhpur. He wants to meet you.'

'To meet me? Why?'

I heard his intake of breath. 'He has reserved you a room in the Royal Hotel for tomorrow night. He says he will meet to talk with you in the foyer at six o'clock.

I stared at the piece of paper. An address was written on it.

'The sadhu gave it to me earlier.' Jahan's explanation sounded more like an apology. 'This person,' he chewed his lip, 'is very important. He works for the Bank of India.'

'Jahan, none of this makes sense. I'm not going to meet someone just on his say-so. Who is he and why does …?'

'Miss Lily.' Jahan's tone silenced me. It was kind but firm. 'You should meet him. It is safe. You will be all right.'

20

I had endured the bone-shaking taxi journey from Asadi's village to Jodhpur. There had been plenty of time to work out a strategy. Hear the man out. Politely decline whatever business deal he is suggesting and fly back to Delhi tomorrow as planned. Now, feeling simultaneously annoyed and curious, I stirred the green cocktail with its red cherry and pretentious parasol. The hotel was all shiny-white tiled floors, gold trimmings, long mirrors and green potted plants. Slick staff in maroon waistcoats loitered discreetly. I could be anywhere in the world. I longed for the India that I had come to know.

A group of tourists, Americans I guessed, were fussing over luggage while waiting for room keys. The tour guide was trying without success to herd them towards the lifts.

Whoever I was waiting for was already half an hour late. Jahan had warned me about 'Indian time'. I would give him five more minutes.

A man strode through the revolving doors. Smart, expensive suit, leather computer case in his hand. Was this him? I sat straighter in the chair and pulled the hem of my dress over my knees.

'Good evening.' A crisp voice came from my side. 'I am pleased you have come.' 'Computer man' had disappeared.

I turned to see two people staring down at me intently. The woman wore an exquisite blue sari bordered with silver. She smiled briefly then averted her eyes. She looked younger than the man. He was probably in his sixties, upright, with greying hair and tall for an Indian. They moved to sit on the sofa across from me. Immediately a waiter was by his side with glasses of chai. My cocktail sat on the table like an accusation.

I chose to say nothing. Let him take the lead. I hated that my heart was beating so fast in my chest.

'You are young. And pale skinned.' His eyes scoured my face, his voice a sneer. 'Your mother was white?'

The woman, who I took to be his wife, laid a bejewelled

hand on his knee.

Fury fuelled my niggling headache.

I stood up. 'I'm sorry. I don't know who you are. You haven't introduced yourself and I haven't endured a hot, dusty taxi journey in order for you to talk about my mother. I don't think we have anything to say to each other.' I nodded to the woman and began to walk away.

'Lily.'

My name followed me. I turned.

'My apologies. I am anxious. Your appearance and your youth took me by surprise. I thought … well, you see … I hadn't expected to have a white … sister.'

'Sister?' It exploded from me.

He glanced around, spread out a hand and clearly expected me to sit back down.

With a snap of his fingers, he hailed a waiter. 'A glass of water.' Within seconds it was in my hand. Cool and clear, I fixed my gaze on the piece of lime that bobbed on the surface.

The bustle of the hotel foyer receded. Only this well-groomed couple sitting opposite were in focus.

'You have been asking about my father. I don't understand why.'

I saw the thrust of his chin, his pained face and the quiver of his lip.

'Ravi. You are Ravi?'

For the first time he offered half a smile. 'You know my name.' His voice quietened. His hand trembled, he pushed a business card across the coffee table.

'Forgive me. I have been rude. I am Mister Ravi Bai. My wife Chara.' He lifted her hand from his side as though presenting her. 'When word reached me from my father's village that a woman from England was asking about him, I was extremely upset.'

He pushed back his shoulders, his eyes hooded, his face dark. 'I asked myself why. It was nonsense. My father has been dead for decades.'

I shook my head. 'No, Mr Bai. Your father died only recently. He was in his late eighties. I am not your sister. Your father never married again. He told me …' I wondered how much to say, 'that your mother, Brinda, was the only woman he could ever love. He was a wonderful, kind man.'

The man's features collapsed. He slumped back against the cushions. His wife made a popping sound and flapped a hand with its painted nails.

Ravi muttered under his breath. A prayer, a curse?

I watched him, my own emotions tumbling. He wore a dark suit, his tie now slightly skewed as he ran his fingers around the collar of his shirt. I wanted to see Asadi's gentle face in his, but I couldn't.

'Perhaps we should start again,' I said, recovering more quickly. 'I have also been remiss. You appear to already know my name. 'I am Lily Salkeld. I knew your father at the end of his life. I wished I had known him for longer.'

He rubbed his forehead. His wife spoke softly in his ear. He signalled to a hovering waiter and issued instructions.

'I am told I am a poor host,' he said. 'I have ordered snacks.' He undid his jacket and twiddled a button until I thought it would come loose. 'You have much to tell me.'

His wife spoke, her voice soft and warm like melted chocolate. 'We are pleased to meet you, Lily. My husband has been very distressed these past few days. You must understand.'

'Yes, of course. This will have come as an enormous shock to you.'

'I don't remember my father. I was only a young child when he died – disappeared. In India it is very hard to grow up without a father. I am now a man of position. Respect has been hard to earn. Family honour is more important than blood.'

The jagged edge of blame sharpened his words.

'Your father lived with deep sorrow and regret – and shame. He also brought love, kindness and friendship to many people. Especially to me. Before he died he asked me if I would realise his greatest wish and release his ashes on the River Ganges. He would not let me agree to his request until I had heard his story.

The foyer emptied, filled again, the residents showered and refreshed, like birds showing off their new plumage. They chattered, laughed, ordered drinks, then peace returned when they filed into the dining room for dinner.

All this time I recounted what Asadi had shared with me,

told Mr Ravi Bai and his attentive wife what I knew. An array of snacks remained uneaten on the table. I nibbled on a samosa out of politeness, but the spicy filling clagged in my throat.

'You are telling me he was a *goonda*. A saboteur?' Mr Bai said it like it had a sour taste.

'He was young. Impressionable. Living in turbulent times. Who knows how any of us would have behaved.' The urge to defend Asadi lay just below my skin.

Mr Bai scoffed. 'We, that is you and me, would have been on opposite sides. That I know.'

I ignored the jibe.

Mrs Bai who had been mostly silent intervened. 'Partition was ugly. Made so by the British and the Indians. Its legacy lingers – Kashmir ...' She linked her arm through her husband's. I wasn't sure if it was a calming gesture or restraint.

'Your father fled to England in nineteen forty-seven.'

'Before I was two.' He snarled his contempt. 'I wasn't even two years old.'

I continued, feeling Asadi beside me. When I faltered over what to say and what to leave out, he helped me, giving me the words. The scenes came back as vivid as when he'd described them. I searched for pride in his son's face but saw none.

It grew late. Only a few people sat around drinking. The chandeliers cast a bright unforgiving light. I wanted to go to bed. I finished speaking, remembering that rainy day in London when Abeki, Adam and I had sought shelter in a café after saying a final goodbye to Asadi at his home.

'Mr Bai looked shattered, his skin tinged yellow, his hair out of place where he had run his hand through it. He inhaled deeply, then released his breath in a long sigh.

To try and ease the tension, I asked the silent couple, 'Do you have children?'

'No,' Mr Bai barked. His wife stared at her lap, unable to hide the tear that slid down her cheek.

He rose abruptly, his hand extended.

'Thank you for meeting me this evening. I can only assume what you tell me is true. If you would be so kind as to fetch the urn with my father's ashes, I will see his wish is granted. I will take over all the arrangements.' He flicked his wrist. 'You may enjoy the rest of your holiday as a tourist. You should see the Taj Mahal. India has beautiful …' His phone rang making us all jump. He scowled at the screen. 'I must take this call.' He strode to the door and disappeared outside.

I released my clenched fists and briefly shut my eyes.

'They call him at all hours. The bank. He is on the board.' Mrs Bai dabbed her face with a crumpled tissue. She leaned closer.

'Please. You will come to our house tomorrow. His mother …' Her eyes darted to where her husband strode back and forth, the phone clamped to his ear. 'She is still alive.'

'Brinda?' I grasped Mrs Bai's warm hands.

'Yes. She is old and frail. I know she will want to meet you. To hear what you have told us.' She squeezed my fingers. 'Come in the morning. My husband has a meeting.' She hurriedly scribbled an address on a piece of paper she took from her bag.

Mr Bai returned and stood over me waiting.

I gathered my bag, stood up and faced him.

'Asadi, your father endowed me with the privilege of bringing his ashes to India. He requested they be immersed in the holy river.' I spoke slowly, holding in the flush of anger that threatened to erupt. 'I felt honoured when he asked me. I intend to see my task through to its end. I respect that as family it is your right to conduct that duty. I will not interfere in the arrangements. I will join you and bring his ashes to whichever place you decide upon.' I took a breath. 'My plan is to return to Delhi tomorrow evening. I will send you contact details. Also, I haven't thanked you for the room. You are very generous.' I loathed the formality of my speech but couldn't trust myself to express it any other way.

His lips pursed. Sweat fringed his hairline.

'Very well. I will be in touch.' He turned and walked away.

Mrs Bai touched my arm. 'He is not a hard man. It is a big shock. He has many worries. Please, you promise to come tomorrow?' She gripped my arm tightly.

'What he said about having no children. It's not true. We have a daughter.'

21

The concierge hailed me a taxi. The driver, a thickset, laughing man wore a Liverpool football shirt. When he learnt I was English he kept kissing the club badge and grinning at me in the mirror.

Within minutes I was at the address. The sand-coloured villa, more modest than others on the road, glowed warmly in the morning sun. Trees, their leaves as large as saucers, dappled sunshine on a small patch of lawn where a water sprinkler rotated.

I knocked on the door. The sound echoed within the house. A young woman, a maid, answered. Her smile suggested she was expecting me. She showed me into a large hallway with chessboard black-and-white floor tiles. An air-conditioning unit hummed in the background. 'I will fetch madam,' she said.

I waited in the cool. Joss sticks burnt in a holder scenting the air with cinnamon.

'Namaste, Lily. Welcome.' Mrs Bai bowed her head.

'Namaste, Mrs Bai.' Today she looked composed, so different from the tearful woman of last night.

'Please, you must call me Chara. My mother-in-law is waiting for you. I have told her a little about why you come. I feared the shock might be too much. Her heart, you know.' She prodded her chest.

I nodded in understanding. My mouth felt dry, my stomach churned. I was meeting Brinda. Everything seemed unreal, like a stage set I had happened upon. A play without a script.

Chara must have sensed my anxiety. She briefly touched the sleeve of my shirt. 'Brinda is frail, but her mind is bright.'

'Will she understand me? Can you interpret?'

Chara chuckled. 'Her English, it is better than mine. It is the subject she taught all her life. Even when no need to work,' she continued. 'She is a determined woman. Independent.' She cocked her head. 'You have no worries.'

We entered a room at the back of the house. The sun shone

through louvred shutters painting strips of light across a patterned rug. Brinda sat in a brocade chair that dwarfed her. Pure white hair matched her white sari. Her face came alive with smiles. She raised a bony hand. I knelt beside her and covered it with mine. Neither of us spoke.

She struggled to her feet and, leaning on a stick, took me to the window. She was tiny, her back bent, her light flowery perfume reminiscent of an evening garden.

She held my arm to steady herself while Chara opened the shutters.

'My Jodhpur,' Brinda said.

The Mehrangarh Fort stood proudly on the skyline in the centre of the framed view. Rooftops stretched as far as my eye could see.

'I lived here nearly all my life. One day I knew my Asadi would come back. Today he has.' She stroked my skin with her fingers.

I squeezed my eyes shut, powerless to stop my tears.

'I am Lily. I can't believe I'm meeting you.' I didn't care that I was crying. Brinda reached up and wiped my cheek.

'Come. Sit close beside me, so that I can hear you.'

The room became shadowed again as Chara shut out the brightness.

The maid brought chai and glasses of iced water.

'You have come all the way from England?' Brinda asked.

'Yes, from London.' My voice still sounded weepy. I took an envelope from my bag. In it was the retirement card and a photograph of Asadi taken at the harvest lunch. He is sitting on his bench looking up, talking to someone out of view. He is laughing; his eyes are laughing. I passed it to Brinda.

She stared at it for a long time. Her finger gently traced the outline of his face. She raised it to her lips then pressed it against her heart.

'He never ever forgot you. He was the kindest man. He talked of you with such love. No one ever took your place.'

She smiled slowly. Listened without interrupting.

'Terrible things happened. Mr Chouhan with his family — at the station — the little boy, Irfan — he died.' I tried to tell her story. The words choked me as I watched her wince. Pain contorted her features. She stared at the photograph.

'Asadi blamed himself.' I had to finish. 'The shame he felt swallowed his mind.'

Brinda seemed to understand what I was trying to say. 'He was herded onto a boat to England. For a long time he was very ill. Later, when he recovered, he wrote to you.'

She shook her head. 'There were no letters. But I moved, with Ravi and Asadi's father. Nowhere was safe. Muslim gangs were looking for him. Why? He was an honest man.' She faltered, seeming to retreat to somewhere else. 'Mr Chouhan. I didn't know that. So sad. Such a lovely family.' She looked up. 'It was because of him I became a teacher. He was Asadi's mentor and great friend.'

Chara brought a wrap and placed it around the old lady's shoulders. A door banged somewhere in the depth of the house.

I showed Brinda the card.

She opened it. 'Can you read it to me,' she asked. 'My eyes are not so good.'

Dear Asadi,

We love you. Not only have you been our wonderful postman and friend, but you are also a great man.

Enjoy your retirement. We will miss you.

I returned it to Brinda and pointed out all the signatures on the page.

Her rheumy eyes misted over. 'His mother's last words to him: be a great man, Asadi.' She clutched the card tightly. 'I always knew he was alive.' She spoke to herself. 'My heart would have known if it was otherwise.' She held out her arm, fingering a gold-coloured glass bangle with a red stone. 'Asadi gave me this. It is only a trinket, but I have worn it always.'

'Brinda never married again either.' Chara hovered at her mother-in-law's shoulder.

'Pah. Everyone, they said Asadi was dead. They wanted me to marry an old man from the village. To give my son a father. I told them no. I would be a mother and a father to my son. The shame, disgrace. I didn't care.'

Chara pulled a face. 'Widows are not treated well. It was

hard for her. Incredibly hard. For Ravi too. I would not have her courage. Today, girls, women, they still suffer ...'

We talked on. Brinda had so many questions. I answered what I could. She was happy when I described the allotments and how Asadi had rescued me, how he helped me to find a path through grief as he had learnt to do. I showed her more photos of him on my phone, told her about Adam and the boys who were laughing into the camera.

'This man makes you happy, like my Asadi made me.' She breathed through missing teeth making a low whistling sound.

'Yes. He does. We speak or text whenever we can.'

Brinda tired, her voice becoming weaker.

'It is time for me to go,' I murmured. 'Meeting you has been more wonderful than I can describe.'

She arched her back with a jerk. 'Kyra is a good girl. You will help Chara? She said my son was rude last night. He has stubborn pride. He cares too much about what others think. I told him I am ashamed of him.' She lay back against the headrest, her breath shallow and uneven.

I looked at Chara for help.

Gathering herself, she beckoned me. 'We will leave her to rest.'

She took me into the garden where we sat together under a tree. Pots of red geraniums edged the lawn. An oasis in this sprawling city.

Across from us, a gardener, his dhoti wrapped between his legs, plucked weeds from beneath the shrubs. Chara was taut; she wrung her hands and played with her rings.

'This is beautiful.' I described the view with an arc of my arm.

'Did you know that Jodhpur is known as the blue city? Beneath the fort, in the old town much houses are painted blue. Some say it is a sacred colour from Lord Shiva, others that it was to frighten the termites that destroy the walls.' She shrugged and withered into silence as if giving the explanation had been an effort.

'Kyra is your daughter?'

Chara nodded without looking at me.

'She is young, like you. Two years she go to the university in

Delhi. Such pride we had.' Her lips tightened. 'My husband would be very angry if he knew I was saying this.' She lifted her head. Tears had smudged the kohl around her eyes. 'But I hear my mother-in-law speak and Asadi's story. They give me strength.' Her chest rose with her deep intake of breath.

'Kyra's professor rang. He say … she has been with boys.'

Chara uttered a single sob. 'Ravi is burnt up with shame. He rant and rave. Says she has brought disgrace upon him, upon our family. That she must never come home. He says he no longer has a daughter.'

'And you?'

'He mustn't learn of this,' she whispered. 'I wrote a letter. It came back. I don't know where she is. I am forbidden to talk of her, even to say her name.' Chara sank into herself. 'His reputation, his position with the bank. He afraid her behaviour will lose him everything.' She chewed her lip. 'Now you will think bad of him.'

'She is his daughter. How can he abandon her?'

'It is hard for you to understand. In India … dishonour is like a disease. The family, the community, colleagues … they think everyone will become infected. Many busybodies, they want to – how you say it? Topple you.'

Chara squeezed her eyes tight then opened them again. 'Please, I am begging of you. In Delhi, you find Kyra.'

I couldn't think. Dared not speak. What Chara asked was impossible. Where would I look in Delhi? I thought of the heat, the teeming streets, the crowded transport. 'I can't …'

'Please, Lily. You are my only hope. Every day I pray. Today I give offerings to Lord Shiva. He has sent you to me.'

I gulped. 'Chara, I don't know Delhi. I wouldn't know where to begin. I am a foreigner. Who will help me?' I didn't know how to tell her I couldn't do it.

'Wait.' She hurried inside.

The gardener had finished his task. I felt him appraising me from across the lawn. I shrank from his stare.

'See, this is where she lived. Many students there.' Chara pressed an address and a photograph of her laughing, pretty daughter into my hand. 'Maybe she have friends who know where she is.'

I took the items from her.

She grasped my arms. 'Thank you. Thank you from the bottom of my heart. Tell her ... tell her ... You will know the right words. I have all my trust in you.' Chara lifted my hand and kissed it.

I knew then that I would have to try.

22

'I show you Jodhpur's fort, see gardens, go to palace. Good price.'

'Pardon.' I realised the taxi driver was talking to me. 'No, sorry. I have to go to the airport this afternoon.'

'Where you fly to?' he asked, tossing his cigarette stub out of the window.

I didn't want to talk. 'To Delhi.' I touched my head. 'Sorry, bad headache.' It was an excuse. I lay back against the tacky, plastic-covered seat. He looked sympathetic, gave up chatting and whistled tunelessly instead. As we pulled out of the road, I saw Ravi's car draw up outside his house. The driver jumped out to open the door and Ravi strode up the path. A near miss! Would they tell him I had visited? I hoped Chara had time to compose herself. She didn't want me to think badly of her husband, but Christ, Kyra *is* his daughter. Maybe she's in trouble, just maybe she needs him.

Night had fallen by the time I reached Delhi. The rambling city hummed as loud as in the daytime with an endless stream of vehicles and gagging pollution. People zigzagged between the cars, tuk-tuk drivers yelled as they were forced to swerve. Stale bread and a dead crow rotted amongst the excreta and plastic bags that cluttered the gutters. Two small children slept alongside their parents only feet away from the roadside and I flinched as a motorbike swerved onto the verge narrowly missing them. I was relieved when I reached New Delhi, the guesthouse, and the same room I had before. Familiar, safe, quiet. I uttered a thank you to Amir, my lovely, funny colleague for recommending this friendly place. Amir, Isaac, Ben, and Jade, soon I would see them all again.

As before, Aisha brought me chai in the morning before she went to school.

'You like Rajasthan?' she asked. 'The desert: is it big?'

I tried to describe the vastness, the peace. It was so far removed from Delhi that I think she struggled to imagine it.

'Where is Delhi's university?' I asked her. 'Is it far?'

'No, not far. The campus is in Old Delhi. When I am eighteen, I will go there.' Aisha grinned and left me to drink my tea.

If I was going to look for Kyra, I would have to start today. I had less than a week before my flight home and I still had to release Asadi's ashes on the Ganges. 'How proud you would have been to have a clever granddaughter, Asadi. And I've met Brinda. She is beautiful and kind. Just as you described her,' I told him.

'Latif, do you know this place?' I asked Aisha's father at breakfast. He squinted at the address Chara had given me.

'It is where the university is. Aisha told me you were asking. You know someone there?'

'No, not really. When I was in Jodhpur, I met the mother of a student. She asked me if I could check on her daughter.'

'Yes. Always the mothers are worried. They want to know, are their sons or daughters eating, are they working hard?'

If only that was all, I thought.

'You could go by metro, or I order you an auto rickshaw. More fun.' He laughed. 'Travel the local way.'

It didn't feel much like fun. The driver, with his baseball cap worn backwards, seemed oblivious to the inches between our flimsy vehicle and the buses and trucks that thundered past. The engine coughed and the exhaust backfired loud as gunshot. In the absence of a seat belt, I hung onto the arms and kept my eyes fixed on the words 'Sri Veera Khali' the Hindu god's name written on top of the windscreen. I prayed for protection.

The university took me by surprise. Paths and trees separated modern, glass-fronted buildings that stood beside the warm sandstone of more traditional structures. Young men and women sat on benches or sprawled on the sparse grass. Others walked, bags on their shoulders, laughing, conversing with their fellow students. It could have been any campus in the world.

I approached a group of girls huddled together. They were passing a mobile phone between them, looking at pictures, laughing. All dressed in trousers and shirts of bright colours with their black hair loose, flowing down their backs.

'Hello, do you speak English?' I asked. 'Do you know Kyra Bai?' I showed them the photograph that Chara had given me.

They peered at it, spoke amongst themselves. I saw heads shake and shoulders shrug.

'Perhaps she live in the girls' hostel,' one of them said. 'You are from America? A student here?' I detected a note of incredulity. I felt old beside them but envied them the excitement, the buzz of learning, the being away from home for the first time.

'No. Not from America. I'm from England. It's a few years since I was at university. Now I work for a charity. Good luck to all of you.' I waved goodbye.

Students milled around, all with somewhere to go.

I found the girls' hostel after several attempts. It was a grey concrete building, similar to the halls of residence in my own university. A young woman with her hair scraped back and wearing a hint of lipstick asked if she could help. Like before, I posed the question and produced the photograph. She studied it for several seconds, glancing sideways at me.

'Sorry. I don't know.' She thrust the picture at me and ran off, her bag banging against her hip.

She'd recognised Kyra. I was sure of it. She seemed afraid. I waited until another group pushed out through the doors.

'Hi.' I stood in their path. 'I'm looking for Kyra.' I waved the photo and kept my voice light and cheerful. 'She's not answering her phone.' A small lie that I hoped would help. They stopped, crowded closer to each other, avoided my searching look. 'I'm a friend of her parents,' I said, scanning their faces.

'She doesn't live here now.' A girl with a pearl nose stud looked like she might say more, but other students bustled from the building and swarmed along the path towards us. 'I hope you find her.'

The girls moved off as one, linking arms with each other. 'Where will I find her professor?' I called after them, not wanting to let this moment pass. The girl with the nose stud turned. 'You mustn't talk to her professor.' Her eyes darkened. She blinked rapidly. 'I have to go.'

They disappeared into the distance. I sat on a seat. What should I do? Something was wrong. A frisson of fear tightened my lungs. This wasn't fair. I wasn't equipped to deal with this situation. Chara should never have asked.

From feeling sorry for myself came the reprimand. When I needed help at uni, Lou was there for me. In London, when I was a mess – did Asadi turn away? I looked at the photo of Kyra. You are Asadi's granddaughter. I have to find you. Where are you?

'Excuse me.' A girl with dark-rimmed glasses stood behind me. I recognised her as one of the group that I'd been talking to.

'If you meet me at three o'clock. I will take you to Kyra.' Her whisper was so soft I could barely hear her.

'Can you? Oh, thank you. That would be brilliant. I'll wait here.' Relief swept over me.

'No, not here. Outside the main entrance, on the other side of the road.' She hid her face behind a raised arm. 'I will find you.'

'Is Kyra all right?'

'Please, no more questions.'

I began to despair as three o'clock came and went. I scanned every young person that passed. None looked like the girl I had spoken to so briefly.

'Sorry I am late.' Gone were the trousers and shirt. This girl wore a long blue robe. She had a grey headscarf wound around her head, her dark eyes just visible through her glasses.

'Come quickly.' She hurried ahead leading me down streets, past women who touted limes and bunches of herbs from squares of newspaper spread on the side of the road. The fragrance of mint and coriander tinged the hot, fusty air. A man with no legs sat begging on a handmade trolley. A few people threw him a handful of coins. Most passed him by.

'We are here.' My guide stopped suddenly. 'You must go to the top of the house.'

'Will you come with me?'

The girl shook her head. 'I can't do that. People will say I too …' Her head swivelled from side to side as she looked along the street.

But this place is so … shabby. Are you sure?'

'I am sorry for Kyra. Please, you will help her?' The girl was already moving away.

'I don't know your name. But thank you.' I soon lost sight of her.

The building looked crumbly and unkempt. Washing hung from a balcony and electricity lines looped in circles and trailed drunkenly down the facade.

The door stood off the catch and it opened with a creak. My heart thumped against my ribs; my legs felt like lead. The dark hallway smelt of stale cooking and cumin. I clutched the sticky banister and made my way upwards one step at a time while my eyes became accustomed to the gloom. At the top of the house, I stood in front of a brown door, the paintwork chipped and scratched. No sound came from within. I wiped my hands on my jeans and wished I could be anywhere else but here. I knocked timidly, then louder, rapping the wood with my knuckles. I listened with my ear pressed close, but nothing. I tried the handle, feeling like an intruder. It opened a fraction but something heavy prevented it from opening further.

'Kyra?' I called through the narrow slit. 'Kyra. Are you there? You don't know me. My name is Lily. Your mother has sent me. She is beside herself with worry.' I spoke into nothingness.

'Kyra. Please talk to me.' I heard the faintest sound of footsteps, so quiet I wasn't sure if I'd imagined them. Brown fingers curled around the door's edge and a thin, frightened face peered out.

'Hello. Hi. Namaste.' My tumbling emotions jumbled my greeting. 'I have come from Jodhpur. Your mother asked me to find you. Whatever has happened she wants you to know she's not angry. Please don't shut me out. Look, I have a photograph of you.'

I heard the scrape of something being moved aside. She opened the door a little wider.

'May I come in? Then I can tell you who I am.' I squeezed in through the space. She shut the door behind me and wedged a chest up against it.

'It has no lock,' she apologised. 'This is the best I can do.'

Was this Kyra? This thin girl with hollow cheeks and dark rings under her eyes? Her hair fell in a straggly plait over her shoulder. This wasn't the beautiful girl in the photograph, the one whose face shone with brightness as she laughed at the camera.

'I am Kyra.'

She took the photo from me and looked at it for a moment. 'I have forgotten who that girl is.' She handed it back to me.

My face must have given me away.

'You are shocked.' She said looking down at her bare feet. 'Come through.'

We went into a cramped square room. A small, dusty window filtered in light. Kyra pushed aside a cover on the only chair and pointed for me to sit down. She sat on a cushion on the floor, her knees drawn up to her chin.

'My mother ... tell me how she is? But I don't understand who you are.'

'Your mother and your grandmother are frantic with worry.'

Kyra wiped away tears. '*Dadi-ji*. She is very old. I cause her such shame.'

'They want to know that you are safe then their distress will be less.' I passed Kyra a tissue and she blew her nose. 'I went to your house in Jodhpur. In England – I knew your grandfather. Your father's father.'

Kyra's forehead furrowed; her eyebrows knitted together. 'That cannot be true. He doesn't have a father.'

'He does, at least he did. He died a few weeks ago. It's a long story. Kyra, why are you living here? In this grimy hole.'

Her face blanched. Her lips barely moved. 'So *they* won't find me.'

'What has happened to you?'

She curled into herself. 'I can't speak of it.'

In her huddled form I recognised a self I knew. The nervous twitch of her lips, the raw hands from constant washing, the picked fingernails. Icy cold spread from my core.

'Have you been raped?' The question plummeted into the hush.

I dropped down beside her, held her hands between mine. 'Kyra.' I lifted her chin. 'Have you?'

238

She nodded. Her head slumped to her knees.

I put my arms around her. Held her until her body stopped shaking, until her sobs quietened.

'You are kind. You don't even know me.'

'But I know what you are feeling.' I eased her away from me holding her by the shoulders. 'When I was at university something happened to me.' I met her eyes, I didn't blink. She stared back. Realisation released her tension. She fell against me like a rag doll.

She talked then. Like she couldn't stop.

It was hard to hear her story. I batted away my anger knowing it wouldn't help.

'Six, seven weeks ago — I lose sense of time. Three of them.' She screwed her eyes shut. 'All night. They pinned me down. They were high ... high on drugs. I only knew one of them.' Her voice faltered. 'He is my tutor's son.'

Her stammer cut into me.

'Are you pregnant?' It was a bald question, but I had to ask.

'No.'

'Good. A grain of comfort,' I said, and we shared a weak smile.

The respite from her misery was short lived. 'I tried to tell my parents, but my father was enraged. He told me I have rained shame on them all. If it becomes known, he will lose everything. He will have to resign from the board of the bank.' I have brought him dishonour, disgraced him.'

'Kyra, this is not your fault. You have to know that.' My fury spilt over. 'You are not to blame. You must talk to him.'

Her face crumpled. 'I can't do that. He is my father. The family ... It is not so simple. Perhaps in your country, but here ... for women ...'

'It's what everyone says. That I don't understand. That it's the way of things, the way it is for women.' I squeezed my head to stifle my scream of exasperation. 'Does it alter the facts? Does it help you? Where is the justice?' I shook my head in Kyra's distressed face.

'Have you been to the police?' As I said it my stomach dropped a notch. What was I asking of her? Did I even know what the consequences might be for Kyra?

'They would not believe me. They would say it was my fault. Like my father does. They do nothing. It would make it worse.'

'And so nothing will change. If women never report it, then it will always be like that. Collective misogyny will persist. Men will continue to get away with it.'

'Yes.' Kyra's murmur sank to the floor. 'It is hopeless. What you say is true. But I don't have the courage.'

'You do. You are young, you are clever. You deserve your place in the university. You deserve a future. Don't let these men destroy you.'

My phone shrilled in the stifling room.

'Mr Bai.' I grasped Kyra's elbow as she shrank from me. I lifted a finger to my lips and put the phone on loudspeaker. She recoiled as her father's voice resonated around the walls.

'Miss Salkeld, I said I would phone you. Our initial meeting was difficult.' He coughed. 'If I appeared harsh, it was unintentional.'

Kyra's head jerked; she fisted her hand over her mouth.

'What is the purpose of the call, Mr Bai?'

'The news you brought of my father was a tremendous shock. Having always believed he was dead, to find out otherwise crushed me.

Kyra's eyes widened. The sight of her gaunt face refuelled my anger.

'We intend to release my father's ashes in Haridwar in five days. It is a town in northern India less than an hour by air from Delhi. I will book you return flights. I will text you the details and where we will be staying.'

'That won't be necessary, Mr Bai. I will make my own arrangements and buy my own tickets.' I struggled to sound calm. I wanted to shriek. Do you know where I am? Who I am with? Your daughter is here, cowering at the sound of your voice. Only loyalty to Kyra kept me quiet.

'You will not let us down, Miss Salkeld.'

'Your father meant a great deal to me. I will not let *him* down.' I was left looking at the silent phone in my palm.

'Thank you,' Kyra whispered, 'for not letting on about me.' She came closer and touched my trembling wrist.

'You stood up to him! But what did he mean? About his

father's ashes?'

'Kyra, it's getting late. I think we're both drained. May I come back tomorrow? We could go for a walk.'

Fear clouded her face.

'Then I can tell you about your grandfather. It's a long, long story. He overcame great tragedy and grief in his life. His genes flow in your blood. He would have been so proud of you. I know he would want you to be brave and face this.'

Darkness had softened the harshness of the city when I left Kyra. Stars littered the sky. Noise and scents were amplified. A dog sniffed at my feet; a mullah called from a mosque. I took a taxi that slowed beside me. I couldn't rid my mind of Kyra's experience. My own memories swarmed. That song, *Live Like We're Dying*. I hadn't thought about it for months. Here it was going round and round in my brain. Jake, the party, the assault. His hand over my mouth; the sour smell of sex.

23

I should've stayed with Kyra for all the sleep I found that night. Tossing and turning in bed, I eventually went to stand by the window and let the cool night breeze brush over me. The city was restless too; people walking, a man sweeping the roads piling rubbish into a cart, a rickshaw driver stopping to hail his mate, the slap of their hands as they greeted each other.

I was up and dressed before Aisha brought in 'bed tea'. She looked surprised but was soon distracted.

'I love your skirt, all the bright colours,' she said, feeling the material.

'I bought it from a stall in Jodhpur. Traditional Rajasthani, the stall holder assured me.' I shrugged, 'I like it.'

In Kyra's dingy room the colours of the skirt looked gaudy, and I began to regret my choice.

On the way over I'd picked up food from a street seller. 'I bought what the man in front of me asked for,' I told her. 'It looked good and smelled good. I hope it's all right.'

She lifted the lid and rewarded me with a smile. 'Spicy chickpeas and *bhaturas*.'

'You need to eat, Kyra.' She pulled a face and picked at the food.

'I have been thinking about what you said yesterday about the police ...'

I didn't push.

'Because of you, Lily, this is a good day. I will get washed and dressed. Then we'll go for a walk as you suggested.'

'Other days, have they been ... really bad?'

She grimaced. 'Except for buying food occasionally I haven't been out for weeks.' She leant against the wall as though her resolve was spent. 'You won't leave me, will you?'

I heard the water running and a cupboard opening. A different Kyra emerged. She had put on sandals, jeans and a white blouse. Her hair, still crinkled from the plait, was pulled back in a ponytail. She was far from the healthy, beautiful young woman in the photograph, but she looked better.

She responded to my nod of approval. 'See, I am brave on the outside but inside ... not so.'

'It takes a long time, Kyra. But it gets easier.'

She touched my hand.

'Your grandfather taught me how to live again. You will be happy one day.'

'You are happy?' Her question begged an answer.

'Yes. I am happy.'

She sighed deeply, 'Today, let's not talk about what happened to me. I want to know all about my dada.'

I looked quizzical.

'My grandfather,' she added.

When we left her room, Kyra draped a scarf over her head. She held onto me. I felt her trembling, recoiling as men passed us in the street. We walked and walked; I told her Asadi's story. Not a shortened version, but what he'd told me. Both the beautiful detail and the horror. I realised how much of it I'd held onto and the relief of sharing.

'This is my history too.' Kyra chewed a stray twist of hair. 'It helps me to know Papa. He is a good father but sometimes he has rages, at other times he sinks into black depressions. I never understood why.'

'Kyra, your mother is desperate. You must tell her you're safe.'

'Tell her for me, Lily. Please.'

'Will you come to Haridwar? Complete your dada's journey. He would have been so proud of you.' I spoke without forethought.

She gasped and stopped walking. With screwed-up eyes, she shook her head.

'I can't. Papa ... He says I am no longer his daughter.'

'That's ridiculous.' I didn't care that the words were laced with disgust. 'Your father is cruel, absurd and arrogant. Don't excuse his behaviour by telling me it's culture. It's not, it's misogyny. What kind of father rejects his child when she needs him most? Has he even listened to your side of the story?'

Kyra's face scrunched. 'Lily, don't be angry. You can't

understand. I wish it were different.' Tears welled. She blinked them away. 'I want to go back now.'

We skirted the university avoiding the students. We watched them at a distance from the shadow of a building.

'What were you studying?' I asked in an attempt to restore her mood.

'I was going to be an optician.'

'Not *was*, Kyra.' I took her hands. 'You still can be.'

She shook me off. We walked back to her room in silence.

Once inside she pulled the bobble from her ponytail. Her hair fell across her face. 'It was hard seeing the university, the students … I shouldn't have been rude. Before you leave Delhi will you come back and see me?'

'Of course.' Helplessness, anger, frustration. All sat in my chest like a giant ball. I had to get out of that stuffy room. I heard the click of the door and the scrape of the chest being pulled across the floor as I left.

The anger wouldn't leave me. I went back to the guesthouse and shut myself away, going over and over the day trying to make sense of events. What had I said? What had gone wrong?

That song again, always that same song. I buried my head beneath the pillow but still I heard it. I recalled the dark days. Black, endless days when I didn't want to get out of bed. And the other extreme when I was wild and crazy. Anything went, as long as it made me forget.

The screen on the phone lit up. Kyra. 'Are you all right?' I could barely breathe.

'Lily, it's too much. I can't go on like this.'

'What have you done, Kyra? Talk to me. I'm coming.' I snatched a bag.

'I feel calmer having made my decision.'

'Oh God.' I collapsed on the edge of the bed.

'I will go to the police. Just as you say. I will tell them.'

'For a minute I thought …'

'Give them the one name I have.' She continued as though she hadn't heard me.

'If those men … rape again, then the authorities will know, won't they? It is too late for me, but I can do it for other women, other girls. I have to.' Her voice splintered. 'I have one more thing to ask of you, Lily …

'Lily. Are you there?'

I covered my face with my hand. 'Yes, I'm listening.'

'Will you come with me? Tomorrow afternoon. You will lend me courage. Not let me change my mind.'

'I'll come. I won't leave your side. I promise.'

'Thank you for not judging me.'

'Kyra, I wouldn't. You know why.'

'Tomorrow then. And thank you for being a loyal friend.'

I stared at the wall wondering what I had set in motion. 'She's so fragile. Please don't make her a victim all over again.' I whispered to nobody and everybody. 'Don't humiliate her.'

The ping of a text coming through halted my growing panic.

As it is your intention to make your own arrangements to attend the Tarpan, I would ask that you arrive in Haridwar tomorrow or at the very latest the day after. Indian transport can be unreliable. You are the custodian of my father's ashes until then. I will take possession of them when we meet.

'Bloody man. Fuck you,' I swore at the mirror; dishevelled hair and a livid face glared back at me. 'Actually,' I shouted, 'I can't be there tomorrow because I'm going to the police station with *your* daughter. To report a gang rape.'

I dialled his number, heard the dialling tone. Held my breath.

'Bai speaking.'

'Mr Bai, it's Lily Salkeld. I want you to listen to what I have to say without interruption.' Something like a squeak travelled down the line. 'You claim to be a man of position, of influence. You had an opportunity to use it. Instead, you have disowned your daughter. She was raped six weeks ago. Gang-raped by three young men, one of whom was her tutor's son. She's moved out of the university and is living in decrepit lodgings nearby. Tomorrow afternoon she is going to the police authorities to report the crime. I will accompany her. It should be you. I had the great privilege of knowing your father. He spoke of his son with pride. I'm glad he will never find out what a coward he turned out to be.'

A crash, a dropped phone, a thrown phone. I couldn't tell. Background noise reaching me across hundreds of miles.

'You have found her. Where is she?' Chara's question faded to a low moan.

'Chara?'

'Is she safe? Lily, tell me.'

'Yes, she's safe. She needs you, Chara.'

The phone went dead.

Tumbling thoughts tore into me, tore me apart. Surely Chara deserved to know her daughter was alive. Ravi deserved my rage, not my sympathy. Should I tell Kyra? But what could I say? Had I betrayed her trust? One minute I was ashamed of my outburst, then flaming anger would burn again.

I reached Kyra's room the next day hardly remembering how I had got there. Tiredness pricked my eyes. Dread lodged under my heart.

'Kyra.' I pushed at the door shoving at the heavy chest. In her room, chaos. A pair of jeans straddled the back of the chair. A shirt lay spreadeagled on the rug, a headscarf beside it.

Her bedroom door gaped open. I slid a hand along the wall and crept closer. She lay in her underwear face down on the bed.

I heard her sobs, shut my eyes and breathed again. Gently I uncurled the fist that gripped the pillow.

'It's all right. I'm here. Has someone hurt you?' I stroked her back.

She lifted her head, grasped my arm, her nails digging into flesh.

'No.' She pushed back sweaty hair. 'I'm so scared. I can't do this.' She wiped her cheeks with the sheet. 'Look at me. I'm a mess. I don't even know what to wear. I've changed a million times already.'

'I think you need a hug.' I held her bony frame against me, her head on my shoulder.

'We'll do it together. It will be a horrible day. But by sunset it will be over. Hang onto that thought, Kyra.' I eased her away and rescued a shirt from the floor. She put it on and sat hunched on the bed like a child.

'Let me show you these pictures of your grandfather.' I sat beside her and found the photos. Her grandfather leaning on a spade. Drinking masala tea. Tying up the beans. Me standing with the first bunch of marigolds that I had proudly picked moments before. I talked about each scene. I described the wind in the trees, the sunshine, like strobe lighting filtering through the leaves. The first frost. I told Kyra about Abeki and her laugh, about Adam and the boys and how they were growing up without their mother. I told her about my own wonderful, crazy mother and how she'd died rescuing a pigeon. We talked, time passed, flies buzzed against the window.

'I'm ready.' Kyra's lips flickered into a briefly held smile. 'I will go through with it. I will. Whatever it takes.' I hugged her again.

She selected a peach-coloured sari and wound it around her body. I brushed her hair, and she fashioned it into a bun on top of her head.

'You look perfect,' I said.

A knock startled both of us. Kyra stepped behind me. 'No one comes here,' she whispered.

I walked to the door more bravely than I felt.

'Who is it?' I called.

'Lily.' Chara's voice, high-pitched, tight.

'Chara. Thank God.' I struggled with the door.

Ravi Bai filled the frame.

'I want to see my daughter.'

24

Ravi Bai pushed past me, a whiff of perspiration lingering in his wake. He stopped in front of the small window, blocking out the light and gulping at the air in bursts, as though too much of it would poison him. Chara followed him, clutching a bunch of flowers. Her pinched cheeks and haunted look made me want to hold her.

A strangled yelp escaped from Kyra; she pressed herself against the far wall, her fingers splayed.

No one spoke. Time hung in the cloying air. Chara slowly reached out and walked towards her daughter who sank into the proffered embrace and buried her head in her mother's chest. Chara stroked Kyra's hair and began to hum a tune. A lullaby. All the time her eyes were on her husband.

Ravi moved closer; he had the same thrust of the chin I'd seen in his father. In slow motion, his features crumpled and emitting the yowl of a stray dog he stumbled into the chair. He extended a trembling arm. Still holding her mother's hand, Kyra squatted beside him and laid her head on his knee.

I felt like an intruder, witness to a scene without words, so intensely private that I was of no more significance than a floating dust mote. I sat on the floor and clutched a cushion.

I'm not sure how long we remained immobile, like statues. Chara had dropped the bunch of flowers; I picked them up and returned them to her. She broke off a white rosebud and threaded it into Kyra's hair.

Ravi extricated himself and stood up, his cheeks wet.

'Miss ...' he swallowed, his Adam's apple swelling in his throat.

'Lily. Call her Lily.' Chara spoke with a clarity that cut through his confusion.

'Papa, Lily has been a true friend to me.' Kyra came and stood close.

'Yes. I know that. We have reason to be grateful to her.' His cough failed to disguise the catch in his voice, but he met my gaze and didn't look away.

'I will try to be honest. Your … outburst last night enraged me. I am not used to being spoken to like that.'

Kyra leant away so that I no longer felt the heat of her body.

'Lily. What …?'

'I rang your father. It was wrong of me. I'm sorry. I was so angry.'

Ravi cut through us. 'You spoke the truth. I did not want to hear it. It was a punch to the head.'

'Mr Bai …'

'Wait, let me finish. In a few short days, Lily,' his glance lingered on me, 'you have rewritten my knowledge of myself. It has been intensely painful.'

He sat back down and beckoned Kyra closer. 'Lily was not the only one who was angry with me. Your mother too was furious. She forced me to listen to what she had to say. Your grandmother gave me no peace. Their words sliced my heart to pieces. They made me reflect *and* forced me to act.' He pressed his closed eyelids with his knuckles. 'We flew from Jodhpur early this morning and went straight to the university. Out of loyalty to you – or fear of me – your room-mate, Sudha, was reluctant to tell us how to find you. Your mother persuaded her.'

Chara and Kyra remained motionless, appearing barely to breathe.

Prayerlike Ravi lifted both hands to his mouth. 'I have made an appointment with the Inspector General of Police. He will see us at three o'clock. I have the name of a top lawyer who takes on rape …' He exhaled like a balloon had burst inside him. 'I will be proud to accompany you, Kyra.'

Her gasp, a cry of anguish.

'But – the bank – the board. What will it mean?'

Ravi raised an eyebrow. 'How did I see any of that as important when my beautiful, brave daughter is prepared …' he opened his arms wide, 'to take on the whole of India.'

Kyra's body shook, her earrings making small, frantic movements.

'*Dadi-ji* is with us.' Chara held her daughter's shoulders. 'She's at the hotel, resting. She wanted to be here for you, her beloved granddaughter. She refused to be left behind.'

'*Dadi-ji. Dadi-ji* is here in Delhi?' Kyra sobbed then. Tears that for too long had been suppressed.

Her mother let her cry, holding her close. 'And she insists on travelling to Haridwar to scatter your grandfather's ashes on the holy river.'

Kyra wiped her cheeks, drowning her sobs in her throat.

'Papa, Lily has told me the story of your father. It made me desperately sad.' Her voice shook. 'For him, for you and *Dadi-ji*. Three lives were broken.' She chewed on her bottom lip. 'I don't want it to be the same for us. I know that what I must do today will be hard. But I will think of my grandparents. I am determined to have their courage. With you all beside me, I will find it.'

Ravi nodded. I could see he didn't dare to speak. He looked at his watch. 'I think we must go. We do not want to give this important man any reason not to see us.'

'You will come too, Lily.' Kyra held out her hand.

'No, Kyra. It is better that you are accompanied by your parents. I'll wait here and be thinking of you at every moment.' I smiled, hoping she would smile back. 'Remember this is for you and for women everywhere.' I kissed her on the forehead and pushed her gently towards the door. She looked over her shoulder as she went down the stairs. We nodded to each other, sharing an understanding.

Remnants of their presence floated in the tension that still filled the room. I forced open the window and let the breeze cool my burning cheeks. Picking up Kyra's strewn clothes I folded them and placed them on her bed. In a cupboard, I found a plastic beaker, set it on a pile of books and arranged the roses in it, their white petals luminous in the dim light.

Each time I glanced at the clock time had hardly moved on. The sky turned from blue to streaks of orange and pink, the light leaching away until the square of colour outside the window became deep indigo. What was happening to Kyra? I wouldn't let my mind dwell there. I shut out all thoughts of what she might be enduring. 'Let her stay strong. Please believe her.'

'Lily.' I woke to Chara shaking me. Pushing my hair back, I sat up.

The single, bare light bulb that hung from the ceiling illuminated three faces. Kyra looked visibly paler; her sunken eyes circled with black.

'Lily, it's done.' Even those few words seemed to exhaust her. She sat beside me twisting the hem of her sari between her fingers.

'You were so long.' It sounded like a complaint. 'I mean …'

'That man.' Ravi combed his fingers through his already tousled hair. 'Head of Police, he calls himself. He kept us waiting for more than an hour. Only because he could. Puffed up with self-importance, he hoped we would go away.' Bitterness edged Ravi's tongue as he walked back and forth across the floor. 'He wouldn't even let me speak the lawyer's name.'

'Hush, Papa, don't torture yourself.' Kyra slipped her arm through mine. 'They will bring in the tutor's son for questioning. They are sure they can get the names of the other two men from him.'

'She was magnificent.' Ravi stroked Kyra's cheek. 'That fool thought all he had to do was listen and then send us on our way. It was Kyra who demanded her statement be recorded. She made him take her seriously, caused him to change his attitude.'

'I saw a doctor … I insisted,' Kyra said softly. 'Just like you told me to.'

Ravi thumped the wall. 'Today I learnt something: the police here have no lady doctors. No lady doctors! In the end, they had to bring one from the hospital while we waited in a dingy room that stank of urine.'

'Stop your ceaseless walking.' Chara pushed her husband towards the chair.

'The doctor only came up to 'Mr Head of Police's' shoulder. As round as she was tall, but she told him.' Chara grimaced as her husband continued without interruption. 'After she'd seen Kyra, she marched into his office and banged his desk so hard a glass paperweight bounced to the floor and shattered. She didn't even pause. Said a report would be on his desk by morning and she expected charges to have been made by then.' Ravi gave a wan smile. 'I'm glad she's on our side. I've never seen anyone so incensed.'

'She was very kind. She said she will do her best to help me.' Kyra's grip on my arm tightened. 'I am … torn,' she whispered, dropping her head. 'I will need surgery.'

'It's only because of the doctor he agreed to bring the brute in.' Ravi shook his head. 'Now I understand how it is for female victims. I am ashamed. You tried to tell me, Chara. I should have listened to you.'

'Come.' Chara took charge and began moving around the room collecting shoes and items of clothing, packing them into bags. 'Brinda will be fretting, and Kyra needs to sleep, We are taking her to the hotel. She can't stay here. Ravi, go and hail two taxis.'

'Lily.' Tears threatened as Kyra held me close.

'Shh. I know. You don't need to say anything.' I eased her away. 'Your grandfather would be so proud of you.'

Chara embraced us both. 'His spirit is still with us. Tomorrow we will release him on his journey.'

25

I stared out of the window at the hazy flat countryside. The bus bringing me from the airport to Haridwar was packed: the seats and aisles full of passengers clutching baggage and children. A smell of tired travellers hung in the air. The woman sitting beside me balanced two chickens in a cage on her knee. Every time the birds squawked, she turned to me and grinned. A longing for Adam and familiarity became a burning pain.

Today will be poignant and sad, but hopefully joyful too. I miss you all so much. Home late tomorrow. Sending heaps of love. XX

Early morning here, the middle of the night in England – Adam would see my text when he woke. I yipped with surprise when my screen lit up.

And we'll be at the airport to meet you. Can't wait. The boys have crossed off every day. I will be remembering Asadi with love and thinking of you all today.

Lily … there's something I want to ask … but I will keep it until tomorrow. XXX

I hugged the phone and turned to my seat companion, giving her a grin that matched her own.

'There are thousands of people,' I said to Ravi and Kyra when they met me at the bus station.

'Mama and *Dadi-ji* are waiting in a rickshaw.' Kyra pointed, shouting over the blaring horns and the shrieks of the bullock-cart drivers who wove their animals through the throng. A bearded sadhu in orange robes raised a withered arm as he hobbled by, his crude crutch tapping on the cobbles. 'I never expected Haridwar to be like this.' I reached for Kyra's hand, reassured by the touch of warm flesh.

Ahead, the grey Ganges forged a wide, straight ribbon through the flood of people who spilt into it – writhing waves of orange, white, turquoise, and other colours: women, their clothes darkened by the water, men in vests or bare-chested. I heard the sound of splashing and laughter, a sound of hope rather than death.

It was hard to keep up. 'Papa,' Kyra shrilled. Ravi turned, saw our struggle and called to the rickshaw walla who swerved into a back alley.

We found a café with the tables set haphazardly in the shade of an earth-coloured building. I sat down with relief and pulled a chair closer as Ravi helped his mother from the rickshaw.

'My old bones are shaken like pebbles in a sack,' Brinda grumbled. 'I have seen this bedlam many times, always I am surprised by it.' She patted Kyra's knee with her brown-blotched hand. 'But my heart is happy because you are here.'

A young boy brought out chai and savouries, rich and warm.

'You should try to eat,' Ravi said and passed the tray to Kyra, but she shook her head. I nibbled at a bread pakoda. Only Ravi seemed hungry.

The sound of live music wafted in the air. 'Listen.' Brinda's fractured voice hushed us. She looked tiny and frail in her white clothes. 'My father made stringed instruments like that. People from all around came to listen.'

'Your Baba was famous,' I said. 'Asadi told me the story of how, as a boy, he went to your house with the schoolteacher to hear your father play. He said it was the first time he set eyes on you.'

She nodded. 'My memories float in the music.' The folds of her skin creased into smiles. 'If I could have a wish, it would be that I should die now, here in Haridwar, with you all around me. Then I could travel on the journey with my beloved Asadi.' Brinda sipped her chai. 'Only the gods can decide.'

If I could have drawn contentment, I would have drawn Brinda with her head tilted, listening to those haunting notes.

I glanced at Kyra who sat twisting her bracelets. She looked caved in from her ordeal yesterday. The tikka mark on her forehead was stark against her lack-lustre skin; her thinness apparent from the prominent bones visible above the neck of her pastel-coloured sari.

'I'm all right,' she whispered seeing my concern. 'Just tired. I'm so grateful to be here. What if you hadn't found me in time?'

'But I did. I am the one who feels privileged.'

Ravi's phone vibrated on the chipped table. He scanned the

screen, leapt up and walked off down the alley, his words lost. Chara gripped her chair and edged closer to her daughter.

The musician stopped playing. A cow with painted horns, one blue, one pink, ambled close, before easing itself down on its haunches a few feet from where we sat. Somewhere a peal of laughter flew from an upstairs window. I watched ants crawl in a line towards our half-eaten snacks.

'This is like nothing I could have imagined,' I said ripping the tension. 'It's the India your grandfather wanted me to see. His India.'

Kyra was watching her father.

He stood stock still, his back turned, holding the phone by his side. I too saw the heave of his shoulders; he spun around and strode back to where we sat.

'They have the man in custody. He confessed under interrogation. There will be more arrests. He has given the names of the other two men.' He batted a fly that crawled across the table and crushed it under his palm. 'It is only the start. There are powerful people who will use any means to pervert the course of justice. I won't give up until those responsible are behind bars.'

Kyra's head dropped. Chara clutched her husband's arm. I held onto Brinda.

Ravi pulled himself upright and breathed deeply. 'Your grandfather's love binds us; his spirit lifts us.'

'And this is his day.' Kyra raised her chin and wiped her wet cheeks. 'Let's not talk about the other matter today.'

'You are right. Everything can wait until tomorrow. Are you able to walk on? We should go to meet the pandit.'

'He's the priest who will conduct the ceremony,' Chara explained to me.

Ravi shouted to the rickshaw driver who was sleeping in his vehicle.

We crossed a bridge, the fast-flowing pewter swell beneath carried debris that I didn't want to identify. Sets of steps leading down to the river lined the long stretch of bank. 'Those are the ghats?' I asked and Kyra nodded.

An enormous white statue of the god Shiva dominated the town and everywhere there were stalls selling flowers or milk and curd, nuts and rice as offerings for the deity. Burning incense sticks sweetened the air with sandalwood and cinnamon.

Mesmerized, I stared at the crowds who milled there. People were undressing to bathe; hundreds were in the water; some were swimming and being carried along by the fast current. Chaos, colour and panic filled my head. I closed my eyes. Asadi had trusted me to do this. How would it have been if I'd been on my own? When I opened my eyes again Ravi was bartering with a seller over the price of saffron.

I called to him. 'I'm going to buy some flowers.' I'd spotted an old lady, sitting cross-legged on the ground, her face lined like wet sand, her hands clawed. In her lap were marigolds, bright and orange against her ragged black robe. 'How much?' I asked pointing to the blooms. She gave me a toothless grin, gathered up the small bunch and held it out. I took the flowers and passed her a few notes. She nodded and tucked them away. Her bony fingers brushed my ankle.

'That was too much,' Kyra said.

'I don't mind. They are for your grandfather.'

We were jostled and pushed as people streamed towards the riverside. Kyra clung to me. Turbaned farmers hauled crops on pushcarts, the wheels scraping and bruising limbs. A group of men thrust through the fray carrying a shrouded body aloft. The covering flapped as they pushed people aside and hurried down the street, wails trailing like vapour.

Away from the stalls, the smell of bonfires and smoke permeated everywhere. I lifted the marigolds to my nose, trying to capture the scent of dew and sunshine.

'All these people.' My heart raced; I tugged at my blouse as a flush of heat swept up my neck. Only with effort did I stop myself from fleeing.

We arrived at a ghat. Ravi looked drawn as he helped Chara and his mother down from the rickshaw. Brinda's smile softened the moment. 'This is a special place, Lily. Har Ki Pauri: the holiest of places.' Tears glistened in her old eyes. 'Here drops of *amrita*, the elixir of immortality, were spilt by the celestial bird, Garuda.'

I wished I could find her sense of reverence. Standing on the litter-strewn steps beside the murky water, the sensation of being an awkward outsider made me want to cry. I pulled my head covering close to stifle the smell of death and burning flesh. Kyra, her eyes wide and staring, held onto her grandmother.

The pandit, dressed in white cotton, slipped the money Ravi gave him into his robe and instructed us to sit on the ground. I pressed my palm against the cold marble platform needing to touch something solid. Disappointment and confusion crowded in. The ceremony began without any introduction; prayers were being said, the priest's rhythmic chanting barely audible in the surrounding turmoil.

I took my thoughts far away.

To Asadi's bench. He was sitting beside me sipping masala tea. A sparrow hopped closer looking for crumbs, downy feathers poking from beneath its wing. The breeze carried the fresh smell of cabbages, ripe blackberries and newly turned earth.

I have something I want to ask you. I would consider it an honour if when I die, you will carry my ashes home and sprinkle them on the holiest of rivers, the mighty Ganges.

Asadi's dry finger touched my lips, his gentle voice freeing itself from his grating cough.

But before you agree, you must listen to my story.

A small commotion brought me back. Ravi had opened the urn and begun to pour the contents into the swirling current. He passed me the container and invited me to do the same. For the briefest moment, the ash clothed the surface of the water. Then it was gone.

The short ceremony over, and the pandit departed without a word, leaving the family holding onto each other. Ravi held out his arm and folded me into their embrace. We stood silent and still, the lap of the waves against the bank masking the mayhem. Ravi lifted his mother and carried her up the steps.

Alone, I moved to the water's edge and took from my bag the shiny black and gold box in which I'd found my mother's packets of seeds, the same box that had kept Asadi's urn safe on my journey across India. I placed it in the river and spread the bunch of marigolds on its lid.

'Goodbye, Asadi. Goodbye, Mum.' My whisper faded in a breath.

The box sparkled, bobbed and turned. I watched it journey on, floating in a pool of sunshine, before sinking slowly beneath the surface, until only the petals of the marigolds were visible.

Acknowledgements

As always, my thanks go to Wenlock Writers on the Edge for their encouragement and scrupulous attention to detail. I am the author, but they are my team.

Particular mention must go to Maggie Bardsley, Jessica Keane, Brenda Carter, Charlie Garratt and Olga Levitt for reading the final draft and to Colin Taylor for his copy-editing skills.

I would like to give special thanks to Sara Johnson, my sensitivity reader. Of British Indian origin, she read my manuscript from her home in Bangalore surrounded by the beauty of India and its warm and colourful people.

ALSO AVAILABLE BY JO JACKSON

TOO LOUD A SILENCE

It is 2011, Egypt is in the grip of the Arab Spring. There is no room for outsiders.

Born in Egypt but raised by her adoptive parents in England, journalist Maha Rhodes recognises a growing desire to touch her roots. Despite her mother's unexpected resistance, finding out who she really is becomes important.

The turbulent political events in Cairo are a catalyst but when she travels to her birthplace she is completely unprepared for the devastating secret she will uncover.

Events draw her into the mayhem. She experiences the abuse and the violence of the revolution and is moved by the Egyptian cause and the passion of the demonstrators. She meets people who fight for change. She faces up to her own naivety and finally understands what it means to belong.

Too Loud a Silence will take you to Egypt. It is a beautiful, poignant, sometimes brutal story of cross-cultural identity, of a mother's love and guilt.

This is a truly wonderful story, a multi-layered novel handled with insight and sensitivity.
Sarah Vincent

BEYOND THE MARGIN

Is living on the edge of society a choice? Or is choice a luxury of the fortunate?

Joe, fighting drug addiction, runs until the sea halts his progress. His is a faltering search for meaningful relationships.

'Let luck be a friend,' Nuala is told but it had never felt that way. Abandoned at five years old, survival means learning not to care. Her only hope is to take control of her own destiny.

The intertwining of their lives makes a compelling story of darkness and light, trauma, loss and second chances.

The strength of this novel lies in its authenticity. A gritty, bitter-sweet narrative that kept me turning the pages.
Sarah Vincent

IT CAN'T GET DARKER THAN MIDNIGHT

A novella

In Sicily, Carlo's father is murdered for a crateful of fish and dies with his eyes open. An old belief changes the boy's life for ever.

His older brother takes revenge, but it is Carlo who is branded by the crime. When the innocent flee, survival has its own consequences.

Will Carlo take the only decision that will save those who matter most to him?

This is a story of crime but not a crime story, of love but not a love story. It is a story of endurance, hope and healing that will stay with you.